Bowt

by

Joe O'Niell

Best Wishes,
Joe O'Niell

ONE

Lying on his back on the boardwalk now and then catching a glimpse specks of yellow moon and flashes of lightning in the angry cloudy sky. He lay cursing but knowing the predicament he found himself in was of his own making. Listening to the forecaster on the radio announcing gale force 9 next 24 hours the lady got it wrong. The storm was here and if he had stayed in the office instead of following the inspector he would have avoided being blown against the rail and falling over and the bicycle landing on top of him or the pedal striking his foot. Willie the Dutchman would be home and out of danger. His great girth and the jolt he took to his stomach left him lying like a beached whale. He was out of breath and unhappy at the gurgling sound he heard coming from his throat. Had tried to hold on to his cap and the cycle. He watched his cap fly high then falling engulfed by the waves but worst the cycle collapsed on top of him. He was trapped lying under the tangle of metal and unable to free himself.

He knew the inspector was out here on the jetty had seen him duck beneath the chain barrier from the office window and knew the way he had been behaving lately something wasn't right. The heap of rotten timber was scheduled for demolishing and he was fearful and anxious. He needed to know why the inspector chose to go walkabout on the unsafe structure. Was late returning and he should have been long gone. Knew the skipper on the supply ship took a risk knowing the weather was not going to be in his favour. The mad rush to the lay barge at the North Sea oil and gas platform, with the final sections of pipe, was a foolish move. And on the grape vine he got word the dock authority advised the sailing could have been delayed for at least forty eight hours or until such time the storm would pass and if the ship had stayed dockside the inspector would still be in the office and not gone walkabout and he would not be lying helpless and unable to raise himself up.

Lifting his arms and clenching his fists he shouted at the wind like a man demented. The pain radiated round his foot moving over his ankle. The burning pain in his right hand, got by trying to save the bicycle, was affecting his wrist and found his hand was now useless. All this he was thinking was happening because the inspector chose to go for a stroll on the jetty.

Least of his worries was her repeating the same mantra about him being loyal to that man. Not paying attention to the people who actually mattered. It was her usual daily say and he was sick of hearing her continually complaining and now more than ever was going to find himself under her feet. Something he was not looking forward to. She was a nark but he loved her in spite of her bickering and havering. The injury to his foot she was sure to be reminding him of the man and in her eyes the man who had all to do with it was this man. Was sure to go on about the man and he was the one to blame for his injury.

The present predicament was his own making and was angry with himself not knowing what would happen next. At least he knew she would be asleep and he would escape the edge of her hateful tongue.

These thoughts were not helping the situation and he was wondering why he was having these foolish thoughts at this particular time. This situation would give her the opportunity to nark all the more and he was dreading the thought of more arguing. In his frustration he called out what a bloody fool he had been, 'stupid, stupid!'

Thinking as he lay he would be found with the daylight dead. Found like a drowned rat or frozen to the boardwalk and not going to see his beloved nemesis Greta again. He wondered what would she do without him? Thirty years of married life had been not so bad but Greta, bless her, relied on him. If he was breathing his last on this piece of rotten timber, was thinking, how she would fare and who would be left for her to vent her bile? He shook his head why was he thinking these foolish things when he should be looking for a solution on how to survive the present ordeal. He heard, according to some scholars, when someone was in the throes of drowning they imagined how their lives flashed through their mind but now he was only thinking of her. 'Get a grip,' murmuring, 'please, please let the inspector get here soon and do not let me die here.' Bad thoughts are taking over and he not being able to help himself he lay wondering, was this his time, was it going to be the end?

Frank was standing beneath the cast iron lamp-post at the dog-leg bend of the jetty looking out on the angry empty sea. The weather changing as it did took him completely by surprise and it was time for him to get off the unsafe structure.

The bracket on the post was loose and the lamp swayed in the wind. The light shining like a spotlight, in light, blackness then light again.

Early evening he watched the supply ship leave and with it's going he knew the time had arrived for him to finally make the decision. A decision what could change his life for good or the other. He knew it was time for hard thinking but of the future? What future did he have to look forward too? An out of work pipe inspector at odds with management, surely, the end of the line as far as they were concerned.

Mind all over the place stay or will he go? Do this or do the other. Only if he could make up his mind. His brain in turmoil because he couldn't solve the problem. No end to the infuriating situation and sleep forefront on his mind. A solution he was finding hard to achieve. Sleep deprivation was not good for his soul. Could not get into his head that worrying just prolonged the agony. Nights without the nightmares was making it impossible to live with. Maybe, he thought, stop thinking about it and it would sort itself out. Was like a drug. Hard to focus on something else instead of bloody sleep. Night after night he was swirling in a vortex down and down drowning.

The waves crashed higher and higher and soon would be above the rail. The rushing sea slammed into the framework beneath his feet and he could feel the structure jolt at every repetitive crash. 'If it collapses my problem will be solved. A long sleep and not waking,' said muttering to himself. Desperate to get away before the structure is demolished he saw himself being dashed onto the nearby rocks mashed as fish food. Food for the fishes was not on his agenda. It was time to get the hell out of it.

Zipping up his cagoule and bringing forward his safety helmet to shield from the stinging spray he walked forward. Head bowed arms clasped across his chest finding it hard to walk. The wind pushed him this way and that way and forced him to stop and catch his breath. Spied the old man lying under the bicycle and pushing against the wind closed in on him shouting letting him know he was coming to his aid.

The weather so unpredictable the rain changed to sleet. The wind roared and the sleet turned to snow. The flakes swirled all around them. The jetty banged groaned rusty metal scraping against rusty metal making an eerie haunting sound. The roar of the wind and the roaring of the rushing waves made him more determined to get both of them away from the jetty. Realising how much of a mistake he had made he was desperate to get them back to the safety of the dockside. The foolish act embarked upon people would say, 'found dead. Shame. Was off his rocker,' others would say, 'they saw it coming.' Knowing them they would say, 'sure we saw it coming.'

'What were you thinking coming out here you should have stayed put. Why did you follow me onto the jetty?' He demanded angrily.

'Yes should have stayed in the office till you returned. Thank goodness you're here,' he groaned wearily and thought the worst. 'Not got the strength to help myself. Was thinking it was time for me to meet my maker. You don't know how glad I am to see you it's good you're here,' he said as he tried to rise and trying to shift the bicycle found it impossible so gave up. Lying back with tears on his cheeks he was desperate and thinking the worst.

'Help me. You got to try. We have to get out of here the jetty is ready to fall and soon be under water,' Frank reminded him.

Cursing the wind and himself because he knew the problem was of his own making. Could see disaster happening and Willie not helping. Now needed the strength to get both of them off the jetty and back to safety.

'Was looking for you had to be on my way and you taking so long to come back to the office. Wondered why you had come out here. You are playing a dangerous game inspector. Can't fathom you lately. These few weeks past noticed you behaving in a strange manner.'

4

Willie tried placing his arm round Franks neck for support. Slumped down huffing and puffing saying he had not the strength to get up and feared the worst and was wondering what poor Greta would do without him.

'Come,' said Frank lifting the bicycle and stepping back beating his arms across his chest and breathing hard. Taking short hard breaths like a weight lifter ready for a lift he stretched his arms and bent to pick him up. Found it impossible. He stood back beat his arms across his chest again. Shrugged and tried again but to no avail. Was feeling finger numbing icy cold. Ears and the tip of his nose froze. His breath ached. Taking short deep breaths bent down and using all his strength, success, helped Willie rise to his feet.

'You thought was going to top myself but no not about to take a dive. Just came to clear my head thats all,' whispered as he strained raising him up.

Will not hear the last of this the old fool will have his story embellished as he relates to all the inquisitive know-alls. Hoping to delay any doubt the Dutchman had by saying what he said to stop him thinking the worst. Surprised the old fool followed him onto the jetty in the first place. Thought he had departed after the ship sailed and the last low-loader drove out the docks.

'The bloody bike fell on my foot give me your shoulder to lean on,' Willie said, his voice pleading, making much of his situation, 'chest really tight. Afraid my asthma is playing up. Thought was going to have a heart attack. Crazy place to be just plain crazy! You should not have come on-to this death trap and I not follow you what were you thinking?' Rebuking but happy to be up on his feet.

Listened to his woes Frank was used to listening to his woes. Day doesn't go by without him bleating and forecasting gloom and doom.

The convincing worked Willie managed to hobble along holding on to the saddle of the bicycle.

Frank steered the bicycle against the wind all the time urging and encouraging him to move quicker. But unfortunately it didn't take long for Willie to start the cursing and complaining about his misfortune and what Greta would say when he got home.

5

The journey was a nightmare and he was fed up hearing him continually huffing puffing and moaning. Combating the foul weather is no joke and he is ignoring the ongoing babbling. Having enough of the constant griping he lowered his head trying to avoid the flakes of snow taking up residence on his face.

Nothing new in the man's behaviour it was well known he would complain at the drop of a hat. Soon he would be rid of the old fool once and for all and that he thought couldn't come quick enough gone forever and good riddance.

The back of his mind was thinking…If the old fool happened to have an accident? Who was there to know? Would be easy. Him and his bicycle over the rail chance would never be found. No, he abandoned the thought. Willie was harmless and would soon be gone out of his life anytime soon.

Thunder and lightning rolled across the heavens. The clouds scurried and hurried as if the gods commanded the sky to fall about them. Realising his breathing was getting worse he took more deep breaths. Lifted his hand and wiped his frozen face. Suffering cold was bad but listening to Willie continuing his unbearable bleating did not help. Harder and harder he pushed and pushed. The swirling snow forced him to go slow slower and slower. Gasping stopping now and then finding it hard to see where he was walking. The snow lay thick and the wind relentless. Again he was thinking the worst and try he must to conjure up the strength from somewhere.

'Willie, think you can move a little bit on the straight? This is difficult enough for me without trying to get you of this bloody place. Swaying like you are doing is making it impossible to keep the bike upright,' shouting above the wind but knew he wasn't being listened to. Was wasting time trying. Better to save his strength and get out of his mind the thought of disaster he was going to succeed in spite of the man and his inability to help himself.

As he neared the dockside he saw the shore captain returning to the dock office and called out to him.

The Captain came running 'Not a good idea to be out here,' he shouted, 'are you mad? What you thinking?'

TWO

The office is a two story wooden cabin in a row of wooden cabins constructed with half their front large double glazed windows.

Not well furnished but adequate. There are four wooden chairs the kind that can be folded arranged around an unsteady wooden table where underneath one leg is a folded empty cigarette packet to stop the table shoogling whenever someone sits down.

There is a sink with single cold water tap. Water dripping from the tap drip drip constantly. No one bothered to fit a new washer because no one takes the slightest notice of a leaky tap and in time there will be no use for the water tap.

In the middle of the ceiling hangs a frayed brown cord with a single light bulb minus the shade and the light making shadows in the four corners of the room.

On the table a bundle of papers and a blue biro pen. Two white mugs containing black cold coffee. A large ashtray stuffed with dead smelly cigar stubs.

Electric kettle sitting on a wooden bunker next the sink. Two white mugs. Four knives and forks. Four spoons on top of four stacked white plates and a small two ring gas burner. One long handled pot and a frying pan. Old sagging leather divan in one corner with a selection of newspapers and open pages showing explicit photos of naked ladies in men's magazines strewn across the seat. In another corner two metal three drawer cabinets one six foot metal locker with doors open and empty.

Willie was sitting examining his foot.

'How you feeling, how's your chest?' Frank asked him after seeing him inhale on his puffer and was surprised how quiet the old man was.

'Getting there slowly. Just my hand. The back of it turning a funny colour.' He said meekly.

Pleased the wheezing stopped but Frank knew it wouldn't last. Would not be peace for long he was sure. Was well aware how Willie operated but for now he was happy to get a little peace and quiet to concentrate on what was important.

Reaching across the table he picked up the biro and gathered the papers together.

'Might have left the place a bit more tidy guess too much to ask,' he said to Willie. Was thinking would be too much hassle. Result of such a request would only lead to them being more surly and he couldn't be bothered with the continuing bad feeling. The more they bickered the more they argued. He knew they were not up to the tasks and wondered why the two where there in the first place. He thought, no he knew, they definitely were not good candidates for this kind of employment.

Looking across the room he saw Willie sitting there and it seemed to him that Willie was somewhere else in his own little world busy examining his injured foot and gently rubbing his leg. He shook his head and hid a smile.

'Should put something on. A lump coming. A lump do you see it and yes okay now. My hand is sore but thanks. Good you showed up when you did.'

He moved his toes up and down and side to side all the time making a fuss and giving out with the tut tutting.

'Your foot looks okay to me. I don't see a lump. Too early for it to lump you'll find out if it's better or worse tomorrow. Twenty four hours or maybe more.'

Willie made a face indicating the pain was unbearable and not relishing the thought it could possibly last for a further twenty four hours. Was having more thoughts about her. Why is he still thinking what she is going to say, oh dear, he's dreading going home.

'I definitely see a lump, feel it, here look,' he pleaded.

'No. Be wanting me to play the good nurse but you are not on. Don't see a lump. Put your boot on it will stop you getting a lump. If you can't manage your bike, well, it's going to be a long walk home. Yes sir for sure.'

'Oh dear! What will she say when she looks at my foot and what can I say if she asks about the missing bicycle?' Thinking the worst he knows she can't stand to see anyone injured and panics at the sight of blood. He is sure to be in the wrong for bringing the problem home. The self doubt setting in he hoped for sympathy but Frank was not in the least bit interested. The episode should never have happened in the first place. If had been more careful things would have been different. Sitting holding on to his naked foot staring into space thinking the worst, 'if only stayed here I wouldn't be in this state,' he said.

'Yeah, see it and it will go yellow,' Frank said as he lifted the mug from the table and chucked the forgotten coffee into the sink with a splash. 'You said it. You should have stayed know how you felt wondering and all. You foolish old man.'

Willie shook his head and came back down from the cloud of gloom, 'that colour now,' he said. He was gently caressing his toes and peering between each one. 'blue and yellow. Hope my toes don't go black? Scary or what!'

Frank was dreading the thought on how long he would have to listen to this saga. Just how long it was going to last his brain was ready to burst. Thoughts in his head if he goes on much longer should have got rid. He can't stand the agony of it all…No, not good thinking dark thoughts not good form. But little does the man know how close he came to having no more worries.

'Maybe get something from the first aid box? A bandage or a plaster from the dock office what you think? I could wait till the day shift come on duty. The nurse starts about nine o'clock. What you think a good idea or what?'

'For goodness sake Willie it's only a bruise. Your foot isn't going to wither and die. It's not going to drop off. Can you please get over this nonsense got to get things done. Stop going on about your foot.' Sick listening to him going on and on about the mishap to the offending foot he's getting restless needs to be gone he still has lots to be done and the Dutchman is not helping the situation one little bit.

'It's okay for you Inspector the accident hasn't happened to you,' said Willie.

Now Frank is thinking Willie is living up to his name the moaning Willie. Willie the moaner.

'Willie moaner,' Sem, Kaiser, his buddy keeps on reminding Frank.

'Must be hellish to work with. Better you than me. I couldn't stand having him around. Do you really need him working with you all the time there in the background like a shadow?'

'He's a product courtesy of the dock authority. I'm lumbered with him till the job is finished. Thank goodness it's nearing the end. Soon be out of my hair. Gone and no more wingeing. I'm fed up with him shadowing me all over the place like a dog waiting for a bone,' saying, repeatedly to Kaiser and reminding him each time the subject raises it's ugly head.

'No, hasn't happened to me and is it not about time you were getting out of here? Soon as I change out of these clothes I will be gone. The storm will not hold me back but do you not think you should be making tracks?'

Stress level is high listening to a lot of nonsense him constantly going on about his foot not on his immediate case. The contract coming to an end a fallout with his bosses not a happy situation. Giving him more to think about being secretive and moody. Not the usual happy go lucky tolerant guy he used to be. Was grumpy, more grumpy than Willie himself. If only he could tell the future but who can predict the future only time would tell.

'I take it Baird and McKay got away okay?'

He asked his wounded companion. Truthfully keeping them in check was a chore he could have done without. Was not sorry to see the back of them. His junior inspectors had been impossible to work with. Was forever checking and had a suspicion one was carrying stories back to management at head office. Found it infuriating he was not able to find out which one was responsible but as from now, now, he was not in the slightest bit bothered. They were out of sight and out of his mind. Gone and thank the Lord for his mercies.

'They got a lift on the last low loader should be on the bus to Groningen and plenty time to catch the City-Link to Amsterdam airport. Took lots of the paperwork with them,' Willie said. 'I've never seen them so happy. Going home put new life into them. You had seen how they carried on. My, pity were not so enthusiastic doing what supposed to be doing. Two entirely different men.'

Willie put him wise but was not happy being distracted from his foot. He returned once more caressing it and carried on with his examination.

'I've signed the tally sheets make sure the copies are sent to Leith as soon as possible in enough deep trouble. Do not let the foot situation distract you. You hear me? You make sure you are in the dock office nice and early to use the fax machine. And expect to be reprimanded by you know who about being out of bounds on the Jetty.'

'I'll see to it first thing. All that has taken place forgot to tell you that your friend Kaiser was here at lunch time. He was in a bit of a state when I let him know you were on the ship. Wouldn't wait said had no time said he had some pressing engagement and would meet with you some time later. But can't remember where or when. Sorry. I forgot just can't remember where he said.'

Sitting on the sofa bending over inspecting his foot he winced and took a sharp intake of breath made a face and sighed.

'There will be a woman involved wouldn't surprise me if it's that is the pressing engagement, 'lucky him, ay,' said a smiling Frank.

'There was someone waiting in a car. Outside the dock gates. Sure was in a hurry made it obvious it was a lady friend.' He grinned and winked and smiled a knowing smile. 'Remember happy memories but so long ago alas,' he shrugged and looked dreamily up to the ceiling. Wondered where it all went wrong. Why he ended up with Greta? He hunched his shoulder and concentrated on the task at hand, his foot.

'Has he left the key for my wheels? Not want to have a locked car problem. Don't want to be locked out at this time. Too much of a hurry far too much still to do.' Said Frank standing and stretching his arms above his head yawning. 'Time to be out of here. No sleep till later this afternoon. What with the boat leaving as it did and having to get back to the mill don't know when I will be done?'

'The key? In the glove compartment,' Willie informed him whilst walking back and forth. Now and then stamping his foot. Saying, 'it's okay now thankfully. Not as bad as thought it was going to be.' For a moment produced a smile. He lifted the mug from the table and took a sip. Spat out the cold coffee threw the remains into the sink, 'coffee is cold,' he said, screwing his face. He put the mug on the table and walked over and opened the door looking outside. 'My goodness, have you seen the like such crazy weather? Bet you'll be glad to be out of here inspector.'

11

The wind was blowing hard. The snow now changed to rain and was dropping like stair rods onto the cobblestones.

'Hope he has left the car open? Not do if the keys are locked in the bloody car.' Frank gave him a long look after witnessing the Dutchman's latest moan about the cold coffee and there not being anything for eating, after, he was the one who ate the last biscuit and scoffed the heated remains of a cold chicken curry.

'Don't think do that,' he said still testing his foot as he walked back and forth across the floor.

'If he has on his mind on you know what he's capable of anything,' said Frank.

'You'll soon know if that's the case. Hope not for your sake.'

'Yeah, hope not. If you think you should not go out into the torrent you can stay a bit longer till it settles. Up to you what you do. You could lock up if it suits.'

By changing the subject he thought he would get him out of his hair and on his way never to be seen again.

'I'll be okay. A chance you could be back if a new contract was in the offing?'

He picked up the tally sheets from the table looked at them one by one and was thinking was not looking forward no way resuming his duties with the dock authority.

'No chance Willie. No contracts. Finished will be gone time for moving to pastures new.'

Changed his clothes. Put his thick woolly socks inside his safety rigger boots then put the boots at the bottom of his brown leather hold-all. Finished dressing reached for his black reefer coat from the hook on the door then put on his black barge cap.

'Well, time to say goodbye,' he offered his hand. Gave him a hug and a few pats on his back.

'A well never say never,' Willie said, 'I'll get going now. Go and see nurse Vera. Ha ha. Have to put the accident in the book just in case of any, you know, complications. You know how he likes to fuss and the way he minces about when busy sure is a joy to watch. You know how he is a laugh a minute.' Rambling on not saying anything relevant. He should have said something for the occasion what he was actually saying was a load of rubbish. Should be saying something like good luck or take care been a pleasure. No, came out with a mouthful of nonsense. Should have said something to lighten the situation but he fluffed it big time.

'Yes, do that in case and say cheerio to Greta. Tell her might come and see her sometime later today, if I can make it. She won't be waiting up wondering why you're late will she,' now he is wondering why he is having this conversation the only thing he wants to be is to be gone out of it.

'Dreamland ages ago won't be the slightest bit interested. Late nights go with the job. You know the situation inspector. It would be grand if you can manage a visit she would like that.'

'A joke Willie? You know my good looks haven't managed to melt her heart of stone. Even Kaiser, who can charm the birds from the trees, can't penetrate her ring of steel. If I get there well won't promise. Know how it goes.'

Willie walked into the storm huddled over the handlebars off his bicycle. He was thinking of his future. Cursing as he walked. The wind scattering the rain-water across the cobblestone'd ground soaking his feet. He was mumbling and wondering what Greta was going to say. Shaking his head as he walked struggling in the wind, 'oh dear,' he said wearily.

'Remember, if I can. Will see later if I can manage,' Frank shouted but guessed Willie never heard. The wind was roaring. The rain coming down in sheets, 'silly old man,' he muttered.

Standing at the office door Frank watched him disappear into the gloom, 'that's that,' he murmured before sprinting raising the hold-all sheltering from the rain. Thunder boomed and cracked overhead. 'What next? Send it down,' shouting as he ran to escape the torrent. Couldn't help wondering the kind of reception the old fool would be in for when he reached home. Greta would be there waiting. Not in bed in dreamland like he said. How Willie puts up with the horrible woman was beyond him. Felt sorry for him although at times could see the back of him. Had to go along with the dock authority when they said was the norm to have one of their employees seconded to the foreign inspection company. A spy in your face you could say but what was there to spy on defeated him. There was no underhand dealings whatsoever. Inspection done at the dockside was necessary. Damaged goods to the lay barge would be time wasted. Holding up production would cost millions of dollars

THREE

Frank got into the unlocked car parked under the light of the lamp-post beside the dock office. Stretching he opened the passenger side glove compartment and removed a large brown envelope. Looked over two sheets of paper then replaced them into the envelope. Reached again and fumbled and found the ignition key. Inserted the key and fired the engine putting the pedal hard to the floor. Revved a couple of times then stopped he had a feeling something was not as it should be. Stretching once more into the compartment he rummaged inside and feeling in his hand the smooth handle of a revolver. 'What the? I will kill the reprobate.' Muttering followed by a string of expletives. 'Dam, dam dam!' Surprised himself for letting loose. His friend will have some explaining to do when he meets him. Why, why the reason for leaving the key in the car had he forgot to take it with him when he parked but the gun? Why the gun was there a more sinister reason and why did he leave the docks when he did? Why the mystery?

The windscreen wipers laboured. A sliver of torn rubber peeking from the metal arm scratched over the glass reminded him of Finger nails scratching on a blackboard. And the scene before him was a pitch black morning interrupted by grey falling rain dancing in the headlights.

Moving forward in the seat he hunched over the steering wheel but the manoeuvre changed nothing. He tried reducing the speed it made no difference either.

Getting angrier and angrier and more confused. Going mad, he's thinking and why is he punching the steering wheel it's not going to solve the situation one iota.

'Am I really going round the bend? If only I could get some sleep. Yeah sleep I need sleep.' He groaned and rubbed his eyes and punched the steering wheel a couple of more times and continued spouting expletives. He said, he wouldn't punch the wheel, exactly what he was doing and the shouting was not giving him any relief from his predicament. He knew, hand on heart, punching the steering wheel was not the solution to the problem. The wipers still screeched. The rain continued to splatter and wash over the windscreen. Now he is sure. He knows the signs a migraine is coming his way. Hoping to reach the mill before the headache gets serious. He knows he's in a dark place but needs to be in a dark place to quell the green lights glaring from the instrument panel on the dashboard. Thinking, would sleep be the answer?

On the lonely road seeing a traffic light showing red where a traffic light shouldn't be. Wondering what's going on as there should not be any lights on this road. In the years he traveled it there never was any and wondered was it going to be the norm?

'Typical council having lights where not needed, fools, crazy people with too much tax payers money spending needlessly.' Grumbling. His mind is all over the place. 'Headache, Road blocks, where will it end? This, a hinder needed like a hole in the head. Got too much to worry about,' muttering to himself.

Cut the engine and opened the window when he sees the copper approaching waving his torch light side to side. Thinking how the holdup is going to upset his routine. Goodness knows what the outcome is going to be and for his heads sake needs to be at the mill. Needs medicine and the time to finish once and for all. Hard to fathom why the police are on the road? Get out or stay in the car. He decided to wait. Watched in amazement as the copper approached. The wind is hampering his stride and he can see him struggling to keep his feet. Turning and twisting he comes with rain washing over his yellow coloured waterproofs and dripping down his hat and down over his knees. Coming slowly. Sloshing through the puddles. 'What,' he mumbles, 'madness...Coppers!' Saying as he shakes his head.

Further up the road two men dressed in similar waterproofs setting up road furniture. Plastic cones stop and go signs and other paraphernalia that goes with the job of disturbing the motorist. Courtesy of the council and the city police department.

Behind the equipment van parked a distance up the road a patrol car with a copper sitting inside listening to loud Cajun music on the car radio. The radio is continually losing sound. The wave length constantly interrupted by a police call the driver is Ignoring. He is snug and warm and out of the storm. Out of touch in his own wee world singing along with the music and not a care what is going on not taking any notice what is going on elsewhere. Nothing matters nothing relevant but listening to the music on the radio.

The copper bent to speak through the car window and the rain from his hat falling into the car soaked Franks shoulder. He wants to know why Frank is out so late and as he spoke he shone the torch into the car spraying the light round and round the car interior.

'You're destination and where have you come from?'

The mood the copper appears to be in he is of the opinion the copper doesn't care a fig where he has come from. His face says it all. Sounding miffed maybe wishing he was somewhere else not here on such a miserable stormy morning.

A bit of a commotion he sees the equipment guys dashing about the field opposite their van chasing after a couple of plastic cones. Escapees blowing about in the wind. Maybe they guys would rather be somewhere else as well he's thinking. The antics of the two men gave him a moment or two of light relief from his woes and momentarily relief from the migraine that now has stabilised. Should be elsewhere and obvious wasn't going to get any sleep anytime soon. 'Is world gone mad?' Muttering and wiping away the rainwater from his shoulder. Cocked his ear listening to the wind roaring in the trees and the rain beating on the car is making it hard for him to hear what is being said.

The cop, repeated, asked the same questions. 'Is this vehicle your own property and where are you going and where have you come from?'

He's thinking, why here, what sense is it being here at this time? The exercise is just one big waste of time!

Reaching into the glove compartment he got the envelope and handed it over, revolver? Hopes it is not going to be discovered. 'Kaiser, Kaiser, Kaiser I offer a silent prayer the cop doesn't search inside the car,' he mused. And if the worst comes to the worst. 'Four?...Come easy!' Followed by a reassuring feel of his underarm holster giving him an added sense of security.

'Get out the car please.' The request is asked in a slow drawl. A weary kind of way followed by, 'you did not say from where or where you are going?'

The copper ambled to the front of the car and leaned over the headlight opening the envelope and shining the torch over the documents all the while the rain is drumming on his waterproofs.

'From Delfzijl docks to the Belford pipe mill,' says Frank holding on to the roof of the car to stop from being blown away.

'What's going on constable this road goes nowhere. To the mill at the end of the canal then nothing but the sea.'

'The mill closed over a week ago,' copper says putting the torchlight full in Franks face blinding him momentarily.

Surprised by the reply he blinked and thought maybe the copper thinks he is up to no good being out at this time in the early morning, 'thinks a gangster I bet,' saying under his breath then shouting to combat the wind, 'yes, know it's closed. Going clear my office.' Says it to reassure he is genuine and not some dastardly or an undesirable foreigner out to do mischief.

Copper asks the reason he gave could be proved?

'Yes, not a crook who you think you have apprehended. One you have caught red handed to give you a step up the ladder. Haven't prevented a heist from taking place...I'm sorry to say innocent sir honest.' Hoping the copper takes the joke in good faith he said it with a smile and a shrug thinking it would lighten the mood. He guessed, didn't work, only prolonging the agony.

'Not funny. Quicker we will be done quicker you and I will be on our way.'

'I apologise it's the weather to blame. Tired. Just finished a twenty hour stint at the docks and not finished yet,' was trying to calm the situation before things got out of hand.

'Vehicle has to be back in forty eight hours. Amsterdam in forty eight hours it's a long way to Amsterdam.' The copper says sarcastically along with a long stare and a hint of suspicion in his voice and for some reason shining his torch in the direction of the police car further up the road. He thought is he trying to attract the other copper for support but after a pause nothing came of the manoeuvre. Obviously the cop in the car has more sense. Why go out into the storm? Perfectly happy where he is.

'In forty eight hours,' he said, turning his head to escape the torchlight in his face and still hoping the cop was not going to find the gun in the glove compartment. Kaiser why the gun? Is the thought on his tired brain. 'Could sleep for forty eight hours maybe won't make it,' says but his words make no sense in the driving wind.

'Take the envelope,' copper shrugged to show indifference hinting wasn't interested or ready to be having any kind of friendly chat. 'Licence give me your driving licence. Sooner you co-operate the quicker we'll be done here.'

Realising he was in for the full treatment. About to be given the whole episode the works and now was not the time to play fast and loose. He knew the exercise was one big waste of time he had better things to be getting on with instead of standing there getting battered by the wind. He is numb and the cold penetrating into his bones he could see, worst luck, flu possibly be the outcome and on top of it all the headache. That would put the cream on the cake he's thinking. This man doing his duty making him stand shivering was now beyond the pale and once again he is thinking dark thoughts.

Handed over the licence thought it would be the end of his inquisition and soon would be on his way.

Copper shone the torch on the licence looked it over then returned it. Wiped the rain from his face and scuffed his right foot through the puddle.

The manoeuvre reminded Frank what a child does when acting up and misbehaving like dancing in pools of water.

Keep it cool keep a level head it would be over sooner than later. Would be out of it. Just let him think was playing along. Letting the copper have the upper hand would be best medicine. Yeah, best to play along and say as little as possible just get it over with and forgo the dark thinking. Soon, this nonsense will be over. The problem the gun. If it comes to what he is thinking, no, don't go there and if he's frisked, two guns, well too bad on someone come what may.

Copper, silent, walked and opened the passenger door shining the torch inside he saw the hold-all. Got halfway into the vehicle and unzipped and emptied the contents onto the seat... White coveralls a white safety helmet. Blue cagoule and a waterproof short length jacket with printed logo above the breast pocket, Leith Inspection Engineers stitched with green thread. The rigger boots fell onto the floor copper picked them up one by one and removed the socks. Shone the torch into the boots and muttered something to himself.

Frank hadn't a clue what it was the copper muttered. The wind made it impossible to make the words have any sense. He held onto the car tighter thinking the copper is done must be time to get going..

Leaving all on the seat and having another scan with the torch the copper backed out closing the door, 'you're British English are you?'

'Scotland not England,' Frank answered wearily. Muttering, 'why do they think it?'

They were interrupted by the appearance of another police car stopping on the opposite side of the road.

'Stay! Don't move,' copper said. He braved the storm struggling to make headway to speak with the new arrival.

'Okay you can pack up vehicle has been found at Schiphol airport.' The voice came from an invisible source. Window was wound up and without waiting for any response the driver sped away showing skill doing a three point turn with screaming tyres and burning rubber it's siren disturbing the peace they were gone.

Within minutes the coppers with the men and their road furniture were out of sight.

The wind buffeted the side of the car. The wipers stopped and he could smell burning. Opening the window with his hand he tried to wipe the rain from the windscreen but no go. His view was still being restricted. Moving closer to the steering wheel he cut the speed keeping his eyes focused on the grassy verge.

Going over in his mind was thinking the reason what reason the police had for being there? Was there dark deeds somewhere near the mill? The road was used by pipe carrying low-loaders on route to the docks and seldom used by others.

Could it be a problem in town? A road block here out in this back of the woods could make sense if whoever they were trying to apprehend had access to a boat. The road was a dead end.

FOUR

The gatehouse was in darkness when Frank reached the mill. The red and black wooden barrier was in the up position and he drove through and parked opposite the doorway to the upstairs offices.

Got out of the car but unfortunately stepped into a water filled hole on the uneven gravel potholed ground. Swearing loudly letting out more of his usual expletives. And the more he swore the more the pain shot through his head adding to his misery. Headache is getting worse. Reminds him of the agony, cold ice cream giving the screaming habdabs across his brow.

Hopping on his right foot to the entrance squelched up the stairs to the first floor and was surprised to see the light shining from the open door at the end of the long corridor. 'Strange,' he muttered, 'wtf!'

When he entered the room his friend Kaiser was there.

On the table was a pint bottle of whisky one full and one empty glass. Two silver handled flick knives and a colt revolver. The shooter lying on the table between the knives in presentation order. And he, he thought, is sitting there looking like the cat who caught the mouse.

Pointing at the hardware, 'nice selection, ay, won't believe me when tell you, Willie, a curse on me. He had a problem with his foot. Was not bothered about him or his stupid foot. Only looking to get sympathy but I just ignored him. Now look. Stood in a hole full of water sure he's put a spell on me the old blaster,' laughed, 'now a perfectly good shoe soaked. How's that for bad flipping luck?'

'Nice to see you too, glad you've arrived safe,' Kaiser lifted his glass and offered a toast, *'prosit'* he said,

Drinking the whisky in one gulp reached for the bottle refilled the glass asking if he wanted a dram but he declined,

'What do you mean safe? Why would not be safe and before I forget, why did you leave your little friend in the car? Was stopped on the road by the cops. What if they had found it what do you think excuse could offer? You take some chances. What were you thinking by leaving it in the car and if I'm not already mad you sure as hell are helping me on the road to being just that bloody mad. I thought the journey here would be a doddle but no such luck. No luck none whatsoever. Cops and the daddy of a headache. What next I ask you?'

'I left it for your protection Bowtow. Listen to yourself buddy getting as bad as the old pest turning into a moaning wtf. Now it's Bowtow the moaner,' smiling, getting a kick a morbid kind of delight from saying what he had said.

None got the better Frank did not take kindly to anyone making snide statements. Faced them and woe betide if making contradictory statements. You have to take the consequences. As a child would act first and not pay any heed. Certainly not to any even one as loyal as his friend Kaiser.

'Pour me a nip while I get this wet shoe off,' said ignoring the remark. Got his socks and rigger boots from the hold-all and changed from the wet to the dry.

'It's bloody freezing in here. Why no heat your office isn't it. Cold. The place is like a morgue and creepy. Listen to the wind outside enough to give you the screaming you know what's.'

'The mill has been closed for a couple of weeks now what do you expect? I'm not a miracle worker. Didn't expect to see you here. Known I would have you know baked you something…Get a bloody grip!'

'The phone is dead you not paid the due? Trying to call but a waste of time. Nothing but silence.'

'You don't listen. What is it you don't get? The mill it's closed no need for a phone or friggen radiators. I'll be pleasantly surprised if the water is still available so no water for the kettle. No coffee never mind a phone. Its dead. Kaput. If you knew what I had to contend with you might show a little bit more sympathy my friend,' chucked the shoes and socks into the hold-all. 'Going to tell me why you are here and stop comparing me to Willie,' he's finding it hard putting up with the agonising situation.

'No phone. Dead and not the only thing that's dead,' said Kaiser.

The statement and the look on his face Frank realises he is about to lay something bad and explain the reason for the visit. Kaiser made the statement and he guessed something more

21

serious would follow. A hunch. One of these hunches he was sure he was not going to be prepared for.

'Okay, spill it slowly, wait, no, why were you in such a hurry to be gone when you were at the docks and why are you here? know I would have seen you later at the Bear. Fetching up here makes me think you've got yourself into some kind of bother or do you have a plausible excuse?'

'Right, will come clean don't want you to worry. Just relax and listen. My date was too hot to miss. It's not everyday such opportunity presents itself. We had to wait for the husband to leave on his travels before it was safe with, you know, couldn't afford to miss the ideal opportunity.'

'Now, you really have me worried. When you gonna take things seriously. When you gonna change from being a Romeo and settle it? Not getting any younger. Time you, you know, gave it up settle down and bloody well grow up?'

'The day it happens will end it all, believe me. Come to think you would be wise to follow my way of thinking. Doctor death may come sooner not later so be prepared to have a jolly time before, you know, get it, understand?'

Watched him pour the whisky and joined him drinking the contents all the while thinking his friend is ready to go on a bender and that problem he could do without.

'No more. Enough for now I have to drive out of here.'

'What's with the police?'

'Beats me. Really surprised at being stopped.'

'Not speeding? Don't say you got stopped not because you were speeding?'

'You kidding me I was crawling. The wipers stopped had to hug the grassy verge to see where I was going. Truly was the daddy of all bloody nightmares.'

'Well, they must have gave some explanation.'

'No. Nothing. Not a clue why was stopped.'

'Funny, sure wasn't an accident or something more serious?'

'What be more serious than an accident? For goodness sake?'

'A murder?'

'No, nothing so grizzly. No murder.'

'They must have said something?'

'You are taking a lot of interest in my incident with the road block you not telling me something have you got something to hide? Cmon talk to me.'

'You think hiding something?'

'Yes, you must have good reason to be here. Are you? What?'

'Am I what?'

'Oh. I give up!' Raised his arms in submission and shaking his head reached for the whisky bottle.

'I need a reason do I?'

'How many times have you shown up here?'

'Can I have another drink not too much to ask is it?'

'Get to it and answer the question.'

'Do I really need to have a reason tell me that and remember your driving.'

'You know you are beginning to worry me don't you.'

'You would say if you knew the reason why you got stopped, ay. Must have some clue why?'

'I knew it. Holding back got something to hide.'

'Not got anything to hide just trying to explain in my own way. It will come clear.'

'Not good enough.'

'Why?'

'Because can read you like a book that's why.'

'I want to share my happy experience and you get all hot and twisted. I know you got stopped know you were worried about me leaving the bloody thing in the car. I'm trying to get you to relax. Goodness sake...Chill. Way your acting I guess headache is gone. Is it not bothering you now? Must be the malt. Good medicine, ay, Relax, you don't want the headache back do you? Calm yourself blood pressure may be on the up.'

'Now, you, you do have me worried get these glasses filled don't think my head is going to take much more of this and you don't have to remind me about the driving.'

'Are you going to listen or sulk? The conversation is getting boring now.'

'You're leading up to something and I would rather get rat-arsed instead of listening to your fairy stories. So, if you don't mind keep the booze coming. You forget it. It's my head. Let me worry about it and the blood pressure is fine.'

'Don't think that's a good idea. The booze.'

'Knew it you're leading up to something.'

'Can go of people you know. Fed up with this carry on.'

'Now it shows. You're going to get on with it, ay.'

'As said, getting fed up with all you're suspicious thoughts.'

'Do you wonder?'

'Wonder all you like but why are you being like this? Let me explain it will come clear I promise.'

'Yeah, wondering. Worried what's next. Can't deal with much more need to sleep but unfortunately know it won't happen anytime soon.'

'I've come here to be with my friend have a session chew the fat but all you're saying is how worried you are. I know you're stressed I sympathise with you getting stopped. Maybe, it would be a good idea, if you learn to relax a bit more it's not my fault you can't sleep.'

'You are up to something.. Are you gonna come clean and get it over with. I don't have the stomach for much more. Jeese, please give me closure.'

'I see. You should calm down and have another drink before you say something you are going to regret.'

'Okay, let me be the first to apologise.'

'I'll apologise.'

'No need. Don't,'

'Well, see what it is.'

'Yeah okay.'

'Are you pouring or what?'

'Jings. You do blow hot one minute then the other.'

'Just get on with it.'

'Okay a truce. I was sure relieved to see the gate open when I got here. Not a clue if you were here or not. Left the docks or gone home just took the chance.'

'Would have been much earlier if not stopped that's for sure.'

'Well, you are here now. Thank goodness. Safe that's all that really matters.'

'There you go again!'

'Again. What again?'

'Leading up to something. You really know how to prolong the agony Kaiser. You got something to say we'll get on with it stead of playing around.' He banged his empty glass on the table, 'some time is it now or later you gonna say?'

'You're going to break a blood vessel if you're not careful you should not let the old pest get on your nerves. I hate it when you've had a hard time with him you take it out on me and it's getting monotonous now.'

'You're changing the subject again. It was nothing to do with him. But better tell you…A little adventure with said man. You better know from me rather you hear it from him. I took a walk on the old jetty and he followed that's it. No more than that.'

'Secret and you accuse me.'

'Secret, what secret, what you on about?'

'Demons, you, if not there to hold your hand. What now?'

'Nothing to worry about not worth mentioning.'

'You were not going to mention it were you, ay.'

'Said my piece forget it.'

'If he wasn't there, no, tell me why he was there.'

'Told you, he followed me on to the jetty. I said it. End of story. All you need to know.'

'Why did he follow you?'

'Oh, Forget it.'

'What reason did he have for following you? I've got to know. Was he the only one following you?'

Frank is looking at him and wondering why he is asking such questions and guessing the punch line is about to come.

'You did check didn't you, ay.'

'I was late. He came to fetch me and said he was worried. Thought was going to take a dive. But you see, no, here getting grilled by you and a kipper, not, so get down to it. What makes you think others are following me?'

'Have a drink and relax,' says Kaiser with an innocent smile.

The wind howling outside. Something somewhere on the roof is loose and continuing to bang like the beat of a drum.

Frank walked to the window and looked out. Nothing but wind and rain in the empty darkness and all the while was wondering what his friend was leading up to?

'The job is finished. What now?' Kaiser asked him.

'Home. What's in store is anyone's guess.'

'Back here?'

'Something on your mind?' Frank asked then said, 'would be an ideal situation if the opportunity to return was forthcoming.'

.'I'm sure you would be welcome. If and when the mill opens again. I heard it could be soon.'

'Well we will see, depends'

'On?'

'Why you going round the houses? What you got on that brain of yours? You know would gladly return if the opportunity presented itself, ay.'

'I heard that's all.'

'Willie, he said you wanted to see me.'

'The docks, yes.'

'The docks, yes and?'

Now he sees a poker face and when he sees it knows nothing will come smoothly.

'Don't worry about it,' Kaiser says, with the assurance of a five year old.

The mischievous look on his face is the warning sign Frank is used to seeing.

'Tell me not to worry about it! You know perfectly well when you tell me not to worry about it I'm going to bloody well, oh goodness sake, you know, bloody worry about it!'

'Boat left and I thought the storm would have delayed the sailing. Will be a good way out now you would think.'

'Why suddenly taking an interest? Ships and boats, you don't like ships or boats!'

'No. Who said I didn't like them of course like them.'

For a moment Frank trying to figure him. Knows something is not right. Try's reading the signs on his face. Knows him and can usually figure him out in five.

'The boat at lunch time why the disappearing act?'

'No time was in a hurry. Short on time you understand?'

'More to it than that I am sure. Hurry, bah. Dames?' Frank said, 'no doubt about it!'

FIVE

The time was…

Archie McDougall the rookie policeman was successful in persuading his station sergeant the boys grandmother, Granny Butler, would be better involved with his upbringing. She had more control and being more strict was better to keep him under her supervision after all he was fed up having to investigate reports day after day thing's this juvenile got up too. The two man station had enough to worry about with drunken fishermen on weekend nights. No need, or time, for the bother of delinquent children and particularly, Butler, the leader of the village gang of wastrels.

McDougall did not think the recent event would be repeated but how wrong he was…His police report…

Frank Butler and Jessie Lyle purloined a row boat and took it out the harbour.

The girl, Lyle , dropped her oar into the water, deliberately, it was said. They both began larking about and it's not the first time the pair indulged in this kind of tomfoolery… Butler…

It got so bad it convinced his mother to wash her hands of him once and for all.

The boat? 'Was just lying there,' they say when questioned.

And definitely this kind of thing happened some times before. Now it has to stop if McDougall has anything to do with it.

Frank rocked the boat from side to side and she splashed him with the water. They cared not a jot how much of the sea got into the boat. If it sank the village would have another disaster to contend with. Bad enough men lost at sea but two bairns drowning outside the harbour not good.

When it was reported to McDougall he mounted his bicycle to investigate the misdemeanour and hurried to arrest the culprits.

The rookie always eager to impress his sergeant and this seemed an ideal situation to get into the sergeants good books. Unfortunately it did not happen very often usually it ended in disaster.

Cycling like the wind he set off along the road. Raising himself up from the saddle now and again glancing over the sea wall he saw them apparently having a great time sailing along on the breeze.

The incoming swell moved them along to the beach beside the entrance to Granton harbour. When they reached the shallow water he jumped out shouting to her to follow. When she did leap the boat turned and moved out of reach. Not that it much bothered them they were having too much fun to take any notice.

Frank was laughing uncontrollably.

Jessie lifted her skirt and tucked it into her knickers and screamed with delight.

Standing up to their knees in the water they both started waving their arms and dancing like Dervishes splashing water over each other as the waves crashed into their legs. Enjoying the madness of it they leaped over each wave as it came faster and higher whooping as they anticipated each roll of the water.

A few beach strollers stopped to watch.

'It's going to Fife,' he shouted pointing to the land in the distance.

'The pirates are going to steal all the jewels and take the gold away to Burntisland,' she shouted, 'ghosts, sailing away the good ship the Black Dog with they pirates to get the dead sailors.' She is leaping over the waves getter wetter and wetter and she is not concerned one bit.

More bystanders come to watch and when the boat sailed off. Curios the pair not taking heed what was going to happen to it. 'Dashed on the rocks no doubt,' a woman to her lady companion.

'Got to be stolen they are not interested in it,' a man said.

'Police should be told, a gent, an old age pensioner,' said.

'It's a dead sailor he's rowing away for his pals,' Frank shouted and throwing water at her more vigorously.

28

'Come on ahead come on,' Jessie is screaming and splashing furiously. The sight of the water over his head and over his face made her laugh so much, she didn't know if it was the cold sea, maybe something else, responsible for her slight mishap. She stopped throwing the water standing with a wicked smile on her face.

He stopped. Looked, wondering what was she up too and in an instant he bent down took a mouthful of water and ran leaping over the waves and when he got close let go a mouthful, splash, right into her face.

'let's out it's bloody freezing,' he shouted when he saw her close her eyes and hold her breath.

She hunched her shoulders and lifted her hands putting her fists under her chin, stood shivering, 'Oh, you're dirty Frankie,' she screamed, 'get you for that.'

She spluttered and spat her spittle onto her sleeve then lunged and grabbed him by the hair pulling him face down into the water.

The move took him completely by surprise. Dealing with a wild cat he decided, enough was enough, so he called a truce, 'taken down the Jolly Roger,' crying out, 'enough! Okay?'

McDougall reached the beach…

'I'll take charge here. Stand back, get back,' says it with a lot of authority whilst walking tall but finding it difficult, struggling to push the cycle through the deep sand.

The sight of the pair stopped him in his tracks.

'Look at you couple of drowned rats do declare what a sight. If only your parents could see you now what would they say?'

Took hold of Franks right ear and held him at arms length then with his other hand he got hold of Jessie's elbow and pulled her to his side.

'I don't suspect there is anyone here responsible for these two children?' He paused, waited for a reaction looked among the crowd. 'I see the parents haven't arrived no wonder at that.' He shook his head, knowingly. 'I wouldn't have expected anything else,' he remarked sarcastically.

'Not me,' Jessie, sobbing and appealing to anyone in the crowd who would give her the benefit of the doubt.

29

'Ouch! Ouch!' Screamed Frank. Followed by swearing and hopping on one foot then the other, 'let go my blinking ear is coming off,' shouting through the pain.

The swearing only gave McDougall an excuse to hold his grip tighter.

'Do you want to die? You could have drowned. What would your mother's say if they could see the state of the pair of you… If they bother to turn up, that is?'

He thought a good rollicking would sort them out. Put fear into them but no chance of that.

'I'm nine so is Jessie. We can swim we widnae droon,' shouts Frank each word in sync with each step of his forced dance.

He was single minded that was that. Anything else was not worth the bother and McDougall he was just wasting his breath.

Another time another adventure when Frank and Mev McPherson, the son of skipper McPherson, the two scallywags, borrowed? a rowboat. Took it from it's mooring behind the cinema, the one in front of the famous dance hall and wrestling venue alongside the water of Leith near the bridge on Great Junction Street.

The dance hall at one time was famous for featuring the big bands of the era and was a happy hunting venue, for lovers, of all types.

Many romances started in the now defunct ballroom and of course wrestling nights a great place to see not just the wrestling but screaming ladies in the audience giving out with their humorous and fruity language.

The pair in the boat, quite happily up and down round and round enjoying a lazy day on the river. They removed their shirts showing the people looking at them from the bridge, pale skinny boyish chests. But such a glorious day is a better deal being on the river rather than in school and they are happy lapping up the attention from the watcher's on the bridge.

Among the crowd, a lady who just happened to be from the village, Mrs, nosey parker, Wilson, who had seen enough. She walked away in disgust at the scene and hurried to report what was going on to the local constabulary. When she encountered constable McDougall, she lost no time in informing him…

'Constable, they laddies, Butler and McPherson, on the water in a boat below Junction street brig. Are you going to do your duty? They wee pests are kipping the school a bloody disgrace what they are up to.'

The nosey busybody felt good, got some kind of perverted satisfaction reporting what she had seen leaving McDougall was in no doubt how she felt about the situation.

Getting on his bicycle and cycling hard it didn't take him long to reach the bridge and was surprised at the number of spectators who gathered to watch.

'My goodness, have you people not got anything better to be doing instead of gawping here giving these two encouragement,' he is saying as he gets from the bicycle, blowing his nose on a large coloured handkerchief and taking a minute to catch his breath after the epic ride. Was there to let them know he had arrived to sort out the situation and in no mood for any nonsense.

Some moved to let him pass whilst others held their ground.

'Get out of it,' woman shouted followed by rude suggestions.

People squeezed closer blocking the pavement the looks on their faces giving him the idea to play the situation calmly. He wasn't ready to cause a riot. Not wanting to upset the sergeant again.

Using his bicycle he forced a passage way through.

'Who was it, who said it? Out with it who said it? You must let me do my duty. Come on, shift. Get out the way and let me observe the situation.'

He sure was wasting his time, none took any notice. His face redder and redder nothing to do with the fine weather. No one owning up to the remark he was determined to disperse the crowd.

'Go for it lads,' shouted a small elderly woman with a loud mannish voice who stood on tiptoes straining her neck to see over the bridge and others shouting encouraging words egging them on as if this was the first time they saw a rowboat on the river.

McDougall, puffed, spluttered, and waited for someone to own up but got no joy. Was a female voice who cried out the offensive remarks unfortunately the majority who were present there made it impossible to find the one who shouted the offending remark. Muttering, was all that greeted him.

Now It was time to show them who was in charge…

'If you people don't get moving away from here will arrest you for causing a disturbance. So, on your way. Come on, move the lot of you.'

That'll teach them, he thought. But didn't work as many still held their ground.

They jostled and craned their necks looking at the delinquents in the rowboat who were enjoying the attention showered upon them.

McDougall was disgusted by their behaviour and in his mind they were as bad as the culprits on the river.

Pushing the bicycle forward he forced a way a bit nearer. Now he could see just what was going on below the bridge. Seeing them cheek to, he thought, was the owner of the boat standing on the river bank shouting and promising their life would not be worth living if they damaged his pride and joy.

The boys stood in the boat one after the other gesturing with their fingers giving out rude remarks. The boat rocked violently from side to side giving the people on the bridge a chance to shout more encouragement, of course, this was all good fun they hoped to see the pair dumped into the water.

When the culprits spied McDougall, who wondered, where they had learnt such language. They sat down, Mev took hold of the oars rowed across the far bank shouting at the top of his voice making a fool of McDougall who mounted his bicycle cycled over the bridge down Coburg street into the cemetery situated above the river parked the bike beside the gravestone of William Gladstone of that ilk and made his way to the dyke looking down on the river flowing fast below.

Seeing him peering over the wall the scoundrels rowed back to the other bank whereas McDougall, he thought, they would go over and leave the boat where the owner would rescue it grab them then he could take charge. Leaving the cemetery he cycled up Coburg street crossed the bridge making his way down behind the cinema.

They saw him and changed course rowing down river.

'That's the last we will see of him. *Old McDougall had a farm*,' sang Frank.

Mev joined in singing at the top of his voice.

32

McDougall on his bike once more cycled across the bridge down Coburg street, helter skelter, approaching Bernard Street. If he did not get them this time well soon he would have them. By golly, would get them come hell or high water, he was thinking, what ever it meant?

The people on the bridge laughed shouted all manner of things the pantomime was attracting more and more spectators.

McDougall reached Bernard street bridge parked the bicycle beside the door of the public house, the last building before the bridge, he walked back and forth looking over the railing down at the water wondering where they had gone not realising they were stationary below him. His frustration was showing and he had had enough with the whole bloody situation he decided to leave.

Mev, holding onto a rusty iron ring built into the stonework that is used as a tie up for small boats waited till they heard McDougall leaving then rowed to the steps on the cut on the wall. Climbing up the steps they stood a moment watching the boat sailing down river. Said a fond farewell. 'Bon voyage,' said Mev but not caring if it sank or it would be rescued.

Out safe and free the pair strolled past the popular bar, the Jungle, on the shore. They lingered a while making fun of a drunk prostitute who was touting for trade at the public house entrance, apparently without much success. She was so drunk her friend came out the pub and tried but failed to get her back inside.

Watching the two woman arguing but did not understand what was being said they walked away from the pub entrance and watched the comings and goings of the various punters, mostly sailors. Tried their luck at cadging pennies here and there and annoying another prostitute who was standing in a shop doorway trying her luck with any men who happened to pass her way.

When they got tired of ribbing the prostitute, who bid them no heed, left with arms round each other's necks. About their great adventure they felt proud. Something to enthral the rest of the gang with. But the icing on the cake…Laughing all the way from the shore when they heard the commotion coming from outside the public house where McDougall parked his bicycle.

What, they reckoned, would he say to his boss when he had to report the theft of his new upright bicycle the only bicycle in the police station. Over at the bridge they saw the crowd getting larger and heard the shouting getting louder.

'You think McDougall will arrest someone want to go and see.' Mev suggested.

'Canny, he'll arrest us,' says a laughing Frank, 'better go now hungry am ready for ma tea.'

'You just made a bloody fool of yourself. Didn't you realise they took a rise out of you gave them more fun at your expense. The owner of the boat is not going to make a complaint and what the school does about the truancy has nothing to do with us, none whatsoever.' The sergeant was furious. Again McDougall was out of line and it definitely wouldn't be the last time. Was finding it hard being a rookie copper. Obviously he didn't fit in and each day something or other would crop up. His slow uptake would find him more and more in the sergeants bad books and he often wondered if he was a suitable candidate or if he had the skill for the job. Wondered daily if he was cut out for police work.

'We have more on our plate to worry about than two bairns having a day on the river see you don't make us a laughing stock again. Get out of my sight. Go and see if you can rescue your bicycle. Do not forget it's police property. Some wag has phoned to say it sticking out the mud below Cables Wynd,' the sergeant bawled as McDougall stood meekly to attention.

'Have to get some sense into that head of yours. More to do can't be holding your hand all the time.'

'I bet was the toe-rag, Wilson, who phoned. He and his mother should keep their noses out of it. The trouble have had with them you wouldn't believe?'

Really low now the sergeant put his candle at a peep was deciding where was the best place to go to get out of the sergeants way.

'Never you mind who it was. Just go. Do something about it and don't come back till you've got the thing settled!'

'How am I gonna resolve it if it's in the middle of the river, sergeant?'

'You have a brain for goodness sake go and use it!'

A slow stroll along Junction street then left into Henderson street was without incident. Thinking of his future and if he can't rescue the bicycle, what will he tell the sergeant if he fails to recover it from the murky water of Leith?

'I need something to rescue a bicycle from the mud below Cables Wynd what do you recommend?'

He asked the guy standing behind the counter and feeling rather foolish for having to ask such a request.

The queue getting longer and the waiting customers in the queue begin making fun because of the loss of the bicycle. News of the local copper losing his bike was common knowledge to all the local busybodies. Possible culprit would be the busybody, Mrs Wilson. This woman was the bane of his life.

'Canny keep his eye on his bike chance have we got,' said the man dressed in brown bib coveralls to a complete stranger in the queue who muttered something scrunched his face but didn't saying anything sensible.

The shop was busy he was in the ship wholesale premises on the street behind the shore. People in the queue not happy the copper using his authority to approach the counter ignoring everyone else.

A man dressed in black bib coveralls and brown flat cap turned to the guy behind him and said, 'chance we got when the cops canny look after their own property and if he doesn't get a shoo on ma boss is going to have me over the coals for taking too long standing here. Know the score know it's like aye?'

Further back in the line a man in a black suit shouted, 'hurry up there. Don't you realise got a business to run this bloody situation is ridiculous'

Lots of laughter from the men in the line.

McDougall, standing there ignoring the remarks was anxious to be away and get the job done as quickly as possible to appease his sergeant.

A guy in brown coveralls said, to the one in the black coverall, 'no patience. Does he not know we've all got to get the business finished. I'm looking for an extension pipe has to be two inches round and this length,' he says stretching out his arm, 'this size…

Canny be a teeny wee bit out cause it will not fit the purpose and ma boss will read the riot act if I get it wrong. Know what it's like, ay.'

'What you need to rescue your bike is a hook to drag it out,' the brown coat behind the counter said wearily He was cheesed off because the queue was getting longer and it was nearing the time for his lunch break.

'You got such a thing?'

'Yes. That's what we sell. Things for getting things out of the water,' he waited, gave a long stare, to see if McDougall would get it. See if he could make sense of what he had said.

'That's good. This bloody trouble has had me thinking what would be suitable then I remembered this establishment.'

'Thought all you coppers had they things for dragging the water for dead bodies?' The brown coat says as he turned away.

'You think I would be here asking if had such a thing?'

'I only want to keep you right. No use spending rate payers money when you have the like. Surely you have something to do the necessary?' said, tongue in cheek and a bit smart alicky.

'Must be a do-gooder who doesn't want to spend the council money,' a voice back in the line shouted, causing more laughter.

McDougall got his grappling iron unfortunately went head over heels into the mud trying to rescue the bike at low tide and was a laughing stock for a long time after the failed episode.

'The bicycle? It's still in the mud below Cables Wynd. And someday when your passing you will see it sticking out at low tide,' Mrs Wilson said to Betty when she was enjoying tea and gossip in the café. After all wasn't she the one who reported it in the first place. Her nose in the air when she thought she had one over the other busybodies.

SIX

McDougall is not very big for a copper. Slender but under his shirt he was you could say someone who done weights and others seen him jogging. A policeman who was out to make a name for himself, even though, his sergeant thought he was stupid and a fool but one day, one day, he would come to his own and prove to the boss that his outlook of him would alter and he would make a go of it. He could even be so good, one day, could just be the guy to end the endless crime in the city. Could see the headlines. Village cop makes heroic arrests. Don't cost anything to dream but maybe one day, one day he'll show them, just wait.

He had these thoughts constantly when out of sight and sound of his sergeant.

Stopping the local toe-rag, vic, the moose, Wilson, one day after his bicycle went for a swim had a slight recollection the moose was hanging about the door of the public house when the incident with the stolen bike took place.

'Hey, when you were on Constituion Street at Bernard Street bridge did you see my bicycle parked at the door of the public house?'

'No, not me haven't seen it... Oh wait. That lump of scrap iron sticking out the mud over there in the water?' He said pointing a finger.

'No cheek from you answer the question.'

'My brother he was there, not me.'

'How do you know what I'm on about then?'

'My brother, he told me. It was him who said it.'

'Your brother said, what did your brother say? I'm positive it was you i saw there and don't you be trying to deny it.'

'What everybody knows,' he said walking away whistling merrily. His fingers inside the straps on the bib of his blue dungerees and now and then gave a little skip and a hop with a click of his heels on his tackity boots and with his right hand touching the top of his head giving a cheeky throwaway salute.

'Are you trying to take the p…' McDougall shouted as the moose hurried away with a large grin on his face and whistling Yankee Doodle dandy as he walked with a swagger into Junction street. Happy, as he thought made a fool out of him.

It wasn't a good day for McDougall. Five minutes later he was accosted by Mrs Wilson, who gave him the sharp edge of her tongue. Accusing him of harassing her innocent boy and blethering on about how useless he was and how he should find better things to be getting on with, like, moving on the drunks who litter the pavement outside the public houses on Junction street. She forever having to walk onto the busy road outside they particular public houses. 'You know the ones am referring too.' Saying out loudly and looking to passers-by to back her up but alas no one is the slightest bit interested.

'The one beside the bus stop. It's a wonder no one has been killed trying to get past on the pavement outside that particular den of rogues. You know what one and it's all you're blooming fault cause of you no doing your duty!'

'I'm doing what paid for and that is keeping the peace missy.'

'No, you ken you're as hopeless as a chocolate teapot. How your sergeant puts up with you is beyond me. Don't you forget McDougall known you a long time. You'll never learn not in a hundred years!'

'I do not have to answer to you. Any complaints take them to the right place.'

The bare faced cheek of the woman hung over him like a black cloud. He knew she would make for the station and be giving her mouth a lot of mileage to the sergeant. Why does he bother he was thinking just best to ignore her and if he spots her in future would be best to high tail it out of her way.

'Missy? How dare you use that term to me. You are employed to keep the peace, I grant you but they drunks standing there in the street are a blight on the community,' she pointed her finger at him angrily and knowing he wasn't taking the slightest bit of interest what she was saying. 'A day doesn't go by without one of my laddies coming in and telling me how you are at them all the time. Why have you got something against them? You not got better things to be doing chasing them. Must be worse than them why pick on mine all the time could show you worse than mine that Butler laddie for starters. Him and his cronies he kicks about with. Aye, them.'

'Mrs, if you chastise your wayward sons more often instead of getting on my case the place, as you say, would better serve the community. So, get on your way and stop havering you silly woman.'

'I'll report you to your sergeant. How dare you say these things to me. Make sure in future you leave my two boys out of it. How dare you McDougall!'

Shoulders straight and head high off she breezed muttering under her breath feeling put out by not winning the argument.

He strolled along Junction street. The woman was out of his thoughts. The sergeant would listen to her he knew full well and also knew he would take her nonsense in one ear and let it out the other... He had nothing to approach himself for because the day was warm the sun shining and everything hunky dory. He walked on his journey slowly nodding and smiling to the people he encountered along the way. Quickening his step made for a favoured café to get a cool knickerbocker glory. After all was a lovely day the sun shining and it was pleasantly warm. Mrs, what's her name? Was out of his thoughts and he knew when he got back to the station the sergeant would have forgot the bother he had had with Mrs Wilson.

If only he could get the bike? Only he could devise a scheme to rescue the thing from the water? Well, that would sure be point scoring and he would gain some respect from the sergeant. If only, but harder than it seems. A couple of hours of peace would be dandy. Keeping out the way was a good idea.

The ice cream was going down well he was quiet happy sitting in the shade of the willow tree observing the grown ups and the children enjoying the day when unfortunately. He saw her coming. 'Bloody knew it,' muttered, 'long time since clapped eyes on her. Just my luck she shows up here when all I want to do his have a bit of peace...much to ask, is it. Goodness sake. What have I done to deserve this?' Hunched his shoulders and crouched trying to make himself look smaller in the seat.

'Hey McDougall.'

'Yeah, can help?'

'Hope so.'

'Well, what you want?'

The woman carrying a basket filled with bunches of heather approaching in a hurried manner.

'Go away, not buying today and no, no need my fortune told.'

'They, flats. The ones they call, think, Oranges. A fire there, quite a big fire.'

'Well, call the fire brigade, go away don't bother me not see I'm busy?'

'Mister, sure they don't call you biscuit seeing you're always on a break.'

'Go peddle your wares somewhere else.' He looked round saw the people taking notice of what was being said.

'I've reported a fire what you doing about it?'

'You've walked here. Walked past all these shops in the street why wait till you see me. What's your game what you playing at?'

'She put the basket on the ground stood with her hands on her hips, 'wasn't bothered earlier. Saw you lazing there thought you should know,' she said brazenly.

Building will be destroyed by now the time you've taken.'

'But reported it to you.'

'What did you see. Describe what you saw a big fire was it?'

'Oh aye. Very big.'

'He looked down the street in the direction of the building, 'don't see any smoke. Sure you saw a fire. Not on something are you?'

'Such as?'

'On your way. You've been seeing things there is no fire.'

'Was so. The bins behind seen the Jani put it out. Thought you should be told.'

'Give me strength,' he wailed as he watched her confront two navy ratings pleading with them to buy some lucky heather.

'No thanks no heather but you got a sister?' Sailor says giving her the eye.

'Goodness never been spoken to like that since the war.'

'The war?' Second sailor says surprise on his face.

McDougall, guessed the guy was too young to have a memory of the war.

'American soldiers. They were always asking you got a sister baby? Trying her American twang. 'But all I wanted was any gum chum or a Hershey bar,' she says.

'And for a bar of chocolate they got?'

'McDougall overheard the remark 'I'd watch it. If you are not careful she'll put a curse on you and what i've heard not wise to get on the wrong side of her.'

'Have you a sister?' The taller of the two sailor asks lifting his right eyebrow and smiling.

'Nothings to fear from us,' other says.

'You've had your fun lads,' says McDougall, leave it, better be on your way.'

'You buy some lucky heather and I'll tell your fortune. You know you're dying to see what the future holds.'

'Tell us if you are going to introduce us to your sister then we will buy some of your heather,' tall one says flashing his pearly whites and giving her the come on.

'Agree and we will see if your lucky heather is as lucky as you say it is,' small sailor says.

McDougall watched them stroll off. The girl between the two of them and the small one toting the basket of heather.

'

Hi Regan, that gypsy pest reported a fire at the back of the flats. Said the jani, you, managed to deal with it no need for the fire engines you coped okay as can see.' Lifted the lid of the large waste rubberised waste bin now instead of green colour mostly burnt black and smelling of rotten eggs and other obnoxious smells from the bin's contents.

'Aye fire right enough. Vandals. Going round lighting fires think it's great fun. Not care the consequences. One of these times someone's going to get hurt.'

'Right enough need eyes back of your head. Okay Regan, won't need to report it now taken care off be on my way.'

SEVEN

Kaiser rekindled Franks memories and he was determined to face his demons. Get the lowdown on the facts with a bit of luck solve his problems. Not taken it lightly that his friend would dream of comparing him to the old Dutchman, there again, thought maybe Kaiser was right. Now the time to man up stop being sorry for himself. If no more contracts came his way, so what. His brother was the only close family he had and if the Leith inspection engineering company had no more use for both of them, well, tough, the Greenes will find it won't pay them to throw their weight in his direction by means of threats no he would be ready. After all, he knew the score and things could only get better there has to be more to life than the present situation. The time to get it straight is when he is home and that would not be be long now.

'Are you going to tell me why you are here drinking my whisky and giving me grief. Not in any kind of mood to play games got too much on my mind.'

'Will you no take a wee dram ma mannie?' Kaiser saying, trying out his idea of a Scottish accent as he slid the whisky bottle and empty glass across the table.

Frank glanced round the room the standing steel lockers are wide open and empty along with the smaller three drawer filing cabinet. Sink is cleared of clutter. The wastepaper basket free of rubbish. Best of all no paperwork. The juniors had done the deed and taken the ledgers with them. 'Good,' he muttered, 'something done right for once,' he afforded a meagre smile. The departing two had been busy without his prompting. Now was thinking fine except a guarantee one or the other was out to impress someone in management.

Sem, Kaiser Van Doreen, was his friend. A dangerous friend some said to be wary of his friendship. People said he could not be trusted was evil an animal. Should be in a cage and the key thrown away. Frank had no reason to be wary kaiser was the only guy who befriended him. Always genuine, since the two had met a few years earlier and more or less in each other's pockets ever since. Certainly up till now he had no case to worry. Not so far.

'Left my wee friend for your protection,' he said, picking up the revolver from the table giving it the once over. Stroking the barrel and spinning the chamber round and round. Held it to his right ear happy with the noise it made. A noise like ball bearings spinning in an empty cup.

'What you think bowtow, nice, ay.'

'Yeah, nice. Come on tell me why my protection and why are you telling me the phone is not the only thing that is dead,' patted the holster under his arm, 'own protection ya numpty. Why would need yours?'

'Listen, you're in some serious mess... Up to your neck in it, to be precise.' Pulled his right forefinger across his throat and made a face ... 'Could have explained at the docks but you were on the ship. I couldn't let old Willie know because, well, you know it would have been broadcast all over the docks. You know how much of an old wife he is. Anyway couldn't wait. Was in a hurry had to be somewhere else you know needs must. Wouldn't do to be caught, in the circumstances, not help my reputation one little bit. That's how you see it, isn't it? Conquests are important for the game. Must understand pally. Yes sir. Have to be on the ball at all times don't you agree, ay.'

Watched him smile. Thought for a moment then shook his head in disbelief at his gaul. 'In a hurry. A dame you and a tart who is on the game some protection. Heard it all now. Fun and games with a pro,' he lifted the glass and filled it to the brim then drank it over. 'Needed that. See how you're driving me to drink.'

'Yes yes, don't need me to drive you to drink you are capable of doing it yourself. You don't need me to start you off. Anyway was a pleasing way to spend the afternoon, until I got the message that is.'

'What message? Get to it Kaiser, you're making a meal out of this.'

'This morning was in the Bear and Pieter, you know the one, was to let you know, two strangers, Deutcher Mensh, were looking for you. Were after information about your kid brother Jamie.The request had me puzzled and Pieter he was vague on the reason.'

'Why would anyone need to know anything about my brother. How the hell does anyone know have a brother. The buck what the buck is going on?' The words came in rapid fire he was angry and resented the fact someone was interested in his private life. No one had the right to poke their nose into his face. No sir and was thinking, why Jamie and what information? He felt the blood vessels in his head tighten and was dreading the onset of another migraine he was sure to come. Would be brought on by what his friend had said. He couldn't take much more of this conversation the way it was panning out. The quicker he could get out of here the better he was not in any mood to hear more.

'The idiot shot his mouth off and told them to look for the gun man, Kaiser, me. What a fool. Should have kept it shut,' he picked a knife from the table and waved it from side to side in a crisscross fashion over his chest, 'will have to be having a word in his ear, that's for sure. Calling me the gun man... How many bairns has he got out of the marriage bed? Cheek to talk of me when he has fired more bullets from his barrel. He beats me hands down.' Rose from the table walked round the room waving the knife in a stabbing fashion.

'Calm down and get to the point. What trouble what you telling me?'

'The word is your saint of a brother and a wee pretty German girl have done a runner. Quite a large quantity of polished stones. Lots. The people who have been robbed of the goods... Biggest crime syndicate this side the American pond.'

Reaching for the bottle he refilled his empty glass moved the bottle back to the middle of the table continued speaking in full flow, 'just out the door and she expected her husband would be back soon, they were there, two in suits. Someone told them where i could be reached. They asked nicely, so, i accompanied them here. Now, you may think it was a stupid thing to do but if you knew what i learnt on the journey. They only spoke together In French. As you know my love for the words. Didn't know I spoke the French. Sure as hell let the cat out the bag would you believe it.,' he smiled, stood shaking his shoulders his palms facing upwards he moved them out and back then forward again. 'Stupid iriot a famous funny man said, didn't he, ay,' resumed his seat waiting the answer.

Thinking how funny his pal had cottoned on to the word, ay. How quick he was copying the things he said. Thought it funny because he didn't realise he said, ay.

'You came with two men In a car, what the, what you done Kaiser, let's have it. Benny something, think is the guy, the funny man if I recall,' gave him the look eager to get back on track. 'Well, numpty not the word for it. Had our cards marked. No prisoners were to be taken and would you believe me if I said good bye Vienna was the tune one was whistling.' Reached for the whisky bottle to refill his glass, 'these drinking thingies are too small have you not got anything bigger than these piddling things,' he shook his head, 'far too small. Take forever to hang one on I tell you.'

Listening to the on going story was now getting tedious, he sighed, 'get to the point. How many chapters in this you gonna tell me?'

Kaiser straightened his right arm lined it up with the sink and took aim.

'Don't you dare,' watched him hamming up the situation he was not about to get on his knees to pick up broken glass knowing how Kaiser operates more than a small tumbler would get the same treatment.

'What?'

'Throw the glass at the sink.'

'No, was not going to do that. You know I wouldn't,' says, smiling, demonstrating with the glass turning it over and over in his hand, 'these things are no use. Okay for Jenever but not suitable for lovely malt.'

Pulled the chair from under the table impatiently planting himself down giving the sign, a look to indicate he was not in favour of the small nip glasses.

'Will you get on with it for goodness sake it's like pulling teeth.' His patience at a low and the situation is going from the serious to the ridiculous.

'Calm down calm down getting there ma mannie. So, we arrived and before they got out I got my little friend and one after the other, bang bang. Behind the right ear. An organisation you've heard of who use this way of disposing and If they gadgies are ever found, we'll, the known brothers will be blamed.

Do you know, unbelievable did not frisk to see if was carrying. Mind you, had a wee bit of a clean up to do, ken me, tidy tidy all the time.'

'Yeah yeah get to it get on with it.'

Nodding and smiling trying his best to prolong the situation hands went through the motion of cleaning and scooping up and depositing, whatever, out, as if it was an open car window.

'Couple of so called hard men. You know me, they couldn't match. Not our league unhappily found to their sorrow.' Lifted a knife and went on 'these are nice though, you think, ay. Why do you think one had two and the other only packed a shooter funny ay. Some people? Yeah canny whack it kin you. Wouldn't like to think they took us for a couple of so called beggars. Us foolish not on your Nellie. What you say up the Clyde in a banana boat? No us, ay.'

'Unbelievable you truly are,' he's aware the story was going to go on and on and thought just let him get going with it let him tell it in his own way and it'll end soon hopefully!

Kaiser moved his finger up and down the blade and the way he did it, was as if it was an every day occurrence. Confident like the old days of the Wild West. Quick on the draw then kill first or meet your maker. Acted the part of the goodie. The one in the white hat the one always in the right.

'I take it you got rid but what about the lassie? Did you find out anything about her? Say anything in French any noise about her?' Asking because he is desperate for an answer he needs to know what he is up against as Kaiser is going round and round the houses and not telling the story fast enough for his liking.

'No, interested in you and your friends pump for information then bring about the final solution,' gave the outstretched arm salute clicked his heels before sitting down cocked his chin gave a wink and a smile

'So we're no further forward we are in the dark clutching and now it looks like you're involved. So what do we do next do you know all ears open to suggestions and they better be good. Can't stand any nonsense this situation is for real.'

Realising how bad the seriousness of the caper is he not happy with his friends laid back attitude. How can they possibly stay safe when he has said the syndicate is the largest in Europe?'

'I've been involved from the time Pieter informed on me and so we will have to be on our guard have to be careful, that's for sure Bowtow.'

'It means we are now on the run. A couple of fugitives, wow, what next?'

'I would say so buddy. Fugitives, we sure are wow is right.'

'You're enjoying this Kaiser. I hadn't dreamed we would be in an Agatha mystery all we need, on the run and you looking for the chase. What are we, hunter or hunted? More night time grief not looking forward to.'

'Oh, get a grip be positive. We will get through this that's for sure. You'll see. It's not as bad as you think. Don't worry you can only die once.'

'Aye aye, says the master of the underworld.'

'Up to speed. Thought you would be here eventually. I didn't think it was a problem…So, took the car round the back to the canal. Didn't bother with the identities they sure to be false. Watched them float away, nicely, face down carried by the fragrant Ems. Sure to end up on a beach somewhere in their own backyard in the Fatherland and if hadn't taken care of it, well, you would have no more worries it would be us dead in the water. In the briny floating with the breeze and easy grub for the fishes. That situation doesn't appeal. No thanks not favourable, no sir, after all love life to take care of,' he said smiling. Reaching into the inside pocket of his reefer jacket, 'I'm positive,' he said, as he laid a pile of British bank notes spreading them across the table. 'There Bowtow three thousand for expenses. They gadgies have no use for money where they have gone. The thing to do now is get rid of the wheels. Pity though, it's a nice motor. Bet it cost a bundle. A lovely nice new Merc going begging. Pity have to loose it.'

'I'll apologise to you for my outburst. I'm really sorry.'

'No I should apologise. We shouldn't fall out over this.'

'I over acted. You understand, ay.'

'Don't worry. I do understand. Was trying hard to find the courage to let you down gently. Hard to come out with the news straight off. You know that don't you. Things will out you'll see pal.' Picked up the glass and drank it slowly savouring the taste. Then he gathered the hardware and followed him out the office put out the light was whistling good night Vienna then hurried along the dark corridor and descended the stairs to the yard.

Frank waited till the headlights of the Mercedes came into view from behind the main factory building.

The rain was relentless battering against the corrugated factory walls. The wind giving out a low drone along the overhead telephone wires and black clouds rushing across the morning sky. The water along the banks of the canal whooshed as a fishing boat sailed outward bound the noise of it's engine slowly going out of earshot. Passing on its journey to the open sea in search of it's hoped for bumper harvest. Dark and eerie buildings, 'good riddance,' Frank said. Home he was thinking but what now what did the future have in store? Watched Kaiser drain the whisky bottle and drink the dregs from the glass. Watched him gather up his hardware. Lights out,' he had said, 'we're out of here,' now thinking will Kaiser still be around or disappear leaving him to find the truth. The whole truth or nothing? Is he going to return home or are the cards going to be stacked unfavourably?

Followed to the outskirts of the town saw Kaiser go left at the roundabout. Wondering what he was up to guessed was on his way to the all night drinking salon, the White Bear, in the small market town of Appingadam. Maybe, he was thinking should have gone himself. May not have time to say his farewells was leaving soon and not the done thing to leave without saying his goodbyes. Would not have much time to be there and knowing once there how long to say goodbye once the drink starts flowing would put his schedule right out. If he can will try but doesn't hold much hope. Feeling terrible he will not have the decency to tell all of them how much enjoyment over the years was gotten in the White Bear.

EIGHT

Frank parked the car at the church carpark. Searched the glove compartment and removed the revolver Kaiser had graciously left for his protection.

Kaiser? He's thinking what is he up to. Saw him turn left at the roundabout on the outskirts of town. The white Bear, that's it, he is on his way to the White Bear. The twenty four hour drinking salon.

The short walk he took to the apartment building the wind and the rain had not let up.. His footsteps echoed on the wet pavement memories of old Hollywood movies took over his thoughts. Thinking about silly times when he would hide his face under a cushion at the scary flicks when he was young watching black and white movie's on a black and white television set. Smiling at the memory pulled his cap down and his Reefer collar closer and glanced round the deserted street checking to see if he was being followed thinking people would be mad to be out at this time and in this foul weather.

A couple of tom cats rushed past spitting and screaming like cats do. Quickened his step as the wind pushed into him rushing him along. Hunched, shivered and groaned at the suddenness of it. Seemed forever before he reached the tenement building and his single end one room with kitchen accommodation.

Made coffee and sat by the table wondering what mischief his friend was getting himself into. Thought over the story about the nonsense his brother got involved with and the girl. Always first to know of any romance his brother got involved in but this time no word came his way of any new girl. The story was hard to believe and he was still thinking just where will it all end? Kaiser, still thinking about him fixed at the back of his mind, was he going to be around or would he disappear to leave him to bare the brunt on his own. Was all too much. Little did he know what was in store when he left the docks. Everything now turning into the dreaded nightmare. Would have to have his wits about him he was certainly on the ball on that fact. Sleep, if only, but knew sleep would be impossible.

Lying on top of the single bed his thoughts going over the recent events finding it impossible to get any sleep. Tossed, up, round, over, turning this way that way before rising to make more coffee. Spilled a large dash of whisky into the mug sat slowly sipping and listening to the lady on the radio talking ten to the dozen in a language he wished he had set himself to learn. Rising from the table walked to the window. Parting the curtain looked out on to the lonely front street. Sitting through the morning watching out the window at the deserted street wondering what his next move would be. Wondering and worrying. Removed the pistol from his under arm holster and grinned, wondered why Kaiser failed to accept that he had his own protection. He smiled, 'bloody man thinks he's my big brother can see why he thinks it's his duty to protect me.' He muttered. A shake of his head again and smiling when he caught in the corner of his eye one of the Tom cats he seen earlier, sitting, crouched under a lamp-post. He raised his drink, 'here's to the victor.'

Late afternoon was ready to leave the apartment.

Crammed the small amount of clothes he possessed into a second hold-all and placed the hold-all on to the bed. Split Kaisers expense money into two bundles and with Kaisers revolver and his own, put them at the bottom of the hold-all. Fussed about the place making sure was leaving the place in ship shape order. The house rent paid to date and the landlord said, at his last meeting, considered him not as a tenant but as a friend and was sorry he was leaving. The guy was also his mine host at the White Bear. The drinking salon where he with his two juniors had been regulars and where many good nights into the wee small hours had been appreciated. He, under the circumstances was sorry to be leaving some good people who he encountered at the Bear.

Done a last look round the apartment getting ready to leave suddenly he heard a soft knock on the front door. He crossed over and when he opened was surprised to see a small girl, with an angelic smile on her face beaming up at him. She done a perfect curtsy. Stood up and handed him a piece of crumpled paper.

He smoothed it... Ma, then K, was written nothing else. He made a face, 'what now,' he said, in a put out sort of way.

The girl, waiting, sporting a permanent gorgeous smile looking up at him made him mellow his mind about the sudden inconvenience.

He knew why she lingered. Smiled back at her and gave her a pile of change from his pocket playfully counting it into her upturned palm.

Her smile grew larger as she cupped the coins in both hands and without saying a word ran down the stair as quick as a flash and was gone.

Shook his head as he closed the door. 'Unbelievable,' he muttered.

Was raining when he reached the street. Though the wind had eased the damp grey skies reminded him of the view he used to get from his bedroom window. A longed for sight of the clouds scurrying above the lighthouse at the end of the Newhaven pier. Constant thinking, reminded by the similar weather patterns between Holland and his part of Scotland. The times when he was young and the times he lay abed waiting and anticipating the oncoming storm. Thought to put the foolishness out his head. Saw a waste rubbish bin on the pavement and ditched the note. He hurried to the church car park. Bells ringing and the faithful arriving for prayers. They rushed about avoiding the other's who shifted here and there, spotting, stopping and starting, seeking the best parking spaces same time annoying the people on foot who skipped out of the way dodging the many vehicles.

He drove out the car park. The drive lasted about five minutes before he parked four blocks away on Market Platz. He waited for some time, watching, to see if he was being followed.

The coast was clear left the car and walked slowly across the square, constantly looking, searching to see no one was on his tail. Approaching the row of shops he knocked on the closed door the one next the window with a red light showing. Watched the fading reflections behind him in the shop window to see if anyone was following from where the cars were parked at the square. No followers the street was clear and silent except for the

51

noise of the wind and the splatter of the falling rain. Dusk coming fast he's thinking how any sane person would venture out in the crazy weather. Knocked once more.

'Ruthie,' he mutters when she opened the door. The vision has taken him completely by surprise.

Took a step back. The heat from inside hit him full on and the loud music swirled above his head. The heavy scent of greasy hot fat from a chip fryer was overpowering but reminding him he hadn't eaten for some time.

Looked her up and down. Her hair was piled high on top of her head. Her lips, painted the reddest he had ever seen and from her neck to her knees she was naked. The scene made him gasp but at the same time thought of hot greasy chips and reminded him just how hungry he was and how much hungry he was for her?

He tried but failed to make a sound of appreciation. The sight of her nakedness, he could make out through the green chiffon skimpy dress excited him? Her slender legs were bare. He took a step back admiring her standing there in her red high heel shoes with her chest, her nipples, reminding him of football boot studs. She looked a dream, he thought – a splendid five foot of desire. 'I cannot take my eyes of your eyes, beautiful. Must be the reflection of your wonderful nearly dress, blue and green. Your hair, my your hair. Your body, not to be missed but, sure gonna miss it.'

Done a pretend swoon with the back of his hand on his brow. Then, the thing men do with their arms palms inwards caressing the curves of the invisible female body, up, waist in, down. Same time making appreciated noises.

'You really like it?' She gushed. 'We got a new girl. Was a hairdresser before she got the calling she has done all the girls.'

'I bet she has.' In his head...Naked flesh on flesh.

Bowed and kissed the back of her right hand.

She ushered him in. 'Look everyone, Frankie,' she announced but no one took any notice they were too busy being busy to what was more important.

The girl behind the bar sitting on a stool watching a black and white portable television set. She was engrossed in an American soap and the actors speaking Dutch, which he thought, was crazy.

Three sailors at a table drinking bottled beer bargaining with two girls who wore the attire, laid down by the rules.

Half a dozen guys sitting alone at tables waiting for the main event to take place or not. Plenty porn movies projected on to the walls holding their attention except for one who was not happy, angry and complaining, the prices in this particular establishment compared unfavourably to similar establishments.

There was a nice selection to choose from he thought at a price. Thin ones and fat ones tall and small he couldn't get the guys attitude at all. Sitting at the end of the bar counting her money was Ma Tracy. She stopped what she was doing and laid her cigarette holder into a large glass ashtray. Without turning she said. 'Sally give him a glass pour a shot of this gin,' moved the bottle towards him the moment he pulled the stool he greeted her with a large smile, 'thanks for that Ma.'

The girl walked backwards down the length of the bar her eyes fixed on the TV. Her right hand, stretched, lifted a half pint glass from the cluster of glasses on the counter below the large mirror and put it in front of him but did not pour. She did not look at him but turned and sauntered lazily back to the TV.

Ma said she was going to do something with that girl. Lazy not the word for it. Was getting too big for her boots but he knew what she said, just words.

Watched her, bemused, he poured the gin into the glass and shook his head at her antics. Watched her sitting on her stool and wondering, just what her function entailed. Was it he thought she in on the game or a paid tv watcher?'

Kaiser was sitting at a table beside the door marked private with his head leaning in an awkward position watching a porn scene projected onto the coloured wallpaper.

The scene in front of him, 'crazy the place is plain crazy,' muttered as he drank the gin, Ma said to have another but he declined.

The angry man came past pushing a pretty blonde girl towards the door marked private. Happy now he thought the man must have got a deal to his liking.

'I can't see what's happening this stupid coloured wallpaper. Who's idea was it to have coloured wallpaper?'

Kaisers remarks meant for Ma who ignored him continued to puff on her cigarette holder and count the money.

'The Queen is in her counting house, stealing the tax mans money,' sang Kaiser.

'You look like my twin,' says as he walked over to where Kaiser is sitting. He was wearing a black barge cap a black full length reefer coat and denim blue coloured trousers. Round his neck a red coloured bandana with a pattern of small black stars. He straightened and smiled, 'got the note then, ay.'

'What's your problem should be saying farewell in the Bear not here with you watching porn and why the get up? But, like your style aye, ay.'

Done a backward shuffle his arms outstretched demonstrating his approval then pulled a chair across from him at the table.

'You can't go near the pub, it's closed it's a crime scene,' whispering, as he moved his chair closer. 'Pieter the barman at the Bear found behind the bar this morning. His throat cut, and no, before you ask,' he waved his right hand anticipating the next question, 'no, nothing to do with me. His head, off. And the noise is the same thing has happened in Oldenburg. A local barman gave out information about the girl and your brother he suffered the same fate. Information from Germany London and maybe a connection to your Scotland. The road block you got stopped at the cops were on the lookout for two men. Unfortunately the trail went sour in Amsterdam. Two Germans wanted for murder. They escaped the dragnet they are not fools we are really up against it.'

'One's in the canal, you think it was these two they were looking for? As you say this is serious. Just what have we got ourselves into or rather, what has Jamie got himself into?'

'No, no the word is two others caught the flight to London. Car found abandoned at Amsterdam airport. There was enough cops there to form a rugby team, useless!'

'Situation is bad. I should go to the cops and get the low down. See what progress if any. Get a handle on it.'

'Go to the cops? No, that is a last resort. No, no coppers.'

'Find out, anything is better than waiting. Not knowing, it's madness.'

'Don't you understand how serious this is?'

'Yes, but there…There could be more.'

'You can't go to the cops you can't trust them.'

'Got to get up to date and play it cool casual like say brother is missing.'

'Have to keep your head down. Goodness sake get a grip.'

It was hard to convince him what was what. Was beginning to try kaisers patience, 'go to the cops? They don't know you are involved. If my information is correct and I trust my sources the police are floundering without knowing the reasons for the murders being committed they have it down to gang warfare.'

'Okay, take it you've got a plan since this morning? Thought I would have seen you earlier you realise things got to be discussed don't you?'

'Wee saint of a brother has brought this on himself. Now we have to be very careful from now on. What is it you're not getting? You have to give me your trust.'

'You think I don't know give me some credit.'

He asked Ma for the gin bottle got to his feet and picked up the empty glass with the bottle then returned to the table.

'No you can't trust the cops. That's that. Will do what we said we would do get it sorted stop getting them in a twist. You'll see we will survive I promise.'

'Okay, are you gonna tell me your plan, or, are you not gonna tell me your plan? Going out of my mind with all this nonsense.'

Kaiser raised a finger to his lips. 'Steady. Keep it down. There are two in the canal and two in London. Two, believe it or not sitting not far from us in a black Merc outside the Bear. Two more, many more, who knows? Will see you tomorrow. Take care of yourself Bowtow. I'm out of here,' made a move on Ma kissed the back of her neck massaged her shoulders slowly moving his hands round to her bosom gently squeezing lingering waiting for her reaction.

'Not at the moment. You sexy boy. Later much later,' she scolded.

'Have you a plan or not?' He is insisting on an answer. 'I need to know the deal,' not happy that Kaiser is not taking the situation seriously and playing the jester at this time is not good form he is thinking.

Waved his hand to silence him, 'Ma will fill you in. Car key, give. A plan, of course got a plan. Shaking his head as he walked towards the exit. 'Be asking if the moon is made of cheese next. A plan, take it as it comes,' says muttering to himself.

'Frankie lover.'

'Yes Ma, come to say goodbye.'

'I know. Sorry to see you leave as is all of us. Nevertheless, we have a going away present for you.'

'A present, for me? Well I never. The sky won't fall in will it Ma?'

'Cheeky devil might change my mind for that you rascal,' gave him the bent elbow treatment and a playful slap on his rump.

Grasping the bar he saved himself from falling. 'Oh no, don't do that Ma, got me all excited. Cannot wait to see.'

'For you dear you can have as much as you wish and the other you can pick free. No charge on the house up to you.'

'First things first do you have the plan? Don't know why he has left you with it and don't see why he has to get you involved in any way. He is playing the fool it's a dangerous game we are embarking on really dangerous.'

'No dear no fool,' her eyes looked into his and she could see he really was disturbed. Tried to console him but she saw in his manner it wouldn't take much to send him over the edge.

'Should not be. Just how many are in the plan?'

'Not many. Now for your present.'

'Gone off it.'

'What', Ruthie asked, 'what, you gone off?'

'Well I never,' Ma says not believing a word of it.

'Haven't the stomach. Too much to think about.'

'You hear that girls he hasn't the stomach. Must be sick.'

'What about poor me?' Ruthie says with eyes flirting and cuddling up against him.

'Must be,' said Sally distracted from the tv.

Must be, what?' A sailor, alone at a table is asking.

'Sick,' shouted Sally.

'Gladly oblige he not up for it,' sailor shouts in anticipation.

'I'll have first refusal,' a skinny weasel of a man interrupted. Saying it as he glared at the sailor who laughed at his cheeky proposal.

'Would do me fine,' a blousy woman sitting behind the sailor said getting in her penny-worth.

'You two can fight it out,' the sailor says to her laughing, 'too much competition for my likes. You can toss for it.'

'Now now' said Ma, 'I know she's a choice commodity. Take your time. Wind your necks in plenty to be had. Be patient till he makes up his mind. This gentleman is first in line,' smiled at Frank, 'see, not nice to have customers squabbling.'

Thirty minutes later he approached the white van the one with black lettering on it's side and was not happy with the situation. Wondering what was in store. He saw the driver get out and walk round and opening the passenger door.

'Hi,' he said 'My name is Beeny. He has left your bags. I'm taking you to Leeuwarden. So, let's be gone,' said somewhat impatiently. Looked up and down the street motioning him to get into the passenger seat then closed the door with a bang.

'Has he arranged for somewhere for me to stay? Ma, a bit vague and Kaiser is a law unto himself got me stumped haven't a clue what he's got on his mind,' looked over his shoulder and saw his bags and he was wondering if Kaiser had relieved him of the revolver.

'Yeah, better not to ask he's a man of mystery. Kaiser, the man of mystery...I like it. Sums him exactly.'

'Tell me about it should have taken the hire to Amsterdam. Got to see someone in Rotterdam it's important I don't miss the appointment.'

'It's okay. The hire people have a drop off in Groningen. You'll make the appointment in plenty time. Kaiser knows what he's doing. Let him do what he's good at don't worry about anything.'

'You seem to be better informed than I am.'

'Well, that's Kaiser for you.'

He fired the engine glanced in the mirror and pulled on to the road. All the while he is having doubts about his passenger.

'Do you know what is planned? He's not let me in on the act so far and I don't know what he's thinking,' anxious, his head all over the place. Getting no satisfaction and for some reason taken a dislike to this guy Beeny. Smarmy in his eyes not appears to be street wise. A no-all who knows no-all. Did not like the guys manner guessed he was trying too hard to impress. Trying hard to show a cosy relationship with Kaiser but really far down the pecking order in the scheme of things.

'We are going to my dads place our wine bar, eh, we sell wine to other bars. I travel most of the week on deliveries was at the Bear last night. Bad news, Pieter the barman. Liked him poor guy. He was good for a laugh poor guy. Can you imagine? What a way to go, wow!'

'Yeah, as you say, poor guy,' but was thinking did he really know the poor guy? Did he know how the guy lived and was he privy to his every day routine or was he listening to gossip and making small talk just to impress?

'You got somewhere for me to kip?' Asked for the sake of changing the conversation.

'You're with me got two apartments above the bar and you won't go hungry. Food is not a problem. We have got a brilliant chef who runs the restaurant. You'll be looked after. No worry you will be okay. A word of warning though, my sister, Nikki eh, er, you'll like her and easy going dad of course.'

Got his his brain into gear thinking is the guy for real trying hard to make me like him. Okay, give him some rope see how far he goes and go along for now. Sister? What about a sister? Well well something to look forward too.

'Sister Nikki? Got good things to say about sister Nikki?' Asked, thinking, might be productive, smiled, well well maybe there is something in it after all to look forward to?

'Oh, forget I said it. You will make your own mind up about her no more to be said.'

'Is she pretty?'

'As I said, you'll find out let's change the subject.'

'Okay. How long have you known him?'

'Kaiser? How long have I known him?'

'Aye. Kaiser. How long? Who else. Who else you think was talking about? If you prefer we could talk about your sister okay

58

by me.' Ask's again, 'How long you been buddy buddy with him Kaiser that is?'

'I don't think you should be asking these questions. After all you are a stranger to me and you are asking too many questions for someone who is supposed to be his friend. What would you say to me if I was asking all the questions about you? Not like it dare say. Not like it one little bit.'

'Not unreasonable should know something about you. After all we are on a journey that's more of a mystery to me, ay, got to give me that.'

'Kaiser moves in some dodgy circumstances. The less talked about…Would appreciate it if no more was said.'

He concentrated on the road ahead hoping he had heard the last from him and was thinking what a stupid name Bowtow? Why Kaiser used the name when he knew the guy's name was Frank. He couldn't see the sense in it Bowtow stupid name. And will be a lot happier when he can off-load this baggage he is forced, yes that's it unwanted baggage Kaiser forced on him.

'Long, get where we are going far is it to Leeuwarden?'

'It won't take long soon be there,'

'How long? I'm waiting why are you so secretive my patience is beginning to wear thin on a short fuse not ready to take much more.'

Stopping the van he turned to look at him, 'Give me a break pal. You certainly are on a trip have to be careful what Kaiser has said to me it is not easy to take in. I'm in as much danger as you are and after all if it hadn't been for your brother!'

'Yeah, yeah if it hadn't been for my loveable…Sweet brother,' he looked away, what now he's thinking. Hoping the journey was going to end soon and be out of this guy's way. Could get rid but then what? 'Kaiser, he got on my nerves! Not take any more of it.' He didn't snap but knew exactly just what he thought he would say.

'Kaiser?' Beeny said, 'Is in so much bother elsewhere this new headache doesn't help. Not knowing if coming or going. Where to look? This way or…Always looking and needing eyes in the back of your head…Kaiser he is so secretive'.

'Don't give me your worries enough of my own just tell me how long before we get where I don't won't to be going.'

Thunder in the distance. Rain shuddered on the windscreen as he watched the wipers go back and forth making him drowsy. Turning sideways looking out the window the trees whizzing past but not whizzing fast enough. Too slow to be where he definitely is not wanting to be!

'You sure are hard to get on with what is your problem?'

'Because I ask a question and you won't open up.'

'You've known Kaiser for a few years now. Why do you need me to tell you anything more? You know how he operates he won't take kindly to spying on him.'

'What makes you think spying? Trying to make conversation that's all.'

To get this guy to lighten up is proving difficult he knew instinctively he was going to have a hard time with him. Ma said, Kaiser trusted Beeny and he was to relax and enjoy the journey. Kaiser , he had it all under control. But, a stranger in control was not satisfactory and how much information did Kaiser let the guy have. Was it safe? If the worst came to the worst could he reach one of the revolvers in the hold-all? He hadn't a clue if Kaiser removed them and he would have to make some kind of excuse to let the guy know he needed to get something out the hold-all without raising any suspicion. Kicking himself for not looking before and should have kept his in his under arm holster. On his person instead of leaving it where it was. Gave up the thought and concentrated on the side mirror making sure the van was not being followed. His friend was playing a dangerous game and how all of this was going to pan out. Why was he going where this guy was taking him? He was his own man and the agro was making for a splitting headache. Needed no one to map out anything for him he was capable of doing what had to be done himself and resented the fact Kaiser thought otherwise. Realised it was his own fault letting Kaiser think he was incapable. Now was the time to alter the situation. Now, was thinking, where is and what is the bold boy up too his reputation with cars a series of disasters. No sense of responsibility. The more he thought about it the more he worried. Would the hire be in good order when the time came for it to be handed back to the company in Groningen? Hopefully not a bill for any damage at this particular time. Kaiser and his reckless driving. What of the people the two waiting outside the Bear. Are they following Kaiser? And would he be able to lose them on the road to Groningen? What about the return journey? The shady dangerous life he led would the men in suits suffer the same fate as the two at the mill. He couldn't wait to find out so tried to get some sleep. How he longed for sleep the last thirty six hours had been hard. The sooner he was out of this van he was thinking sleep would be his first priority. Settled in the seat and closed his eyes. The rain battered against the windscreen. Overhead the thunder rolled across the sky. Beeny playing the music loud on the radio. The singers are Dutch and the usual he does not understand a word. Now he finds it is impossible for any kind of sleep. Getting peace and quite and a chance to sleep he knew, now impossible. He is wondering about the forthcoming meeting with Captain McPherson. Wouldn't be long now to be homeward bound out of Rotterdam.

'Can't find anything better to play on the radio? Something we both can understand instead of that rubbish. Western say?'

'I thought you wanted to sleep not listen to the radio?'

'No chance. That racket above and the rubbish you're playing.'

Beeny scowled and fiddled with the various wave bands each time the radio spewed out foreign stations.

'Oh, forget it. Get the station you were on at first. I'm wide awake now.'

'Is there no pleasing you?'

'When are we getting to this so called destination can't be far seems forever.'

'Soon.'

'Then I'll meet your sister?'

'Oh, for goodness sake go to sleep.'

'Not with that nonsense. Find something better or turn it off. The music got louder...'You deliberately trying to mess with my head? Said get it off! You deaf or something? How long got to put up with this racket, off, put it off!'

'Sorry, is there no pleasing you?'

'You will be sorry if you don't turn it. ....Off!'

'Said sorry. What more do you want? It's off. Now you can sleep. You sure are impossible to get on with. Go to sleep.'

'Sleep, it's no use now. Jeese, why does my life keep giving me a problem about trying to get satisfaction from sleep my clock is all out of timing.'

'Relax, soon be there.'

'Good, about time too. Asleep you wake me.'

In his minds eye he is imagining a scary black and white movie and the appearance of a creepy haunted mansion. Wouldn't be surprised to seeing a driveway meandering off the lonely road and each side lined with dead gnarled leafless trees. Then suddenly the appearance of a large black bat changing into Count vampire or something like it. Not a surprise to see skulking behind, a werewolf or a giant hairy beast on two legs with red bleary eyes and arms dragging on the ground.

Thunder continued above and the lightning sending angry fingers streaking through the clouds. Darkness engulfed the road ahead and he was thinking more dark thoughts. Beasts and ghosts with five fingers, monkeys paws and creepy, Peter, hovering. Old movies watched as a child has a lot to answer for.

The wind is blasting the side of the van. Beeny seems not to be very good at controlling under the severe weather conditions. 'You want me to take over cause you truly are hopeless. How long you been driving?'

'Long enough. Don't worry soon be home.'

'And you're sister?'

'What's with you?'

'If you're not going to talk about…Well, you brought it up in the first place. Give me the crack on this elusive sister. If you're not prepared to spill then get out of the driving seat. I want to arrive in one piece at this place not anxious to be at. Said already, Rotterdam is were I have to be want to be safe your attempt at driving is giving me the runs. To put it nicely, I'll drive so stop the van. Rotterdam soon you say. Thank goodness!'

'You think would let you drive. Think again,' he says, slow and calm and sitting tighter into the seat concentrating on his driving.

'You're driving is the pits never seen such rubbish driving.'

'Rubbish or not it's the only way you going to get there!

NINE

Patrick is a few years older than sister Mary though both are in their late forties and unmarried. Mary is the dominant one of the two. She is the brains behind the success of their business dealings, running the agency, factory workers, dockers, oil and gas pipe inspectors. Employers who deal in contracts above board or otherwise. According to some of the gossip talked about by their non friends.

When he was a teenager, Mary took him under her wing after loss of both his parents. She done it to help her childhood friend, Mary McKenzie, who approached her on the behalf of her unofficial wards, Frank and Jamie.

'The poor laddie on his own with a wee brother to support can you no give him a job know how hard a life they bairns have had to put up with.'

She asked, when her friend was having a drink one night in Maggie Shaws. Mary Mckenzie's public house near the slipway at the pier.

Mary Greene obliged. Franks mother was also a schoolgirl friend of hers and the three had been inseparable. The proverbial three of a kind but as a grown up, Mary Greene, was devious and an uncaring person. Mary Mckenzie was still friendly with her on a long distance basis. They hardly ever met which suited Mary Mckenzie fine. The occasional occasion was when they would exchange pleasantries when they met up out shopping or on the few occasions in Hells Kitchen the Maggie Shaws ladies bar.

At fifteen years of age he joined the labourers removing rust painting red lead on the underside flats of derelict barges. In those days there was no such thing as health and safety. The vessels to be used as line barricades somewhere in a foreign land. It was suggested the barges to be used as artificial reefs to help the regeneration of the sea bed in tropical waters. 'Pity,' the worker's would say, 'why can we not go with them could do with a holiday in the sun.'

Ah well, they were realists could dream dreaming didn't cost anything.

Through the years the Greenes promoted him he reached the heights, senior inspector. Fluent in the inspection of concrete and paint could say a bent for quality control. His skill was welcomed in the oil and gas industry. The skill he had, good or bad, used to go anywhere the Greenes secured contracts, legit, or otherwise. Could tell by look if a large round rusty section of steel tube was properly shot blasted to remove the rust. Coated to the correct thickness of black coal substance, dope, on some occasion mixed with blue flaked asbestos and could tell at a glance if the correct thickness of concrete was applied to the finished section of pipe. These things he learnt after many years of experience and hardship in some places he would not wish on his worst enemy.

The Greenes building is a blue painted wooden structure with a rickety wooden staircase leading to the second floor entrance. Paint peeling on the walls it looks like a snake shedding it's skin. Come to think about it, the snakes are inside the building, their names, Greene, Mary and Patrick.

The windows once had a sea view but now covered in black paint. Shabby and run down the premises look out of place beside the once busy harbour.

The office is looked after by the janitor, Jock, night and day, Watson, available to the Greenes twenty four seven days a week. He's the dogsbody, go for and hard man. The gadgie who lives on the premises. A creepy giant of a man with a bald head and a very large nose and equally large mouth. His language is coarse, loud and prone to bragging, some would say, couthy. Not to be met on a dark night. Not if you are on your own, It was said.

The Greenes? They live in a luxurious sprawling bungalow off the Queensferry road sitting at the entrance to five acres of wooded countryside and not far from, in their opinion, an undesirable council estate. The palatable residence where many of their deals are carried out, maybe, where some of the bodies are buried? Police? Some say, they have no need to be afraid of the police. Mysterious going's on over the years and nothing proved.

'It's six thirty, Patrick phone a taxi. Got to be in the Rainbow Rooms on the shore at seven running late.'

A demand she wanted doing straight away but he ignored her, as per usual. Playing dumb was par for his course and all the time hiding the rage he harbours inside.

She sat on her large blue coloured divan in the middle of the room surrounded by copious amounts of female luxury, party dresses strewn beside her, in different colours mostly red, her favourite colour.

She lit a cigarette and hurriedly downed her coffee from her dainty blue and gold rimmed coffee cup then plunged the cigarette into the saucer. Scowling as she destroyed the cigarette in the process.

'What you going to do with those scumbag Butler brothers? You keep hedging and dallying. Something has to be done about them and if you don't hurry and decide others will be called to do what you are delaying,' he threatened, 'plenty volunteers can be called on to sort the mess, but delay, don't understand you Mary? The time is now to be doing something about it.'

'Oh, for goodness sake, Patrick, give it a rest. Give me peace. Will deal with it in good time. How long are you going to keep bugging me?'

She lit another cigarette, her hand shaking, she is in a rage, and so angry that she immediately stubbed the cigarette into the ashtray.

'Give it a rest, a rest! You've been putting it off forever. Get a grip of yourself Mary. They have cost us a fortune when are you going to get round to it?'

Standing in the middle of the room waving his arms letting her know how much he was upset at the lack of progress. He stood there in his dressing gown, shaking his head from side to side, small and skinny, his eyes on stocks looking a sorry picture of one, oh so pathetic 'Get a bloody grip, Mary' He shouted leaving the room in a rage slamming the bedroom door behind him.

She knew how he performed. He said things like this when he knew he couldn't win any of the arguments and she constantly made him feel belittled by ignoring him.

65

'Have more important things to be doing don't need you going on and on can't stand you bleating,' she shouted after him as he disappeared from the room. At the end of her tether and angry because he is useless and she is the one who is left to deal the cards. Not only useless but he's a coward to boot. A devious and an untrustworthy individual known by her from a very early age.

He returned to the room and sat beside her lifting his arms as if he was going to embrace her. 'Sorry Mary but you have to let me have my say. You are losing your grip. Weakness, they'll say you are weak.'

'You've had your say Patrick too many times. It's me always me who has to deal with the consequences so if you please give it a rest will you?'

'Oh, Mary, that's not fair. I've done good before. Was me who got the bridge contract don't forget,' he said, putting on the act trying to get, 'there, there dear, all is forgiving.' He pleaded but she scorned him and saying how she was fed up with all his carrying on. This tactic was used too many times and she was not in the mood to appease his ego as she was more interested in getting away before she would do him some harm.

'And what a turn out that proved to be,' she reminded him.

'Well, how was I to know?'

'If you mention Butler again, Patrick will swing for you so stop it!'

'On that old sow Mary Mckenzie's say. It was you who engaged them in the first place. You are always quick to lay the blame at my door. Now I've got one on you how are you going to get out of that, ay Mary, tell me if you dare.'

He would like to say more but hadn't the nerve to say it. Had lit the fuse and when Mary was lit up there was nowhere for him to hide and he had to accept the consequences.

She rose up her eyes widened and was showing her teeth and just like a female cat she got into position ready to pounce.

Lowering himself into a defensive position, he looked, waited for the rain of blows he knew she was capable of delivering.

'No Mary no don't hit me. I'm not well. I'm sorry,' squealing like the rat he is.

The blows she inflicted on him on previous occasions, his sister, would have been at home in a victorian correction centre.

'Well suited for a correction house,' he was quick to say when speaking with his cronies in his local watering hole after a skinfull of the amber liquid.

His plea worked. She relented, 'pathetic,' she said. Was not worth the effort was in a hurry to be gone but would take note for next time. Waved her finger, threatening. The look she gave him was enough to put the fear of god into him.

'Stay keep your distance Patrick. No time for this. Stop your shenanigans have to be away from here and you are keeping me late. Will deal with you later. Promise. I will explain later. Stop going on.'

For the moment he escaped her wrath but he never learns he started once more.

'What is so important that you have to go out tonight? You never let me in on anything. Thought we had a partnership but you always keep me in the dark and had enough. Things will have to change round here sister Mary. Mark my words. Will be a day of reckoning you'll see!'

'Your word Patrick? Your word isn't worth a cent get away to your bed. Get out of my sight and make sure you leave the lobby light on little boy so you won't be afraid when you're left alone in the dark.'

With fists clenched she calculated the distance to his chin taking aim to give him a right hand uppercut.

'You would like that Mary. Keep little brother out of sight, nay nay na nay nay,' he said moving his right hand up and down in front of his face.

She changed her mind about the uppercut. 'Don't be childish Patrick. Got a meeting with two foreign gentleman have to go can't afford to be late.'

'Yes run Mary run. Don't keep your fancy man or is it fancy men? Not good form to keep them waiting!'

She screamed, 'Oh, don't start that again keep your trap shut. Don't know anything and the less from you the better.'

'Know all right don't think I don't. I've known for a long time about you and that Mary Mckenzie woman.'

'The meeting will be to our advantage Patrick. Will make sure of it,' she said as she made her way into the hall picking up the phone.

'Mary Mckenzie, indeed,' she said, then, 'taxi, taxi, yes?... it's Mary Greene, need a cab to take me to the Rainbow rooms on the shore. Yes, quick as you can.'

She replaced the phone, walked out into the garden to wait. The smell of the flowers was over powering. The heavy scent of the roses had a calming effect and the spat with Patrick was now forgotten

'Mary Greene. Don't you be bringing any strangers back here you hear me? Won't have it will have no fancy men in this house.' He was at the door giving out the bad mouthing and bringing her back down to earth it was business as usual.

She stood a good distant from him making him feel safe. Tomorrow could take care of itself she was thinking.

'We'll see who is in the right you wait.' Shouting so loud the near tenement dwellers would know they were at it again.

'The Greenes, last night, you hear?' The locals would remark to each other when they met.

Nothing unusual in this behaviour was a regular occurrence between the siblings and a wonder they stayed together for so long.

After a short wait a black hackney cab drove into the driveway.

'That was quick driver,' she said as she opened the cab door. 'Rainbow rooms please. Fast as you can in a hurry.'

Patrick was in the garden saying she better not be late.

'Suck off,' she said rather loudly.

'I was on the Queensferry road,' the driver said, 'got you on the radio. The shore is it?'

'Yes! Not deaf are you?'

'In a bad mood lady? You are some people. Why is it always end up with punters like you? You have certainly made my night if I may say so.'

He was surprised at her attitude and the use of the word she uttered.

'Having trouble with the old man are you it sure sounds very much like it?'

'None of your business. You're paid to drive so drive.'

'Thought I seen you. Greene, yes Greene. How the mighty have fallen. Know you can take the wife out of Newhaven but not take Newhaven out the wifie. Know who you are. Thought I recognised you. Greene, yeah Greene. How the mighty have fallen,' said again, 'you can, take a lassie out of Newhaven but impossible to take Newhaven out the lassie.'

'Awe shut it and drive don't want to be late.'

'Dearie dearie me,' he muttered shaking his head, 'you do meet all sorts and I get a fair share you better believe it.'

'You said you knew me, how's that? Certainly don't know you. Would remember it it were so.'

'My aunts. Four of them live in Newhaven.'

'And how does that square the circle?'

'My old aunt Phamey same school as you.'

'You saying I'm old?'

'Aren't you?'

'Cheek! You won't get a tip for that young man.'

'Didn't say you were old asked if you were old?'

'I will not answer that question. Keep quite and get me to the shore. Drive carefully and watch the road.'

When they reached the restaurant she said, 'how would you like to earn some extra money driver?'

'Extra cash? I'm okay with that. Do you want me to rough someone up?'

'No nothing like that.'

'If that's what it is it will cost you plenty.'

'No do not want anyone beaten up.'

'Well let's hear it then. See if agreeable.'

'Want you to wait.'

'That's it, just wait?'

'Yes. As simple as that.'

'Let's hear it then. You want me to just wait?'

The tall man stood up from the table.

She hurriedly approached apologising profusely. 'Sorry,' she said smiling same time flustered.

'You are late,' man said as he resumed his seat.

69

'We do not appreciate being late,' his companion said.

She produced a sheet of paper from her handbag and pushed it across the table towards them

'What is this?' The first asked.

'A contract we do not sign contracts,' said the other, 'if we do not do the deal we have what you say…Other fish to fry.'

'Need workers to make it work contract is essential,' she said, a slight pause then a flutter of her eyes..

'Trust, we deal In trust.'

'Yes, all well but need a written contract,' she offered a biro pen but he ignored her offer.

'Getting a tip top deal nothing for you to worry about'

'You're wasting our time,' his companion said.

She gasped,'are you trying blackmail?'

'You need workers don't you?' First man said.

'Supply workers not the business of blackmail,' companion says in a way she takes as a threat..

'Looks to me your at it.' Looks round waits to see if back up is on its way.

'At it? What does it mean at it?'

'You know perfectly well.'

'Forty first class workers you have no worries. We are ready to go all we need from you is a date to start. We shake or we are out of here,'

'We shake', she nods and gathers the pen and the unsigned contract.

'Are you ready Miss Greene? Your taxi awaits.' The driver cries out as he approaches.

'Okay driver, coming,' smiles a smile of relief.

'Did well driver things getting a wee bit scary good you came when you did.' Saying as she enters the cab.

'Where you want to go now,' the driver ask's.

'Anywhere for a quite drink,' making herself comfortable in the seat.

'Preference?' He says.

'Oh, you must know where. Somewhere nice and quite.'

'Not this time, bit late to find a quite place. Why not go home to your husband.'

'Husband? Not got a husband just a brother.'

TEN

Three thirty after midnight Binky Mason brought the, KELLY REMMY, into the harbour. He was tired and grumpy and fed up as he sailed his little fishing boat through the harbour entrance. Sheer luck in time to beat the fog unfurling like a carpet behind him. Seven lobsters and three large crabs made for a disastrous night. Was thinking he may have a change of fortune if he shifted his pots nearer to Inchkeith island. Better to try new fishing ground as nothing could be worse than the disaster he just endured. Yeah, good idea. He would try the next trip when the fog bank lifted he was sure it would be a better solution and nothing to lose if he failed again. As he steered the vessel towards the tie up he saw a large square object inches below the surface and his first thought was comparing the object with a shiny mottled back of a giant Manta Ray but he soon gave up the thought thinking it was a ridiculous notion to think a Ray would be beaching up in the Newhaven harbour. Missing it with room to spare he tied up and climbed the iron ladder onto the slipway.

What the heck? Took his hat off. Scratched his head as he looked back at the object in the water. Strange, some kind of metal that shouldn't be there. He was thinking how lucky the escape as it could have been a further disaster to the so far horrible end to a rotten adventure. With no seafood for his customers he would have some explaining to do to keep them happy in their disappointment.

'Vandals at it again. Time the harbour police got a grip on the situation and done what had to be done to keep the nerds away from the place and keep the boats safe.' He let go his displeasure by shouting across the harbour his voice echoing as the horn at the lighthouse started wailing and the fog came rolling in like a door closing the harbour entrance, 'just in time,' muttering, 'lucky to make it.'

He turned to go, suddenly, it seemed from nowhere he heard a voice he recognised. Someone speaking to himself. Ghostly words interrupted by the sound of the horn. He squinted and saw him approaching. A shadow appearing from the gloom. Rubbed his eyes peered into the fog…'Jakie, you old bowtow scared the life out of me. What are you doing here?'

'A saw it. Honest saw it, aye did, a saw it,' he said as if he had just woke from a long sleep and after a bad dream.

Binky looked, surprised seeing behind the old man a jumble of empty fish boxes beneath a scramble of fish nets piled into a build makeshift den four to five feet in length and height propped up against the harbour wall.

He pulled the front two boxes apart. 'Jakie, what the ….What are you doing dossing here gave me a scare,' he said again, 'you old bowtow. What do you think your doing here you can't sleep here the harbour master will get you locked up.'

He pulled on another box and the whole edifice fell into a sprawled heap.

'Ma house. You've tumbled down ma house. What will a do now you've crashed it to the ground?' Then he said in a scary voice whispering as he turned around looking to see if they were alone. 'Binky a seen it a tell you a seen it with my own eyes. A seen it a seen it honest.' He was rambling looking up at the sky and holding his arms aloft as if to prey. 'Ma judge is ma judge honest wis a horrible thing.' He went on and on all the time peering into the fog getting close up whispering.

'What, what did you see have you got the jeebies again you silly old bowtow. What was it a monster or you seeing rats and snakes again you old fool!'

'No, no a seen it a seen it Binky honest,' unsteady on his feet swaying from side to side, 'what can do help me build it up. You will Binky, ay.'

'Forget it you canny stay here.' Took his arm helped him walk away from the edge of the harbour wall and the danger of a drop from the fifteen feet high pier into the water. Couldn't risk the old fool toppling over into the rising tide it would be the last thing he needed after his rubbish trip and having to explain another rotten disaster.

'People are fed up putting up with you. It's time you were put away Jakie. A nice roomy loony bin would suit right down to the ground,' he said not happy with the present situation he found himself lumbered with.

Holding Jakie by the scruff of his collar Binkie guided him forward. 'Walk straight. For goodness sake keep straight. It won't take long till we're out of here if you keep going. Do not stop go forward keep going.'

'A car driving down the slip and into the water saw it honest.'

'A car? I nearly rammed a car? Keep on you silly old man keep going we have to go and wake Mary McKenzie and get her to phone the police.'

Opening the door slowly Mary Mackenzie peeked from behind and when she saw who was responsible for disturbing her sleep she exploded.

'How dare you come to my doorstep do you know what time it is?' She clutched at the neck of her dressing gown and slammed the door shut, 'go away. We are closed. Do you know what the time is?'

'Do you know what the time is Binky?' Jakie slurred his words and swayed to and fro the way drunks do. 'No room Binky. No room at the pub. Go to another.'

Binky turned him round and shoved his back to the wall trying desperately to hold him as he knocked once more on the door.

'If you don't leave I'll call Archie McDougall. So you better be on your way,' Mary shouting from behind the door.

'For goodness sake keep up,' he said. Holding tight trying to keep him from sliding down the wall. He reached and extended his arm and with some effort grabbed him by the shoulders, 'stay up and keep quiet,' he said then started to knock again on the closed door.

'I'm not letting that man in here. Go leave him where you found him. Enough of him last night. A flaming pest, bothering folk to buy him drink. Take him away not wanted here go away,' she screamed and slammed the door once more.

Crouching he shouted through the letter box. There's a motor in the harbour Mary. Please, can you phone the police ?'

Within the hour Chief inspector Rooney and detective sergeant McDougall and a female constable were on the case in Maggie

73

Shaws girls only parlour, the room known what the locals call, Hell's Kitchen.

'Now then Jakie. Give it to us again, You saw a car?'

Rooney, tired, fed up like he had all the world on his shoulders needed to hear a more convincing story from the old soak. Needed to make some sense of what he was being told as the alki was rambling and how many more times did he have to listen to him saying he saw it with his own eyes. Longed to be somewhere else and not here listening to a senile old man saying repeatedly he saw it with his own eyes again and again.

'Give me strength,' he said, raising his arm and pointing. 'See if you can make some sense of what he is saying sergeant,' he moved to the bar and pulled a stool sat down and shook his head watching disbelief at the proceedings, 'get a handle on the story get some sense out of him.'

'Aye aye, said already.How many more times? Awe Mary, you no give me a wee dram. My throat, awfy dry. In need, need a swally?' He said with the voice of innocence and a spectacular hangdog look on his face.

Rooney gave her the nod. 'Give him a drink Mary indulge him. The quicker the better and we will be out of your way. I've given up sergeant see if you can make sense what the old fool is trying to tell us can't make any sense of it whatsoever.'

'Mary returned from behind the bar handing Jakie a large glass of whisky.

He smiled, 'danke!' He said, astonished at her benevolence. The large whisky certainly gave him something to perk up about.

She gave him the long stare.

Jakie admired the whisky and savoured the moment.

'It was luck that I did not hit it.' Binky said to McDougall.

Jakie downed the whisky in one and continued. 'A saw it with my own eyes. It was horrible and goodness me never wish to see a repeat was really horrible.'

McDougall, he wasn't listening he was tired and fed up with the whole rigmarole.

Jakie wiped his lips on his sleeve along with a satisfying slurp in the process.

'The motor came down the slip,' he said, rolling his eyes and waving his hands in a circular motion. His brain going through the thought process. Slowly the words lingered as he milked the scene and wondered how to get Mary to come up with another?

Mary thought, if he is stalling for more drink his bahooky is oot the windie.

'Another one came behind it,' he continued, 'the man got out the motor and the next man in the next motor helped him get the drunk man out the back of the motor and put him in the front seat.' Here he paused then said, 'they put down all the windows then they watched it drive into the water. There told you seen it. My own eyes and can't say any more it's what I saw, honest.'

'At last! Bloody last we're getting somewhere.' Rooney said, looking at McDougall with a satisfactory smile as if he had solved the mystery of a long unsolved crime. He pointed to the door. 'After I organise things at the harbour get him locked up and see if you can make more sense out of him when he's sober.'

Small crowd gathered watching the police divers assist the mobile crane at the pier in the recovery of the car from the calm water in the harbour.

'My goodness,' Rooney said when he looked inside the car, 'there's a lassie on the back seat. You know who she is sergeant?'

'No, don't recognise her but the one in the front,' said McDougall as he looked up at the onlookers above on the pier. He took out his handkerchief and wiped his face and said, 'the wee laddie, Butler. It's Jamie. My goodness what's the score here? Who would believe it, the wee laddie Butler.'

Rooney moved off to greet the doctor coming from his car.

McDougall walked away with his head bowed, 'what a tragedy. I need a drink. We're done here inspector. Mary McKenzie will need to be told she is the only nearest kin I know. And how she will take it? Going to be hard.'

Twenty minutes later, McDougall writing in his note book.

Mary, crying. Finished her third whisky and her hand shaking as she held the empty glass letting the woman copper know she was ready for another.

'Who you think done such a thing sergeant saw him a while ago drove up from London seemed fine to me was all excited about his new girlfriend poor quine. Said they were enjoying their holiday what a shame just a bloody shame!'

'Did you meet the girl Mary you know her?' Rooney asked.

'No never. Was excited can't believe what's happened and wonder how Frank will take it he's on his way back home.'

'Sure are you coming back here?'

'Yes. Why wouldn't he? Captain McPherson was on the phone he said it.'

'There should be a clue to her identity in the suitcases we found in the trunk of the car but will have to wait, forensics, in the mean time it's a waiting game,' said McDougall.

'Are you sure you can't tell us anymore Mary you are telling us everything you know any little detail will help.' Rooney had one of his hunches. Was certain she was holding something back. She hadn't responded to his question when Frank would return he had expected more from her but she cut him short.

'No, said all. Got to say, aye, all for now. No more questions got a pub to run will you please leave,' wiped her tears and took command of the situation, 'leave, nothing more to say. Come back later got to get my head round what has been going on. I need time to work out the ins and outs.'

Within minutes the squad car arrived. McDougall got Jakie to his feet. Grabbing him by his coat collar he marched him quickly out the door. 'Transport at last about bloody time,' he said to the two policemen who got out the patrol car.

A small crowd mostly fish salesmen from the fish market, stopping on the way to Betty's café for the usual all day morning fry up wondering what the situation was all about but McDougall was in a mood he had no time to listen to any of their questions. Pushing forward he guided Jakie to the waiting car.

The crowd were not happy seeing the old man being huckled by McDougall. Some voiced their displeasure. McDougall held on tight to Jakies collar pushing forward ignoring the crowd.

Jakie, taking advantage he asked, 'could do with a wee swally Archie. You know, enough to get the faculties moving. There's nothing better than a good nip to give me a good kip.' He was hoping McDougall would relent and take pity on him. After all he had known McDougall since McDougall was a scallywag.

'Now now Jakie had enough drink to last a while. The boss would have me over the coals if I gave you any more. Keep moving don't want to start an incident here. World war three will not start on a Newhaven street I assure you. Keep going. The quicker the easier it'll be the quicker you'll be done with and quicker get you know, off my back!'

He struggled to get him into the police car. The more he tried to get him in the more Jakie resisted and the more the crowd showed their displeasure.

'Just a wee one afore we leave. You're not feart of him. He's nothing to worry about I ken all about him give me just a wee one to help with the shakes. You know how it is go on one won't break the bank. Mary will understand. Can you no take pity see ave got the shakes. Just one wid dae it. Just one.'

He was asking but all he was doing was making McDougall more determined to get him into the car, 'now that's enough of that need you sober to tell the boss what happened at the harbour. You better be on your metal cause he's not one to be fooled. He could make your life a misery if he thinks you are at it. Now, get in the fekin car. I'll make sure you get sorted when we reach the station. I promise.'

McDougall, he was threatening with an unsavoury outcome hoping his threat would work he had better things to be doing instead baby sitting drunk undesirables and the crowd becoming more rowdy made him fearful of the outcome.

When the squad car pulled up outside the Leith street police station after a successful getaway without incident. Jakie was snoring his head off and it took two coppers to haul him into the police station.

ELEVEN

The desk sergeant was not pleased with his latest lodger, jakie, the thought of more paperwork did not appeal.

''Why did you bring that thing in here he is stinking the place out. Why oh why plagued with such fools.' He looked up from the desk. 'Rooney! You have been at it long enough to know you leave them out on the street. Bloody disgrace you fetching him here.' The outburst made him feel good and he smiled and got on with the paperwork. On reflection it was good nobody was around to witness his outburst because now he felt rather foolish. Shook his head sighed and gave a couple of short dry coughs into his right hand and looked-sheepishly round his empty domain.

'Tell how it was. You heard a car so what made you look at the car what were you doing at the time, you awake or asleep at the time?'

Rooney sat opposite asking the questions. Next to him a woman pc ready to take down the answers in her notebook.

Downstairs in the cellar of the building. The walls, dark blue glazed tiles. There is no heating in the room it is cold and damp and there is an unpleasant smell.

Jakie, thinking there could be a dead rat lurking somewhere even as close as under the wooden table. Put his fingers to his nose and blew hard. Wiped his nose on his sleeve and made a gurgling noise at the back of his throat. Rooney gave him a look, sniffed the air, 'disgusting,' he said. Was not happy being there couldn't tell if the smell was stale air or coming from the man who was obviously still in the throes of the drink. He turned in the seat looked at the woman cop for a reaction. She was staring at her note book ready to write, hoping, the interview would be over quickly she couldn't wait to be out into the fresh air.

'Don't remember a need a drink. Got a drooth. You know my throat is awfy dry. Can the quine get me a wee whisky I know you like it yourself!'

Rooney stood up and buried his face in a large green square handkerchief. 'Let him go we are done here,' he said as he hurried out.

'Get someone to fumigate that place,' capturing a unfortunate constable encountered as he walked up the corridor, 'we know where to find him get him out of here.' Done a quick shuffle to his right to get out the way of the lady cop who dashed past. He hoped she was not about to throw up because he was in her line of fire.

All alone in the interview room Jakie was left wondering if they were away to get him his swally but soon found out his Christmas hadn't come. Was too early for Christmas. They did let him go however.

The daylight hurt his eyes he was in Henderson street being released from the police station. Standing and pondering were he should go next and who did he think was good for a nip who he thought would take pity? The foot of Leith walk has a number of watering holes and one in particular is always good for a drink if one has a good story to relate. Someone there is sure to be sympathetic after his ordeal. Unfortunately his luck was out.

'You can get him one drink. That's all.'

Glesga Mary, was acting go between to get him a drink. The barman wasn't shifting but he did agree after much wrangling with her and her pal, Marlyn, to limit him to one drink only then he has to leave. He was not wanted here and the barman did not want his customers upset.

'Take pity on the old man.' Marlyn pleaded. 'You can see the state he's in.'

'Locked up in the nick. You would like a wee one, would you think,' said Mary.

'A do not think being very hospitable. Denying him a swally,' Marlyn chipped in. 'Aye. No very hospitable are you?'

'I'll show you some hospitality. Out the pair of you you're barred. Take him with you. I can't have my regulars upset with his nonsense.'

'Come on,' Marlyn pleaded again. 'We're good customers in here you know that, ay. You don't want to loose good paying customers do you?'

'Aye,' said Glesga Mary, 'if we tell the grape vine, well, you don't want to have an empty pub, do you. You get the message, ay.'

'Don't you pair of slags threaten me. Is it blackmail you're after it want work here. If you don't get out and take the drunk with you...I'll have the hounds on you if your not out here in five. Make your mind up.'

'You want hear the last of this mark me and you'll know what's what Ringer Bell. I'm giving you fair warning hounds or dugs call them what you like but mark my words!'

'Aye aye. Glesga Mary you and who's army? Get the hell out of my place you're barred don't come back and take your marras with you. Out now!'

'I know,' Glesga Mary said, 'the Cosy Corner we will make for there.'

Five minutes walk he enthralled them with his experience in the police station and how he made a fool of the two of them, McDougall and Rooney, but was thin on the reason why and said how many times they got him in he wouldn't spill.

Puzzled at what he said they tried to get more out of him but was a waste of time trying the impossible..

When they entered the pub, the Cosy Corner, a dispute between a couple of girl regulars was on the go. The manageress managed to separate the pair holding them at arms length trying to get to the bottom of the argument.

'Her', one said, 'she started it.'

'No, the other said, 'it's her fault.'

'She stole his money,' the first said, 'I couldn't get paid because of her. Tell them, go on. Where did I find the money in the toilet that's where. You crouched and fished the bundle where it should not be where it was in the first place. It's her should be kicked out not me, her!'

'No no it's her fault,' the supposed friend said.

'Shut your mouths,' the lady boss said, 'out you go and don't come back you are not welcome in this establishment from now on you're barred!'

Four men playing dominoes stopped to watch the fun, 'this is far better entertainment than the Cappy concert on a Sunday night,' one of them said.

'Aye, and it's free,' his neighbour says taking a long look at one of the girls who's skirt is ruffled round her waist in the melee.

'That brings the memories back, ay,' said another.

'We playing bones or watching this pantomime going on? Time she barred awe they slags and give us peace.' A disgruntled one said shaking his full head of hair.

'You don't keep quiet you'll be out on your ear as well,' lady boss said, still in the process of calming the wayward girls.

'And this pub is called, the Cosy Corner?' First man said sarcastically.

'Better the name would be, Queens and pros,' another said, laughing.

Landlady gave them the long look, 'not happy? You know where you can go.'

'We playing or moving?' First man said as he pushed the chair back ready for leaving.

'Good. And don't come back. Rather have this pair than the likes of you,' she said. Then, 'Clementine, sit there,' pointing to an empty table, 'And you, Sweet Pea, over there and stay well out of her way.'

'We're leaving,' said the disgruntled man, scattering the dominoes over the floor.

'Go to Berts,' says Marlyn after witnessing the argument, 'a better class oh gadgies at Berts. Would not put up with this load of tripe let's get going.'

'Awe naw,' Jakie wailed, 'barred at Berts, och, not going get a swally anytime soon. What has a bowtow to do, tell me that?'

'Barred at Berts, where are you no barred,' asks Glesga Mary.

'Lots, no barred in lots,' he said, hesitant. Stopped walking put a finger to his lips, let me think? Plenty, aye, plenty.'

'Name one?' She asks waiting.

'Next one we go in, what's it going to be?' Marlyn asks as she begins to walk.

'Maybe aye, maybe naw,'he said.

'What's it mean, aye or no Jakie?' Fed up now wants to be rid of him.

'We going to get a drink, or not?' Glesga Mary asked Marlyn, 'leave him. Lets go to Berts. Got us barred because you wanted to play the goodie goodie.'

'And you. You agreed don't forget not just me.'

'Me? What about, what am a going to do?'

Listening to them discussing as if he was invisible. He's got the hangdog look of innocence on his face again.

'Please yourself. Do what you always do,' Marlyn says, 'fed up. Wish we had never met you. You always cause grief we are out of it.'

'Newhaven, go back,' Glesga Mary says abruptly and giving him an innocent smile whilst feeling guilty.

'Aye, Glesga Mary you would leave me here wouldn't you. Ken ave no money.'

'Here,' says Marlyn, giving him a handful of notes, 'Get a taxi.'

'We are standing here discussing what to do with this old …. Why? You know he'll spend that money on drink, what are you thinking?' Glesga Mary is not happy.

Arm in arm they took off along the street and looking back…

'Aye, your right Glesga. Shouldn't have done it. Jakie, we'll see you later we are going to Berts. You get a taxi or whatever. Do what you want.' She shouted over her shoulder.

'No leaving me here girls. Your old pal, your marra. Don't go please not leave me.'

Too late. He stood pondering what he was to do now he's been dumped by the girls. Someone somewhere would take pity. Took off in the direction of Micks place and soon pushing the door to gain entrance past a couple of lovers smooching who barred his way into the bar.

'Now then Jakie,' said Mick, 'behave or you know. Out on your erse so be warned. No nonsense and no going on the tap for someone to give you a swally. Be keeping my eye on you.'

TWELVE

When Kaiser met Beeny and after he left Ma Tracy…

'Let your father know I will see him tomorrow or maybe the next day if everything goes alright and make sure my pal is safe. Get going as soon as he comes drive safely want you to arrive in one piece.'

He was taking no chances. Frank would maybe get an idea to do a runner and be involved in something he couldn't handle on his own.

'I'm not a child Kaiser give me some credit. I know what's what. You go about yours and let me to do the business my way,' he reacted angrily, 'why do you always put me down getting fed up with you always repeat repeat sick of it.'

Kaiser after a few yards turned gave him a two finger salute.

'On yer bike ya loonie wee ratbag. Get doon the strath and mind ye dinnae cull ony coos oan the wie,' he said trying out his version of a Scottish accent.

Beeny circled his right forefinger round and round his temple. 'You're an idiot!' he said. 'I couldn't understand a word of it. You want to give it up not in the least bit funny. A Scot, you're not Trying to impress your pal won't work and going on about this Scottish guy…Why do I have to babysit him? Why not take him with you?'

Watched him get into the car was not surprised he received no answer.

Kaiser drove to the car park at the church waited ten minutes sure was not being followed returned to where the van waited and from a safe distance saw Beeny leave with Frank. Satisfied they were not being followed he returned to the White Bear.

Police gone things back to normal. People just going about doing what they usually do when they are out strolling and window shopping round and about in the small busy market town of Appingadam.

Almost at once the wind whipped along the street rain fell in torrents sending the people scurrying for shelter.

He got out the car opened the bonnet withdrew the dipstick. Walking to the rear he rummaged about in the trunk. Looking round the surrounding area he spied the Mercedes parked further up the street. Going back to the front checked the oil wiped the stick put it back into the engine block closed the bonnet ignoring the fact he was soaked to the skin. Got into the car drove slowly up the street. Picking up speed keeping watch through the rear mirror smiled when he saw they were following. His right palm hit on the steering wheel a couple of times, 'gotcha ya numpties,' he shouted with delight, 'ya pair of numpties,' again and again continuing to hit the steering wheel. His mind was in overdrive. The plan was complete and he knew exactly what was what and what he was going to do about it and the storm was thinking was going to be to his advantage if it lasted all day. An ideal situation to settle what he had in mind at the final destination. The storm would keep the busybodies off the streets and he would be away from prying eyes.

Twenty minutes and thirty kilometres later he handed over the car to the hire company in Groningen.

He waited till the girl mechanic went over the car and gave him the okay that everything was in order and he could complete the handover in the office.

Leaving the forecourt he saw them beside their vehicle deep in conversation and when he walked out the forecourt turning left he saw them slowly walk behind him.

The short walk in the driving rain to the railway station was without incident. Thought they might have tried to get him in the street but they kept pace at a safe distance. He hesitated before going into the station. Now and then glancing back as he walked and like him they braved the storm with heads down hands keeping collars close to their necks walking bent over struggling to keep upright and determined to do what they had to do.

Entering the station he made for the gents toilets and like the concourse the facilities were empty.

'Perfect and no people...Oh the sight of an empty train in an empty station,' he whispered. Muttering, 'two blind mice, two blind mice one dead rat two dead rats.'

Looked in the mirror above the sink. Smiling turned the tap on and let the cold water run through his hands. With his wet forefinger he went through the motion of cleaning his teeth. Smiling repeatedly at his reflection, he knew they would soon be here. He had things as he wanted knew just how they would rue the day...Turned the water off crossed to the towel machine on the opposite wall pulling till he got enough towelling to dry his hands, stopped, waited with his back to the entrance he stood stock still not turning when he heard them entering.

One waited while the other looked into the row of empty cubicles banging each door shut satisfying himself they were alone.

He turned holding the revolver.

'On your knees,' moving the gun from side to side followed by, 'you want to pray or are you non believers?'

They looked at him with scorn on their faces. Neither spoke.

He counted a silent one to five, asked,' are you comfortable on your knees,' no time to answer the gun roared it's message. The one on the left between the eyes and before the body collapsed to the floor he moved forward and placed the gun on the others right temple. Bang, dead meat!

The blue and white tiled floor was awash with blood, deep red flowing blood.

He skirted past the bodies going to the row of sinks. Turning on the hot tap washing his hands with a wry smile looked in the mirror trailed wet fingers through his blonde hair.

Seeing the condom machine in the mirror on the wall behind he turned off the tap crossed put coins into the slot pulled on the drawer taking out two packs then returned to the cadavers.

Car keys, coins...Three hundred British pound notes. No identity. One had a silver flick knife the other a Walther PPK 380 pistol.

'Nice, truly was worth the effort,' was his response, admiring the prize before tucking it into the waistband of his trousers. Returned to the dead men placed a condom pack into the top pocket of one body then into the inside pocket of the other. Wiped his revolver and placed it in the dead mans right hand squeezing the forefinger on the trigger. Waited. Stood above them looking down, shook his head, idiots,' he said and made his way to the row of sinks.

The sound of silence was overwhelming. Turning on the hot tap once again he washed his hands. The flow of water sounded to him like waves crashing on the shore and the noise of the gunfire bouncing off the tiled walls the echo to him was irrelevant. The sudden rush of blood to his brain increased the moment he succeeded. The plan worked and he had known exactly what he had to do and the result was a perfect hit. Drying his hands on the towel and for some reason he thinks of food. Was perfectly calm. How easily the deed had transpired it made him wonder if the pattern would repeat. Now, he had better thoughts on his mind

'Hi, Jossi high everyone.' Greeted her and the few customers in the café bar. The one across the way from the railway station.

The particular venue played a huge part in the Dutch underground movement in World War Two. His activities followed on from his grandparents who distinguished themselves at the time. Remembered with much kindness many stories of their daring deeds stayed in memory fostering a hatred of the atrocities gestapo in particular. Gruesome stories that were locked into his brain.

'Hello Kaiser love. What will it be dear, whisky is it?'

She smiled. He noticed the twinkle appearing in her deep brown eyes. Knew instinctively just what she was thinking. 'Yes please. And would like a plate of pork chop and potatoes or as they say across the border, schnitzle mit kartofel please.'

'Ten minutes dear,' she said, 'have you been busy you keeping it for me, dear, have you?' Shook her ample bosom from side to side. 'We've missed you,' she said, ' been a while dear.'

'Certainly been a while but you know welcome is the hunter home from the hunt,' smiling and with a cheeky nod of his head had the idea planted in his head.

She straightened the top of her blouse ran her finger down the cleavage letting him know what he had been missing and what she was thinking and he thought could be a lively night of passion on the cards.

86

'Business as usual Jossi. Business as usual always on the go. Planted a kiss on the palm of her right hand finishing it off with a playful bite.

Blushing, pulled back her hand, saying, 'did you hear the car backfiring loud bangs you hear them. We looked outside but it had gone. Chrissy over there, silly girl, thought it was fireworks,' pointing to the redheaded sitting in the dark secluded corner. 'Fireworks? No, not a holiday or anything but definitely heard the two bangs. Fireworks, don't think so. Where she got that idea from?' Shook her head.

'Hi kaiser you free tonight lover can you spare the time?' The redhead asked giving the signal she was pleased to see him.

Smiling, walked over and as he sat down he saw Jossi, with a scowl on her face retreating into the kitchen. Knew the move upset her and thought, not going to get any food now, as Frank would say, 'left, wi a face like a well skelped erse.'

Two days later, 9.40am, at the ticket window back in the railway station buying a single to Leeuwarden.

Keeping tabs beside the platform sitting alone on a bench watching the policeman clear away the line of yellow and black banded no entry tape from the toilet area and a few minutes later the policemen with the paraphernalia were gone.

A young blonde station attendant walking about the station in the process of sweeping up any rubbish she could find. A wizard with the brush she bent to use the shovel and did a little side step, scooped. Deftly deposited the proceeds into a canvas bag she had hanging with a leather strap from her shoulder.

'Is there something wrong with the toilets?' Asking when she came near. His brain in forward gear and thinking he could maybe make a conquest. Wishful thinking but realised he hadn't the time. 'There was a shooting,' she replied putting the shovel on the ground leaned and placed her chin onto her clasped hands on top of the brush, 'like a gay affair went pear shape police are keeping it quiet, queer that? No publicity, not saying you know what bad publicity can do...Brings nosey parkers.'

He smiled, obvious she hadn't a clue what had taken place, 'have a safe journey,' she said, without your leave picking up the shovel and strolling away whistling a tune from Wagner and keeping time with the brush tapping on the floor.

Here was someone who enjoyed her labour he was thinking.

The train left on time he was sitting in the restaurant car turning the pages of the morning paper looking for anything being out of the ordinary at the local Bahnof. His breakfast consisted of coffee and croissants. Pleased with himself now and then glanced out the window and seeing the sun shining in the cloudless blue sky. He blinked at the brightness. Closed his eyes for a second then smiled carried on reading, flush, definitely feeling pleased with himself. Noticed two old ladies opposite giving him the glad eye. He turned the pages. Any minute now he thought.

'It's going to be a lovely day,' elderly lady greeted him.

Stopped reading squinted across the top of the paper a wry smile nodded in her direction but thinking, go away silly old woman bother someone else but he smiled in her direction. His mind is on other things and doesn't need a distraction.

'Are you going far young man, a holiday, lovely weather for a holiday. Isn't it?'

'It's a lovely day for sitting on the beach. Isn't it?' Said her elderly companion. Smiling broadly and nodding to the other who smiled and nodded her head pleased with the suggestion.

He of course thought otherwise.

'We are looking forward to having a few days by the seaside,' the first said.

He smiled and gathered the newspaper left the dining car walked along the corridor glancing looking for a vacant carriage. Needed to be on his own. Not in any mood for any kind of chit chat with silly old mares much on his mind for idle chit chat.

On his mind, what would be waiting at his destination has to stay alert.

'Well I never. What a rude young man.' The elderly lady said to her lady companion who nodded in agreement. 'Not one to be trusted I dare say,' her friend replied, then both sipped the coffee from their dainty coffee cups.

'Yes,' he muttered on entering the empty compartment, 'it's going to be a very nice day a perfect day, perfectly satisfactory.'

Settling on the bench seat he lifted his legs and stretched out. He closed his eyes and placed the open newspaper over his face.

Some time later the compartment door opened. The guard, coughed. Cleared his throat and was hoping the body spread out on the seat was not dead. He hesitated before approaching and uttered strange gurgling noises, 'er, sorry to disturb you sir, five minutes Leeuwarden coming up in five minutes,' he said, slowly inquisitively and relieved when he saw the hand remove the newspaper. Relieved when he saw the body move and thinking, dead bodies and paper work thanks but no thanks.

'Thank you sir,' kaiser said, 'sorry if gave you a fright. You have to understand had a busy night last night, needed that little sleep. But on reflection sir don't know why I'm explaining my actions.' Swung his legs over and sat up and folded the paper all the while giving him the once over.

'No need. Things came across in these carriages you couldn't explain not even to your mother,' saying before leaving.

Kaiser waited before sliding the door open and having a long look both ends of the corridor just as the train came to a halt.

Waiting in the station the elderly gentleman beside the magazine stand reading a newspaper now and then glancing at the crowds coming and going from the trains and in from the street. Was particularly interested in the passengers approaching the ticket collector at the exit gate on platform 2.

His raincoat has seen better days. Grubby and rather long. Is wearing a bowler hat and got on thin rimmed spectacles perched on the end of his nose. He's carrying a brown leather briefcase and a rolled up brolly hooked on his right arm.

Seeing him come from the train he folded the newspaper he was discreetly hiding behind and walked to meet him.

'No dear boy. You ask but expected it would be first on you're mind but no nothing in the press. Seems no one is interested in queers doing what they're good at. Fancy boys. They won't be missed I'm sure but their families. Feel sorry for the families. But there you are takes all types I'm sure.'

'Thanks very much for that Uncle. Not expected it to be in the newspapers today. But uncle, explained. No, not as you say, not fancy boys.'

'Possibly tomorrow's editions,' he said, shaking his hand. 'If you say so.'

Across the road from the station and only a short walk they approached the black painted shop front with it's grey dusty coloured net curtain hanging haphazardly in the single window and looking as if the closed bookshop had gone bust a long time ago. In times of the Second World War this was a secret meeting place for those who engaged in good deeds against the Bosch.

Uncle opened the door and scooped up the mail from the wooden floor.

Kaiser took a deep breath as the smell of musty books overwhelmed him. He parted the beaded curtain at the back of the shop and entered the single room. Bed in the corner was unmade. Small fire basket in the fireplace looked cold with overflowing ashes. Piles of rubbish in the grate suggested no fire for a very long time. He rubbed his face and gasped as his stomach heaved. Saw the bottle on the table, a half empty bottle of gin. Lifted the pint glass from the table and blew into it then wiped it with his handkerchief before filling it to the brim and gulping it down.

Uncle chucked his coat on the bed and sat down at the table. Odds and ends, rubbish, destined for the bin or the fire strewn on the table top. Still wearing his bowler he lit a cigar, 'she get in touch?' Asks whilst giving him a sour look.

Kaiser refilled the glass with the gin and thinking, here we go. Going to get it again. Same old argument. He hurriedly drank the gin over then reached once more helping himself to another.

'Can I get you one? You look as if you could do with one,' hoping to delay what he knew what was coming next.

'Asked if she had been in touch? Need you to forget Karli for the moment. Have to go and see, Edgar Kline. Got information on what happened in Oldenburg. Why persist, why do you play such games when you going to settle? Your still a young man is it not about time to be making something of what's left of your life before it's too late.'

'Like this you want me to end up, like this?' Banged the bottom of his empty glass on the table, 'you are the last person I should be listening to this place is a tip!'

'Exactly, you do see how it is?'

'I know. Why do you always go on about it? Why always an argument?'

Uncle trying to get him to come to his senses, 'change your way of life instead of the cloak and dagger nonsense you get involved in will end up on your own with family nowhere to be seen. If they want something they'll be in touch. When they get what they want they will be gone something else they need they will be back for more. That's the way of it. Can take my word on it. Not good being old and useless no bloody good whatsoever.'

'That's it Uncle Winter. You know how it goes. What having a family is about. You must have many happy memories to think on why always so gloomy and grumpy? Sure time now to lighten up. Enjoy your retirement for once.'

'Yes, being on your own has ups and downs and is something to be endured. It is something I don't wish for you or any of the others who you have got involved in your mad schemes. Where is it all going to end I ask you? This new adventure will end in disaster if you are not careful. Why, you so hell bent on getting involved with this man, this Scotsman's affair? Not as if he is family, is he?'

Lifting the gin bottle he poured the gin into a thin bone china cup gaily painted with red roses and yellow daffodils he supped whilst thinking and as he supped showing his displeasure at what was said.

'You know don't you? Jungle drums I suppose,' said Kaiser.

'Yes, she phoned don't think it wise for you to go there.'

'There are things I have to do there.'

'Such as?'

'You don't have to bother yourself about it. The less people know about it the better. I will be careful and you can't let anyone know about it.'

'She knows. Are you convinced she's reliable?'

'Karli? Course she is reliable why are you asking such a thing? I'm really surprised at you.'

'It's just worry. You don't know how much I worry. Getting past it and you can see what you're coming to maybe not just now but the day will come. My word on it.'

Kaiser interrupted, 'I know I know. I'll wait for the day but for now will keep more in touch but just now things are really getting on top of me promise. I'll phone more often when things get easier.' He knew he was in for a long night and was going to have to put up with Uncle constantly bleating.

Late evening…'Will go and see Kline for an update?' Uncle sighed, said, 'one more drink then bed, sleep. You can have the settee. Find a pillow and a blanket in the cupboard,' he pointed, 'over there if you are staying?' And in the morning you'll…'

'Uncle, give it a rest. Heard you the first time, sleep, go to sleep.'

'Harry's place, you'll be going there when you leave?'

'That's the plan.'

'The next move London suppose,' Uncles last words on the subject.

Met Edgar Kline in a café near the rail station. The ideal place to see the coming and going's of people. An advantage to keep his eye out for any danger. Easy spot to see strangers as it were. Watching for men, usually tall and in the habit wearing the tell tale identical black hats and black suits.

Breakfast consisted of of white bread spread with hazel-nut chocolate and cold meats. A shallow dish filled with, hagelslag. China pot black coffee and two small glasses of Pisang Ambon.

'Why London?' Edgar asked.

'Because have a duty to my friend.'

'Karli doesn't think it's a good idea things need settled here.'

'Okay, to what you say but can do more good in London. People here will be up for, you know. Don't need reminding.'

'Tony, he will meet you though still think it's a foolish move you're making.'

'Germany can wait have to get to England. I'll learn more there. Karli and her contacts will keep me informed.'

'She is walking into danger? Some of her previous efforts, well you know how many scrapes we've had to get her out don't think you can leave it to her can you not put London off till a later time?'

'Uncle Winter asking the same bloody questions not trusting her to do the right thing. I will be seeing her shortly. No worry. Just you be careful. Will be in touch.'

Made his way to the taxi rank beside the rail station.

Harry's place if you will, Stacy,' he said, surprising her as he slid silently into the rear of the private cab.

'You're back,' flustered and stammering she twisted round ready to scold him for the sudden appearance, 'gave one hell of a fright coming in like that but glad to see you, you blaster,' she threw at him supposedly angry but all the while smiling.

'Yes, back, old haunts.'

'Will I see you this time round?'

'We'll see, maybe. For now keep your mind on the road.'

'How do you know what I'm thinking?'

'I think I know what you're thinking.'

'The Elderado hotel is along on the right?'

'You up for it?' says cheeky like waiting her response.

'Do you have to ask?'

'I'll have to have a rain check on your proposal.'

'That's not wanted to hear, you say, yes, not knock me down, you certainly know how to let a girl down gently you bastard.'

'Another time promise too much on. If you knew how it is.'

'Half an hour you can manage half an hour?'

'Too easy. Your proposal is sounding desperate. Putting me off. Not in the mood brains scattered.'

'Well. Now heard it some lame excuse.'

'My thoughts at the moment are somewhere else.'

'Not had that problem before I seem to recall.'

'Have you heard from Karli?'

'Yes. She is concerned about this thing in London and like me doesn't agree it's a good move at this moment in time.'

'Things have to be taken care off.'

'Why you and not the Scotsman, why?'

'Do you really have to ask? Surprised you asked it.'

'Beeny, certainly not happy.'

'Beeny? Okay find some exclusive place to park and we'll settle this conversation here in the back?'

'You want before the hotel? Kaiser you are a glutton that's for bloody sure.'

Elderado hotel, midnight. He is drinking coffee with two German plain clothes policemen.

'It looks very much like the balloon has gone up,' the short fat man said smirking with that know all look on his face.

'War has been declared the innocents being murdered,' the tall thin man speaks with authority in his broken English high tone manner.

'What can I do?' Kaiser, says, 'you guys? What about the…'

'Police?' The thin man interrupts, 'gang fallouts they think fallouts, er, yes.'

'Oldenburg. You should be returning with us not going to London,' fat man continues where the other ended, 'you would do more good if you came and fished out why?'

'Money and diamonds. Trail goes to London. You two keep watch, go but keep in touch. I will contact you in due course.'

'And if…' The thin one looking to his partner for guidance.

'You handle it'. Kaiser says, now getting bored with the two.

'And, if I can't?'

'How many are we up against? Other asks, clearing his throat.

'Just be careful. I know you can be relied on to do the right thing.'

'We don't know what we are up against. How many do you know?' The fat man asks the question again, 'any idea at all what the situation is?'

'Keep a low profile just trust each other to do the right thing.'

'We know it. Ears to the ground all we can do at the present-time,' said the thin man, 'taking dangerous chance liaison with you.'

'That's it. No heroics too valuable for that,' Kaiser trying to ensure them.

'Where can we get you?'

'There is talk of Scotland not London.' The other sniffs the air with a superior shake of his shoulders.

Kaiser looks at him and thinks he done the sniff because the mention of Scotland.

'You don't contact me. Go through the usual channels,' says looking to the other.

'No way. Can't involve Beeny or Karli?' The thin man sounds puzzled, 'not to be trusted?'

'Edgar Kline.'

'Kline, not Uncle?' The thin man now surprised at the answer.

'Why him,' his friend asks somewhat perplexed.

'Get on your way it's time you left,' Kaiser says fed up with the grilling. Excuse he thinks. Typical Deutchers needing always to be in charge. Bullies each one.

'Explain why Kline?' the thin man demanding an answer, 'something not being said?'

'Go, to Germany keep a low profile. Things getting hotter and hotter you got to be vigil. Have to root out and get results.'

Thin man poured three glasses of schnnaps handed them over and sat down on the end of the bed. 'I don't like the idea. We are taking big risks this organisation has, like a spider, the web is huge and growing.'

'You, lives are a risk. Have been you know, how long?' Moved to the cabinet and lifted the bottle and refilled their empty glasses, 'I need you two to be careful.'

'Yes yes. We are on it,' thin man said looking to his friend who rose and reached for the bottle. He turned to look waiting for Kaiser to say something.

'Not a good idea to be having any more,' Kaiser tells them, 'have to keep on it as Otto says, a clear head for the journey.'

'East. Some work required east,' Otto is spelling it out when they hear a knock at the door. They look at each other wondering why at this late hour someone is knocking. They fall silent. The two look at Kaiser for an explanation.

'Enter,' Kaiser calls out reaching for the door.

Man dressed as a waiter comes into the room pushing a trolly laden with covered dishes. Food kaiser hasn't ordered.

'What's this?' He says. Bewildered as the trolly is parked and the man fusses sorting out a feast for one.

'Ja, riktig. Muss nach osten gahen,' Otto says again and rising from where he is sitting to examine the plates of food.

'Wrong room mate,' says Kaiser, thinking, what is going on here. He's looking at the waiter suspiciously.

As the waiter stops and looks he fusses and is apologetic hurriedly replacing things on the trolley.

Otto, his hand on a chicken drumstick drops it on to the plate as the waiter is fussing. He looks at Frank as if to say he was going to enjoy.

The waiter turns, looks, produces a silver flick knife from inside his white jacket and a revolver in his other hand. He stabs Otto, once, twice, three times in succession in the neck.

Kaiser gun in hand aims and with one shot drops the man to the floor.

'Go,' he says as he turns the waiter over. Looks up 'nothing to say who but got an idea who has sent the message. Get going. Leave things to me. A quick call will see things cleared up.'

'Otto is dead. What you going to say to the chief? Don't like to be in your boots when tell Mr Oldersum the news. The fool got wrong man.'

'You go back to the hotel.'

'Me, to do it?'

'Only way out.'

'Not my fault the idiot got it wrong'

'Want to stay safe you have to do it or…'

'No. Leave for another time.'

'You want to be like Otto you fool!'

'Too risky. Too soon.'

'Should have done when you were there.'

'Confusing happened so quick surprised he got it wrong. Had to go along with the result. Couldn't think what was best. Not let him be suspicious.'

'I pity you. Mr Oldersum will…

Fingers tap tapping on the cradle of the phone.
'Hello, hello!'

THIRTEEN

'How long to get to where we are going? I ask and you answer in miles. What kind of an answer is that?'

What was it he had said fifty six miles or so. You work it out he is thinking the guy is thick and he can't get his brain into action.

'Not far now. We should be there in twenty minutes not long.'

'You don't want to talk about your sister do you?'

'If you're tired you can get some shut eye. I'll wake you when we get there.'

'Must be some dame your sister why don't you give me the lowdown?'

'You'll see.'

'I get it. No lowdown on Kaiser. No lowdown on your sister. Make sure you wake me when we arrive be sure and remember.'

Please make it soon he is thinking sooner not later. He closed his eyes and settled into the seat. Was no use asking anymore questions thought the guy was not worth the bother, tighter, than you know what and to get some sleep wouldn't it be just dandy knowing full well sleep was impossible.

You get the luggage,' said Beeny, 'I'll arrange the food.'

'At last he said,' rubbing his eyes.

'You did sleep,' Beeny said sarcastically.

'Not long enough. And no no food for me. A room show me a bed please!'

Late evening the noise from music and the loud voices from the bar below his room not helping and the dreaded demons resurfacing.

Brain was all about events that had taken place. Memories of long hours on the dockside. Low-loaders parked nose to tail waiting to have the concreted pipe sections lifted by the mobile crane onto the deck of the supply ship. Dockers everywhere scrambling on and off the ship like rats swarming to escape from a fire.

McKay, was the tally man. Checking the numbers inside each section of pipe and Baird on the dockside looking for any damage on the pipes to be reported.

Willie, bemoaning the fact that after a long time working with him…Working on the the instructions of his main employer the dock authority. He was now due to resume his duties under the guidance of the shore captain. A man he disliked immensely and was now giving thought to early retirement. If he could only persuade Greta to go along but then, no wait, not such a good thought after all couldn't see himself under her thumb. Better take a chance with the situation as is.

To say the events had been chaotic was an understatement. More akin to bedlam. Baird and McKay possibly in Leith and no doubt one or both spilling their feeble accounts to the Greenes.

The supply ship outward bound to the lay barge in the North sea he watched it sail and a reason he couldn't fix in his mind. Why he did it but he did do it. Took the long walk on the unsafe jetty. The police road block the meeting with Kaiser led him to wonder when was all going to end. Was he going to be given another contract in six months time or was it time to jack it in. Was his future in jeopardy or will it all work out right. He and possibly Kaiser maybe could solve the mystery of his brother and the girl who could tell. Kaiser and London? What was he getting into. Would his own luck hold. The future would take care of itself a sure guarantee there was no doubt on that score.Thinking these things was foolish. He was in danger and what Beeny had said about Kaiser and the meeting Kaiser had with Uncle Winter. Beeny and the conversation he had with Karli on their return was not good news to his ears. Would Kaiser withdraw on Uncles say- so? Was the game up in the air and would Uncle Winter succeed with his argument and convince Kaiser to abandon the idea of going to London. The thought is a nonsense and turning his brain to jelly, he sighed, 'wtf!'

Trying to sleep the noise a distraction. Burying his head under the pillow made no difference. Later, early morning he heard the last of the revellers leaving and thought at last peace to sleep then he realised no chance to sleep, a soft tip tap on the wooden floor. Barefoot steps came crossing the room.

Lifted the pillow, squinted. Head in turmoil desperate for sleep. Reached to the bedside table, his cold hand clasped the butt of the revolver. Put his head back under the pillow and waited. Peeped from under the pillow and saw the light shine through the open door and the slim naked body approaching, 'what now' …Muttering, 'what the….Now!'

'Move over,' she whispered lifting the cover and sliding hurriedly beside him. 'I can't sleep for the noise either,' she said, purring in a funny little way and snuggling against him.

He felt the warmth of her young supple body and liked what was happening but for good measure said in a voice to condemn the adventure, 'for heaven sake can't a man get peace to sleep?' A slight pause, coughed, after another pause, 'a well, the name's Frank take it you are the one they call, Nikki?'

'My, that's hard. You expecting me,' she said, slowly and seductively.

He smiled slowly slid the revolver under the pillow, 'well,

you Nikki, or not?' he waited. She giggled, purred 'what's in a name?' She said.

Lunch in the bar they were sitting on the long chummy seat below the stain glass coloured rose window. They dined on frog legs and plump snails swimming in a concoction of butter and mustard sauce. Her father Harry said the french mustard was the best compliment to the snails and would be a gourmet delight one Frank would never forget.

Harry was enthusiastic about it and went out of his way to assure him but Frank, Frank was doubtful if he would ever eat the things again and that was his firm thought to the suggestion.

They followed the starter with French fries and frikadellen washed down with the house red. Picked at a selection of nuts and cheeses from a large blue coloured plate decorated with three Dutch girls dressed in old fashion costumes. The girls are sitting on a snowy bank below the sails of a windmill. Two Dutch boys skating on a frozen pond and a lone black and white cow looking over a broken fence enjoying the scene A small plate decorated with fine painted green and red bunches of grapes and on the plate real bunches of red and green grapes.

Father Harry the pot belly old man with the bald head and round red face sat on a stool at the corner of the bar playing his accordion to the delight of his customers. Close together they danced embracing each other on the small square lit-up coloured dance floor. The glass panels glowing orange from the coloured bulbs. The dancers smooching happily as they slowly danced round and round.

Others enjoying the midday dalliance sitting at tables under the low red glow of the coloured overhead lights giving a warm cosy feeling to the darkened restaurant.

Their conversation was interrupted by seeing Kaiser enter the place, 'I know, bit late,' he said, breezing over to their table, 'had business to attend but like the bad penny, here fit and well. Don't suppose you missed me anyway did you?'

'Oh, yeah, never mind, two days late. Hope your business was worth it but not to disappoint had a nice time as well waiting your return,' said Frank.

'Nice to see you too Bowtow. I see you have muscled in on my favourite girl. Well hello Nikki. Missed me by any chance, no, come to think it you have a nice bright shine in your beautiful eyes. Not tired dear? Up all night have we or have you been having sweet dreams that would explain, ay.'

He kissed her cheek. She pulled back, 'haven't missed you,' she said…'One can only have sweet dreams if they are asleep but lucky me,' she hit back, 'as it so happens was up all night. Tonight will have sweet dreams, maybe. Though glad to see you're back. How long will you be staying this time, long, all-nighter perhaps,' fluttered her eyes placed a snail between her teeth made a rude slurping noise before swallowing then made a long reach with her outstretched arms moving her breasts along the top of the table making much play as she extracted another snail from it's colourful shell and placing it between her lips making a longer slurp.

'Stop that. Behave yourself,' said Frank, 'have things more important to discuss here don't want to be disturbed. Go away and play somewhere else,' gaving her a friendly push.

'Was enjoying that,' she squealed giving him a slap on his arm in return, 'best thing this morning no doubt about it,' fell back on the seat laughing.

Kaiser was wearing a brown single breasted suit a pink open neck shirt and a thick gold chain round his neck. He sat down at the table and watched Karli, the voluptuous, black eyed waitress with the hour glass figure arrive at the table with a welcoming smile.

'My, look good enough to eat. I've missed you honey. Have you missed me, expect not. Take it you want some food?'

Whispering into Kaisers ear she lingered a second with her tongue letting the others see exactly what she was doing.

'Yes, yes to your questions,' Kaiser said, ' see you later. Bring me what they've had and don't forget the wine,' watching her leave gave a long low whistle at the going away view she presented.

'Things went smoothly no worries up till now is fine,' he said, just a little bit flustered at the way Karli had greeted him.

'Care of the wheels I know how good you are at getting rid, don't want any comeback over a hired car and the shadows did you manage to avoid them? Of course that is obvious seeing you are here and in great form as usual,' said Frank.

'Yes, don't even give it a thought. Taken care of. Finished, kaput, nix worry. Next question all ears. But one unexpected interruption I had though not worth the mention. Stop thinking of work we are hear to have some fun.'

He demonstrated by waving his arms smiling looking at the surrounding company was the usual crowd nothing to worry. Was sure hadn't been followed from Groningen. Knowing if they had followed they would have shown themselves by now. He was certainly sure things couldn't have gone smoother even the Elderado hotel was successfully taken care of.

'Have a question,' said Nikki, 'how did you two happen to meet you certainly are a strange combination. One Dutchman the other a Schottlander…Schottlander mit der doodlesac where's your, up your kilt?' She fell back on the seat holding her stomach laughing. Kicking out giving a view of a long well proportioned leg.

Frank pulled at her skirt to cover her knees, 'behave.'

'Easy,' said Kaiser, watching her making a fool of herself.

'My father was on my grandfathers farm,' he continued, 'at the bottom of the lane two German sentry boxes guarding the way into town. One morning to get the cows for milking dad saw the soldiers had gone rushed to the farmhouse all excited and told them the Germans had fled. Granny grandad and father cycled to town when they got near they heard strange music in the distance. Further on they saw the townspeople dancing in a field to the sound of bagpipes, your doodlesack, Scottish Canadian regiment relieved the town. Goodness knows where the drink came from all were drunk as skunks. If the Gerry soldiers returned the whole kit and kaboodle would have been recaptured. Bottles of gin lying everywhere full and empty a great time had by all. Father said the Scots were the best in the world no surprise I have the best friend. Easy to see don't you think he said it was the best day of his life…Except for meeting my mother of course and that is a story for another time.'

'Will raise a glass to that,' Frank rising unsteady on his feet arms waving from side to side wine spilled out of the glass splashing on the table. The other's made fun saying he was drunk as a skunk which he denied profusely said the Germans would never have got their hands on him.

'What. No whisky? not on, one bottle of whisky, no Karli better, two bottles.'

'Didn't take you long Kaiser to be up to your old tricks,' she said, putting three small glasses and the bottles of whisky on the table.

'I'm free tonight,' she said, walking off and giving a playful wiggle on her, bahooky turning her head to look back sporting a large come-on smile.

Beeny came from the kitchen squeezing past the dancers. His face, you could say, on recognition, he had just eaten the mother of all sour lemons.

'Ready to go now are you fit to go Kaiser? I've three wine deliveries to make in Rotterdam have to be on our way. Ready or not,' said hurriedly. Watched Frank flirt with Nikki and wondering what they were laughing at, laughing, her like a girly teenager. Fed up with the laid back attitude they took and was anxious to be gone out on the road back to things that mattered.

'Your not leaving me are you Frank?' her eyes rolled and her hands clasped her cheeks. 'Not already, not now. Not when we have lots more to do,' laid her head on his arm, 'boo hoo, boo hoo you can't leave me please don't go,' she straightened looked longingly at him crossed her arms on her bosom pretending to be suffering a broken heart.

'You'll find someone as soon as we leave. Stop play acting,' said Kaiser with a playful rub on her you no where, bahooky?

'Are you going too?' She said softly, seductively, when she let go of Franks arm.

Karli joined from the bar.

'You are going Kaiser? Was looking forward to tonight,' reminding him.

She grabbed his arm, 'not letting you go. I've waited too long can't disappoint me. No way not now. What does a girl have to do? Please Kaiser, please,' people looked thought she was over the top putting on a show.

Harry stopped playing the accordion when he realised what was taking place then he began to play *We'll Meet Again.*

'Play *Lilli Marlyn*,' male voice sounded out from the dancers.

'You kidding, *Lilly Marlyn*? Don't you dare!' Cried a female voice.

Someone started a slow hand clap. The dancers carried on.

'Have we got twenty minutes? A few minutes is not here nor there is it Beeny? You know how it is.' Kaiser said, more demand than a question.

'Twenty minutes is neither here nor there so be quick,' Beeny replied with a look and a shrug showing he wasn't pleased at the delay.

Kaiser ignored him, did what he wanted to do irrespective of Beeny.

FOURTEEN

'Quick thinking I thought we were not going to be able to talk. Beeny is in one of his daft moods and can't fathom him at all just lately,' Kaiser informed Karli.

'Think your friend has something to do with it. To me, what it is,' she replied.

Upstairs in the apartment. Kaiser poured the wine, 'drink slowly,' he said, 'have to wait at least twenty, you know, twenty minutes. Reputation,' he smiled and clicked her glass, 'good health and stay safe. Soon, hopefully we will *meet again.*' He smiled and she saw the gleam in his eyes. Fun she thought maybe if I tease worth a try.

Kaiser saw the signs but unfortunately no time to risk another spat with the spoilt boy Beeny it was better to wait for another time. Arguments was not what he was after better to play it nice and easy for now.

She thought about it but realised she wasn't going to be the one to start any bad vibes among the crew and got on with the business. 'Saw my friend, Trudi in Willemshaven. Information was correct. The yacht is there again the routine is simple. A round sea voyage to Cape Town then Durban and a longer stay at Port Elizabeth before returning to Willhemshaven.

'Drugs and laundered money exchanged for gold and diamonds some bloody operation. Must be someway we can get the right information to nail it?'

'Yes, Oldersum is under orders from his wife who is the brains behind it all.'

'Is it true the woman is Burke's cousin?'

'Yes, sure is and Irish, Trudi confirmed it and trying to get as much information as she can because her boss at the cleaning company has been told not to send the same cleaners to the yacht. Strict instructions from Mr Oldersum.'

'His goons you're saying they mean business?'

'Yes. There no doubt about it, vicious. Change of the routine is certain. Someone I know and you know disturbed a cabinet on board putting papers back in the wrong sequence. Was not the thing to do. The man went off his rocker don't think we can rely on any more information coming from that source. Oldersum, will not let it go will keep digging till he finds out who was responsible. My friend will have to lay low for now have to take a holiday keep well out of the way. But stubborn you know how she is. Going on past results. Worried who will be sent to the yacht next. Should ease off for a while see a disaster in the making,' she says as she his filling his glass, 'you drinking or driving? I've other things on my mind.'

'Not driving and don't want to know what's on your mind just tell me about the German police?'

'Turning a blind eye. Many fingers in this particular set up.'

The casino in England. The English police have a mole in Burke's Mayfair, establishment. Has the German police got anyone inside the Oldenburg place?'

'If so will be a friendly one. Been told too many celebs in there off their heads with drugs. A private club. Police can't or won't do much. Run like a well oiled machine. The Oldersum bitch certainly knows how the game is played to her advantage.'

'I've no time to go there and suss it out. Too much on my plate at the moment. Frank is desperate to get to Scotland. The situation with his brother has got him on edge and would not surprise me if he has a breakdown. He's becoming impossible to keep from asking too many irrelevant questions.'

'You will have to keep a tight grip. Can't afford to have a loose cannon upsetting the, so called, if you can call it, norm.'

'I've seen him when he looses it.'

' Oldersum they say earned his iron cross the hard way.'

'Murder comes easy to him. His henchmen are all in the same category. In feet first not think it out but in time you know the saying catch the monkey but carefully.'

'Yes have to be careful,' said Karli, 'his people are really vicious. The daughter and her guy may already be under the daisies. Seems the wicked stepmother has pulled out all the stops and nothing will get in her way to find the two of them. I pity them. Silly girl what was she thinking?'

'When I'm through here and finished what I have to do in Rotterdam I'm going to, London. Will see Tony and find out the situation.'

'Yes no secret. Uncle on the phone. Tony mind you and give him my love. And tell him to keep batting...Don't you bother asking he will understand.'

'Batting, thats a new one on me.'

'Do you want me to make the arrangements? I said don't ask. Tickets. Hotels. Or you know?'

'You have some filthy mind. But the deed is done made the arrangements in Groningen it's all done and dusted, sorted.'

'The pot calling the kettle, know how it goes,' she said.

'I've got to find out about the pair who escaped the police and flew to London. I had two, no, make it four,' smiled, 'not a worry now. But how many more I don't know. A mystery. Be very careful is the watch word or so says Edgar Kline.'

'Who was responsible for the murder of Pieter? Is it the ones who are now in England or the ones in Oldenburg? I've lost count.'

'You've lost count I've got the same problem.'

'You saw Uncle when you arrived was he well? Got no joy from him when he phoned. The shop? Is the business holding up, no, guess asking the wrong question. I think I know the answer to that one. Will have to make time to see for myself been a while since saw him but any excuse will do to forgo a visit.'

'Better make it quick the shop stinks needs someone to look after him. Shame he is going on what he did in the underground against the Germans. Now is recalling the memories. Suggested he should write his memoirs.'

'Offered to have him with me but you know how set in his ways he is. Good at giving advice but not willing to take any.'

She walked to the window parted the curtain peeped out. 'He's in the van bet he's miffed at you for taking longer. He'll be giving your friend an ear bashing. Moan moan moan, typical Beeny.' She came over put down on his lap. 'How about giving him something to really be miffed about,' she teased, 'still got time. Let him wait and suffer. Don't envy one bit going on a journey with him.'

'I've no time just now. Will have to get going. Had a long talk with Edgar Kline he put me wise to what the score is like in the Oldersum set up. The situation is really bad the Bowtow really in it up to his neck. Oh dear. Shouldn't have said that could've phrased it better not nice to talk about necks. Little brother has sure started something really big. Don't think Bowtow realises just who we are up against. Have we got shadows following? Only time will tell.'

'Why Bowtow why that name?'

'Born in Newhaven, Scotland, endearment to anyone born there I believe or so he tells me. No cause to doubt and anyway has a certain ring about it.'

'Some twenty minutes?' Beeny said. Of course was his usual unhappy self. Sitting in silence and not looking forward to the coming journey. 'Okay if we get on our way? Nothing more doing no further delay. Sure we can get going? Positive there is no more instructions to be doled out, we can go, can we?'

'My my Beeny we are in a strop. Dearie me just drive if you please.'

Beeny switched on the engine and the radio and drove onto the road in silence.

Frank closed his eyes.

'Soon be there,' said Kaiser.

'Do we have to listen to this rubbish on the radio?' Asks Frank.

'Go to sleep,' chirps Beeny.

'What's on your mind?' Frank asking Kaiser.

'I want to hear the radio not listen to you two,' said the sulking Beeny.

'If you have nothing better to say then I think we two will oblige by trying to sleep,' said Kaiser and giving Frank a large smile followed by a wink.

'Not sleepy not now. Want to hear what you've got on your mind?' Frank said.

'On my mind? I was going over it thinking what a nice, er, that twenty minutes had was something not to be forgotten,'

'Oh, here we go,' said Beeny, 'not going to tell us the sordid details are you?'

'No, nothing sordid about it.'

'That's not what Karli would say am I wrong?' Beeny shot back at him.

'Excuse me but I don't wish to know,' said Frank, 'maybe sleep is a good idea. Should be able to sleep, after, you know up all night with you know.'

'Not wish to know what you got up too with my sister so if you please. Please go to sleep.'

'You two going to go at it or is peace about to be declared?'

Frank ignored him and closed his eyes.

'Good,' said Kaiser, 'I've a lot of thinking to do.'

'And after, Rotterdam? What next, where do we end up?'

'You do your deliveries Beeny and Frank has business to attend to.'

'Us? What about us?' Asked Beeny.

'There is no, us. Get it through your feeble brain.'

'I thought…'

'Gentleman please!' Frank cried out.

'You thought wrong.' Kaiser said, 'Just concentrate on your driving. You thought! Thats your problem your always thinking.'

'Franks smiled, still with his eyes shut, 'wake me when we get there,' says it with a long yawn. 'Roll on Rotterdam!'

'You do know the arrangements, ay?' Kaiser quizzed.

'Think I've got it clear,' Frank answered. 'Or am I doing too much thinking also?'

'You want…?

'To take command?' Frank interrupted. 'You asking?'

'Got to be clear in the understanding,' said Kaiser.

'Thought you wanted quietness and you wanting sleep. Not going to have an argument are we? Please be quiet and let me concentrate on doing the driving. You two are beginning to get on my wick if you must know.'Beeny said long and slow.

'We're sleeping, sleeping,' said Kaiser. 'But concentrate on the road. Keep watch if you think we have a tail you wake me if I'm sleeping. You can do that can't you?'

108

FIFTEEN

Late afternoon they stopped in a street full of rundown tenements overflowing rubbish bins on the pavements. Groups of men loitering drinking tins of beer noisily arguing with each other. Down and outs sitting about sipping their desired swally from bottles secreted in brown paper bags. Others walking up and down. Woman gossiping children playing the games children play.

Nothing much changes, Frank was thinking. Truly this place the ideal ripe for demolition kinda place. Like slums in Leith. Overdue for a makeover but not if it is made a hash of like some in Leith.

'Welcome to Rotterdam,' said Kaiser when they got out the van, 'go on in and register. I'll bring in the luggage after I see Beeny on his way.'

'You want me to go in there this flea joint? With all these newspapers lying here strewn among these rat infested dustbins? Give me a break is this the best? Is there nowhere else? Surely, oh why bother!'

He was looking at the mess at the entrance, 'I've seen some joints but this doss house takes the biscuit. If it's like that here I wouldn't go anywhere near the rear entrance in fact don't want to go anywhere near or in the building!'

He was remembering a certain Leith derelict building that had been converted into a male only hostel. A haven for the many with drink and drug problems. He remembered the dank damp smell made his stomach heave and now was experiencing the same again. 'Some place this typical Kaiser,' he shrugged. He knew in his head it done no good to complain. Started a slow walk toward the entrance and was wondering just how bad it was going to be inside.

'Get going it's okay I'm a regular in the joint Register while having a word with Beeny letting him know the next schedule.'

Beeny was delighted and smiled as he watched to see what was coming next. Was gloating at Franks obvious displeasure at the task in front of him.

Kaiser smiling not letting him in on the joke giving assurance everything was okay although he was a little surprised Frank reacted the way he did.

'What do you expect Frankie? There's no such thing as five star hotels in this dockside metropolis. Nice inside, you'll see.' Beeny shouted as Frank lingered before going up the steps.

Reaching the top step he was deciding to chance the revolving door or retreat back to the van.

'Is he in for a let down when he gets in there, ha ha ha, you'll get it when he finds…ha ha ha you ….. Kaiser,' said Beeny taking much delight at Franks discomfort and hoping more of the same would befall him before they parted company soon and forever.

Frank pushed on the revolving door squinted across the empty space that greeted him. He saw her and perked up. What does Kaiser have going on here and he thought there maybe be a little bit of an adventure if he played his cards right.

'A room for two please,' he said giving her a big friendly smile as he approached the same time having a long look to where she was sitting behind the booking desk. He turned slowly and clocked the surroundings. The décor in sore need of a makeover. More of a demolition job would be favourable he was thinking. The wallpaper peeling here and there and a putrid smell of dirty water, the kind of smell reminding him of a washing machine needing a full inner clean- out descaled or preferred put on a bonfire

He sniffed caught the odour of blocked drain it was the way he turned his head, one sniff, bad, another turn of his head, really bad…Taking short breaths and covering his nose with his handkerchief, 'what the?' Mumbling to himself. Wrong to think his handkerchief would mask the words but she heard and the look she gave could have sunk a battleship.

She rose up eyeing him showing her dislike and he thought the first encounter was bad news he definitely got started on the wrong foot.

She placed the newspaper she was reading on her seat, 'Is your companion male or female?' she asked and in a moment smiled. Her face lit up at the thought whatever it was she was thinking whilst hovering with her pen ready to enter the details sordid or otherwise onto the hotel register.

Taking a backward step he tried to figure her out as he listened her voice sounding a little husky and all the time he was wondering was it a man or a woman? Ah well maybe later he would find out or not and of course she must be used to the smell so if he was to succeed he better get over it as well. Would she be worth the bother smell or no smell?

He couldn't see how she shaped below the desk. Reckoning, she was in her late thirties. Her hair colour mousy brown and surprisingly a pleasant smell of rose water meandering from her bowed head. Was it to hide the horrible odour he couldn't say but the reek of the other...

Turning her head slightly to the side she waited for his response.

He was wondering why she was wearing black rim specs it wasn't as if she was ugly. A nice mouth a small cute nose has to be a woman he thought men have bigger noses. She reminded him of a young lady school teacher he had a crush on many years ago when he was an awkward teenager journeying into puberty. Oh, the memory so long ago. He remembered something else not so pleasant. A time when he suffered boils on his neck. Wrapped in white bandages f... no bint would give a second look not when you were a leper in their eyes. He put the memory out of his mind and continued to concentrate busy admiring her white blouse under her black jacket where three buttons undone and could see most of her small bosom. Is it she or is it the other was what he was giving his thoughts to.

'A gent, a gentleman,' he answered with a slight awkward stammer hesitant and definitely thinking of something else as the glimpse of her breasts distracted him.

'Pardon?' she said, followed by a knowing sort of smile one that proposed, okay mister, nothing new in that and gave him a broad smile 'seen it all before,' she said, 'what was it you say Sure would help if you spoke up and no nothing surprises me.'

'Male friend I said a gentleman,' he got back to the thing in hand. Decided to stop dreaming of what could or not could be?

'A gentleman you say, the rate will be five hundred and fifty euros per person paid in advance,' she said abruptly giving the broadest of a sly smile. 'Room nine first landing. The rules are on the door we don't tolerate loud music.' Turning she retrieved the key from the board on the wall and handed it over.

He felt the warmth of her soft fingers as he took the key and savoured the slight squeeze and sly come-on smile she gave him. Dangerous, he thought, he's getting signals but are they right or are they wrong?

'Can you arrange some sandwiches to be sent to the room? Bottle beer. Jever pils, if you have it?' He stammered distracted.

'Ham or cheese?' She asked quietly.

'Both would be fine if it's not any bother,' couldn't fathom her change of attitude stepped away ready to climb the stair to the first floor.

'For the refreshments that will be another five hundred euros each in advance,' she announced stopping him in is tracks. Her tone changed again getting back to the business in hand.

'On my reckoning the beer and sandwiches cost as much as the room. Are you trying to rip me off?' His previous thoughts vanishing into thin air with the demand.

'What two gentleman do in the privacy of the room is not my concern not a charity,' she said coldly.

He couldn't see if she was scowling or having a laugh at his expense. Reaching for his wallet he watched her stand erect and stick her chest out then saw her running her hand through her hair seductively removing her specs noticed her eyes where light green with a hint of blue reminding him of Ruthie except spotting a slight a hint of dark shadow under her chin.

'Hi darling you missed me?' said Kaiser as he came hurriedly into the foyer.

'You're money is not needed put your wallet away mister,' she said to Frank then 'Can arrange for company later mister Kaiser?'

'Later Maisie. I'll see you later gorgeous,' he dropped the luggage. 'Plenty time for fun when I get organised okay?'

'I forgot about you,' said Frank.

Kaiser took his arm with his two hands pushed him toward the stairs

'I can manage,' said Frank, 'don't need your assistance.'

The room stank of dampness the smell of cigar smoke got up his nose. 'Good grief Kaiser, why have you picked this rat hole. Might have known you have something dodgy going on, agh. If you don't get these bloody windows open I'm gonna die in this place. And what is it with you? The dame? I saw the way she acted when you appeared.'

'Love Bowtow, love. Good at it,' falling backwards onto the single bed, 'do I feel a little bit of jealousy moving in my direction?' laughed, 'don't worry Bowtow won't happen bet your kinky boots on it.'

7pm Beeny burst into the room.

'You'll never believe this,' he said excitedly as he sat on the single bed. Moved Franks legs to one side giving himself room to sit.

'Did you knock? Never heard a knock did you hear a knock?'

Frank looked over to Kaiser waiting his answer but got none so he said, 'well did you? No. The door,' he said nodding to the door. 'What next you left the door open. Not locked anything could happen in this joint give me strength what have we signed up for?' It was obvious not happy. Things piling up in his mind was at a loss to deal with Kaiser and his laid back attitude plus the return of Beeny was not helping in anyway.

'Relax. Let's hear what he has to say. Go on Beeny spill,' said Kaiser.

'Beeny thought you were on your way home why have you come to this den of rapture?' Frank sighed. Closed his eyes, 'why oh why has this rat hole not been pulled down? Why has the street not been demolished beats me what a place. Couldn't see myself living here for long bloody ridiculous.'

'You won't believe what got to tell you,' Beeny said when the banter between the others stopped, 'was on my last drop off at the Angel hotel talking with Alfred the head kitchen porter asked about Erica the pretty young German girl,' his voice went up when he said the girls name, 'she is from Oldenburg.'

'Who? Erica? I didn't know you were into young fraulines Beeny you rascal,' said Kaiser rising from the bed giving him a playful slap on his back.

'Get off.' Beeny making much of shrugging his shoulder and taking hold of Franks foot and shaking it to get his attention.

'You have to hear me out listen will you it's important.'

'Go on then. The quicker you say the sooner I'll get some sleep.'

'Alfred said the girl left the hotel no longer going to work there. Left without any warning. Left with her boy friend. You will not believe it. It was a Scots boy name of Jamie. If that is not a coincidence don't know what is. It happened a couple of weeks ago but where they've gone is not certain.'

'Has to be him how many Scots guys do you know with the name having it off with a wee German lassie,' said Kaiser.

'Must be and from Oldenburg. The lad has visited every time is here in Holland, Alfred said something about her introducing him to her folks. If that is not a clue,' Beeny continued. 'I don't as I said know what is. Good clue to start with or what? We going to Oldenburg are we?'

'Is there a phone in this dump I've got to make a call,' said Frank rising from the bed without hesitation and rushing to the door.

'Down there,' said Kaiser pointing at the floor and following him. Beeny got pushed over in the melee.

'Hey, watch what your doing. Wait I'm coming too.'

SIXTEEN

Pier 11, Rotterdam docks.

Shoogled their way up the swaying gangway boarding the supply ship the, Maddie Lyle, leaving Beeny in the van.

Eckie, Captain McPherson, had already agreed to meet before he received the phone call from Frank. Was a bit surprised to get the phone call thinking it was Frank cancelling the appointment. Was relieved to find it wasn't.'

He is not a blood relative but such is the custom adults are considered to be related. The kind of people who are always willing to help in any way they can to fellow villagers. Frank and his brother had sailed many times as youngsters on school holidays with captain McPherson. Now they were grown men he still welcomed them on his trips to the continent. Turned a blind eye to any of their schemes as long as they did not involve him. They were on their own when it came to getting ashore before the custom men came on board. He was well known and liked by the people who he does business with on his regular sailings between the port of Leith and the port of Rotterdam. People found him to be a good ambassador for the shipping line of, *KILLGOUR IMPORT AND EXPORT,* a well known company in Leith docks for over a hundred years.

'Did he come and see you?' The skipper asks, saying, 'he was going to visit the last time he came over excited about seeing you as it had been a long time since you saw him said he had something important to tell you.' Poured three nips of whisky invited them to drink. 'Sit lads sit down. It's nice to see you again. It's been a wee while since a clapped eyes on you yes a wee while.'

'Coming to see me, when?' Queried Frank.

'A few weeks ago I take it he never made it from what your telling me.'

'No, he never showed. Wonder why he didn't show? Could have done with a visit. Would have cheered me no end. Getting to know the girl. Would have been a bonus. A new one fast worker ay, some boy right enough!'

'The scoundrel. I knew there was something bothering him. Something to do with the lassie. A wee German quine. So, you didn't know anything about her?' The Captain said surprised.

'No, not a clue.'

'Heard about her,' said Kaiser.

'Unfortunately he never came back. I did get a phone call from her. She said they where taking a sightseeing holiday in a hired car going to Paris then on through to London and home and for me not to worry. Said it was all right they would see me when back in Newhaven.'

'At least now we know he is safe', looking and nodding to Kaiser, thanks for that good news at last.' Frank said.

'Thank goodness for it.' Kaiser repeated with a wink, 'as far as it goes call is weeks old remember let's hope it's still the case, you agree and I hope right.' He slid his empty glass across the table just a wee bit out of reach of his hand.

'You want a refill laddie?' the Captain asked taking the hint and carefully watching as he slowly pours a thimble drop of whisky into the glass. There that'll do you fine I'm thinking. Enough to wet your whistle laddie.'

'Fine,' says, 'thanks plenty,' said, hiding his disappointment. Wondering how long the conversation would last. Was desperate to be out and away. Knows Beeny will give him more grief because he had told him to stay put in the van they would be quick and not take long the business would be done in the shake of a lambs tail or words to that effect.

'Do you know something what is your concern?' Put the whisky bottle in the cupboard ignoring Franks empty glass.

'We think he's got into a wee bit of bother about the girl, that's all,' smiling and not needing to elaborate on the situation. Certainly not to give a reason for any concern whatsoever.

'It's not an elopement not relatives chasing them. It's not a shotgun occasion don't tell me it's that bad not good if family doesn't agree. Seen it before. Love does some strange things.'

'Gretna Green may be the final destination,' Kaiser looking over smiling at Frank, waiting for a back up to the suggestion.

'Must be the distraction then. Definitely intended visiting you but now we know the answer. Good luck to them who's like them.' He lifted his glass. 'A toast to the runaways to them a happy union.'

Frank was glad the Captain accepted what they had said. 'Lucky, aye,' he said.

Kaiser, his eyes focused on the locked cupboard hoping the Captain would free the bottle.

The pilot came up the gangway making his way to the bridge.

The mate stuck his head in the cabin door, 'pilot is here skipper, time.'

Having a good look round and wondering why he hadn't been invited for the pleasantries as he was partial to a dram and felt left out.

'It's up anchor time. The pilots oan the boat we have tae git going,' he said, closing the cabin door, slowly.

'Have a safe trip Bowtow.' Kaiser shouted over his shoulder walking to the waiting van and the moody Beeny. 'See you soon buddy take care.'

The engines throbbed into life Frank made is way below to the cabin

A docker on the quayside let go the mooring ropes.

The engine roared into life. The prop churned the water and the boat throbbed.

Thunder roared across the sky. Streaks of white lightning peeped at the edges of the dark menacing clouds.

'How do they expect me to sleep,'said Frank muttering to himself, 'with this racket going on nothing changes. A cabin on top of noise and a cabin below noise help ma boab!'

Following morning, 'taxi on the quay.' The mate informed him when he finished breakfast in the seamen's mess and ready to leave the vessel when the Captain joined him.

'Morning skipper. Best nights sleep for a long time he lied. We ready to go ashore. Pity couldn't stay for one more night. Peace to sleep worth it's weight in gold a good night sleep. No one knows that better than me.' Suppose get a rousing home

117

coming. Will have to organise a lock in at Mary's place. You'll be there won't you Captain?'

'No not going ashore. Got a quick turn round unfortunately. I will see you next time,' then he said, 'good luck with your wee brother.' He gave him a hug before going to the bridge. 'Be careful and don't be hard on him. Understand? Okay, know what a mean?'

The mate poured coffee and sat down. 'Take it your brother never showed.'

'No. Did you manage to speak? What kind of state was he in you remember. Know it was a while ago. Got me puzzled hope to catch up with him soon.'

'Yes, good. He was full of it. Couldn't wait to meet up with you was crazy about the wee lassie but bit hesitant at meeting her parents.'

'I don't understand why he never showed.'

'No? Not even a phone call he didn't call? Surprised really surprised at that.'

'No, that's what's bugging me.'

'Funny, ay. Since it was all good news.'

'Good news? About her most likely.'

'No, the way I understood was going to come into a windfall.'

'Did he explain where this windfall was going to come from?'

'Naw, kept that bit close to his chest It was something big I guess. Won't be seeing you there tonight either. Next time that's a given.' Handed him a bottle of whisky, 'skipper wants you to have this,' he said, 'must be feeling good. A free bottle my what next?'

'Taxi you say? Better not keep it waiting.'

'See you soon,' stood up and made his way forrard.

He gathered his luggage and made for the gangway. Saw her standing behind the taxicab. 'Wait,' he said to the taxi driver.

'Clock is running,' driver says, anticipating.

'Hi, Lena. Surprised how you knew?' Put the luggage on the ground giving her the broadest smile. Will send him away yes or no?'

Taxi driver in a strop crashing gears heard as he drove away.

'Drinky poos first,' she said.

'Your pleasure,' he said.

'No Frankie. Your pleasure dear.'

'Long time no see,' he said.

'Remember? What a laugh it was. You remember?'

'The case of the Tanker? How could you forget that episode?'

'Guard at the gangway wouldn't let her on board. Laugh? Said she was crew. Spoke to him in Norwegian. Laugh? Never made so much money in her life. Memory of her being so tall and the Chinese sailors so small. She's gone now rest her bonny soul,' she said.

'Aye, and the security guard got a roasting from his boss.'

'I remember his feet never touched the ground.'

'How you remember that time?'

'Had a few well maybe more than a few money making, good money making times at they docks.'

'There was, wait, wasn't you by any chance…?'

'Me? Wasn't me what?'

'Chucked of a Sparta grass boat into the water. Wasn't, was it? No couldn't have been no, say no!'

'No. But remember wasn't the first there was more chucked into the harbour without payment. Three or four I remember.'

Enough of the all our yesterday's. What you think.'

'You're home?'

'No, yours.'

'No go I'm afraid got a live in lodger.'

'Send her out.'

'Who said it was a she?'

Can't, not mine.'

'Yeah, understand. Under the circumstances,' she said.

Circumstances? What the hell she on about, he's thinking.

SEVENTEEN

'Beeny get to a phone fast as you can drive let's get out of here.'

'There is one at the hotel,' he says as he fires the engine, 'what are you up to now more intrigue no doubt,' upset not being invited to join them on the ship and another who was miffed at missing out on the refreshments. 'No, not the bloody hotel. The walls have ears one at the flower market go for that. Move it and don't ask just do it. You've got to stop second guessing me'

The old dame was wearing a flat hat and had a tartan shawl round her shoulders was carrying a clip board. Specs shifted to the top of her head she lifted the phone from its hook under the half canopy on the outside wall of the building.

Kaiser leapt from the van when it screeched to a halt.

'Help lovely flower seller there's a fatal accident someways down the road. Need to phone an ambulance,' he snatched the phone from her hand and ducked under the perspex half canopy.

She removed the pencil she held in her mouth. 'My goodness anyone hurt can get help in the market can go…'

He stopped her…'No it's okay. I've got the phone no need for you to get involved no need for panic. Don't fuss all under control misses lady.'

She stepped back stayed in earshot listening. Her eyes shot up from the clipboard was angry realising she had been duped.

'Yeah Tony, it's me...sure yes...no fine meet me the flight will arrive around noon. Thanks pal will see you… the weather, oh dreich, yes dreich...a Scottish word…

Sure…I'm learning another language…and London? dreich! might have guessed, bye, bye.'

The flower lady rushed him waving the clipboard, 'you lying whelp of a bitch,' screaming, 'lost sales because of you you lying mongrel.' If a man would punch your face. You knew there was no accident. You lying…Done an old lady out of making a living would you. You shister. You whelp of a whore! I'll see you are punished for doing what you done to me.'

120

'If you don't stop screaming you old hag you who will need assistance. It will be you who needs the ambulance you old boot,' he said, calmly walking to the van.

'I'll report you to the police.'

'You do that granny you think I give a… ' He said as he got into the van.

'You've been busy keeping that quiet. Going to London. When did you decide on that move truly hid that and me left out in the cold again.' Beeny said downheartedly.

'Just drive. Booked the flight when I was in Groningen so get out of here. Get going before the men in the market form a posse and give chase we need a head start so go. Never mind the speed limit. Just go.'

'The hotel? You devious bastard you sure kept that quiet.'

'Yeah of course the hotel where else? And don't you be calling me devious.'

'Take it I'm not invited?'

'That's correct and not in the mood for this just now just you watch the road.'

The journey to the hotel was done in silence. Beeny once more deep in thought fixing how to get kaiser to change his mind. Being moved aside was happening too often in his estimation and now this guy Frank he was sure was behind it.

'Maisie, get my bill ready be down in five,' he said, when he walked past the reception in the hotel.

'Leaving so soon Mr Kaiser? Oh dear not long this time.'

Her face changed from a smile to one of disappointment.

'Next time darling. Next time longer will have fun the next time promise.'

'Remember. There is no charge. You had the beer with the sandwiches on the house. Just bring the key when you come down. Remember for the future.'

His hand on the sulking mans shoulder pushed him towards the stairs, 'don't wish to hang about here get my luggage and take it with you haven't time to mess about at the airport don't want to be hanging around the carrousel at London airport waiting for luggage. Seaside, tell your father gone to the seaside.'

'Why?'

'Do it stop sulking.'

'Not going to let me finish?'

'You are not a child Beeny. Or the BOWTOW would say. Yer no a bairn stoap fassing yersel. Or something like it. Goodness, grow up.'

'Could help out?'

'No. You can't. Do what I said. Everything is taken care off.'

'I'm going to say it again. You've changed since this has started. Why is all about the Scotsman? You have stopped taken me into your confidence and I would like to know why am being sidestepped or sidewinded or something?'

'Sidelined, the word is sidelined. Get over it.'

'Now Amsterdam suppose have to drive you there. Could easily leave the van and get a flight ticket no sweat just say okay and be on the phone home to let them know.'

'How many times!'

Thought maybe think it over change your mind.'

'Not your wildest dreams change my mind. Heed what I said already going it alone don't know how long will be required.'

The journey done in silence. Kaiser can't work out why Beeny is acting foolish? Even if he agreed was doubtful a ticket would be got at this late stage. Thinking as things are shaping up his days probably numbered. Can't go on putting up with his childish way of coming over always on the down side. Not there to hold his hand. Realising it will be hard to say not wanted on voyage surplus to requirements. But say it, well, will be said.

EIGHTEEN

Tony Gissertini parked alongside the taxi rank at London airport. His stature you could say is overly large but tall with it. He fits into his oversize grey check suit with a little to spare would take one look for the average joe to guess he was an American. His black fedora pulled down over his eyes and his flash red pattern tie. Makes him stand out from the crowd. Son of Italian immigrants living in New York. In previous years was a cop in the murder business. Detective sergeant in a rundown precinct in a rundown part of New York. Lease lend, you could say. He helped in a case in the Netherlands where he was successful with the help of the Dutch police on an international drug bust. Cleared out a crime ring with full honours. Helped put many away for a long time. Dutch but mostly American gangsters taken off the streets of Dutch towns and cities. He was fortunate to fall in love with Meerka a pretty blonde, an Amazon female, cousin of Kaiser. One of the many in the cosy clan of streetwise friendly people who's lives were made famous by dealings in the Dutch resistance in the Second World War. Tony resigned from the police department when he got married. Both agreeing to set up business in England as a one man private detective agency with her working as his secretary. Now nearing fifty years of age and Meerka passed. He was looking for an easy life with early retirement. He was the kind who had plenty fingers in the proverbial pies. Well known in the gang haunts of the notorious East End to friends in the London city Met division. Quick to turn a blind eye or turn a trick any which way, when the opportunity arose.

'This makes a change not having to pick you of a deserted beach on the coast and you arriving without any merchandise why you travelling skinny?'

'Well with your contacts hope we can sort it out. I'll give you the details later. Now could do with some sleep if you don't mind can't remember when saw a bed. I'm bushed,' he said settling into the seat and closing his eyes. 'Twenty four hours give me time and everything will be clear.'

'Your pal Billy Main, the silly eejit doing a stretch up in Manchester says you can have the use of his flat while he's away. Said, you can have the use of his clothes. If you want that is. Know how he loves his clothes. He's one smart cookie that boy. I think it would do you well to take advantage of his offer. You being the same build and all. He has clothes a plenty and lots never worn by him yet think he gets to keep the clothes he wears in that other legit business modelling. Little do they know how he makes his living from his real endeavours no sir.'

'What has he done to get a holiday? Thought he had learned his lesson the last time he got banged up?'

'Done for wrecking a boozer in the, East End was looking for some guy who queered his pitch. But you know Billy, came of worse doing six months for his trouble. Three witnesses the fool he didn't clock them there in the background. A scumbag bent no good son of a bitch barman, gave the judge plenty to go on. If you are going to hang around till he comes out he will need you're help to make retribution. You know what is required. The amount of people you help sure is astonishing. How you find the time to stay one jump ahead. You must have an angel on it. Yes sir, on your shoulder.'

'Sure is a fool. Looks like missed him again. Can't wait for him resurfacing.The apartment will be fine but I won't need any clothes.' Opened his eyes and yawned, 'made arrangements with Martha Fraser tomorrow. You know brown suitcase full of the necessary.'

'Yeah the dear Martha. Of course her favoured emporium. I haven't seen her in a long time,' after a pause, he said 'it's on the back seat in the paper bag.'

Turned and reached behind lifted the bag spilled its contents onto his lap, 'a little beauty' he said, 'Waltham p.k with ammo. This was good enough for the high command good enough for me, but now, they are becoming a wee bit quite common. I got one just the other day, matter of fact. Yes just the other day,' he smiled, 'that was a good day all round really good.'

'You would certainly know about it.'

'What do you know about an Irishman, a louse, Irish. With the name of Burke?'

'Burke, no nothing, should I know about him?'

'I thought your pal Rutherford would keep you informed.'

'No nothing about an Irishman and what should i know?'

'Danger, is dangerous you keep well out of his way. Pump you're pal for information get the lowdown but be careful.'

'When have you ever known me not to be careful? We're nearing the flat do you want to get out here or will I drop you at the door?'

'Here will do fine. I'll walk the rest of the way be in touch see you tomorrow.'

'Hi,Tony,' the wag behind the bar greeted him as he pulled the stool to sit. He was in the Blue Star, the joint across the road from the park. It was evening the following night. Place was full of the usual sad sacks with their partners, or some other people's partners, this place is the type of establishment for gathering easy peasy information. 'Hi, Tracy, how you diddlin?' He gave him a front and centre front row seat look at his tonsils as he yawned. Rubbed his eyes as he squinted with a ninety degree head turn clocking the joint.

'My you do look beat. Hope the lack of sleep was worth it? You naughty boy,' he said clearing clutter from the bar left by a previous tippler.

'No such luck my friend. Up all night because duty is always on the go. When you've stopped gassing give me my usual if you please.'

'Must have been one hell of a night. Not with it are you? Fragile are we dear. Hope you're not going to kick off a real grump when you're like this.'

'Kick off, me, tut tut. What put that idea into your head my drink if you please. Won't be asking again so finger out spitting feathers here so move it.'

'Yes dear but do you see the scrubber at the end of the bar… No, don't look just now be casual…Do you see her she's been asking for you. Her neck must be in a right state been twisting and turning every time the door opens and in and out of her handbag fishing for something. Certainly got it bad whatever it is. Someone has got her upset the dark glasses she's wearing, my, a sorry sight. Looks as if she is trying to hide from someone or something.'

'I see her, what's your beef Tracy you fancy her?'

'No lover don't think she's a whore. No, not on the you know the game,' he said shaking his head handing him the bottle of beer.

'Well why the interest, you got the hots? Can tell you're taking an interest she sure looks your type. You better be careful. If your man, Bunty finds out, he will kill you me thinks. You on the turn, wow!'

'No interest it's you she wants silly boy. He moved down the bar, 'silly boy you're a silly boy.' Puffing his lips and with his right hand threw him a few kisses.

A couple moved from their table and walked past him making for the exit.

He lifted his drink walked over sat at the vacated table.

The lady at the bar left her stool joined him giving him the biggest smile.

He smiled... thought how quick the act changed from doom suddenly to happy happy. He took a long quizzical look at her wondering if Tracy read the wrong signals then twigged... 'Kaiser! you certainly fooled me you reprobate hook line and sinker you sure fooled me for a moment yes sir certainly did that. You got me sure buddy but the shoes? The shoes are your downfall. If it wasn't for the shoes. Friend you are a treasure never would have reasoned, hell those shoes.'

'The shoes, dare you look at my legs you pervert,' he glanced round at the clientele who heard his outcry. Some stopped what they were doing to give their attention and the expression on some said it all, indifference.

'This gentleman is interested in my legs what do you think of that?' he shouted and waved his arms making out as the injured party.

'You can't wear flat shoes in that getup,' said Tony, 'trainers, you can't wear trainers you will never learn will you?'

The blonde floozie in the nearly dress at the table next to them whispered. 'Is it a man or a woman?' Her eyes fixed on kaiser trying to make sense of the situation. It was a sure fact this was her first visit to the den of anything goes establishment.

The guy she was with shrugged continued to massage the back of her right hand. 'What does it matter? You know the deal, it's normal what goes on in here don't let it bother you just look at me, it's me you should be interested in not them. Only me not these degenerate queers.'

'Feel uncomfortable. No place to bring a lady.' She got up and made her escape.

The boyfriend rushed after her waving her little handbag. 'Wait, you don't have to go. My friends are here. Making me, your making me look a fool,' shouted after her. Too late she was out the door and into a taxicab waiting in the street. He emerged just as the cab left. He shouted after it but it didn't stop. Looked inside her handbag and took out the few pounds then for some reason had a long sniff inside before throwing it into the gutter. Slow amble to the bar shaking his head side to side. Thought he felt a tear. Right hand to his cheek wiped the wet away.

'Never mind,' said Tracy when he was inside 'have a drink on the house.'

A butch tart making her way out stopped to give Kaiser the once over. He refused her offer. Was looking not bad for a man in drag except for the offending footwear. Had on a short length auburn colour wig, dark specs...Blue jacket. Red blouse with a thick gold band round his neck and medium length green pleated skirt, his shoes and no stockings. A dab of lipstick with a little mascara, seen, when he removed the specs giving a hint of mischief in his baby blues.

'Refuse to wear high heels make me waddle. A fat duck walks better than me. But got you, right if it hadn't been for the feet?'

'Down to business,' situation got back to normality, 'spoke with my friend after I left you yesterday Tom Rutherford he's looking into the killing of a known fence who suffered a nasty... f….. gaping hole in the neck. Nearly took his head off some sight imagine walking in on that after you've had your breakfast not even the bravest would wish to see.'

'Know of two others who fit the bill bet it's the same people who are responsible and what you say confirms it.'

'People you say what makes you think it's the same people?'

'I'm on the trail why I'm here get to the finish once and for all to end the game.'

That Kaiser would be thinking it as a game gave Tony the reason to smile and he was wondering just what his part would be, in the game?

'Another fence. The dead mans partner is scared out of his wits. Wants police protection he's squealing like a pig like he's being castrated. His take on the situation, a young lady known to the dead man delivered a parcel got paid in cash lot of money and not the first parcel she's got rid off no sir.'

'Is it a German girl by any chance?'

'Believe so left the office with a hold-all stuffed with the filthy lucre. Said she was going to Scotland with her boyfriend let the fence know when they were going. Said it when leaving his office. The partner overheard the conversation love and trust between villains so much for partners.'

'Should not have said where they were going what a foolish thing to do.'

'Found him on the floor when he arrived at the office the next morning. The sleepover was a regular occurrence as he was forever hanging one on. Got the shock of his life when he realised was not sleeping. What a sight.'

'Body with a severed head not everybody's cup of tea'

'Yeah gruesome or what Rutherford has found out the boy is a courier. They've left a lot of angry people behind got a lot of blood on their hands. Although, they haven't done any killing they sure are involved. Rutherford was under the impression that the Dublin born Irishman is responsible and i'm of the same conclusion.'

'Burke is it, Burke, guy I asked you about?'

'Yeah Burke. Runs a nightclub in Mayfair a high class joint. Casino and restaurant full of pimps and the usual drug dealers. Rutherford has a man inside. He hopes, really hopes. Tell you I'm sick of hearing him repeat the word, hope. Soon he will get results. When I know you will know. I'll make sure you are in the loop.'

128

'Well pal it looks as if I'm on the night train to Edinburgh will be in touch thanks a bundle for your help Tony.'

'Not dressed like that no way will the jocks, they won't let you into the country dressed like that.

But do keep in touch. Before you go you can pretend to give me a loving kiss got the queer behind the bar curious. Watch out though, he, she, might be on the pull... A girl, my my!'

Tapping Kaiser on the bottom when he got up from the table he looked seeing Tracy showing an interest. Would he give kaiser a farewell kiss? No, thought the better of it just to play it cool casual like.

When kaiser left he had doubts reckoned was holding back not telling the full picture. Some things had been said made him wonder why he seemed to know the couple would be followed to Edinburgh dead mans partner said Scotland never mentioned Edinburgh was not like Kaiser not to be more inquisitive. If when he meets up with Rutherford he was hoping to get more information. Maybe the parts in the jigsaw would fit into place. London had always been a haven for the gang culture. Murder was common place why was Rutherford not getting a grip on this Irish guy, Burke? Murder could be the usual and usually when a random murder is committed it could be pinpointed to someone close to the unfortunate one or in the case of a gangland crime... Let them dispose of each other no sweat. Coming from the continent is something else. A trail of murder, brutal murder has to be something big. Is Interpol on the case or is Rutherford not giving out the full facts is it a case of corporate murder and why is Kaiser so invasive is it to protect him answers and questions should have been shared more freely.

'You not get it?' Tracy said, putting a bottle of beer in front of him.

'What?' He said and not pleased.

'My my. Oh dear, said no did she?'

'I didn't ask for this,' he said, pushing the beer bottle at him.

'As I said, dear dear.'

'Get this rubbish cleared from the bar and get me a whisky,' he barked.

'There is no pleasing you, is there?'

'You will please me by getting the... out of my face!'

129

'Okay I'm going can take the hint. Sure you don't want my help, know, upstairs. The girls, soon get that smile back again.'

'Darling the only help you can give me is keeping it shut,' put his forefinger to his lips, 'when I need assistance will be first to let you know.'

'Paul the post took the stool next to him, 'she giving you a hard time? Couldn't help overhearing the conversation.'

'Hi Paul, nothing i couldn't handle. You want a beer? Tracy, a bottle of beer for Paul and see if you can do it without you bending our ears with your nonsense.'

'I hear Billy is due for release anytime soon.'

'Yeah. But how long will he stay out?'

'Not very wise is he, the stupid things he gets up to.'

'Young and foolish. Kids, never learn!'

'I couldn't but hear you going on about Burke. This guy is no pushover. Been getting away with it a long time.'

'You got the dirt on him?'

'Be careful,' looked around. Tony could see apprehension on his face. 'Can't use what i say.'

'It's that bad?'

'In here best less said the better.'

'Nothing to fear friends here.'

'You think? More fool you.'

'What's on your mind people like you and you know friends here not a worry.'

'Think so. Don't trust him,' looks long at him behind the bar, 'don't put trust in him. He's living a lie took me a while but got the lowdown a while ago.'

'Paul, what are you? Is being a postie a cover. You gonna say if on to you or what?'

NINETEEN

Hurried from the bar made for the phone box at the park.

'Hi karli. Yes favourite one sorry it's late. Have I interrupted any thing special… Yes I wish I was there with you to,' paused, thinking a time when they…no, he thought the memory although pleasant now was not the time to dwell on long forgotten memories of illicit passions.

'Tony,' she says, 'no darling nothing special. Just watching the television. What can I do for you didn't expect to hear from you till next week.'

'The boy arrived safe,' he paused again then said, 'wait a moment Karli phoning from the box at the park a couple of fancy queens lurking too near.'

Standing in a compromising position close to each other beside the park railing in an obvious embrace. They stood under a hanging bush only a few feet away from the lamp-post and next to the entrance gates much too close to the phone booth.

He was sure being so near they would be able to hear his conversation.

'I saw you two in the bar across the way you following me? Would not like to think that's what you are doing.' He took them completely by surprise.

They came apart from each other in a disheveled panic. He got one by her arm and looked menacingly into her eyes. Growled at her making her think the worse.

'Sorry mister. We were only having a bit of fun.' One said as she adjusted her breasts. Smoothed her skirt under the blue see-through plastic rain mac.

'Some people,' said her companion, 'why can't you mind your own?'

This female was wearing a pinstriped suit, on her head a flat grey tweed cap. Round her neck a whiter than white silk scarf.

Tony pulled the revolver from his under-arm holster grabbed the woman by the lapel of her gentleman's suit. 'Do you know what this is?' He placed the gun under her chin on seeing the fear in her eyes thought she was going to feint and wondered if he

131

was being too hasty after all it was a female he was dealing with. Never before this kind of occasion came up always held these ladies in high regard. Let go watched as she trembled, still close enough to get the whiff of stale cigarette smoke and equally stale perfume. Worst, her breath, her breath reminded him of rotten fish. He turned his head and for a moment thought going to throw up and what would that say to the girls? Not manly no sir.

'This double action revolver. You see it if I pull the trigger It will blow you're head right over the park fence. Then after it bounces on the grass. I'll do the same to your lover. Now, who sent you?' Stepped back gasping and needing to spit.

'No one sent us mister no one i swear it only having fun that's all honest,' she is saying in a pleading way, 'have no right to treat us this way, not a cop.' Struggled to get free from the vice like grip he had on her lapel.

'Get out of it and if see you again will kick you down never mind up the street. You get it? Now get going. I don't want to be bothered with you two again.'

'Okay mister we understand you won't see us again. But, my, what a strong grip you have. Really strong…want to change your mind have some fun?'

'What does the name Burke mean to you tell me never mind changing my mind!'

Now scared out their wits looked at each other wondering is he for real and are they about to breath their last? …'Burke,' the one in the suit asked her friend,

No they hadn't a clue what the fat American was asking.

'Nothing about a man, Burke,' they said in unison.

One said she thought someone with the name Burke ran a high class casino up town though she had never met him only what she heard, like.

'Nothing, honest, nothing.' The other said, 'never heard of the man Burke.'

'Don't get in my way again remember what I said?' Watched them hurrying away into the park. 'Just a pair of queers Karli. Just two Queens having fun but smelling, agh, like the underarm of a sweaty stoker,' he said, when he returned to speak on the phone in the booth, 'quiet now. Gone into the park guess to finish what ever.'

132

'My goodness that was scary better find somewhere else to meet. Better get out of here it's not safe too many strange people,' said the woman in the rain mac,' where do you fancy for a holiday, say Scarborough or Morecambe?'

Her companion hunched shivered kept looking over her shoulder every few yards,

'You decide can't think straight let's keep going.'

Near the exit they heard rustling in the bushes took to their heels running as fast as they could till they got out the park. 'Safer in the crowded street,' the one in the suit said, 'and I think a holiday is a good idea.'

'What do you know about Scotland just come off the phone to my contact in Holland Scotland was mentioned Edinburgh in particular you holding back wouldn't like to think things were not being said,' asking when he phoned Rutherford.

'Don't know what you're on about it was you you're the one who was interested, not me. I've said already out of our ball game let them sort whatever.'

'Okay, got to go people waiting to use this phone see you.'

'Wait, another, have to tell you, has been another.'

'What?'

'A prostitute. Same as the others.'

'Neck? Are you saying by the throat?'

'Yes.

'One of Burke's?'

'Yes, hostess from the casino.'

'A prostitute? Others, were not or maybe yes?'

'Yeah, not prostitutes. But you know same as the other ones. Same as, you know.'

'Know why?'

'How the hell would I know why?'

'You don't have a clue do you you're bloody useless!'

'It's definitely same as the other's no clue why it happened?'

'Maybe she was doing what she shouldn't have been doing. I'll have to go people out here are waiting on me getting out of the booth. Bye.'

'No. Wait. I know your friend Billy is out.'

'Yes, heard. Good behaviour I believe. And so?'

'Information…Can you, well, pick his brain must have learned a thing or two.'

'You really think going to use him for you're sake what you, dam cheek.'

'Don't start. Get off your high horse be to our advantage.'

'You're advantage you mean.'

'You know what I mean. Anything, how small is better than no information.'

'What's in it for me?'

'What you mean to our you know mutual interest.'

'I won't reply have to go. A frustrated female is hammering on the glass window of the booth'

'A menstruating female, wow! How on earth you know that?'

'Ha ha good-bye.'

'When can we meet make it soon.'

'Soon. Usual place.'

'Not that can't be seen there.'

'Behave yourself never suggest there. Gee, certainly you are a snob.'

'Billy. Sure are you won't be using him?'

'No nark of your own? What do you pay these people for, oh no don't say you don't pay. You're a cheapskate Rutherford.'

'Why use mine when I can use yours. Funds you know how it goes.'

'And me the funds where you been all my life?'

'We need to get smart have to get to the bottom of what's being done.'

'The whole of the London Met and you come crying on my shoulder.'

'This is special.'

'Special what you mean special?'

'You don't need me to spell it out.'

'Have to go gonna get lynched if don't get out of here bye. See you soon.'

Back to the blue star. Was crowded he got a stool at the end of the bar. Waited five minutes to get served wasn't in any hurry, saw Billy enter.

'You want a drink,' Billy asked, 'usual,' he said nodding. The barmaid Derba gave them bottles of beer and a come on smile. Billy said was up for it. Tony told him to behave himself, 'go elsewhere if you need to do the business. Not to be trusted. In here not good form too close to home.'

'You heard,' said Billy, 'a tart, one of Burke's that's what was said. Going the rounds putting the word out.'

'What is it with this guy Burke, you know?'

'Nothing new there.'

'Meaning?'

'Surplus to Burke's needs.'

'Requirements?'

'Yeah, do what your told or do one.'

'Kill them! What is he running an abattoir?'

'You had any dealings with him?'

'No. Relying on you to give me the lowdown,' pushed his empty beer bottle to one side. Caught her attention and asked for two more. 'Stop it,' he said to Billy.'

'What,' surprised, 'stop what?'

'Saw what you done. Stop ogling that tart.'

'You do appreciate been locked up. A man. You know! You going to think going to be celibate all my life?'

'Drink your beer and listen. Kaiser is here. No, was here. Used your flat in case you were wondering if anything was out the ordinary?'

'Left a note. The place tidy was okay. Didn't have any wild parties.'

'Good, now this is serious. Listen to what I'm saying. Drink your beer and stop looking round the place. Nothing in here is good for you. Sex from this place is a no no. Can't have you involving me with anything to do with sex. Remember this is my second official office don't want you having any problems with the girls in here.'

'Am drinking am drinking. What you want to know?'

'Lowdown that's it pay attention. There is lot going down and maybe some work on to you. Don't be getting into something that's going to give you another holiday. You got to realise your sheet gets longer the longer the sentences are going to be. You don't want that do you and Burke, a handle on him for starters.'

'Burke? In the dark as well. I'm afraid.'

'Afraid? Why afraid?'

'Silly, not afraid of him just means no never set eyes on the gentleman. Think I pick... You...upstairs?'

'I said behave yourself. Go somewhere else you must know other places.'

'Time got there feeling will be gone.'

'Get your mind off the subject. Concentrate.'

'You need information, me, second thoughts don't see why I should spill my guts and you take the pleasure offloading. Giving information to that pig. Well if it got out words came to you from my way to his way. Understand what up against?'

'Surprised taking that attitude Billy.'

'Burke as far as I know gets the know all more than a bee reports back to the hive the places best for to collect the pollen.'

'What the hell you on about. Bees, honey?'

'Took a mini course Bee keeping in the stir. Very informative I'm thinking of taking it up as a hobby.'

'Drinks Billy. Get the drinks in,' sat back let his eyes wander taking in the surrounds. Billy, he was thinking, not gonna come up with the goods anytime soon and relying on someone so young he was having second thoughts. Billy was madcap and prone to foolishness. Maybe not such a good idea.

TWENTY

Out of the taxi and was surprised to see people in the street stopping to stare no welcome home or glad to see you back. No, nothing from any of them. Finding it strange he had known most of them since childhood. Not a hello or any kind of welcome strange behaviour why had they stopped to look not as if he was a stranger. Hadn't suddenly dropped from outer space ready to wipe them out. Why he wondered? Why was he being ignored by the people who knew him most of his life and why did they put in his mind visions of the living dead, leering zombies.

'How's it going Dan how are you Joan?' A nice welcome hello from him to the couple who stood on the opposite pavement but no response watched in awe as they took to their heels. The other living dead suddenly took off glancing back as they hurried away. Stood for a moment shrugged got the house keys from his pocket and opened the door. Lifted the luggage from the pavement looked up at the bedroom window saw the sign below it, MAIN STREET, blue letters on a white background the feeling rose in his chest he was home to the house of so many memories.

John is father a fisherman from a long line of fishermen going back to the first who came to the village in the dark ages. His ancestors managed to survive the ups and downs of the good and the bad times. Time was the healer though sorrow would never be forgotten of the many relations and other's in the village who died at sea in pursuit of the white fish. His mother Jeannie could reel off many stories she heard as a child herself being from a long line of fishermen and fishwives. Stories about the custom of baiting long lines with mussels gathered in all weathers. Although the memory of skint knees and skint hands got from prying the whelks and the mussels from jagged rocks was not such a happy memory.

Sitting beside a roaring fire in the winter listening to story's was the norm in those days. Mother would be busy baking and father at sea or when home celebrating a good catch most likely would be in the pub.

Granny Butler was a fisher lassie like many others from the village who followed the east coast fishing fleet in search of the herring, the silver darlings.

Hard work for little pay. Working in all the weather nature threw at them. Cold hands got cramming the herring in wooden barrels filled with salt.

Granny remembered they were hard times but happy times. Comradeship of the girls was a treasure. The singing was a known fact the lassies were good at belting out a tune. The reason giving was good fresh sea air gave them a special lilt in their voices. The truth is out there because in the past the village fishwives choir was good enough to sing for her majesty Queen Victoria and Granny Butler was quick to remind people of the fact. Ah, but gone now are the days when one could walk from the middle pier to the west pier at Granton harbour over the steam trawlers. The same was true at Newhaven harbour when you could cross over the fishing boats from one side of the harbour to the other. Things certainly have changed for the worse. The fishing fleet is now gone not many fishermen and no fisher lassies left in the village.

He moved from room to room. The place was tidy someone had been busy there was a good selection of food in the fridge. The radiators were warm someone had switched off the central heating thought Jamie had been in the house and pleased to think his brother had been there and had in his mind the idea to rib him about his new romance he knew exactly where to find him. Took a shower then shaved and dressed before making his way to Maggie Shaws hopping to get to the bottom of why he had been snubbed by the people who acted strangely when he returned to the village earlier.

The customers in the bar fell silent when he entered. Getting the feeling as if he was intruding on some sort of secret society accepted what strangers feel when they have the nerve to come into this hallowed place invading their private space.

Robbie the barman approached him pulled a pint of beer, said, 'on the house Frankie, welcome pal.'

He lifted the drink turned seeing them looking at him he was ready to ask why then, Robbie dropped the bombshell.

'I'm really sorry about Jamie. Too bad what's happened.'

'Sorry, what have you to be sorry about?' he said, puzzled.

Looking round the bar seen things got back to normal carried on with their conversations no one was interested in what Robbie had said.

'You don't know do you, Frankie?' He continued a peculiar expression of guilt on his face. Shaking his head and feeling stupid he realised he had spoke out of turn. Why do I do that he thought. Why do I always open my mouth when should learn to listen and speak when asked. Jumping in with two feet without thinking how stupid is that.

'What do I not know Robbie going to keep me guessing?'

'Your wee brother Frankie thought you were aware what happened, ay'

'What, what has happened you seen him. He is not in some kind of trouble is he?'

'Dead Son. So sorry to be the one to tell you,' lifted an empty pint glass retreated down the bar over cleaning with his cloth, 'idiot,' he mouthed while shaking his head.

The news hit like a thunderbolt he reeled back and managed to catch hold of the table behind preventing crashing to the floor.

A young man and girl companion sitting at the table caught hold of him.

'Watch it.' He shouted. The drinks and the glasses splattered on the floor. His partner screamed. Some stared thinking the silly quine was being accosted. Others thought the noise she made she was being murdered.

Some sitting near jumped up caught hold of their drinks looking to stay dry.

Mary Mackenzie was coming down the stair leading to the bar from the upstairs apartment seen what had taken place.

'Bring him up,' she said to two regular fishermen coming in the bar from a boat who's thoughts were on the first welcome drink of whisky and beer.

'I'm really sorry Frankie,' Robbie said again lifting the hatch to let them pass to the door of the upstairs apartment. 'Me and my big mouth thought you already knew what happened.'

He couldn't apologise enough but now he thought he was grovelling and making himself look rather stupid.

'Heh Mary, what about your fancy man he won't take it lightly to you having another gadgie in the house.' A female shouted in a loud voice as she opened the door to climb the stair. Remark brought lots of laughter from the punters but she ignored the foolishness of it and continued up the stair to the apartment.

'Fine' she said, 'thanks,' to the two fishermen, 'ask Jonny, tell him to give you a drink on the house. Thanks again for your help,' she said on her way to the back stair and wondered how she was going to give out with the facts as she knew them. McDougall had hinted a suicide pact. She had her doubts. The way Jamie acted she saw how enamoured he was with her. There was no way anything so bad a suicide was on his mind. Was a rubbish idea on the part of McDougall. Him and his big mouth the idea off it will go round the village like wildfire. The know-alls will have a field day spouting their propaganda to anyone who is daft enough to listen not knowing the full facts of the disaster. She knows how they react. Good gossip makes for interesting story telling. Seen them, old woman holding on tightly to their shawls round their shoulders giving their tongues plenty of exercise.

'Will you take care of him?' Asked Robbie catching her arm.
'In a while. I'll explain. The facts. Hell when we going to get them. McDougall has lit the fuse the ejit. Him and his big gob should have known better.'

'Sorry me and my big gob blurting out the way I did.'

'Easy mistake. How were you to know. If not you surprised hadn't heard it earlier.'

'The reason giving, you think that is the answer?'

'No. Would like to kill that Archie McDougall!'

TWENTY ONE

Loud banging on his front door woke him. Head was somewhere else. His mouth was a cesspit. Not surprising the amount he had put away. It was enough to float the proverbial battleship. He looked at the clock on the bedside table and murmured who the hell is at the door this time in the morning,' before he got out the bed she was standing there looking down at him.

'Used my key. You're with us then, ay, see you certainly packed it away last night,' helped to ease him from the bed. 'How you feeling after the shock you okay?'

'Why did you bang on the door Mary when you have a key frightened the life out of me don't know if coming or going hard to tell,' sitting on the edge of the bed nursing his head. 'Help need the hair of the dog. Get me a whisky please Mary.' He stood and pulled his dressing gown over his pyjamas, 'if I don't get a drink this minute. I'm going back into the pit to sleep it off not got the strength to chuck you out so will you please leave me alone. Come back later. If you give me a shot of whisky I'll put up with you then you can stay.'

Head was reeling feeling bad with the drink wondering asked if he made a chump of himself, 'considering the reason, de facto that is,' he said. 'Can't remember a thing after leaving your place. Suppose now it's a case of me eating humble pie. I'll need to apologise to any I got on the wrong side off.'

'No. I will not get you another drink you never learn end up like uncle Jonny if you're not careful. Get ben the scullery and I'll make a pot of coffee. Your having it black till you sober up. A shot of whisky! I know what you mean you have had more than enough you and your... a dram my bahooky a dram. Who you got on the wrong side off, jeese. I don think that will worry you. No, don't think so.'

'What happened Mary? How did it come to this how come he ended up in the harbour does anyone have a clue or see it happening?'

'No, no one but expect you'll hear soon from McDougall. Guarantee he will be out to find out what you know about it all.'

They were seated at the kitchen table was on his third cup of black coffee. Head suffering was thinking no more drink, or, not for a while. 'My goodness Mary can't make coffee it's like black pitch it's disgusting!' Spat the liquid into the cup made a face Mary thought it was him who was the more disgusting spitting into the cup, looked at him in astonishment tut tutted, 'disgusting drink it. Famous for my coffee never had a problem with my coffee your mouth too much drink you imbecile when will you ever learn? Wasting my time here.'

'Aye Mary you make great coffee great tea as well so what want a medal?'

Looking at him busy feeling sorry for himself she shook her head, she wouldn't give him up desperate to get him to snap out of it, 'mystery to me what they were doing anywhere near the harbour i thought they had gone away on holiday,' looked into his eyes seeing his hurt.

'Thought you said you were going you are beginning to embarrass me.'

'In a minute be out your hair.'

'The girl was in the car you said, they, didn't know she was in the car?' Turned his head waiting for an explanation.

'Go and see ArchieMcDougall. Surprised not been in touch. Knows your back it's unusual not to be hovering like a vulture waiting for scraps. His boss is sure to be on his back. What has happened is not something wanted here. Not in Newhaven.'

'When did it happen, sorry can't get my head round this someone was here in the house thought it was him.'

'Three nights ago. Saw him the day before it happened. Something on his mind. Tried to get it out of him. Too secretive. Gave me a large envelope said to post it to Eckie Mcpherson. I was to post it one day after they left wherever it was they were going. Honestly don't know but he should be back in a few days. I was not to wait to give it him but post it. Jamie was strong on it went on and on post it has to be posted he insisted.'

'You still got it?'

'No afraid not posted to the Captain care of pier11, Rotterdam docks. Me, it was me was in the house came to check everything was okay after what happened. Let Archie McDougall and his boss Rooney in to snoop didn't say if they found anything'

'Three nights my god was with Nikki having it on. Having it on when this was happening. In outer space in a world of pleasant dreamy ecstasy.'

Realised too late should not have said what he said not to Mary. Saw her eyes flashing angrily wondering what will she say how would she react should have curbed his tongue. Silly but couldn't help blurting it out. And Lena, what was he thinking?

'Not needing to hear details sordid or not. Keep your love doings to yourself only curious to learn who this Nikki is?'

She reminded like his mother would have reacted. Oh dear standing with folded arms a scowl on her coupon, there she was, Jeannie Butler to a capital T.

'Make up your mind Mary you're like an old washerwoman down on your knees scrubbing with one ear cocked listening to the latest gossip.'

Hands on his head again. 'Head is gonna burst give me a dram Mary take pity wouldn't treat a dog like this.'

'Welcome home Frankie got more respect for a dog. If you are going to act like a bairn be going. I'll wait till you come to your senses so if you need me you know where to find me. You know how to find me ay. Give you drink no you're not on!'

Rising from her chair, 'don't leave it too long get yourself together. Goodness sake drink yourself to death for all I care get over it.'

'Come on Mary.' Too late she was gone slamming the door behind her.

'Ah well she'll come round' he was muttering. 'I'll give her more dishes to wash that'll keep the old cow happy.' He poured more coffee into the cup splashed the whisky with an unsteady hand steadied his shaky arm gulped down the drink in one, 'that's better. The hair of the dog is, better. 'My, Lena?' Muttering, remembering what she said, circumstances, 'the c..! She knew but said nothing.'

'Mary have you seen anything of Jakie Ross?' McDougall asked when he encountered her in the street.

'Me, anything to do with that excuse of a waster? No way!'

'Please Mary. Have you seen him?'

'What makes you think i'm responsible if I knew where he was and don't what makes you think would tell you?' Avoided him by stepping to his right.

He stopped her by holding her arm she struggled to get free.

'Don't take it like that why have you got into such a state only asking if you had seen him the inspector wants a word. He's on my back as usual. You know how it is but if you must,' stepped aside unaware her mood caused by her visit to Frank. She was walking slowly deep in thought when he stopped her. What a fool he was making of himself fearful he wouldn't get over the shock take more drink than was good for him. The demon drink done for many in the village over the years seen it all sadly before so many times.

McDougall certainly was taken aback by her attitude. What, he was thinking, has got into the silly mare, something bad must have rocked her boat and was not about to delay her any longer had had the rough edge of her tongue before and sure didn't want to have a repeat. Better to leave it alone and see her later when she was in a better frame of mind. 'Alright Mary thought you could help you haven't seen him fair enough, just don't know where the old fool has wandered off too?' Was apologising but she wasn't listening, was all about Frank and was annoyed at McDougall for his untimely intervention. 'I've said already not seen him. Now if your done get out my way got business to run and you're keeping me out of my road let me pass.'

'What's with you woman not be civil for once. Hope you don't treat your punters like this what's with you're attitude can't you see I'm trying to apologise.'

'If my punters see me talking to you they'll be the ones with attitudes. They will desert my place like snow of a dyke so go and bother some other of your snitches and leave me alone.'

'Mary, all asking is have you've seen him that's all. Better to get to him before, you know, Rooney. Who's reading the riot act if you must know.'

TWENTY TWO

At the harbour McDougall was talking with the rookie cop. 'She asked me what I meant when you see it?' I said, 'what you meant when you see it?'

'Don't you pretend you are looking out for him,' she said. 'My my what next you'd sell your granny given half the chance get out my bloody way. I had to take that from that bloody woman!'

Scratched his head and wiped his face with the tail end of his tartan scarf, 'bloody wummin,' he said. Then followed, 'Need you to be observant you know the old guy Ross? The one who saw the car in the harbour need to find him keep your eyes open and get in touch straight away.'

'I've seen him wandering about but not recently. Don't think he is here today haven't seen him anywhere here today,' said wearily, hoping the sergeant was going to leave him alone to get on doing what he was doing and not trailing him, spying. Found people to be more friendly when they saw him round and about casual like. A different story when McDougall shadowed him people kept their distance seeing the two together preferred to do the job his way, alone. Sick to the back teeth of him constantly on his case. Was thinking of putting in for a transfer he was forward looking and all he could see was a career stuck at Newhaven pier. Ambition better served in a city not in this forgotten backwater.

They strolled round the market. The restaurants was busy lots of children running round the pier screaming like children do playing games getting in peoples way annoying everyone they encountered. Hide and seek was a favourite game if they hid near empty fish boxes they would go home smelling of rancid fish an experience McDougall knew full well the smell would be hard to get rid and linger a long time. There was no washing machines at his mother's house in those faraway days.

The rookie was fed up with the sergeant always on his case preferred to get on with the job on his own not have McDougall always on his back was hoping this visit would be a fleeting one.

They stopped and watched two fishermen unloading boxes of sprats from their boat onto the slipway.The gulls overhead creating as much noise as the children screaming and swooping circling eyeing the scene for leftover fish.

'Why do you think when people see two coppers out and about they turn away going back the way they came?'

Walked on, slowly in deep conversation but stopped again when they saw a van arriving and the driver loaded the boxes.

'We've had the problem since time immemorial people don't trust the police you will soon find that out.'

'So far found the people round here are sociable. The locals are okay. Don't know about the visitors who come to neb what's going on,' rookie said.

'The boats draw crowds in the good weather suppose it's normal people are interested. Anyway, enough of the chatter. I need you to keep your eyes open when your walking about this place. Be careful if you think anything looks suspicious get in touch with me day or night not Rooney me'

'Such as, what you mean suspicious think something dodgy is going on what is it I should watch out for pick pockets druggies what? The people round here are mainly locals don't know. Can't ask every stranger, what you doing here?'

'Just do as I ask. You see the old alki Ross move him on. Keep him in sight and do as I said get me straight away. Don't let him know you are on to him. Just don't let him get onto you got a habit of sleeping on the boats in the harbour knows when they are coming and going been getting away with it for years. May be a drunk but don't underestimate him knows his way around the houses if you get my drift.'

The rookie bewildered thinking why was the sergeant was so much interested in Jakie Ross and why tell him anything when he knows the inspector is the main man and why is McDougall making a secret of it? Chase him if you see him. Keep him if you see him he's not very clear what he wants. He pondered again why the sergeant wanted the old guy and It seemed to him McDougall was desperate not to let Rooney be informed and that he felt was strange behaviour coming from the chief honchos bag man and dogsbody.

'Seen him hanging about Maggie Shaws reminds me of a little dog a Jack Russell used to see in the Main Street. Oh, a few years ago now sure if I wrack my brain will recall the little dugs name but sure was a funny wee thing.'

He hoped by changing the subject McDougall would be a bit clearer with the instructions knowing how he came looking for Ross so something didn't add up?

'He used to hang about outside the butchers,' he went on, 'begging for scraps. I watched him go on his daily run mooching outside the various shops was a comical wee dog and a friendly wee thing everyone had time for it.'

'Knew the dog.'

'I wonder what happened to it disappeared from the area.'

'The owner made a lot of money with that wee dog was so smart it could tell the difference between beer and lager to see it in action was a joy. Not only a joy but a con. The guy who owned the dog, Shuiey, made the bets with the mugs. Would go into a pub, any pub. The owner, Shuiey, and his pals fleeced the mugs left right and middle, aye he hooked them good. The money he made wow. Make the wager get them interested. The dog was removed from the proceedings next a saucer of heavy put on the floor, a good two feet, a saucer of lager. Everything in place the dog would be brought back sniff each sample then go straight to the lager every time kid you not the owner along with his cronies made a fortune out that wee dog.'

'Maybe it read the label on the lager bottle,' he said, trying a joke.

McDougall, thought he was an idiot, 'read the label give me strength,' he muttered. 'Whatever happened to it? One day it was there but suddenly no more, gone. Got run over by a car in Main Street. The driver took it to the vet who put it down he said the wee dog was drunk. Had it's fair share of lager. Wee dogs and lager a no go.'

'Must be a lesson there, don't let your dog out on its own. Specially after it's been in Maggie Shaws shebeen.'

'I could do with one right now but Just you think on what I told you, get me, only me when you see Jakie Ross.'

'Hi Mary are you feeling better you all right sorry got you upset earlier.'

'Do you want a pint or are you on duty not that it makes much difference Sergeant,' she pulled on the handle filling the pint glass giving him the look preserved for the ones she has no time for, dislike or not, puts up with them needs her sales to be in the black not the red specially when McDougall expects his pint is free gratis.

'Don't know to ask or not if going to get my head filled with your bile or what not know how to take you certainly are a puzzle lately,' screwing his face forcing a smile in anticipation of her acceptance of his apology.

'You want this drink or no if no you can go somewhere else to ask your stupid questions and before you ask not seen him.'

'Okay, got it,' moved from the bar sat at a table near the door.

Some he didn't recognise standing close in deep conversation at the end of the bar three men he thought looked like city gents. Each with a brief case and wearing expensive suits. The curiosity got the better lifted his glass sauntered over. When he got near they saw him coming they hurriedly knocked back the drinks made for the exit in silence. Mary looked what he had done astonished what had taken place and when the three departed she rounded on him, ' think you better leave as well not happy with accosting me in the street but now you're chasing my customers away drink up and leave' Eyes we're on him was about to speak changed his mind surprised at her attitude was not prepared for any more of her outbursts put the pint glass on the bar walked to the exit not turning knew her customers were stabbing him in the back. Who, he wondered, who were the strangers and why were they here in Mary's place? Out on the street he spied a black saloon car taking off fast in the direction of Leith.

In the cafe asked Betty if she saw the three men. 'Did they come here often in before or throw any light to what they were after?' Knew was nothing to do with the fish market the market was long closed. Finished much earlier in the morning deserted for hours. Speculation getting him down just who were these characters and what were they doing in Newhaven. Things, it seemed to him funny things happening lately.

TWENTY THREE

9.40am police woman Sissy Maitland hurried down the steps at Rochester police station just as Detective sergeant Rutherford was getting out of an unmarked police car.

'Hi Sissy. Why are you in mufti you going on a date? You look good enough to eat who's the lucky guy?'

'Sorry to say, with you,' said scornfully 'and Walker wants you yesterday is banging his head off the table I would be careful what you say better get your act together. I've just left his office wants you but doesn't want you if you get my meaning. Certainly in a bad mood you better be on your best behaviour.'

She scowled, he smiled, she knew she was talking to the wind.

'Up there thinking down there for dancing,' he said pointing at his head then at his feet. 'Lets face the music,' he sang doing a soft shoe shuffle, 'let's get it over with,' he said opening the door to let her walk through. 'Never noticed that before,' he said giving out a long low whistle the way some men do.

'Can you not take anything serious sergeant Rutherford? For goodness sake. For all the time known you when are you going to grow up?'

She hesitated and pushed him to the front and followed him up the stairs.

'Reminds me going to see the headmaster hope Walker hasn't got a cane. Don't want to see you over his desk, oh, maybe not,' he whispered but she heard what he said.

'I won't respond to that remark not playing your game. Grow up and behave it's serious, Walker, you know.'

She opened the door and followed into the superintendents office who was giving someone on the phone a real ear bashing and when he saw them he exploded, 'Rutherford! Not wanted down here when perfectly good officers at my disposal. You guys at the Met are taking the you know what if you think we are not capable. The less see of you the better,' letting loose.

Rutherford interrupted in mid sentence said, 'I understand chief not my idea to be stepping on anyone's territory only doing what told. Not my choice better things to be doing and sorry if treading on anyone's toes.'

'Don't interrupt me and don't call me chief.' He bellowed making it clear was at the bottom of his Christmas list possibly not on it in the first place.

Maitland took a step back he's heading for a heart attack if he doesn't calm down looks as if it will be soon she was thinking..

'Stand still Maitland,' shouted, not happy with the proposal. Their full attention was needed wanted no nonsense from either of them why they sent Rutherford to his station was beyond him. His own men were as good or even better than Rutherford. Stretching his arm pointing beckoning her to step forward nearer his desk then, 'stay still,' exasperated.

The outburst, never witnessed such behaviour before took her by surprise not sure why wondered what the reason?

Rutherford took her hand guided her to his side.

'You two get out of my sight do not I say do not get involved in anything no matter what it is. Any trouble call for backup. I don't want a one man band cocking up the investigation that has already taken place do you understand me Rutherford and get you're ugly mug back to where you came from as soon as your through with the Irishman. You, Maitland you be here in this office as soon as he drops you back. Do you understand me? Now get out. Mark my words I'll…' They were out the office fast not get the rest of his sentence but got the gist of his wrath.

'What was that about? I've never seen him like it before,' Sissy asked when they were driving out the car park.

'Not seen anything wrong with his head,' said Rutherford, in all seriousness.

'What are you on about?' She turned giving him the look the look woman are good at when they don't get the point.

'Head, table,' he said pointing to his head, 'you…'

'Grow up heard it all before your jokes are old hat,' closed her eyes, 'what an idiot you are,' let the words out slowly snuggling her back into the seat.

The name atop the ornate iron gates in large gold painted letters no one would fail to be in any doubt they would be entering, MOUNT KENNY.

'Press the button on the square box next the gate,' he said when she got out the car, 'the one next the gate the one hiding there in the ivy on the wall ask whoever to give the okay to breach the hallowed ground.'

A gruff male Irish voice answered her buzz. 'What? What you want you an appointment need an appointment to get in here private property.'

'Police wish to speak to Mr Burke.' informed the voice, 'Mr Burke if he is available not take long short interview to help with our enquiries.'

'Hold,' voice said.

Looked at Rutherford, 'I'm on hold.'

After what seemed forever the voice was back, 'come.' The gates swung open smooth and silent. 'Wow! Some place splendour or what?' Seeing the mansion when it came into view along the tree lined driveway 'And they say crime doesn't pay wow is right,' He wound down the window and spat on to the ground. She, stared, 'disgusting, you really are, grow up. That's no way to show your displeasure.'

'Master will see you in the library,' with brogue thick as a pint of black stout the maid admitted them into the hallway her fore finger pointing at the floor then knocking on large ornate wooden double doors 'stay, don't move, the command barked out like an army drill sergeant.

'Does think we are a couple of dogs?' Maitland whispered.

'Hound dogs,' he said, trying a low growl.

'Ha ha. Not funny,' she said.

He glowered, 'keep it shut when we get in just keep your nose in your notebook. I'll do the necessary,' whispering from the side of his mouth.

Again gave him the long look. 'Wow, who's an angry little boy. Who is having a moody?' She rubbed his shoulder 'Oh dear,' she said.

'Sergeant Mr Rutherford and lady police woman,' the maid announced.

Maitland thought definitely acting like an over enthusiastic sergeant major the way she shouted in a loud voice as sergeant majors do.

Rutherford looked round the room amazed at the luxurious surroundings, gotten, he knew, by ill gotten gains.

Burke, standing left side of the ornate marble mantelpiece rearranging a couple of small Chinese figures. Flames gently drifting up the chimney in the huge old fashioned fireplace.

' Aggie put some coal on the fire put more life into it you silly girl,' he said, nodding to the small lumps of coal heaped in a brass scuttle on the corner of the hearth, 'more coal on do your duty you useless girl. Should not have to be told,' demanded like an overbearing parent scolding a wayward child. The maid ignored him bent the knee to the old girl. 'Anything for you mam can I assist in anyway,' stood up stepped back waiting a response showing her back to the master.

'Leave the fire,' the old one said, 'go arrange a pot of tea for our guests,' dispensing the command from her throne, a high back red leather chair were she was busy knitting.

Maitland, sensed the old lady was not happy with the intrusion.

'Please, nothing for us won't take up much of your time,' said Rutherford.

'May I offer you something stronger?' Burke asked, moving some liqueur bottles on the cabinet beneath the book shelves lifting slowly scrutinising the labels on each bottle his back to them was thinking what on earth do this pair think they are up too how dare they invade my privacy.

'No thanks not on duty,' Rutherford said thought a pound for every time the sentence was said he would be rich indeed. He was admiring the large oval shaped room the walls filled floor to ceiling with books. Plush modern and antique furnishings blue and white dishes placed around the sitting area arranged on small designer tables standing on thick individual multi coloured wool carpets. Four large glass cases jam packed with Roman miniature clay figurines mostly gold and silver objects, goblets and trinkets lying next and on top of each other haphazardly placed.

'Rutherford?' Burke said his thoughts in overdrive stood posing holding one arm across the middle of his stomach the other raised with his forefinger to his lips repeated, 'Rutherford, a yes, are you not from London the Met what brings you to the

Kent coast don't see how i can possibly be of any help?' Turning slowly still in the pose position smiling waiting an explanation.

'Not you sir. You're mother,' said Rutherford, 'may be able to give us some help with our enquiry,' looked away studied the woman's face giving out with his best smile waited what seemed forever until Burke intervened. 'Mother Angelica how can she possibly help?' Stammered and stuttered giving the impression he was suddenly taken by surprise he outstretched his arms pleading thought it ridiculous to be asking his mother such things. Put on an act acting as though he was the mild mannered dim witted country gentlemen.

No way was fooling Rutherford who definitely was not taking in by his pathetic performance. He waited till Burke finished his theatrical turn was thinking that the game was up thought he was on to him. Better be on guard got the feeling the coppers hunch knew Burke was not pleased with the questions being asked. The maid and the old girl out of place in this palace of splendour found himself in a complete daze in the surreal situation thinking they going to get out of there without any trouble was foremost on his mind.

'It's okay Kenny,' old lady said, shushing him lifting her knitting needles starting to click click ten to the dozen. 'The sergeant must have something bothering him,' said, bowing her head and concentrating on the knitting.

'Just a couple of questions if you don't mind,' smiled tried the good cop approach all the while wondering if they were in any sort of danger.

'Your from the Met?' Burke said placing a shot of sherry on the table in front of his grey haired mother. 'Why has the the local police not done this why have you come all the way from London?' Looked at Maitland with a cheesy grin smiling a sickly creepy smile.

The maid took up a position at the door.

Sissy thought he was the devil in disguise. Looked at the fireplace the dying coals straining to go up the chimney was thinking his performance put on to paint a picture of someone who was caring. Not fooled, something wrong about the sorry specimen who craved attention. A ghoul, something about this sorry individual crying out for attention needing to be under his mother's control needed her approval also thought that the man was bent but she could take it any which way it pleased him it was his own desire. A little smile crossed her lips,'my my,' she muttered.

Rutherford guessed the man was fishing what next is this clown of a sleaze ball going to come up with what does he think came here for a picnic, does he think came here to his beloved Mount Kenny from the smoke for a cosy chit chat?

'An incident which occurred in London,' Maitland broke the lull.

Rutherford gave a slight cough she observed the angry sign.

The old woman fixed her attention on a ball of green wool fallen on the carpet at her feet. 'Aggie,' she called to the maid who was standing at the library door, 'get this ball of wool from the floor.'

The maid came to the chair. Retrieved the wool putting it on the table walked took up her former position.

'Maitland watched the maid. Wondering if she was ever a prison guard and if so in what prison?

'Rutherford coughed to get her mind back on what they were there for.

'What can Angelica tell you about an incident in London?' Burke said to Maitland giving his full attention with a scary stare in his eyes.

Rutherford interjected...'If you don't mind sir don't want to take up much of your time just let me ask my questions we will be out of your way.'

He touched his nose giving her a look that she was being told to be quiet to shut it. Attend to her little black book leave him doing the business.

'Let him get on Kenny. I'm curios, what he wants from me let him have his questions,' his mother said laying the knitting on her lap.

'You visited a jewellery shop one day last week when you were in town. Can you tell me if you saw anything out the ordinary when you were there.'

The answer he knew would be blarney. He didn't believe she would tell the truth the whole truth and nothing but. The answer she was about to come up with he knew she would be lying. Her answers would be just he guessed, blarney.

'Is this why you have come all this way to ask could have phoned never saw anything out of the ordinary. Tell, no nothing whatsoever.'

She looked away. Started the click click clacking on the needles. Without lifting her head said, 'if that's all bid you good day Aggie show them out if you please. Kenny get Aggie to show them the door.'

'Then tell my driver to get the car,' he said.

'Just one more if you please,' Rutherford said, anxious to get a result before leaving, 'ask why you visited that particular shop? Late on that Wednesday and if I remember, do remember, it was a very wet evening.'

'To collect a bracelet that was fixed my wrist is shrinking and needed a link taken out,' she said, pushing the wool along the needle counting the stitches.

'That's all to ask. Positive there was nothing, nothing out of the way?'

'She has answered don't see what else can tell you,' Burke interrupted, 'If you are finished,' he said pointing at the door. 'Aggie they are leaving and if you please Aggie show them out.'

'Yes sir,' said Rutherford, 'Chance we could speak with your driver only with your say will soon be finished and on our way that's it done.' He knew nothing would come of this visit but his boss was right Burke would get the message. Now the wheels were in motion and they were on to him. It should not take long for Burke, hopefully, will make a slip up and someone somewhere in the organisation sure going to have second thoughts and hopefully come forward. At least this was the thinking behind the cooked up exercise.

Sissy shot him a look wondering what he was up to she wanted to be out of it. The longer they were there she thought, walking into danger.

'Certainly,' Burke said, 'you'll find him in the kitchen. I'll get Aggie to take you there. Goodness knows what help he will be able to give you. Oh well, if you must. Will require the assistance of my driver you have five minutes,' he said wearily.

155

The wheels man looked like a tired old wrestler who had fought his bout, round fat and tall with a bashed in face two enormous cauliflower ears thick rubber lips, sitting at the kitchen table his bashed nose inches from the paper studying a horse racing form sheet.

The spacious well equipped kitchen fitted with all the modern appliances and windows with a view over the posh gardens, two gardeners busy doing what gardeners are supposed to be doing.

Rutherford had his doubts where they actually gardeners or something else not in the garden when they arrived. Was it time for action had a worried frown on his face checked the gun in it's holster under his oxter giving him a moment of knowing he could handle the situation if it arose.

A large fat cook who possibly could have been another retired wrestler was busy at the cooker stirring something in a large copper pot. He thought the smell was lentil soup and reminded him he hadn't eaten since early morning.

'Can i get you anything to eat or something to drink?' She asked, turning and smiling at Maitland. Who was also thinking the delicious smell was making her hungry and it was time to be getting out of there. She was not happy with the set up. The eerie silence reminded her of a visit to the morgue.

'No thanks,' Rutherford said distracting Maitland from her thoughts, pulled a chair sat opposite the bruiser reached his hand grasped the racing paper and had a quick glance at the horses names then said, 'you took the lady to the smoke on a visit to a fence didn't you Malky?' Looked into his eyes as he slid the paper back across the table. Knows of this guys record of violence knew the petty crime was as long as his arm. Asking the question he knew wouldn't get straight answers.

Sissy by this time is desperate to get out but wondering, Malky and Rutherford?

'I've nothing to say to you Rutherford don't have to answer any of your questions. Why you and that floozie over there,' he pointed to Maitland, 'why youse here makes your journey a waste of time,' lifted the cup with his banana fingers. Retrieved the racing paper. Belched and slurped like something a pig would relish... 'Wasted time coming here nothing to say nothing to say to you so sling it.'

'Okay Malky just wanted to confirm you were there on the day and if you saw anything out of place when you waited for her ladyship. Malky no harm in it,' started to rise motioned to Maitland on his intention to leave.

'Was in the car,' he said, stopped, realising he made a hash of it sure enough.

'You fool the cook said angrily. Watch your mouth. He won't, you know Burke.'

'Okay you nailed it,' he said, sheepishly feeling foolish. His right hand smothered his face as if he was wiping it with a wet flannel wondering what Burke would say, knowing, what he had said. And mother Burke, not one to be taken lightly. Now was fearful. Maybe, he thought it would be better getting instead of staying was fearful and rightly so had knowledge of ever long shadows no desire to be caught some dark cold rainy night in the shadows of a deserted alleyway

'So you were there that is all wanted to know. No sweat it wasn't hard was it? A little bit of cooperation goes a big way for the future, Malky.'

'If you mean the two queers I stopped going in didn't do them any just told them to come back later, that's all. They haven't made something of it have they?'

'No Malky that's it. Nothing more.' Thinking the moron had fell into his trap and maybe Burke would have a fall out giving his driver time to think about things.

Could be he will be in touch soon? Rising from the table caught her eye, 'let's go its time,' he said and wished them good day, 'we'll meet again no doubt Malky. See you soon expect.'

'I wouldn't you know if see you first,' he replied getting back to his form sheet.

'That was not very productive,' she said as they walked to the car trying to keep up with his long stride.

'Know the old girl is buying with laundered money. We have established the two queers as the gorilla mentioned were at the place. They were not queers but hit men,' he said. 'The fence who died had written the name Angel, in his ledger. Angel, Angelica one in the same. The Burke's are sure part of, no, are the London link. Not part but high on the hog. Devils in disguise

157

a shister as my pal Tony would say. He is not far of the mark is on the mark.'

'All Irish in that house?' Maitland asked as she caught her breath. 'Was that scary or what didn't know we had the Irish mafia over here. Are they all Irish mafia in that place. The cook, gee the size of her goodness me.'

'Looks like it except for the driver. Suspicious seeing him employed by the Burke's. Been used as a heavy. Need someone put in hospital he's your man. Know of his misdemeanours. Catching him red handed well something else.'

Aggie appeared from the house, 'wanted the phone sergeant,' she shouted as she came running behind waving her arms round and round like a windmill.

He returned to the house and the maid said he could use the phone in the kitchen where the cook was still stirring the copper pot but said like Malky nothing.

'Hello, Rutherford here.'

As he spoke he heard a click knew the phone was tapped heard heavy breathing then the caller said, 'I want you back,' it was Walker. He heard another click before he replaced the phone on it's cradle. 'Trouble?' She asked, when he got into the car. He started the engine. She could see he had a face on. The one he puts on when he is not happy knows not to ask too much when he is in this kind of mood knew how easily he could go from one extreme to the other this was a time for the other.

Gazing out the window any minute heard all the expletives before and waited.

'Have to get to a phone,' he said.

'What was wrong with the one...'

'Bugged' he said cutting her short.

'Expected it,' she said, sneaking a smile a shake of her head looking at him giving a knowing smile feeling superior. 'Knew it. Glad we got out before anything unpleasant took place.'

They stopped at a phone box on the way back to the police station.

Rutherford was five minutes in the booth. 'Another one same as the other's. One the grey haired sweet old lady visited getting her bracelet fixed. The old rotten excuse for a human being,' he said getting into the car. Didn't take long, started his ranting ages before calming down to give her some welcome peace.

'The sooner get something on Burke be the day for rejoicing might even ask you to marry me,' he said, 'good idea don't you think?'

'Can we go back and make an arrest?' she asked ignoring his suggestion.

'No nothing get back to London straight away.'

'But not even to help with...'

'Leave it Sissy. My boss says it's too early to make an arrest. Too much at stake. How many deaths before we make arrests , just don't know?'

'When is a good time?'

'Meaning.?'

'To get to the bottom of all of this.'

'Oh!'

'Oh What?'

Thought you were giving me a surprise?'

'Surprise?'

'I said, marry you.'

'That would be a surprise!'

'Worse things have happened.'

'You off your head? Last man I'd marry. What makes you think would marry someone like you?'

'Oh, we'll take that as a no then?'

'Not coming to see him, Walker?'

'My boss wants me back said already and why you change the subject giving it a thought are you?'

TWENTY FOUR

Sissy climbed the stairs to the top office anticipating the reception she was about to have with her boss who she was hoping was in a better mood.

'Well, let's have it then take it Rutherford behaved himself? No mishaps and no comebacks from the Burke's?' Not about to have the phone on fire, well?'

He smiled and sat back waiting her response. The phone rang. He picked it up said nothing just listened. His eyes rolled in his head he squirmed put the phone down. Here it comes, she was thinking. Why suffer this madness?

Waited for the storm to happen but surprised what he done next. Sat back and folded his arms and smiled at her. She could see is face conjuring unpleasant thoughts she was sure. Appears calm and not wanting to light his fuse said nothing.

'Get your notebook out let me see it take it you used the bloody notebook? It should have been in your hand when you entered so let's hear it missed an appointment waiting for you. Give out exactly what happened?'

'Nothing to report sir. Sergeant Rutherford done the interview was downgraded to the kitchen.' She lied the look on his face, now could see the storm coming.

'What! You got nothing get out of my sight.' He screamed slammed his hand on the desk, 'Might have known Rutherford would pull a fast one out of my sight and want your report on my desk in the next hour so get on with it.'

She was out of there as fast as her legs could carry before he burst a blood vessel was under the impression whatever she done would never satisfy him and wondered who was responsible for her being paired up with Rutherford in the first place? Never felt so unwanted Walker was making the job not worth a fig.

'A coffee please and have one of those iced buns, thank you,' she said to the young woman who served the food. She walked down the lane paid the lady sitting at the till at the end of the food counter. Lifting the tray and looking round the canteen she saw her friend sitting at a table reading a women's magazine.

'You look bushed,' her friend greeted her with a smile.

'Tell me about it Linda,'

'Had a very fruitful day? You know, fruitful,' she said with a knowing wink.

'Okay dear tell you about it if I knew what are you going on about?' She puffed up her cheeks letting the air slowly escape before removing her shoulder bag then her hat and placing them on the table shaking her head ruffling her hair, 'much much better needed that what a stinker of a day. Sometimes wonder what I'm doing in this job there are more villains in here you can throw a scabby cat at. More here than outside.' She glanced round the canteen lifting the cup slowly sipped the coffee. 'You know how it is,' she said, shrugging screwing her face in disgust. 'What a nightmare don't know the half. Honestly.'

'Out With Rutherford? Time he was taken in hand.'

'Was lucky to get out of you know who's office,' Sissy said, throwing her head back looking up at the ceiling, 'will have a heart attack soon you can take bets on it. Rutherford he seems to rub him the wrong way. Wonder why he dislikes the sergeant so much definitely got something against him you know what it is?'

'Walker was at the Met before he came here was bad feeling there been ongoing for a long time. Bad blood a long time in the making. A very long while ago.'

'Well tell don't keep the secret to yourself lets hear,' pushed her cup and saucer out of reach leaning forward with her elbows on the table looking to see if anyone was near enough to hear. 'Come I'm excited never been excited since well if you could remind me, please do.'

Linda reached and placed her finger on her lips, 'Please', laughing, 'no not that don't need to know about your sex life.'

'My sex life when was that nothing to talk about.'

'Were sergeants together at the Met on surveillance outside a warehouse near London docks and got separated when the fun started. Walker caught one of the gang when he was putting him into the van he saw Rutherford speaking with a gang member but Rutherford let him go. Not good move according to Walker who thought Rutherford was going to have the man in the van

161

alongside the others. Walker suspicious and reported him. At the enquiry Rutherford walked guy was his nark and was responsible for the tip off in the first place. Walker not accept the verdict sure he thinks Rutherford a crook doesn't trust him. Walker,' pointing upwards, 'up the ladder and ended up here, Rutherford, well, still a sergeant and blames Walker. Good job they never meet hate each other. Can believe it.'

'Makes sense mystery solved. Well not hanging about here got a heavy date tonight be going I'm off my love to your kids,' gathered her hat and bag, 'see you, bye, got to get the slap on have to look my best.'

'Fancy being his doxy do you Rutherford?'

'No not him.'

'It's not the boss, Walker?'

'Your being silly now,' another look round to see if anyone is homing in on their conversation. Word would go round like wild fire if they happened to be overheard. And her reputation would be shredded by the, as she says, the under washed.

'No, what makes, old enough to be my grandfather,' she says with a shrug.

'He's same age as Rutherford would go with him wouldn't you he is handsome wouldn't you say?' Linda, carrying on with the nonsense of it.

'No he's not Walker could easily give him twenty years. What are you on? What your on get me some, handsome, you kidding?' Walked hiding a smile.

'Maitland, you wanted up stairs. Old man. Would not want to be in your size fives,' Sergeant McKay got to her as she was leaving the building.

'Why you covering up for Rutherford?' Was sitting, no, was lounging in his chair calmly asking her the question.'

'Covering, me sir? Don't know what you mean.'

'Complaint from Burke. The Irishman not happy why did you say you had no report and left it to Rutherford?'

Sissy was surprised he was quite no shouting and wondered what and where he got his information?

'Sir?' Doesn't know what to say next. Is fearful of what the outcome is going to be. Pulled herself to her full height. Took a deep breath and looked into his eyes.

He sat forward waiting on her saying anything but nothing came.

'You thinking of moving?' He said smiling.

'Moving? No sir. 'Not thinking of such. I do not know why you ask?'

She left under a cloud. He wasn't so unpleasant and she expected much more. Why, what was the meaning he had asked the question all about a move. If only she could get hold of Rutherford. She could see her reputation going down the tubes, first with the sergeant and second what her boss was hinting at?

Hurried down the stairs ignoring the sly remarks thrown at her by the coppers she met on her way. Rutherford, was on her mind. What had he been up to and what had been said?

Met Walker's secretary on her way out the building… 'Abbé, just left him, Walker. What's happened expected a showdown but no such thing going to let me in on the secret?'

'You expected a rollicking?'

'Believe it. Morning talk hell late today sweetness and light. Something not right!'

'Got a call from someone put him in a good mood surprised me also. Peace and quiet all afternoon, bliss.'

'A hint?'

'No, haven't the slightest.'

'Would, wouldn't you tell if you knew you would?'

'Don't know but wish he got more calls like it really put him in the best form seen him in for a long long time believe me'

TWENTY FIVE

'What will his next move be?'

Rutherford explaining the situation he had at the Burke's mansion. 'Who knows chief but sure rattled his cage can hope something will come out of it soon. The man, Malky I found him in the kitchen got his feet under the table there.'

'The old lady are you sure about her if you are right well give you more time to have the yank on the case but make it look as if he is helping you on a friendly basis can't have the press sniffing out we needed help from a down and out has been private, what they call them, is it, shamus or hard shoe. Oh you know what the saying is just be careful. The driver you saw him did you get sense from him and the cook got my theory about that one. Cook my, no, don't need an explanation.'

'He's not that chief you underestimate him. He's got what it takes. Eye, is the word you're looking for private eye.'

'See what else he's found out. Get up to scratch. What he's got from the funny guy up to date news you know. Oh get out of here out of my sight.'

'Yes sir but no more walker's patch you know how he feels about me and Maitland that was not good pairing.'

'He's phoned already. Yes he's not happy. Raging but leave him to me.'

'Don't like the sound of that you got something to tell me you cooking something?'

'Maitland could be an asset think you would make a good team as I said, leave it to me, we'll see now get out of here.'

Late evening on the phone to Tony explaining the events of the visit to the Burke's place in the country.

'Yes Tony a real eye opener. The old dear is the prime factor Burke is nothing but a lackey.'

'I'm a bit pre occupied at the moment.'

'I thought you sounded a wee bit out of breath.'

'Not as young as used to be. But will manage.'

'Be careful heard about people like you.'

'What about people like me?'

'Your age.'

'My age?'

'Yeah, keeping up. You know. Hard. Up at your age? Need to take it easy for a bit. Goodness knows what you get up to in that dive you habit.'

'Engineer will be here tomorrow…to fix the lift…darn stairs.'

'Are you joshing me knew you were past it and here is me thinking.'

'Think on. You have the mind of a sewer rat Rutherford.'

'Have you heard on the QT anything worth reporting?'

'I should be asking that.'

'Your grass?'

'Has nothing surfaced after you visited the Irishman?'

'Only, in deep, you know by who.'

'And you took the girl with you. Who's idea? Like a fox in the hen house. Walker was sure to appreciate I don't think. If were you I would stay well clear.'

'I'm not freelance like you have to do you know or get on with it.'

'Die! Not much chance is there didn't think so.'

'You mean?'

'Like the generals lead from the back. A taker of chances you're not.'

'Don't get me started you are starting to get my dander up.'

'Good, at last a pair at last excellent.'

'A pair a pair of what?'

'Things you hit with a bat. Jeese what now don't know about getting your dander up got a friend in Scotland who has a friend who would say dander more of a dunder heed. Okay good bye but don't ask me to explain it.'

'What you on about?'

'If you need to ask, well, don't bother.'

'A dander or a gander?'

'Now it's you who is acting queer.'

'Don't be ridiculous.'

'Well are you going to explain?'

'Explain?'

165

'Yeah, you know. What the hell your talking about?'

'A dunder heed a dunder is a stupid person and a heed is your head a noggin that thing you've on above your neck.'

'When I was in Scotland a dander was going for a stroll.'

'Wait. When were you in Scotland didn't know you had been in Scotland kept that under the radar.'

'There is lots of things you don't know about me.'

'Okay will you explain or get off the phone ya bam.'

'Ya bam? Why do you say, ya bam?'

'Bampot. Youve heard the expression you must have goodness sake!'

'Sure it's a form of endearment I think.'

'If you say so. Give me strength!'

'I know what should give you. You've said you hadn't a clue about the man Burke. Think back when you were in Ireland on the case of the diamond thief remember it was Burke but as I recall you cocked it up.'

'I trailed him to Dublin from London.'

'Yes and lost him in Kilkenny.'

'How you know about that?'

'Never mind how. A lot you don't know about. I have the ways and means. Your not the only one who knows the time of day.'

'Sold Lady. Cant indulge you with the information but a very expensive necklace or was it a bracelet? Anyway he took the dough and done a runner with the goods. Other people were after him too late someone was there before me got there first.'

'Drowned in the river NORE and you never saw the body.'

'Never saw him. Just a name Burke.'

And how many Burke's in Ireland? Ya Burk!'

'Oh get of the phone goodbye. Usual place, meeting, usual, tomorrow?'

'If anything new lunch time.'

'Okay.'

'Listen, instead of the park somewhere else.'

'Phone me.'

TWENTY SIX

'Mary thanks for taking my call last night been here in the station for a couple of hours since off the night train. No no one on my tail no, Yes Mary sure. You'll recognise me okay. Look for a gent in a tweed jacket a flat tweed cap and a cut down fishing rod got it strapped to a large brown suitcase. I've also got a large black and brown hold-all. You can't miss me. Yes Mary won't leave here. Yes. See you soon, thanks. Bye. Till later, bye.'

Within the hour he was in the parlour above the public house.

'Mary you must not let anyone know I'm living here with you need to keep a low profile,' he said making himself comfortable in the leather easy chair slowly sipping a cup of coffee. Looked round the room wondering if it was such a good idea after all. Hearing quite plainly voices in the bar below now wary of what he could or couldn't say. If he could hear what was going on below someone might hear what took place above. The situation was important the only thing in his favour was the apartment had a private entrance where he could come and go freely. In and out hopefully without being seen by prying eyes.

'Yes understand but don't you think Frank should be told you are here. What if, god forbid, he finds out? Some old biddy you know. In the street saying your living here. He would be here like you know, fast.'

'No, would defeat the purpose will keep him safe don't worry will not know I'm behind him all the way. Don't you worry,' he repeated seeing the doubt on her face.

She was worrying about what the outcome of this fantasy would accomplish fearful of any more dead bodies appearing.

'Got trouble getting my head round this. Why is it happening why all these murders? Why poor Jamie and the quine had to be killed? Why did McDougall tell me it was a suicide pack doesn't add up. Suicide, no, not think so.'

'Quine?'

'Girl, quine a girl, loon a boy, well that speaks for itself, boys, bloody loons!'

'Frank said you were someone precious maryMary not let you think that's what he thinks but the way you have had him and his brother in your thoughts all these years a special person Mary,'

'Well by the by known them all their lives ma and pa like family. I've only done what had to be done others who are all in the same frame of mind to children just like them nothing special all family.'

'Soon it will come clear to you. You are worrying needlessly. Just carry on as usual. Mary please, don't want to keep repeating but things will work out soon.'

'How soon is soon? when will it happen when do you think the police should be told about this mess? You must be able to tell the story after all you have been in it from the beginning.'

'Impossible Mary,' thinking how the heck can get her to leave it alone. Doesn't need this old lady pumping for information asking too many questions is not used to this kind of behaviour what he has in his head is for him alone. 'Things connected to the underworld murder committed in three countries. I know of. Who knows how many more there are? Not forgetting doesn't matter what continent you are in Police are police some good but afraid some the opposite. Believe me when say seen it all. Stories to sicken you. Gestapo! You don't know the half of it.'

'But, surely you have to trust them.'

'No Mary trust no one. Not even your best friend. Have to work behind the lines that's how it has to be.'

Trying to convince if she held on to the believe everything would be sorted but was hard to convince. Now hoping she would hold steadfast and not waver. Much at stake has to get it into her head she must be very careful a disaster if she was responsible for the wall crashing down around them.

'It's going to be hard for me to keep this to myself. What if let something out? Don't think can trust myself specially when speaking to him.'

'You'll be fine Mary. Just curb your tongue you'll be okay.'

Now it looks like she is not getting it. Maybe it was wrong he's thinking for him to hitch up here had doubts looks like he is walking into a horror situation of his own making.

'He'll be suspicious if I keep out of his way. He will think I'm avoiding him and that will make him all the more determined to get to me. He expects me to be his daily help and if I don't turn up, well, he'll be round here in a flash worrying. Just hope don't make a hash of things.'

'I will be coming and going at all times day and night so don't want you to worry. I'll try and be as quite as the proverbial church mouse,' he said to delay any fears she may have.

'You'll remember to use the side entrance don't go through the public house. Too many to wonder who you are.'

'Mary I will be invisible. Bet you if enjoying your wares down below you will not know it's me. By the way talking about wares have you nothing better than this so called coffee?' He was looking at the drink cabinet in anticipation. 'No my lad not for you. Remember must have your wits about you always. Doubt, you are a stranger and the people here are really nosey. The first sighting will have the news spread like wild fire guaranteed.'

'Guess the manner of small villages don't worry yourself.'

'Some will stare others will stop and ask why you are here? Where you're putting up? You'll find they are not slow in coming forward.'

'I'll be careful. Don't fret used to having the third degree.'

'All am saying is don't be getting too friendly with the nosey Parker's.'

'Okay I get what you're saying. But listen, won't be needing you to make meals for me i will make my own arrangements. Maybe just the occasional breakfast if here at the time but don't be putting yourself out on my account. I promise not to be getting in your way will not be upsetting your routine.'

'All right but make sure you eat properly won't be putting me out.Would happily cook for you though if you're sure It's up to you.'

'Will be coming and going. Sometime not showing when you expect me. Better leave me to my own devices, okay.'

TWENTY SEVEN

Betty's café drinking black coffee, Night and Day, crashed open the door coming in like a whirlwind. Like a drunk man stumbling on unsteady legs and when he saw Frank he straightened to his full height approached grinning like butter wouldn't melt in his mouth. Squinting and looking menacingly at the customers who were sitting at the tables.

'What are you doing?' Betty screamed 'open the door if you please. What the hell do you think your doing you oversize moron?' He frightened the life out of her. Not only by his abrupt entrance such an ugly individual would frighten the bravest of people.

In her hand she held a plate filled with the usual Scottish breakfast, eggs, tomato, hash browns, square sausage, rashers of bacon and a potato scone. Unfortunately she let it fall and the plate smashed on the floor the contents ending up scattered.

The monster ignored her pulled the chair opposite Frank.

Customers got up from their seats and hurriedly left.

'Come again,' Betty called followed with, 'bloody moron upsetting my customers'

She walked out from behind the counter demanding an explanation but was ignored.

Frank who looked at the intruder hoping he would apologise but thought wrong.

'If your friend doesn't behave himself Archie McDougall will be on his back mark my words get him told if he's not going to order anything you can tell him to get, now, this minute.' Waved her finger pointing and jabbed Franks shoulder Ignoring the intruder as if he was invisible. Then without another word she walked dipped below the counter to clear the mess from the floor.

'Mary Greene wants to see you not happy with you Frankie my boy raising hell. Just to warn you son be forewarned,' bruiser said.'

Two busybodies watching with delight stopped their yapping when this was going on started gossiping again spoke so loud the customers who were still in the café couldn't help but hear what

170

was being said, Kelly Broon and Rogan, Josh Innes, at their usual table letting their tongues go on the loose without concern for whoever we're definitely better broadcasting outfit than the local broadcasting station if dirt to be found they would be odds on to find it scoop it up and dish it out.

'Mary Mckenzie has a fancy man know cause I seen him.' Kelly said, 'a fancy man not privy to that?' she announced with glee a wicked knowing smile.

'Naw, your wrong a lodger. A woman know cause saw her didn't know that did you Kelly Broon, you seen him didn't you, Mary Mckenzie's fancy man, ay. Am right or am I right Betty?'

'Have it your way,' said Kelly 'a saw a woman.'

'You are both right,' Betty says, ' seen both so there.'

'Two?' Josh said, 'well, never two are you kidding me?'

'Have you pair not anything better to be getting on with instead of gossiping like old fish wives? Why don't you get out of it and annoy some other buddies sick to the back teeth listening to your outrageous stories.'

'A fine way to treat your customers,' said Josh.

They got up from the table and walked out the door into the sunshine.

'Come again,' said Betty, 'see if you can make a cup of tea last longer than half an hour next time and bring up to date news,' followed with, 'silly old mares. Make the place look untidy like only you pair can do but come again if you please won't hold it against you rat bags!'

'I'm really sorry about your brother,' Night and Day said.

'Thanks for that. So the holy one summons me? Well tell her I'm busy at this time and when I have space in my diary maybe if I can will fit her in.'

'Yes, yes Frankie. Know your feeling but you know how it is with the pair of them.'

'You going to put my arm up my back? March me into her presence?'

'You know couldn't possibly let that happen it won't happen. No son not about to do that. Come when you can. I'll explain to Mary the spoilt boy you really have to avoid you ken that son don't you the spoilt one.'

171

'Mary is vicious you know how devious and untrustworthy she is but Patrick is a kitten,' said Frank, 'not a cuddly one but nevertheless a kitten under her spell. I don't have much to worry about. His threats are not to be taken seriously. I'm not about to get on my knees to satisfy his or her egos.' Putting a brave face on the encounter but truthfully he wasn't looking forward to the upcoming meeting.

'Will see you right don't you worry boy you can rely on that. That's my word.'

Waiting to see what is going to happen next other places to be a visit to the Greenes not on the agenda. Seeing the man soften his demeanour thought to show how unafraid he is and choose is words carefully be more brazen with it. 'Thanks for that but remember will hold you to your promise,' stared into his eyes giving the impression not to be messed with in any way.

'Been putting up with them for years needs must but saying that you are unaware that your old man and me were pals for years in our wee days always looking out for the two of you ken always had ear on the ground and if the Greenes are involved in anyway you'll be first to ken let you know. Sure you'll know.'

'A doubt about the Greenes you gonna say?'

'Too much already must be going don't leave it too late to show give her time to get over her beef,' rose up tried a smile, more of a grin. His tongue peeked from the side of his mouth, sliver of a slaver oozed from his grey false teeth gathered on the corner of his bottom lip done a loud slurp grinning as he walked hunched like a great ape to the door.

'Come again. Leave my door in it's hole p l e a s e!'

He stopped and stared. Looked her up and down. 'Wummin, know your place,' said with a voice like thunder.

'My door is going to part from it's hinges,' she stood with both hands on her waist directing her gaze, 'You! Yes you! It's your fault and thinking it's time you were barred, Butler. No more of your undesirable friends can't stand them scaring my customers away how you attract them,' shook her head eyes blazing, 'like a magnet!'

Tried a smile not knowing if she was going to order him off the premises at this moment, 'don't look at me nothing to do with me. No, didn't invite him he's just the bearer of bad news could have done without him turning up,' he's appealing to her better judgment. He hunched his shoulders wished he was somewhere else but calmer now the man had left. Was an unexpected visit he could have done without.

'No, I'll give you that,' she said, 'what a chancer that man is a good thing doesn't come here often nerves wouldn't be able to stand it. How the Greenes employ him I don't get it. Brute of a man,' shake of her shoulders stood grimacing.

'I'm sorry Betty afraid as much as you were,' going on the defensive standing ready to leave before asked to leave.

Pointed to the table told him to sit sallied behind the counter returning with a cup of tea and bent close. He could feel the warmth of her breast near his cheek. A smell of rose water. Just for a moment, Rotterdam, he never found, was it, or was it?

'What's with your pal Mary,' she said, 'got a man in her old age or they old gossips talking rubbish?'

Wee bit surprised how she reacted and was it deliberate. The tip of her breast practically in his mouth. Careful maybe reading the signal the wrong way better ignore see what happens next. Said, 'heard the gossip but really non the wiser but a good way to get her back up if asked and like getting Mary's back up.'

Betty lifted the cup to wipe the table jiggled the saucer the tea spilled over on to the floor.

'What's up with you?' jumping up went through the motion of wiping tea from his trousers if the trousers were wet or not looking at his shoes. Wet shoes brought the memory of the old Dutchman to mind.

'sorry, sorry was an accident. You all right not burn you did I How stupid of me. Here let me get a wet cloth to wipe.'

'No, no need.' She is apologising, he thought, not as bad as she makes out but other thoughts he had gone out the window he was wary of her actions it was rumoured she was on the lookout for a suitor for her what he knew of her retarded daughter, Dilly. 'I'm fine,' he said, 'are you all right been on edge since I came in what is it Betty you can tell me you would say if anything was wrong have you not got over him. Night and Days visit?'

'You attracting some queer people since you returned home that's what on about. Trouble. If want trouble get that loon

173

Butler. Trouble following you like a bad penny. You and people talking,'

'Why did you say attracting people what people? Riddles why you speak in riddles got something to say well let's have it. Don't keep it to yourself let's here it!'

'Oh some strangers The latest foreign gadgies. Two Germans, think they were, definitely foreigners.'

'You sure? Looking for me?'

'Yes twice in here not so bad if they ordered food or drink, no, you was all they wanted. Glad to see the back off them not a enquiry agent. Food it's food I sell food!'

Mind into overdrive, Germans looking for him. Have they caught up are these the two the ones responsible for his brother's death?

'Not seen them again think they were tourists.'

'You only saw them a couple of times think they've gone?'

'Yeah. Friends of yours are they.? From the continent? They never left a message. Twice they came but no message. Seeing you had been away for so long I guessed couldn't have been important they never came back.'

'Three something years in Holland three years and more.'

'That could be it. Dutchmen they could have been Dutch not German,' she said.

Thinks, she doesn't know it not got a clue. Doesn't knowher erse from her elbow! 'Don't you know the difference Germans or Dutch?' If the two were Dutch it could be Kaiser and Beeny they could be here on his case he was thinking and pleased and surprised at the thought.

'Use the phone Betty need the phone.' Excited knowing what Kaiser said. Would see him soon he remembered but not hearing from him was a worry it was not like Kaiser to be silent.

'Okay,' she said, 'the phone in the back but dinnae make it a habit dinnae allow customers take advantage but seeing its you.'

Made his way to the back room office surprised to see was used a bedroom come living area small and cosy with a business desk and the phone sitting amongst papers spread haphazardly across it. Half finished cup of coffee A plate with the remnants of someone's breakfast and an open woman's magazine.

Dilly in the king size bed woke when he entered. 'Frankie you come to see me? Was expecting you. Wait, will get dressed.' Stretched her arms above her head yawned shaking her hair vigorously the long black tresses tumbled to her shoulders as she watched him her mouth open tongue peeking from her red smudged lipstick lips and smiling seductively waiting for his reaction.

'Hi Dilly come to use the phone.'

'Anything you want?' She blushed he smiled. 'The phone, Dilly just the phone.' looked long admiring the view. She said something but he missed what she had said as he watched in disbelief saw her childlike dive under the bed covers.

Shrugged picked up the phone dialled a few minutes heard her voice, 'Karli, Kaiser, is he there? Tell him need to speak to him been a while since heard said he would keep in touch but nothing,' said the words hurriedly breathlessly in anticipation.

'Nice to hear you. Sorry about the sad news, Kaiser? No. Not here he's not here at present gone to the seaside,' she spoke the words slowly, cautiously.

'Damn! What's the reason for him going on a visit to the seaside?' News not wanting to hear a visit to the seaside? 'Sorry is he on some kind of business or holiday, in particular, a woman say? Know what he's like.'

'A woman? Don't make me laugh. No not a woman.'

'Sorry.'

'Why you sorry?'

'For saying damn sorry for that just so important.'

'Well heard more harsher words so don't worry about it. Yes he makes me so mad sometimes said worse believe me dear. Not know honestly don't know,' she said, he thought she lied?

'Was wondering why he went off to the seaside myself you can't rely on him says one thing then does the other. You know how it goes don't worry on my behalf used to his ways believe me.'

'Have you a number I can reach him?'

'Afraid. Don't know. Could be anywhere might be Spain likes going there but really don't know. Anyway it's nice to hear from you know what you must be going through and hope things get sorted soon, bye.'

'He's not here in Scotland is he? You would say wouldn't you?' His words said slowly saying in a way to out think her he was suspicious of her long pause. He waited for her response but got none, 'Nice to have spoken to you so if you hear from him will you tell him need to speak with him knows how to get in touch. Thanks Karli, bye, bye,' he wondered if she was still there cause he got no response, just silence.

Replaced the phone turned when he heard her giggling saw the bed covers move her legs in the air flaying as she resurfaced 'Ma!' She screamed, 'you said you were going to get him to take me out you lied he has one,' another scream dived under the covers sobbing.

Moved to calm her as Betty entered in a frenzy not expecting to see him so near she stopped looked smiled the kind of smile of satisfaction, 'See, cosy with each other, my, surprise surprise,'

'No, you're reading it the wrong way.'

'My eyes don't lie perfectly well what is going on here.'

'No. Nothing going on. You wish assure you all was doing was the phone. Speaking to a friend. Heard her sobbing enquired if she was okay that's it.'

'Out of here, now!' Her thoughts gave way to anger.

'You know. For goodness I wouldn't do anything so stupid Betty,' he moved quickly from the bed looking at her trying to explain.

Put her arms round her sobbing daughter. 'Did he touch you darling tell me? Bad to you there there,' softly soothing stroking her hair and giving him the long stare.

'The state. Can't honestly say she understands do you?'

'Just leave speak to you later go you disgust me.'

'I'm going nothing happened assure you and it never will goodbye. Ask her. If she's capable that is.'

'

'Okay go and wait I'll come through.'

At a table in the empty café sees she's got the closed sign on the locked door. What I'm going to hear don't want to hear it he is thinking the worst.

After ten minutes watching the clock on the wall behind the counter waiting and listening to screaming words and soothing words then complete silence she came. Standing expecting a mouthful of unpleasantnes. No, she's smiling what's coming? He's got to play his cards straight, 'you thinking of blackmail, forget it. Had no desires anytime past or present on your daughter say what you're going to say get it over with I'm out of here.'

'Just sorry,' she said.

What the… what is she up too going from hot to cold devious as only she could be. Sat down, she said nothing, watched her go behind the counter preparing some coffee and sandwiches.

'Eat you wish or don't eat up to you,' said and smiling as she approached him at the table, 'forget it. What happened back there. Read it wrong sorry.'

'Is that you're idea of an a apology?'

'No,'

Open the door and let me out.'

'In good time.'

'Keeping me here as a prisoner?'

'You daft? What purpose would it serve?'

What on earth. What she got on her mind? He's thinking.

'Won't be telling Mary that,' Betty said.

'Why would I do that?' He was looking at the locked door.

'Seeing how much she dotes on you,' she said sitting down.

He looked into her eyes. The combination of green and grey and possibly a touch of blue they reminded him of Ruthie. That was a good thought but her what game is she playing. Maybe a trap? The daughter is ripe for plucking but he isn't the one to be the one to be doing the plucking. She, like a spider ready to trap but he was not going to fall into her trap. He unconsciously picked at a sandwich on the plate. 'Customers will not be pleased,' he said nodding towards the door.

'Speak with you later,' she got up and walked and unlocked the door. We will continue this when have the time. Come back at closing time.'

'No. Said all. No more to be said.'

'Apologise? You want me to say sorry when you brought this on yourself, ay.'

'No apology needed.'

TWENTY EIGHT

'How the hell,' Mary said, 'do you get the place in such a state.' She is showing her displeasure as per usual, 'why do you chuck everything in the sink instead of cleaning as you go? Simple, see, use the cutlery the dishes the pots and pans then you wash them. It's easy better than having a mountain of plates all this rubbish growing here,' she's giving it big licks, picking things out the sink. Hot water splashed everywhere, 'Loons? You're useless goodness you've only been back a few days. Do not understand how you live like this!'

'Aye aye Mary, keep it down. My head is somewhere else,' reached for the whisky bottle about to pour she grabbed it out his hand he saw the anger on her face,' no Mary, no, please!'

'When you going to learn have to get a grip Frankie son.'

'Stop clucking,' took the bottle from her poured whisky into the glass, head back, whisky down the hatch, made a sound as if the amber nectar burnt his throat same time shivered, 'that's better.'

'Going to end up like uncle Jonny if you don't pull yourself together can only afford one pot man and you are a wee bit young to end up doing that job.'

'Think so Mary give me some credit, Jonny Mack, give me a break.'

'Well a good woman might have made the difference instead of him getting married, the bottle, all I see is you taking the same route it's plain don't need a glass ball to see it.'

'Oh Mary give up. Is it not time you were going got nowhere else or someone else to be fussing?'

'I'll get when ready just finish what am doing then be out you're face.'

Returning to the sink, bang, clang, bash a symphony of pots being created.

'Awe Mary my health sake can you please do it quietly?' Held his head feeling very sorry for himself.

'I'll make breakfast when finished. A nice plate of bacon and eggs, black pudding and red, fried bread black coffee, that'll soon sober you up.'

'You'll kill me Mary the grease will do for me.'

'By the way,' she moved beside him at the table, 'a wee bit worried about Jonny Mack just lately he's acting funny.'

'What's he up to not as bad as Jakie Ross is he?'

'Started annoying my customers. The strangers not the regulars. Collects the empty glasses wipes the tables gives no time for them to finish their drinks. They get the impression wants them to finish up and leave he's hustling and me losing my punters. Got to get to the bottom of it wondered if you would have a word with him, ay, you being close an all.'

'Not me won't listen to me you'll have to put your foot down Mary after all you're the boss.'

'Talking rubbish asking have they seen the southern cross at night? Don't think he knows what's what.'

'The southern cross at night why?'

'Seems if they play along are ex merchant navy takes a liking but if they don't know what the hell he's on about lifts their drink wipes tables like that,' she demonstrated, 'people are demanding another it's becoming an embarrassment regulars are ribbing him they are looking for extras as well making a fool out of me.'

'What's the answer? Maybe he needs the men in white coats.'

'Lit the Milky Way,' she says wearily then goes on, 'Queen Bess any idea?'

'Need to stop giving him his ration of the swally looks as if he really needs to be seen by the guys in white coats.'

'How you persuade him to do it a law unto himself think he's going back to his youth. Memories of years at sea. Just like you're dad. Always knew what he was about to say, ay. A good woman might have done him the world of good if only?'

'Yes, okay Mary you've said a good woman will make the difference but would it?'

'Going on about the Table mountain in South Africa and the bay. Really acting funny. It's all getting me down. They daft questions becoming monotonous my customers to think about.'

'Mary getting ready to go out so if you don't mind places to be people to see.'

'Get on with it am not keeping you will go when ready. You won't need feeding? Don't know why a bother ma bahooky.'

'Queen Bess you said don't know? Honestly? Port Elizabeth in South Africa. Must have heard the rubbish talked by the seamen punters in your pub,' removing his dressing gown as he walked to the bedroom turned looked and gave her a large grin said, 'have to be sure your customers? Mary, protect your punters, ay?'

'Can go off people very quickly can do with less of your snide remarks.'

'You know how to treat the situation. You don't need my penny- worth to give you a solution know what to do get rid.'

He heard the door shut with the usual bang.

'Gotta be careful,' muttered, 'one of these days she will be gone and sure to miss her just gotta treat her with some more respect that's all,'

Things on in his mind sitting caressing a glass of whisky. 'No, why upset the apple cart not appreciate a change of my behaviour not a good idea I think not.'

Later in the day Frankwas in Mary's place. 'Had a wee talk with jakie to see what could get out of him and the story he was peddling for the ejits to buy him drinks.'

'Make any sense of it?' Robbie asked him.

'No. Same rubbish.'

'You think he's not telling it straight?'

'Know what he's like,' said Frank.

'I tried asking him but got nowhere. Cost two whiskies but no luck. Feel so stupid what said. No one any the wiser. When they going to get grips with your situation? When will it end?'

'Agree it's a mystery Robbie.'

Robbie lifted his empty glass, 'a refill but not a word to Mary. She won't take it kindly me giving free booze pal or no pal,' smiled shook his head and winked.

TWENTY NINE

'Came in to see McDougall,' Frank approached the desk sergeant in the Leith police station, 'wants to see me,'he said.

Not lifting his face from the ledger, 'Sergeant McDougall?'

'Yes sergeant. Came to see Archie,' let him know on good terms better to let them think you are friendly for as little time as possible was thinking.

'You Butler?' Stretched his full height stuck out his bulging stomach, 'well are you or not? Got more important things to be getting on with.'

He could see the man was a good contender for high blood pressure watched the colour of his face change from slight purple on the broken veins on his nose to cheeks redder and redder obviously not coping with the paperwork. Unhappy with the untimely unnecessary intervention of street punters coming into his domain 'Mr Frank Butler in a hurry can see him or not?'

'All in good time,' turning the pages slowly supposedly, looking for something important to find in its hidden depths.

'Tell him got better things to do instead of waiting here fiddling my fingers,' he moved from the desk towards the exit.

'Hold on there don't be hasty tell him yourself,' waving his hand to stop him from leaving, 'wait your name rings a bell you the guy?' Two burly coppers pushed past as they came in from the street the sergeant didn't finish what he was about to say.

'Heh Butler, McDougall is looking for you,' one said as they passed on their way up the stairs. 'Wants to see you about the old alky Ross. Says you are hard to find in a foul mood. Would watch yourself if were you.'

'Something or other on his whereabouts,' the other copper said in a loud booming voice.

He watched them go without waiting for his response.

'Canny win,' he said to the desk sergeant, 'why so important all of a sudden?'

'If you hold your horses was about to tell you he is at the morgue. Will be there till two this afternoon. You've got plenty time to get to Stockbridge. Plenty of time if you leave now.'

He knew what the sergeant was about to ask and was fed up having to explain to all the nosey people who wanted to know the sorry details.

He got out before he responded to the question and before the sergeant had time to quiz him. His only thoughts now where's the nearest boozer.

'Can confirm this is, Jamie Butler, your brother,' holding the face cover a little way above the body, 'Is it?'

'You know perfectly well it is Sergeant.' Said moving after a quick glance.

'Come on Frankie got to ask.'

They moved to the next slab McDougall exposed the face of the girl, ' you know who this girl is?'

'No don't know. The one with Jamie? I've not seen her before,' moved slowly away with head bowed looking down at the floor and wiping the wet from his eyes.

McDougall replaced the sheet.

'Yes it is, shame, such a pretty girl and so young, so pretty.' Shook his head as he walked past in silence making for the exit.

Gave him the sensation of a shiver going up his spine and thought why was McDougall acting so caring. Very unusual he was thinking as McDougall returned and lifted the cover from the dead girl again.

Pretty lass,' he said taking a long peek at her face, 'waste of a precious young life. Got happened beats me. Real crying bloody shame,' is repeating to himself in a low whisper.

'Did they have their throats cut is that how?' he asked disturbing the man's thoughts hoping the truth would be out once and for all.

'You know I can't tell you. Why are you asking such a question? What kind of question was that to ask?' Gave an angry response not appreciating the untimely intervention.

'Oh you know what it's like. Rumours are all over the place. Killed or a lovers pack? The quine was her relatives chasing? Is that how it goes Sergeant?'

'Listen Frank,' looked round making sure they were alone… 'They were killed but not how you think they were so let's get out of here.'

'What's your tipple?'

In Tamsons the local pub in Stewart street.

'I'll have a whisky a double to steady my nerves.'

'I'll fetch them,' McDougall said approaching the barman, 'two doubles of my preferred and a half pint and one for you if you please Ian.'

'How were they killed?' Asked as McDougall sat down but got ignored and it looked like McDougall was now unimpressed.

He thought it's like drawing teeth and thinks the conversation is over. Will have to play it casual from now on.

'Not drowned as you plainly saw. No marks on their faces no water in their lungs and not garrotted as you thought. Don't know why you asked that question who have you been speaking with what information have you received? Now that's it no more.'

'Not drowned well how?'

'The doc. Thorough with the examination found tiny holes between the big toes injected with something nasty. You going to lighten up. No more questions.'

'Before the water?'

'Yes, the truth of it,' swallowed his whisky took a sip of beer. Looked round the bar saw it was quite busy for the time of day didn't recognise anyone. Lowering his voice to make sure they were not heard said, 'done elsewhere. Truth is we haven't a clue as yet. The old guy, no. Now as I said enough.'

Got the impression to end the conversation memory having a time lapse. 'Jakie Ross, you know, the alky. The one the gadgie who's known you before you were old enough to be a copper,' reminding him, 'knew you from your school days surprised you forgot,' observed the guilty look as McDougall averted his gaze.

'Aye, right, Jakie yes that one no his observations have come to nothing worth while. Useless. Not safe to take the word of an alki should have known before asking.'

'The girl you know who she is?'

'Yes, Boy von Oldersum. German gangsters daughter. A real villain the London police are on his case with the help from police on the continent he's a real nasty not to be met on a dark night would fit well with the gestapo.'

'Natzi, you say a Natzi?'

'No, said nasty not Natzi, nasty' said as he took a large swill of beer. 'That's it.'

'How do you know this and what's, it?' Seen his eyes searching round the place and wondered who or what could make him so interested on the going's on in the place?

'Trust me have information can't relate,' rose up and crossed to the bar. 'Same again please Ian.'

'The luggage? Someone said there was luggage in the trunk. Any information in the cases or too early to release the findings?'

'Still waiting to find out the contents of those soon find out what forensics have to say in due course.' He placed the filled glasses on the table and sat down.

'Forensics? When do you expect will be finished with their investigation? Soon you think I will be getting his effects back?'

'You'll be informed when to collect them let you know in good time don't worry.'

'Funeral. Got to arrange the funeral.'

'Yes you'll be informed in plenty time. I'll make sure you get informed when the time comes. Drink up. Needed somewhere else,' downed the drinks one after the other, 'Hurry up you going somewhere else like Berts are you?'

'What about the quine what will happen to her and no not going anywhere.'

'Stepmother coming from Oldenburg to claim the body out of our hands.'

'Thought cases of murder the body to be buried where it happened she not going to be buried here?'

'You're asking too many questions, me, just as much in the dark as you are so that's enough finish up.'

'Any chance they could be buried together? According to Mary Mckenzie she put two and two together and got five, a romantic notion they were going to be wed. But knowing Mary well You know how she is.'

'Not see that happening son. Too many complications in this case. Time will tell what the outcome will be. You're drink,' pushed the glass towards him, 'wanted elsewhere,' agitated shifted on the seat watching the coming and going's frustration on his face.

'You wanted to see me about Jakie? What you want from me I don't know afraid can't help you there.'

'Who said, wanted to see you about Jakie Ross?' Resented the question big time.

'Looks like he's playing the memory game something on his mind. Something not as it should be. He is getting wise to him and wondering what is behind his behaviour. Time for him to stand his hand and buy a round of drink maybe with more drink McDougall would slip up let him know some of the questions he was seeking answers to. What puzzled him was why did McDougall mention Berts how did he know about Berts bar has he been spying? Is this more worry? His mind is troubled who can he trust or not trust, puzzled, more of a nightmare and has to be careful to be safe from now on.

Approached the blonde with the over size chest, hanging, nearly hanging, outside her blouse. 'Whisky his preferred and a half pint heavy and a pint the same,' he said not looking in her deep brown beautiful eyes.

'Said had to be going did not have to bother getting me another drink. Not listen do you.'

'Frank saw he was more in a tizzy than before. What the hell what is he up to. He couldn't work out and wondered why he was so desperate to be gone. Put down the drinks on the table ignored the rebuke.

McDougall looking at the people who were sitting and the ones standing at the bar but especially watching the door he appeared anxious ignoring him he wondered what plausible excuse to convince he had to be out of there.

'One more before you go can't say never bought you a swally and not in the business for anything it's not a bribe.'

McDougall on his feet checking the door suddenly sat down drinking the beer. Wiped his lips ignored him his eyes fixed on a stranger who entered.

'You got it bad whatever it is what's the reason? What is troubling you why are you looking for Jakie Ross why is he so important? Why suddenly the man of the moment you letting me in on the secret are you?'

Not listening he was giving a long smile to the guy who entered and hurriedly came and sat beside him 'You're late,' he said to McDougall.

'Excuse me, Frank said,'don't you see we are having a conversation who are you and what do you want what's your business here?' Angry at the intrusion. Answers he needed, answers shouldn't have to be put off by a stranger. He had a notion to punch the living daylights out of him knew impossible not with the copper McDougall on the premises.

'I've been waiting might have guessed would find you in here. What's been keeping you?' The stranger said a frothy girlish sort of way, 'you know got a schedule to keep,' ignoring Franks outburst.

'This young man is helping me with some of my enquiry's confidential so won't be doing any introductions.'

'You don't have to tell me. Got no interest in what you're up to. No nothing whatsoever.'

'Are you gonna do the decent thing?' Stranger asks, 'and get me a drink?' He shifted nearer went sideways on the bench seat looking longingly at McDougall.

'What you want?' Frank asks as he rises curbed his anger and looked at her who was waiting for his response, 'I will oblige,' he said admiring the view she was presenting.

The guy turned clasped his hands placing them on his closed knees. 'Not sure what do you recommend? I'm not in the habit taking drink from strangers. Mam, she always warns me. Beware of strange men,' a smile a swish of his long raven black dyed hair and the look that seems never ending.

'F…Me! come off it fun boy what is it you want you want a drink or what? It's not twenty questions.'

McDougall got up from the table blustering and flustered said, 'not used to this kind of carry on it's embarrassing we are finished here let's go,' steered his friend towards the exit.

At the bar not looking at her blouse but into her eyes heard the ruckus and saw McDougall pushing the unfortunate man out the door who was shouting something about a drink and why he wasn't getting one because after all he was not the one who was late was he who was late so was entitled to have a drink.

186

'Later a drink later,' McDougall pushing and shoving him out the door towards the steps leading to the street.

'Do you want this whisky or not?' she asked. Hurrying to serve another punter same time smiling at him.

'You drink it,' this time he is looking longingly at her eyes then at her blouse.

She put the drink under the bar, 'will,' she said giving him a coy look, a come on look, 'a bottle of the stuff in my flat,' winked her left eye, 'finish at ten.'

Looking up and down the street didn't see McDougall. Wondered what was going on. Astonished how fast the pair had disappeared. What he was doing with the handsome boy was not any of his business. He never thought after all the years he had known him that he was that way inclined. McDougall? Maybe he thought was but there again maybe he wasn't? The problem now was a black Mercedes car parked along the street. He decided to go and suss it out but as he got near it took off. The same car he had seen before he was sure of it. Watched it turn round at the top of the street and came passed him going fast driving into Kerr Street along to Raeburn Place. Retraced his steps nearing the pub he witnessed a tramp causing a disturbance heard a shout, Natzi. A tall man bigger than Jakie Ross and was wearing an old army great coat. Was carrying a grubby green blanket and had on a brown balaclava. He couldn't get close as a large crowd gathered to witness what was going on. Couldn't see if he knew who the man was. Decided to leave and let Ian the barman from the public house sort out the commotion.

Into Inverleith park to kill time waited a good hour watching the men mostly old gadgies and boys sailing model yachts. Swans and ducks not happy for the inconvenience. Ducks making most noise as the sail boats came into their domain. Wings flapping but only flying short distances splashing about in the water. The swans on the other hand graceful and not in the least put out by the event.

THIRTY

Bert's bar was packed with punters he couldn't see an empty seat the crowd standing at the bar made it sure a long wait to be served so decided to go somewhere else instead of waiting for a chance to get to the bar. When she stepped up to the mike well he wasn't about to stay and listen.

Wee Lizzie was ready… 'Hurry on,' she announced.

Hurry hurry on hurry on you played the ace
Now it's you're place to hurry hurry on
Speed along speed along fly a plane catch a train
But hurry hurry on

'I'll just hurry out of here,' he said to the nearest customer standing at the crowded bar..

Five minutes later in the STEAM BOAT at the Citadel. Quite a stir upsetting the punters the resident large grey parrot was out it's cage flying about annoying everyone. The lady boss wasn't concerned not wishing her pet to be harmed telling them it would return to the cage when it was ready in it's own time. Came to rest on the bar beside him reckoned it was in a stressed condition didn't move so he grabbed it. 'Make sure the cage door is open,' to the landlady as he walked along till in line with the cage..

She thought he was about to give the bird to her how wrong she was. From his side the bar saw the door of the cage was open took aim threw the parrot straight in. It went in so fast, crash, it's feathers flew everywhere. The punters cheered. The landlady was not amused seeing her pet lying on the bottom of the cage exhausted. Gave him the look waved her arms shouted at the top of her voice, 'what you think you're playing at said to leave it alone!'

'Poor Polly,' punter cried out, what now if it's dead no more fun and games.'

'Shut it,' she said, then at him, 'out your barred!' Screamed At him, 'don't you come back Butler you're barred!'

He never heard much of what she said because the punters were laughing so loud.

'It's alive isn't it? Some people. Expect I won't get a swally not now? No not expect it', he walked. Was silence in the bar they all watching her comforting her parrot.

He strolled along Bernard's Street to Mick's place over from Rabbie Burns statue and ordered a pint.

'Would you believe only came out for a quite drink. No wouldn't believe having to dodge a wee quine who seems to follow me about you know the one, the wee singer. Go to the Steamboat she bars me. Her and her parrot. I ask you. You better give me a double of the usual Mick need a pickup for ma shattered nerves.'

'Shattered nerves well that beats all. Hearing things about you my friend some bad but mostly, you know, the usual.'

'Such as.'

'Getting into bother that usual.'

'You would think they had better things to be getting on with. Not on my back all the time.'

'No me goes over my head too long kids remember. What is said well talking about you they're leaving the other you know, alone, ay. Worrying though you not to be seen with.'

'What now what has been said?'

'The gossip would've thought you heard.'

'Heard what?'

'Forget it drink up. Don't let it bother you.'

'Bother me why should it bother me?'

Mick smiled and walked to the other end of the bar chatted to the two ladies, ladies of the night, served them their drinks.

'Finish up and go,' he says, 'them two sitting by the door,' they turned to look, 'plain clothes watch yourselves.'

Came back up the bar.

'Stick out like a sore thumb,' Frank said to Mick who shakes his head, 'Why do they bother?' Frank says, 'everyone knows

189

who they are. Think some day the penny would drop. Couple off ejits. Bloody coppers on the make you bet.'

The ladies on the way out had a quick quiet conversation with the plain clothes. 'If you want something to be doing you'll get us along you know what street. We will watch for you,' the blonde said cheekily as her pal pulled her out the door both giggling like a pair of schoolgirls.

Laura behind the bar heard what was said, 'they two quines are taking a chance telling them over there were they were off to,' says in a whisper to Mick.

'You mean the cops?'

'Aye, they want to watch what they're doing.'

'None of our business.'

'Yes know but nevertheless.'

'Serve the punters and Dinnae let it fash ye,' said to her as he bends his head to Frank and whispers, 'the pair oh filth sitting by the door you recall seeing them before? First time had the pleasure in here. Not the usual.'

'Thought you…'

'No first time in here.'

'Not local you think specials?'

'Up town gadgies, yeah, could be.'

'Why giving you the attention you got any idea?'

'You asking me?'

'I'm getting used to seeing shadows following me. Infuriating not got the guts to approach and end it.'

'Think you here after you?'

'Well not after me or maybe for after.'

'What for after?'

They're going, look, not trying their luck with me.'

'Frankie please no trouble,' he whispers and summons Laura, 'follow them see what's what but be discreet.'

Five minutes later, 'followed along behind good distance. Don't think they spotted me, ' Laura reports.

'Gone then not waited outside?'

'No. The girls are standing at the corner but the cops crossed over and went a different way.'

'Not a worry Frankie not on your case my friend.'

190

THIRTY ONE

It's awfy good what you are doing for Frank,' she said, 'I'm afraid something is going to happen to him.' She never felt this anxiety since her two uncles failed to return after a storm and the fishing boat never found.

'That's what friends are for but think he can look after himself don't you worry.'

'Wish I could believe what you say. He's just a silly loon. Jumps before he thinks. Goes in at the deep end always has to be the leader of the gang.'

'I'm on his case and far he's doing things the right way,' said Kaiser. 'I'm happy so far hope it lasts.'

He gave her shoulder a rub hoping to make her feel a little less frantic and assured her things would work out. 'It will not do for you to make yourself ill worrying all the time the outcome will take care of itself so please don't worry Mary.'

She got up from the table, 'sit still,' she said, 'have your breakfast some eggs and coffee they won't take long or would you prefer to have a nice cup of tea?'

'Saw him in Stockbridge. Followed him. Nothing much to report he met the Sergeant what's his name?'

'You mean McDougall that waste of space. Him and that other copper, Rooney. Nothing but a couple of no users. What do we pay our taxes for bloody disgrace and the skinny malinki Rooney is as much use as a chocolate fire guard,' she said, trying to make a joke out of the situation. 'Is it tea or coffee? Was up to me would put a thrissle doon his troosers and give him something to dance about no bloody use the pair of them. Oh how they make my blood boil!' She shrugged and made a face.

'Yeah McDougall that one Met at the dead place. You know the place the morgue after went for drinks. Seemed okay with each other. Tea please Mary, milk, no sugar. In the pub quite a while they were.'

She got busy with the frying pan Filled a plate with two eggs and a jumble of bacon and two sausages one fried tomato plus a potato scone and put the plate on the table.

'Get it into you will do you good. Eat it all want to see an empty plate. Listen wee bit of a puzzle. I got this mysterious letter yesterday. I don't know why it was sent to me,' fished the envelope out the pocket of her apron shaky hands trying to open it, 'not a granny, blast! Here you take it gave him the envelope pulled the chair to sit beside him finger stretching hand pulling trying to get some life back into them.

The envelope contained a half page from a child's crayon drawing book.

'Simple Mary half page colouring book nothing unusual, 'If you know what to look for. It's meant for me. Good job you kept it,' he spread the page on the table smoothing out the wrinkles.

'Well when seen the London postmark could count on one hand how many times got a letter from England why I kept it to let you see if you could explain it. After all you have just came from there. Didn't know who could be sending me a letter from England surprised when seeing the post mark. Postie another busybody sure to be surprised at me getting a letter from that place you can imagine.'

'We'll see Mary,' studied a moment. 'Your granddaughter signs off with T age 3. My friend Tony three means three deaths.'

'I've told you don't have grandchildren none whatsoever.'

'Yes Mary I know,' eager to explain she he thought a bit slow. 'A coded message just like spies?' face lit up when he mentioned spies, 'yes now you've got it Mary easy as I said work it out.'

'Like a film we goodies or baddies? Liked that film with the Fat Man when he was a detective.'

'Fat man? Oh yes Finkle Jones that one you mean.'

'No the Fat one, him.' she said. 'If it was not so serious all this getting into murder and things. Goodness, my what are we coming to. Goodness?'

'See the house the house has four windows and three have red curtains. One without the red crayon another clue again for three deaths as well as the picket fence yellow crayon on three wooden parts but none on the fourth part.'

She moved her finger across the crayon on the picture.

'Right now you're getting it. Now you see the three sea birds above the house two have black crayon rubbed rather thickly while the other has no crayon. This tells me the colour black speaks Gestapo. The two who are responsible for the killings are Germans. Tony is aware of this fact his contact has told him they have flown out of London. We already know this. On the back of the envelope is a pencil drawing of a mayfly.' The look of astonishment on her face made him smile and he thought she was still pondering Finkle Jones.

'Wow,! Germans. War has been over a long time now. To me that thing on the back looks like a daddy long legs. Germans, Gestapo, what next?'

'The drawing like a three year old child would do,' gave her a sour look for interrupting him, 'the mayfly means the nightclub in Mayfair Mary. Number on the door of the house a round nothing, zero, no joy so far Tony is not getting information from the police about the club.'

'No surprise there then. Not that I understand what the thing about the club means anyway,' looked for an explanation but he went on.

'Address Mary your name,' handed her the envelope.

'My name and address nothing out the ordinary,' she said, looking puzzled.

'Again Mary look closely.'

'No, no don't see what's special about the address.'

'Look see how it's spelt with a K instead of a C.'

'That's how it is it's right it's correct that is my name.'

'Granny Mkenzie Mary it says Mkenzie not Mckenzie,' he said spelling each letter out loud moving his finger on each as he spoke gave her the envelope to look at again. 'K, Mary K for Kaiser you get it?'

She fumbled the reading specs from her apron pocket, 'your right how did not see don't think would ever make into any kind of spy,' she laughed. 'No too stupid to be a spy.'

'With a little bit of time and patience it's possible you could learn to read the signs just time and patience.'

'Too much time running a pub that's all good for. Leave the skullduggery to you and your ilk your better at it.'

'Ilk? Goodness me what on earth?' Raised his arms waiting for an explanation.

'People like you you are ilk. People who know what they are doing not old duffers like me. Now if you don't mind, thanks for the lesson got to get on. Things to be seeing. I'm dreading a meeting with him but heed what you said. You take care will see you later. Please be careful, my nerves won't stand anymore bad news. All bad at the moment.'

'Mary got to learn to relax. Nothing bad will happen assure you. Go about like normal. That's all you have to do.'

'Worry worry not easy. The pub door every move someone in someone out my heart is in my mouth. What to do if you are there and he ambles in. Never know when he is going to appear,' she said giving him the impression that she has lost it and he is wondering how she manages to sleep at night.

'You expect many more correspondence from England?'

'Maybe. I can't honestly say.'

'Just, you know it's getting harder to explain to people.'

'Mary go on as you have been doing.'

'A sudden influx of letters from your friend will have people talking. The postman well he is not known for holding his tongue. Especially when he his propping up the bar. Remember the war time saying loose talk cost lives.'

'Get what you're saying. Just go as normal.'

'Better said than done afraid.'

'To keep your mind at ease I will phone Gissertini and tell him no more letters. How does that sound to you better?'

'Good idea.'

'Yes should have thought it best way.'

'That takes care of that.'

'Glad you think so Mary.'

'Yes one less worry to worry about.'

THIRTY TWO

The fax he received from the Greenes with their congratulations on a job well done, was a blatant lie, night and day, spelling out about the two of them made him realise they had already made the decision about his and Jamie's future. Won't forget the smile on the old Dutchman's face, when he presented him with the fax early morning at the dockside office saying maybe a new contract was forthcoming on the grape vine heard the pipe mill about to get a big contract from the Americans. A pipeline down on the Mississippi River and other projects that come with such work somewhere in Kentucky. So a job well done was maybe a hint he could be working in Holland very soon. The old man Willie was pleased to say it could possibly happen again. Would be great if it came to fruition. What he knew for fact was to be wary knowing the history of his employers.

Suffering the morning blues his fourth cup of coffee after waking in a drunken haze by the previous nights booze session in Maggie Shaws. His meeting with McDougall came to nothing realising when interrupted by the boy in the boozer the one in Stockbridge, McDougall had made much of the intervention to put him off suggesting a different meeting he was ready to attend said he had made him late for the appointment and took no time pulling the boy out the pub to the street doing a fast disappearing act. The black car the Mercedes was it the reason McDougall vanished so quickly. He couldn't tell too slow coming from the pub she a happy distraction at the time but cost him time. If only kept what was important, well, she was important, nevertheless cost him dear.

Unhappy memory of a two year episode in a foreign pipe mill reminded him of what the future could hold was thinking why, why do this? Working fourteen hours seven days and nights non stop till a contract is completed and when it's completed he would be sent to another destination be it inspecting pipes paint on bridges or paint on new built ships in shipyards anywhere in the world where the Greenes saw fit to send him. With recent events was unsure what was before him. Was the police going to get results? Was he in any danger would the Greenes henchman watch his back or still a target and why was kaiser out the picture? If he never saw a rusty length of steel tube or ship fabrication again so what! First thoughts now was to get to the bottom of the mystery. Why was these things happening to him and why was his brother killed? What is it about diamonds and who is pulling the strings? What was it about a gangster his brother and the gangsters teenage daughter?

'Oh, still with us are you?'

Came in sounding disgusted by his behaviour. Was drunk talking nonsense lots of falling about and friends no better loud singing getting on her nerves the more she tried to stop them the worse they got.

'Mary why do you keep spying on me will to have the key back from you could have been in bed with Dilly!'

'Chance would be a fine thing time you came to your senses. Haven't you taken any notice what was said any quine seeing you last night would run for the hills as fast as that cartoon thingy, you've seen it.'

'Oh, you think so. Thank you very much for your support. I thought you wanted me to be out of your hair. Thought you were going behind my back trying to set me up with Dilly, Dilly dimple that Betty's half wit. Now come to think of it, the café to think about. Yeah who knows it's a wee gold mine.'

'For goodness sake act your age.'

'It is. You have to agree to that a gold mine.'

She twisted her lip, glowering, deeked the mess in the sink started on an encore of the second chorus of pots and pans. 'Dishes and pots to be rescued.' She scolded for making fun of the situation took off her coat rolled up her sleeves. 'I've heard of pearl diving but this is ridiculous. Have to start charging if you persist in living like a tramp. And heh you nothing wrong wi

Dilly a nice caring wee quine could do a lot worse mark my words a lot worse. A ken full well what am saying.'

'Hear you. Got a fancy man, Mary?' he said, changing the subject.

'Me, fancy man? Where you glean that wisdom from never heard anything so daft in all my life.'

Busied herself by sloshing water over the dishes had her back to him so could not see the broad smile on her face. 'The amount of clutter in here tells me you're not starving yourself, dishes dishes dishes what a life.'

'Is it a fancy man or fancy woman, or no?'

'Don't you dare!'

Spun round to face him her smile gave way to an angry outburst, 'only one woman in my house and you know who that is.' Could not believe what he said. 'How dare you think such a thing ashamed you would think that of me.'

'What I heard in the café the other day.' Trying to apologise but she grabbed her coat and hat and stormed out, bang, the door shut, 'Mary, Mary for goodness sake don't...'

The pier at lunch, time a couple of gadgie's spinning for mackerel. The two in good fettle their wooden fish box lying at their feet held quite a few wriggling tails. The water flashing silver in the sunshine as a school of sprats panicked in the attempt to evade the predators.. Now and again the calm water disturbed by the resident seals gorging on the bounty. Pair of black cormorants were in competition with the screaming gulls for a share of the feast. Rising up high and descending from the clouds with wings close to their bodies nose diving into the water.

It was free entertainment for the many who took enjoyment in the slaughter of the fishes. And was a rare sight a wonder to those who saw the seals for the first time.

One woman remarked, was a better day out than going to the zoo. Saying, it was a lot cheaper. A middle aged man, who heard her, disputed her assertion he said, 'the prices at the restaurants was not a good deal and not worth the money. Trying to feed seven bairns wis a joke.'

She reacted angrily and said, 'he should take his bairns and his wife if he has one to the zoo and he would soon find out.'

He replied, 'would soon find out what the price of fish was cos he was going to take the bairns there but prices at the pier, bah,' he said, 'stuff and humbug.'

'Dinnae ken why they bother,' the woman said to her woman friend.

'Waste oh time don't know why you involved yourself with him,' friend said, giving a short sniff and a little tilt of her head.

A seen it Frankie. Telt the cops what it was all about.' Sitting with his brown boots dangling over the slipway inches from the water.. The tide was high sky cloudless the sun shining. A good day for lazing about .

'You won't a swally?'

He offered his tin of lager shaking it from side to side saying 'no much left son but your welcome. Kent you were going to be here would've brought more. Could've had picnic. The tins here cost an arm and a leg so won't be buying,' hinting.

'No thanks. A picnic when the last you had one of them? No. Here to ask can you go over it again tell me what you saw positive what you said was it a true account?'

Sitting beside him looking down at the water dangling his feet moving his legs back and forth.

On the water a large round circle of blue, purple and green colours, a small fuel spillage from a fishing boat The colours moving slowly in the gentle swell, sideways and forward, mesmerising. His eyes fixed on the moving colours. The silver on the little fish flashing in contrast as the came to investigate, not entering, scampering and making the whole thing a joy.

'Had a bool, you know a marble in they colours,' Frank said, remembering longing for days of the past easy happy times.

'Really nice they colours ay,' said jakie, 'reminds me when was a laddie and me and ma pals went swimming at Royston beach. The ink from the ink works used to get into the water from a wee discharge pipe hidden in long grass. A steady trickle I remember. The sun, aye, seemed always to be very hot like,' he pointed to the colours lazily floating slowly in and out on the swell thinking and reminding himself of the long past. 'They colours are like it was,' looked over to the opposite harbour wall watching men stacking lobster pots for a minute said nothing, then, 'no beach at Royston all factory buildings now. It's a crying shame. Water is reclaimed. Now land for buildings. Reminds me of the hot water quarry at the gas works. Great place for a swim used to go in bare buff. Never had a cossi. Naw too poor. All us laddies so poor. But yer ma knew when you went in there for a dook. Yer ma not daft. She knew all right. Nothing got past her heard and seen it all before. No doubt about it.'

'How was that Jakie? How did she know she a mind reader?'

'Naw, saw how clean you were when you came in for your tea. She would say... 'you've been in that quarry again!' Then give a right good wallop when pulling your shirt out from your trousers could see the weals on your belly.'

'Weals on your belly? What weals? How come you got weals on your stomach?'

'Gas Frankie. Hot water coming from the gas works into the pond. Waste water the norm and maybe waste gas? The steam, my, like being in the jungle. Kept hoping Tarzan would appear from the trees but he never did.'

'The fishermen on the boats got ice from the ice works along there.Remember when was small. Played there quite a lot. Trawlers in the harbour got tons of the stuff.'

'Aye, but no more the works are just a memory. No more like the lemonade works. Aye, happy days right enough. Not even a boat and no harbour all gone.'

Frank sat up and moved a little to ease his back and shook his shoulders. 'Someone strolled over my grave,' he said leaning backwards opened and shut his eyes in succession. The blue sky made him blink. He closed his eyes and was seeing white stars in a black background. He sat up and rubbed them a few minutes his sight was back to normal, 'horrible feeling that,' he said, 'thought was going blind.'

Nearby couples sitting dangling their feet holding hands, tight, in case they had a mishap and went for an involuntary dook. Bairns running around with nets on poles and coloured buckets giving their parents concern in case they toppled into the water and went in for a dook.

Dangerous place to be playing their games the many children unsupervised. And no chance they would be able to scoop up sprats with their little nets. These things are suitable for playing on the sand at the beach. Buckets and spades at the ready to explore the rock pools but no good for catching anything from the slipway where the water is a dangerous place for children to be near. Plenty little ones but not enough adults to supervise the boisterous ones.

He watched in silence at the boats making ready in the harbour. Men working the nets and stashing ropes. Lobster pots being made ship shape for the coming lobster hunt. Watched the seagulls diving after the sprats. Heard the children screaming with delight. Was a happy scene. All in all one of calm. Families were enjoying the day unaware of the turmoil he was going through. And the short episode he was remembering. Happy childhood days. But not now. Has to get back to the present and the future. The worrying part is still to come.

'McDougall is looking for you. Take it you gave the coppers everything they wanted, did you? Nothing forgot you would tell me ay.' Got onto why he was there. Happy memories all well and good but now it was the nitty gritty time.

'Am no as daft as they think. Am daft the right way look after me numero uno. What you say that thing, ick, you know what a mean. Always number one. No daft. Daft the right way son,' he drained the beer and threw the empty tin into the water'That's it nothing left. See if you had said could've had more, that's the rub could have should have you ken brought more.'

The small circle rainbow colours remaining below separated then came together again circling the beer can.

They sat a few minutes longer in silence taking notice of what was going on around them. The sun warm. The sound of the seabirds and the children making for a nice comforting feeling and giving him just a teeny bit of respite from his worries but knew his demons were a long long way from being resolved.

'Yeah, yeah but what did really happen? Are you sober enough to recall the incident?' He brings the conversation back after the lull. Needs to get more information. Needs to be told as it really happened. Jakie is shrewd, a drunk but he knows the time of day that's for sure. Sure, Frank knows, it's a given.

200

'Aye, never let that scab Rooney know all the story. Didn't suss there was another man in the car but all saying. Ready to rise but Frank got hold of his arm and held him still. Jakie looked at him and was surprised at the move he made.

'You sure? Thought you said just two men?' Was taken aback by what he said.

'Aye, two g,s,o men and another in the back of the motor giving commands *achtung al is fertig heil Hitler*,' saying it out loud. He got loose from Franks grip and stood up raised his right arm shouting out so all who were near could hear.The people stopped what they were doing to look at the strange man. The small boys and girls ran around in circles laughing and goose marching copying his antics and screaming in high pitched voices.

'For goodness sake Jakie what you playing at?'

Hustling him away from prying eyes and apologising. Telling people how sorry he was for his friend acting strangely. They were going and there was nothing to fear.

When they reached the junction of the slipway at the road end the young rookie copper approached them.

'Just a minute you two. It's been reported to me you have been causing alarm back there on the slipway,' tried saying with authority if he had a deep voice it would have sounded with some authority but unfortunately had a rather weak sounding voice. A voice that lacked authority and Frank thought the guy is in the wrong job and he couldn't see him lasting for long.

'Sorry constable. A wee bit too much liquid lunch. The hot sun you know it's made him a wee bit tipsy. I'll see him home. I will make sure he's all right.'

Ready to calm the situation was relying on the copper to accept the excuse maybe the fine weather would mellow his attitude knowing him from past occasions was a pushover a timid specimen of a man. Always on the lookout for McDougall so he could escape out of the sergeants way.

'Are you taking the wee wee?' said it as if he thought Frank thought he had come up the Forth in a banana boat, 'This old soak might have had too much of the sun but if you think gonna believe he's no pissed and causing a nuisance you better think again. Not good form to be upsetting the locals.'

'Okay constable. Got me banged to rights as the saying goes.'
He's giving him the friendliest of smiles.

'You're the guy the brother of the guy who was… Fished…'

Jakie interrupted him, 'yeah,' saying and slurring the words,
'I'm the guy that telt the guy that I was the guy who gave the guy
a big black eye,' then swinging a fresh air punch and would have
fallen in a heap if Frank hadn't got hold of his collar. 'Say it go
on say it. The Leith police dismisseth us. The Leith police
dismisseth us. If you canny say it it's you who's drunk no me.'
Then he started to sing, '*was up for being drunk in the high street
one night when a woke in the morning a got such a fright.*'

'That's enough Jakie it's not funny.'

'*In and oot the windie in and oot the windie in and oot the
windie shouted tig your het.* Aye the Auld yin's are the best
Frankie son the best. Lunatics asylum you know it, *the lunatic
asylum I did go in and oot the windie.*

'Keep a hold of him or will get assistance to lock him up,'
rookie eyeing the spectators who gathered nebbing to see just
what the situation was.

A little girl four or five years of age her arms wrapped round
her father's left leg looked up at the rookie and stuck her tongue
out followed by a big smile showing the middle gap in her teeth.

'Mind taking your child away from here sir not nice the child
witnessing such behaviour. And the rest get on your way nothing
to see here. All taken care off.'

'Yeah, that's me constable,' looked down giving the little girl
a smile, 'was just thanking him for the help he gave the police
should not have given him a tin of beer not knowing how much
he had supped before. Let me take him away. Will see he causes
no more bother.'

'A told you son,' said Jakie, 'sounds like he who was in the
back of the motor honest,' he whispered, thinking was out of
hearing of the constable.

'Okay, get him away from here. Families came here today to
take advantage of the fine weather not to see the likes of him,' he
said pointing and directing them to get going away from the pier
same time shooing away the spectators who were reluctant to be
moved. Frank took the opportunity to skidaddle while the copper
was busy dealing with the busybodies. Listening to Jakie he was

surprised how he appeared to be worse the way he was rambling and talking nonsense. He decided the nearest place to sit him down and get coffee to sober him was Bettys café.

'Too busy to put up with him can you no see how am run of my feet with the people wanting served at once,' said Betty when she stopped them going into the café. Staring at the drunk, 'my my the state of him. Where did you find him? Or did you get him into that state? It wouldn't surprise me one bit Frank Butler not one bit!'

'Have to have somewhere to sit him down so I can make sense of what he is trying to say to me. He's got more to his story Betty. He's holding more information than he's letting on,' he pleaded, 'got to get him to talk.'

'Well somewhere else cause there is no room here. You can see how busy we are,' she said moving them away from the open entrance to the café.

'There was me thinking you would understand. How wrong no chance.'

'No room at the inn there's no room at the inn, Frankie. Can we no go to Maggie Shaw?' Slurring his words swaying on his feet making it awkward to control him.

'You'll need to take him elsewhere. Look at him.' Her arms clasped across her middle, angrily, take him away from here don't want him upsetting my customers.'

Walking up the Whale Brae holding on to him tight as he stumbled about as if on a small boat in a swell two sheets to the wind as they say when it appears someone has had a jolly good drinking session.

'Am sin die wi misses Mary don't think she would take kindly to me having you fetching up on her doorstep Jakie do you?'

Held his arm, 'walk right walk straight. You can't fall in the street people are looking. Sober up for goodness sake play the game and get a grip. How you ended up in this state you were all right at the pier.'

'The pub Frankie go to the pub. Are we going to the pub any one will do a could go a swally,' slurring his words all the more.

Desperate to get him settled thinking where he could take him to get more information out of him.

'We are going to mine,' decided after much thought, 'try and pull yourself together walk straight your going back when you should be steering straight ahead.'

'The wrong way Frankie Main Street not up the brae'

A hopeless task twenty four hours trying to make sense all he got was nonsense. Short bouts of sleep the demand for whisky made for a long tiresome time and havering not a night to be repeated. 'I give up if you think stalling you have found yourself a safe billet think again. Waffle all you like but you'll have to make tracks out of here. Places to be so get going if you can recall anymore get in touch but get your face out of here now. This minute had enough of you go!'

'Right Frankie boy. Thanks for your gracious hospitality can you not see a way couple oh shillings will do it.'

'No no not giving you any money. So you can get out of here.'

'Right son out yer hair now. Going going gone that's me know when am no wanted.' He left, straight and stiff sounding out chorus of feeble coughs. 'No trouble you any longer. Ken when no wanted but nice to know who your friends are and mind pay you back when can, wont forget.'

'Aye Jakie, remember. You think of something with more clarity look me up.

By the way you remember the other day you recall being in Stockbridge getting hassle outside a pub? There in the street. You must remember there were quite a lot of people nebbing. You remember?'

'Naw, not me. Never been in Stokeree for a long since.'

'Your positive you were not there not just saying?'

'A said it was not me honest wasn't there.'

'If you had been there would you tell me if you saw a nice big black German car. A Mercedes black with tinted windows?'

He thought he could trick him into remembering seeing how he disliked anything German. All he got in return was a grunt and the front door slamming shut.

The information was sparse. Trying to find fact from fiction would have tried the patience of a saint but without a doubt there was definitely a third person in the car who was dishing out the orders. The two in suits were German he was positive about it but the third man he said was Scottish. Was positive he was local but he did not see into the car and was clueless to the identity. A reference to g.s.o. men he insisted repeating were the underdogs German service orderlies, who done the bidding of others the undermench, according to Jakie who professed to know about such things from his army days serving overseas in Europe.

'Oh well upwards and onwards. A little help is better than none at all,' he muttered opening another whisky bottle.

The next afternoon Mary was back. 'I've come to tell you McDougall is looking for Jakie' about the fracas at the harbour. Honest, why can't you leave him alone. What has got into you, hounding him like that?'

'What fracas, what you on about?' Bloody place nothing gets past her. His brain was in overdrive might have known she would get the lowdown from someone.

'You and him at the pier.'

'Yeah we were.'

'Upsetting Betty not to mention the bairns on the slipway.'

'Not Betty no way upset her. Jakie thought it a good idea to put a show on that was all. Who gives you this rubbish?' Nothing but duff information.'

'Worse news. You could be in more bother. The quine, Nettie Nestles found raped and head, goodness, head cut off.. Her pal left her in Commercial Street. She was found corner Constitution Street. Another dead. Poor quine! Police all over Micks place. You were seen speaking with her in Micks. He has kept your name out of it for now. Be wise stay out the way. Will sure be on the hunt for you sometime soon I bet. Something sure to be said, guaranteed aye.'

'Cops! Had to be but now not as we thought not cops? Mick got it wrong. Certainly I spoke with the girls that's true.'

THIRTY THREE

The military band coming to the end of the concert. The sun is going down and the people are gradually leaving in little groups. Was trying to fix the music of the Blue Danube in his head. A drib drab sequence of lights going on in the houses round the park a light here one there another one here one there.

'You left it to the last moment Tony clearing up now.' The ice cream lady in the ice cream van said, 'the last ninety nine of the day saved for my favourite bambino,'presented him with the over filled cone and the chocolate bar standing proud in the middle of the ice cream.

'Thank you, a diamond, Landa.' Reaching he took the ice cream from her outstretched hand, 'you make my life so happy what would I do without you?'

'But not happy with you. He's waiting. Know where.'
She pulled the glass partition secured the bits and pieces round the shelf in preparation for driving out the park. Turning to look lifted her hands to her mouth and mouthed the silent words, 'be careful love you.'

'Let's get away from this area don't like being so near the conveniences could be talk,' said Rutherford, 'and you are late where the hell you been hung round here too long. I thought you were not going to show was ready to leave.'

The park the usual meeting place where they melt in with the crowds. Two gentlemen a park bench reading their newspapers doesn't attract anything out of the ordinary. Tony agreed to the park as the meeting place convinced Rutherford it was necessary. Coincidentally a short distance to his usual den of undesirables the Blue Star public house.

'Someone has croaked the mole we had planted in the club. Burke has got away with it again. No bloody witnesses was out of town again. Burke is no fool he's a real slippery b……

The prostitute I told you about found with her throat done in the same manner. Said she was a possible contender to be added to Burke's list is now confirmed. What to do with this diamond caper is anyone's guess. We will never find out that's for sure.'

'So that makes four?'

'No, makes five. One in Germany one in Holland now three in London.'

'Your Mole?'

'Yes, same as.'

'And not forgetting two in Scotland now makes seven. I guess a lot more before we get a handle on it.'

'Yeah. Could be. Lots don't know about should have pulled him out of the joint earlier would still be here.'

'Hindsight a great thing. How were you to know can't blame yourself there is no future in it.'

'Got kids too Imagine dying with your head nearly severed what a way to go?' Shook his head silent a couple of minutes remembering.

'Snap out of it do no good dwelling on it.'

Walking past a waste basket stopped and chucked the last remnant of the ice cream cone. Disgusted felt the anger swelling in his breast, 'think it's unlucky to be counting the dead. Time you suckers got a grip on the situation,' turned from the basket got in the way of a girl on a bicycle. 'Watch out you old age nutter!' Screamed, 'nearly had me on the ground you old goat'

'Not my fault you silly girl!'

She shouted again with the usual teenager speak they know how best to communicate as she came to a sudden jolt. Stared for a moment stood legs each side of the bicycle. Lifted one leg over. Hands on the handlebars pushed walking ranting about perverts. Looking over her shoulder saying how they shouldn't be in the park in the first place.

'Typical,' he said as he watched her cycling away saying something about old goats.

'You nearly bowled her over should look what you're doing. Keep your mind on the present. We've two jack the rippers on the loose again and you know what the outcome of that episode achieved Zilch!'

'You sure made a suck up of that the world knows that too well and the last heard of the hit men is they moved into Jock land. My friends friend lost his brother and his girlfriend because of them. Are you really convinced Burke is using German hit men and if not who?'

Brushed himself down after the confrontation with the screaming teenager, 'got ice cream anywhere on me?' Wiping himself down having a long look at his shoes going on about his near miss with the girl.

Rutherford watched him going through the routine said, 'convinced Burke's mother is behind it in this country. I've found out the German girl who died in Scotland is the daughter of a German gangster who just happens to be the husband of mother Burke's Irish niece. The girl spared the knife for some reason wonder why and no don't see any ice cream. Please this is serious. Ice cream? Cmon can't be seen here talking to you got to be going,' he walked and left him fussing over his clothes and his shoes, 'no time for this nonsense,' he said.

'Wait a minute. You're saying the girl was not done getting her throat cut she was done clean,' trying to get his head round what he was being told. 'Seriously taking it very serious indeed.'

'You're spot on these Germans are going round in pairs. Getting rid of anyone who comes into contact with anything to do with the diamond trail. We've now got knife fanatics on our f...... hands.'

'You mean anyone who contacts the dealers are done away with so the trail is cleansed? It doesn't make sense why kill the dealers?'

'Beats me. No such thing as a mouse in a house or one queer in the you know where. Always more and bent dealers are ten a penny easy to replace.'

' You got a real headache on your hands. Not care about the scum who are being eliminated but not like that poor cop who was sliced. Do you have any idea about the leak?'

'Yes, fool was having it away with a female copper. One I've known for a long time. One who just happened to accompany me to the Burke's mansion in Kent. Should have observed the rules of no fraternising. The Burke matriarch spotted them when she was on her round of the dealers. Her driver who drew her attention to our man. Mother Burke remembered the girl. We have her, Sissy, squirrelled away in a safe house for her protection. Why the pair happened to enter a café used by

Angelica Burke is one in a million chance. Beats me why they took that particular night for a liaison? Fate suppose.'

'That's the mystery for sure.'

Walked to the exit gates stopped outside taking notice of the heavy traffic before crossing the road.

'Time for a quick one?'

'Are you kidding me can't sully my reputation being seen in your company. Heavens above. People would talk can't take the chance no thank you.'

'Ha ha ha very funny, ha ha, see you.'

'Before you go,' catching hold of his arm. 'The mother of the girl who died in Scotland not her real mother her stepmother. Remember the story of Cinderella and the uglies? Well fast forward to modern day come to light there is bad feeling. If the father dies his money and assets go only to his girl not the uglies. The mother was desperate to get rid of her seems she wanted to spare her husband from the gory was achieved clean. With a needle. Our mole got information in the club before he was done overheard the conversation by two of Burke's henchmen. A sort of compassionate interval when the wine was flowing thought a plot was imminent.'

'Division in the camp nothing new,' said Tony, 'maybe a takeover.'

'Yes but not Burke. Angelica Burke pulling the strings.'

'Ciao. Keep in touch pal... Angelica Burke?... Well well.'

'How they hanging Tony?' Tracy asked clearing the clutter over-doing a bar wipe and making much of it 'punters what a bloody mess they leave. Pigs. wouldn't want to see how they live. Filthy pigs see how it is filthy beggars.'

'Fine Tracy fine. Hanging how they should.' When he put on the act he knew was building up to something. Taking time to get round to whatever he wanted to say by fussing. 'Stop acting like an old woman. Get my drink. If you have something to say well bloody get on with it.'

Busy bar noisy making it hard to hear the banter. The music from the box in the corner helped him make up his mind to get a drink finish up and get out the place.

'Well how was it, good? Was worth the while was it dream my dream boy?'

'Now now Tracy you know not to ask gentlemen do not kiss and tell.'

'You looked soo cosy together,' he said, 'still not sure what she was, it or was it? She followed you out. Well well old Tony has struck it rich right enough.' Stood with his arms clasped across his chest and giving himself a little hug whilst sporting a huge grin on his face.

'No Tracy. You got it wrong. She did not leave after me she left before me was still sitting over there at that table when she left,' pointing to the table in the corner saw the expression on his face change to one of astonishment.

'I thought I could have sworn the pretty little blonde followed you out,'

'No Tracy. The doll was with was a brunette not blonde. She left before me. Maybe you were busy with other things got confused so come on for goodness sake stop the crap get the bottle no time for this tonight. Make it single malt.'

Thought be rude and he would go away and bother someone else.

'Okay take what you say but sure the tart followed you out and thought you had made a conquest that's it. Was sitting over there with a grey haired old dear and I thought, oh great, the boy has got it made. Pity. She left the old girl on her own, lonely all alone sitting there sipping her sweet sherry.'

'A dame with an old dear in tow? Did not see any old dear or a blonde, no, no blonde. You sure it was the same night?'

This is getting ridiculous he was thinking have to get out of here the noise is unbearable. How do they stand it goodness knows how they do it?

'Yes Tony it was definitely the same.'

'The lady I was sitting with wore a head scarf and when she removed it she had auburn not blonde hair getting mixed up darling.'

Now becoming bored with his constant inane questioning.

'No, a yes, remember you are correct. We didn't know if the one who was sitting at the end of the bar was a man or a woman. Yes you joined her at a table I did not see her go. When you left the blonde with her companion sat at a table behind you. You got up to leave she left following you. That's why thought she was with you. I'm sorry Tony. I'm a right fool,' gave himself a little tap on the cheek shook his shoulder, 'silly fool you silly me.'

'No sweat give me a beer then love you and leave you. Sorry to miss the blonde. The way at the moment could have done with some female company,' well end of conversation should be the end of his nonsense he thought. 'Go and give me peace go serve someone else do and annoy some other sad sack,' he muttered thinking Tracy was out of earshot.

'Dear dear punchy tonight. Feeling lonely are we dear. Got the blues baby may if want could arrange something?'

'Not even Tracy the offer take a rain check.'

'Do you know come to think shortly after you left a big bruiser in a chauffeur uniform came in and escorted the old girl out. Maybe he had come from an old folks home. He could have been an attendant collecting her after her day out. The blonde could have been alone? Not with the old woman after all.'

'Yeah, that's maybe the answer. An old dear from an old folks home out for a jolly. Must have been past her bedtime or back not to miss the Bingo.'

'Can't stand here gossiping with you all night Tony, Be seeing to my other customers see you later dear.' He moved to serve a blonde sitting on a stool further down the bar.

'At last,' said Tony. 'Be good see you.'

'They call you Tracy don't they?'

'Yes dear that's me. What can I get you?' He knew instantly she was the one who followed Tony out the bar the one who he thought was with the old lady.

'I'm in danger can't explain it there is someone in here who wants to do me harm please help me.'

He could see she was frightened. Droplets of sweat on her brow the mascara smudged under her eyes. She kept looking around. The white handkerchief she held showed traces of black powder. She was scared her expression like a rabbit caught in the headlights.

Tony was leaving.

'Wait here don't go. Stay I'll be back,' said Tracy.

'Out, must go,' she gathered her purse and lifted her dark shades from the bar, 'it's not safe for me to be here have to get out just go with me take me out.'

'No wait. I'll get my friend to make sure your safe. Just stay till I come back.'

He summoned a barmaid, 'this is Derba she'll look after you.'

He walked up the bar raising his arm. 'Tony Tony love. A minute please wait it's important.'

'Goodness me. Is there no getting away from this,' he muttered was only two steps from the exit when he was collared.

'The blonde one at the end of the bar she's the one who followed you.'

'You sure? Positive?'

'She is frightened for her life. She thinks someone here wants to harm her. Do you think you can help? Please do something and get her out of here.'

Tony clocked the barmaid holding the woman's wrists and it looked like the blonde was trying to escape but the barmaid was holding on tight.

'There's a vacant table out of the way over there by the corner get her there. I'll see what the fuss is about. I'm curios to know why she was following me and, try to be discreet there's too many nosey people here. Do it discreetly. Don't want any of your punters getting involved.'

Let her go Derba,' said Tracy when he saw the marks on the woman's wrists. 'Watch I said. Watch not use force these marks are like cuff marks what are you trying to do to her?' He pushed her aside. 'Others needing served go. He thought of giving her a slap but abandoned the idea thinking if he give her a backhander she was quite capable of hitting back so better not try it not in front of the customers.

The barmaid pleaded to stay.

He saw the hate in her eyes as she looked at the woman and mouthed something.

He didn't catch what was said. The blonde got it and was frightened more than ever.

She was rubbing her wrists and checking the scratches.

Tony caught hold of her as she fell against him.

'Please help me got to get away from here,' she whispered.

He saw how frightened she was the look on her face was an indication, he guessed, hadn't had a proper sleep for a long time.

'Sit over here,' said, helping her to the table. 'Tracy wants me to assist. Tell me what's bothering you. You are safe now. Don't worry. You'll be alright.'

Tracy came to the table with a cup of tea 'Drink this dear it will do you good.'

'Can we go upstairs?'

'Sorry, no, it can't be. Upstairs is occupied at the moment sorry.'

'Where do you advise?'

'You're asking me? Tony dear you know more about this kind of thing you must have somewhere up the east end where you can take her.'

'You come with me miss guarantee you'll be safe.'

'Go with him dear you will be in safe hands.'

'Yes. I'll go. Anywhere, please get me away from here. I'm in danger here quick let's leave.'

Looking round couldn't understand why she was so afraid. The people in the bar were the usual. He knew them and none there were a threat. Except he was not sure of the butch barmaid who was determined to keep the girl from leaving.

Within minutes, 'I've got a cab. It won't be long till you're safe believe me dear.' Tracy said, helping Tony to more or less carry her to the waiting taxi.

Tony managed her into the taxi. She was sobbing. Fingers twisting round her wrists and rocking back and forth on the seat.

'Not long now not long till get you safe.'.

Tracy watched the cab leave. Soft drizzle falling from the starless sky. Hunched shivered and rubbed his hands together shrugging as he walked slowly to the entrance and suddenly saw a shape appearing from the shadows. Burke he thought. Watched him cross the street to a waiting car a white Rolls Royce. Could be but wasn't positive hesitated looked and saw the car leave shook his head coincidence he thought. He walked and closed the door quietly. Approached the barmaid, 'what you think you were doing carrying on like that?' Saw the hate in her eyes. She smiled. He thought more of a sneer pushed past without speaking but still smiling.

'That's it you're finished get your things and leave. You are out of here do not wish to have you here anymore!'

'Going anyway. Made my mind no need for you to say it!'

'You phoned the Irishman?'

'What what you say Irishman?'

'Yes. Don't stand there lying to me you phoned earlier didn't you. You told him she was here.'

'No.'

'The Mother? That's it you phoned Angelica.'

She shook her head in defiance, 'you're playing with fire,' sneering and showing hate in her eyes she pulled away from him. 'I'm giving warning. The Burke's will not tolerate the way you have used me. They will demand and will get their dues you can be sure on that score. I've gave giving you fair warning!'

Watched her leave. Hurriedly pushing past people in her way.

'Think she came out best in that encounter,' murmuring as he walked up the bar and lifted the phone.

'Bunty dear. This excuse for a barmaid, Debra… yes the Irish one. She in cahoots you know' Looked round cupped hand over the speak part of the phone, yes, Burke. Good you got it for definite. The Mother? As well, oh dear. How come we not got the handle on that information. You did not do sufficient take on the background. No dear not blaming you just a shock that's all. Had to get rid. Someone round to her place keep an eye. No dear do it. Seen Burke here outside. Find out if he turns up at her place. Burke dear be wary. Less he knows the better. I'll explain later dear. Yes get on to it love you. Bye.'

THIRTY FOUR

12.40 am. Rutherford knocking on his door.

Not happy with the intrusion Tony struggled to get out of the bed. Goodness sake you nearly had the door on the floor did you have to knock so hard what's the time just got off to sleep what do you want come in. Excuse the mess the cleaner is on strike,' dragged on his dressing gown sleepily rubbed his face ruffled his hair. Yawned and farted apologised for his stomach.

'Wake you did I? Did not think you would be asleep,'

'What's so important this time,' stretching and yawning. 'You no bed to go to better have a good reason.'

'This place is a tip enough clothes lying about here you could have a jumble sale it's time you shelled out for a cleaner.'

'Just make space on the chair get yourself a drink and sit down and say why you are here?'

A long look round the room to see where he could sit, 'what time was it you got back,' before he got the answer, said, 'how can you live like this?'

'Easy. You should try it sometime. Don't worry. I'll get round to it eventually. But why are you checking on me have to stop meeting like this my neighbours will talk. Wondering why I've a visitor at this god forsaken hour.'

He poured two glasses of whisky from a decanter.

'Sit down and drink tell me your problem, why, if you can't sleep why the hell are you here?'

'You had words with Bryony Walters earlier this evening?'

'Yeah, correct was worried Burke was out to do her harm.'

'And you didn't think to tell me?'

'No didn't think. Didn't think it would interest you at this time. To get more from her that's why smart arse! Arranged to see her this afternoon.'

'Did you know she was one of Burke's girls?'

'She told me last night but was not up to telling me much because the problems she had couldn't make much sense out of her didn't want to push her anymore got her holed up in a room in a joint up east. Got her out of Tracy's place was in a sorry state believe me.'

'Not any more you haven't was found in bed. Looks like an overdose.'

'You think Burke is responsible?'

'Well, it was you who was with her you tell me. She must have gave you something. Why was she running and how she get the marks on her wrists, before you saw her or did you not see any marks?'

'I've said she was in no condition to spill was going to go easy going to let you know when got her story straight. You would be the first to get the full story when she was compose mental, oh, you know what I'm getting at. The marks, before.'

'Nothing doing now. We will never get to the bottom of it. Look like Burke going to get away with it, again. Off the bloody hook again!'

'Has she topped herself?'

'Not at this time no witnesses no one in the flea pit you dumped her in saying anything. Nothing unusual there know what it's like.'

He downed his drink waved his hand 'this place see why you never brought her here should be ashamed living in squalor.'

'Not that bad get to it eventually, Important clues anything unusual, no, don't think so. Stop criticising. You are useless you know that Rutherford? Here another drink. No clues expected and if had brought her here she would still be alive that's in hindsight. Now don't remind me!' Was on the attack. Watched him sit mouth open ready to speak shake of the head sat back in the chair outburst took him off guard reached for the whisky.

'It's too early. We will have to wait for the report. Really nothing to go on give me time and hopefully something will turn up. You know by now what the situation is you know how it goes. Bits of the puzzle soon fit hopefully.'

'Hopefully,' he repeated. 'Hopefully? Give me strength,' he poured more whisky and gulped it down. 'Why the hell do you come out with all these excuses when are you going to do something positive?'

'What do you want me to say you're no help and not forget spent more time. If you had arranged to meet me straight away this might not have happened. But yes hindsight know all about it to my shame.'

'Don't turn the fault on me. Told you what the situation was. How was I to know how fast they would get to her.'

'We don't know if that is a fact but someone might throw some light when talk to the you know the one in your drinking den. Someone there knows something hope to find out as soon as possible mark my words.'

Uncomfortable in the chair lifted a handful of clothes from behind and chucked them onto the floor and shaking his head, 'disgusting, disgusting' he says squirming.

'You mean Tracy? Tracy the... funny... Can't you give him his....You know.'

'Okay if it pleases you Tracy that's the one.'

'When you see him ask about the old grey haired lady who was there on a jolly. You'll find it was, Angelica Burke, I'd bet my life on it.'

'When were you gonna lay that on me? You knew the old bag frequented the place and only now you tell me what were you thinking?'

'When you tell me how you knew?'

'A sure tip off. An anonymous phone call. The night hawk confirmed you registered the dame after nine and left nearer ten. He was a bit vague about the exact time.The phone message was after eleven. No one else seen in the place after you left according to the night hawk.'

'How was it done drugs or something more sinister?'

'If you knew how much had to stop my boss from coming here to arrest you was practically on my knees begging to let me handle it. He wanted you to tell why she needed to die. The reason, why she died? He's got you on suspicion. Lucky for you succeeded. So you can give me some more of your treasured malt. Have you anything to add not keeping things to yourself, are you?'

'Help yourself. Are you going to give me the lowdown was it drugs?'

'An empty bottle of sleeping pills. That's it at the moment all am saying. Going now and thanks for the drink. See you friend take care. Bye.'

'My my, aren't we the early bird, was it worth it?'

'Morning Tracy give me my usual beer.' The early morning tipplers were minding their own. Like zombies staring into space if any had the audacity to open up a grunt would be all that would be forthcoming. Was well aware of the situation here in this place. Morning through evening and late night nothing changed.

'I've come to see your Irish girl,' glanced around. 'Don't see her what time is she expected or is she on duty up stairs earning early no doubt.'

'You mean Derba. Not here anymore sent packing. Gave her the marching order after you left last night. Couldn't have customers serving me with lawyers. What she done to that poor girls wrists, wow! Couldn't let that go.'

'That's all I need. Where can I find her if not up,' raised his head eyes fixed on the ceiling above.

'Should have known she would be trouble. Paul the post was in earlier and the discussion was about what happened last night. Knew her for some time said she was on the game and surprised when he saw her working here. Thought she turned straight and anyway it was none of his business what she was up to.

'Yes Tracy, everyone knew she was on the game. All well and good but were can I find her you employed her cause she's on the game you're no innocent bystander.'

'You can't dear boy. What's the time and ignore what you said,' looked at the clock on the wall. 'It's ten after ten sent Bunty you know my husband, Bunty. Sent him round to her slum with money. Her weeks pay wanted her gone not wanting her showing up here again no way going to put up with her.'

'I need her.'

'You do like a hole in the head you need her.'

'Yes, but her address. Are you giving it me or what and while your at it a whisky. And information fast.'

'Oh you won't find her there at that address. Bunty phoned at nine thirty said she was not at the address any more. The old hag who ran the place was furious she left owing a months rent.'

'Just my luck. What else did postman Paul have to say he let on who she worked for. You know who her pimp is any idea was it Burke?'

'No.' Tracy said, 'No idea but wait a minute. The blonde did you know the blonde was Irish? Paul did say he knew the girl was another one on the game a feeling the two knew each other. The name Burke he did say and I thought I saw him after you and the girl left not certain not sure if it was him.'

'You think you saw Burke but you're not sure! Bet that is why your barmaid held on to her so tight had something on her must have contacted Burke.'

'Tony you naughty boy you never said if…'

'Yes, the two were Irish. You are changing the subject.'

'Sure knew got it from the slut and did she play up? Wow!'

'What else did your postman tell you?'

'Only the blonde was high class.'

'You mean she was expensive?'

'You bet could have been a film star.'

'She's lost her looks now. Sure we're talking about the same dame. A film star?'

'Well, that's how they end up drugs seen it all before.'

'Was she a favourite of Burke's was he into her?'

'Tony dear thought you knew the situation.'

'What did you think knew what situation get it off you're chest.'

'The word is he is in love with his mother not a nice person. The information in here. Well ask you! Heard things that would curl your hair honestly darling.'

'So you do know of him Burke. Have known all along. Why you kept it secret and now your telling me he's a pervert. Call it like it is. Got to know what up against never set eyes on this guy Burke but would sure like to meet him.'

'Oh for goodness sake Tony. You don't know what you're letting yourself into. Of course know about him. I've got my squealers like you dear. Meet him? No don't advise it. You keep well away dear.'

'Just you remember we are not having this conversation. Understand me get it.'

'You know A1 in my book hope it stays that way no falling out on my part.'

'Yeah and you make sure it stays that way,' drank his whisky put a finger to his lips pointed, 'remember should have put me wide to Burke,' watched the expression on his face. Tracy did not know how to take the threat.

Later approaching the telephone box outside the park gates across the street from the Blue Star spied a teenage girl leaving the booth was glad to see no surprised to see inside had not been vandalised. Muttering, 'three bloody phones entered and all bloody vandalised. What pleasure they get... don't know.'

'Hello is that you Mary? It's me, Tony, speak to him?'

'Yes Tony hold on.'

Almost immediately, 'here, what's new Tony?'

'It's all kicking off more grief than you can shake a stick at. How's it your end this guy you know the guy, Burke, getting away with murder down here.'

'All quite at the moment not showing their hand here not yet. Except what has happened earlier. Like I said. Hope not going to be as bad as it is down in the smoke so you take care down there. The old girl worried about some old man who gave information to the coppers and has now gone walk about.'

'This guy Burke has a lot to answer. By the way the word is his old lady is the one who is in charge you know anything bout her. Who would guess it the old lady.'

'No but the Oldersum dame is expected here soon to make the necessary for the girl. What about Rutherford? Has he got another stooge in Burke's place after the last fiasco? Stupid an experienced copper shouldn't have died.'

'Rutherford? don't get me started. Take care, pips,' replaced the phone on it's cradle. Felt and fished a little black notebook out his overcoat inside pocket. Thumbing through found then dialled a number. Waited letting it ring till he realised Rutherford was not in the police station.

Strolled through the park thinking maybe Rutherford could be there but no so decided to return to the Blue Star to gather more information.

Nothing new. The place is full of the usual clients and after one drink he decided to phone Kaiser from the phone box at the park.

'Another one, says Kaiser the same! A girl this time a pro? Let me tell it straight. He's in a pub...Yeah yeah this Micks place. Seen speaking with one of the girls?. Two coppers who are not coppers? They thought they were police but no not coppers. Real police confirmed it.'

'Your pal,' says Tony 'Let me get it. Your pal leaves after the girls leave. The police who are not police follow your pal. I'm getting this right, yeah? Has he been collard, no. Why? Because the bar keep when quizzed keeps you're pal out of it. The punters when interviewed keep their mouths shut am I right you could read it. Simple plot in a thriller.'

'Yes, that's loyalty for you. I was there followed him was no way he was anywhere near the two girls.'

'Bogus cops has to be.'

'Got it in one. The bar owner Mick was suspicious of them. Why they thought the men were cops in the first place beats me. The local cops any wiser? No. Don't believe the theory of the guys pretending to be coppers and Frank is safe for now,'

'Stranger and stranger,' says, 'how much more is coming. Day after day another and no one got a clue. Strange not the word for it. Why the Scot's not up in arms is beyond me.'

'I'm trying my best with no help whatsoever.'

'Sure you are. Doing more as far as can see doing more than him, don't need to mention his name f...... useless!'

'When we going to see a result your guess got me stumped.'

'The Scottish police not showing any signs?'

'Just as much as the English.'

'That says it all. No bloody good.'

THIRTY FIVE

You have to give me more?' Rutherford said.

Sissy Maitland by his side not happy with the questions.

Police woman Gillian McInnes laid two cups of coffee in front of them then joined them at the table sitting alongside Sissy. She was more interested reading the evening newspaper turned the pages and licking her finger each page slowly as if she was somewhere else not in the least interested in what was taking place between the other two.

'I've said already what I know sarge not left anything out give me credit I want to know what happened to him as much as you do wouldn't be human not to find out.'

Put down the cup of coffee on the table lit a cigarette. 'Why did he leave you alone in the café. What did he say when he got up to go did he look as if something was bothering him? Did he not want you to know what was about to take place?'

'No, said. Nothing out the ordinary. Thought he was going to the little boys room. That's it was just surprised thought he stood me up was as mad as hell when he failed to show honestly don't know what happened.' With eyes pleading she wanted to know when she would get out of there and back to work.

'What going to tell his wife and kids? Daddy went to the toilet got his f...... throat cut! That would have gone down well don't think Sissy. You must have seen something not left anything out are sure? Important to give the full facts you know it. Walker and my chief are reading the riot act.'

'Not again, what you want from me said all. That's it don't know anymore. How was I to know Angelica Burke was going to come in and see me there before I could do anything about it.'

'You know was undercover. Wouldn't surprise me one bit if you did.'

'No, hadn't a clue.'

'Well that's something suppose. But what good did it do why oh why did you go into that particular restaurant? Hundreds to chose and you go into that one.'

'What now can't stay cooked up here go off my rocker having to be dubbed up here. You might just chuck the key away now. I know how game is played rather get back to work better taking my chances out working.'

'You'll be safe here. We'll give you twenty four round the clock protection.'

'If the Burke's want me it won't matter where will succeed wherever here or out there. So get your, oh, detract your finger and get me out of this situation!'

'No will not happen. Your boss is not happy know how he is. The way it has turned out is just an unlucky throw of the dice you know him he won't let it go. Wants an enquiry. Like a hound dog with you know a bone and that's what he is after my f...... bones dear one.'

'Nothing new there then.'

'Be patient get some reading material to keep you busy. You can always play poker with the others time will go quicker than you think. Plenty tv to watch. Should not get bored think it as a break a short holiday.'

'What about your pal Tony? Get me a shift with him. An under cover job would do. I'm sure you can arrange it. Why don't you put it to your boss to get me working.'

'You're a police woman what the hell are you thinking? Undercover? Watching too much cop shows on the tele.'

'Not much of a police woman being stuck here that's what I'm thinking.'

'Will not risk my career on your daft schemes.'

'You don't have to let Walker know.'

'And if he finds out what then?'

The woman cop said nothing. Gave him the look and licked her finger turning the pages of the newspaper slowly same time shaking her head.

'Who cares about walker,' said Sissy with a scheming smile and a wink to the w.p.c.

'No need for you to be catty is your chief,' Rutherford said, trying his best to get her to see sense but she is dragging her heels.

'You can make it happen on the quiet.'

'And my boss,? What about him what do you think he would say? Get your brain settled.'

'Your your own boss aren't you? Keep telling me so say nothing.'

'You can go off people you know. You gonna get it into your thick brain what you propose is unthinkable.'

'For someone with your record… Cheek isn't the word for it.'

'My record who have you been speaking with?'

'Well don't tell your granny to suck whatever it is she sucks if that way inclined.'

'Eggs,' Gillian says, 'your granny sucks eggs. Not my granny though. What saying expect with no teeth everybody's granny will learn to suck eggs.'

'Her talking eggs makes me hungry. Why not take me out for a meal. Won't cost you a dime you can have it on expenses.'

'Nice try. Something will be provided.'

'Worth a try. Anything to get out of this place.'

'Stop scheming.'

'Me? Beggar the thought but you wouldn't want to be held here would you no you wouldn't.'

'This conversation is getting boring the more you open it the more am ready to get out of it.'

'Oh excuse me for boring you.'

'You know what it is don't get me wrong you are not boring me just the conversation is boring me.'

Looking at Gillian,'understand a word of it you think he's taking it to heart too much. Ask you. You think the conversation is as he says, boring?'

'Forget it. Lost track when eggs came into it and now hungry about time someone was ordering some food,' Gillian said.

THIRTY SIX

The walk along the shore road beside Granton harbour brought back memories for Frank. Some good some not so good. On the right of the road from the square the old railway lines where the coal wagons would be raided, coal for nothing word from house to house quicker than you could say, well, you know the saying. The woman the men and children of all ages out on dark nights scrambling over the open tenders loading hand carts and prams. Like ants scurrying here and there could disappear as fast as lightning just as the lookouts gave the word to scatter. Geordie, the old sop of a cop whose beat covered the harbour and the shore road would be spotted coming from the gatehouse at the harbour entrance was said he knew what was going on and was in cahoots making sure he got his ration. And not to be forgotten the many raids on the potato wagons and the whisky wagons who knows the surprise seeing goodies stored inside, always someone who had a knack of undoing the locks on the sliding doors of each wagon. There was also the time when a coal tender overturned at the dock entrance and a guard got trapped and killed no looters that time they did show a bit of sympathy.

Further on to the right of the road the spare ground once the slipway were he learned the craft of scraping the rust from the bottoms of old barges painting them with red lead paint no such thing as health and safety in those days.

On the left of the road the lighthouse workshops the sheet metal company where a childhood friend was an apprentice finished his time and emigrated to Australia never to be heard of again. Old military Nissan billets taken over by the fish processing company now deserted and derelict. Across the way from the Nissan huts we have the sorry sight of another derelict building the office's of Greene and Greene the paint peeling from the walls like a snake shedding it's skin.

225

It was time for his showdown was not looking forward to the experience he knew what the outcome would be before the event and was ready.

'Don't sit down not be here long not a pleasing thing to say.'

She turned her head looked at Patrick who sat alongside her.

Her opening remarks reminded him of standing in front of the headmaster waiting for the punishment to be administered. Oh dear, she's giving him the chance to spout his worst he thought and what will this idiot come up with rubbish suppose.

Patrick said nothing looked over at night and day who was sitting on an old worn out sofa stuck out the way in the corner of the room who also said nothing but shrugged opened the palms of his outstretched hands and grunted got up retreated to the back room mumbling.

Frank eased the weight from his left foot to his right foot waiting, the silence overbearing looked round, up at the ceiling, over at the worn out sofa, better place to be better things to be doing why can't she get on with it.

She looked and smiled.

He thought where have seen similar scenes she's coming over like an old movie, a snake, Queen cobra getting ready to strike. Her piercing eyes giving him the creeps will have to be on his guard stick it out and will soon be over.

'You know you have cost this company a lot of money don't you?' Smile slowly changing to a frown wrinkles increasing the road map on her face Chin sticking out like the one on the wicked witch he remembered in another old movie.

His turn to shrug was about to speak when she said…'Closing down production not only lost us money you lost us further contracts with that bloody agency. The money they have lost is astronomical and all down to your actions.'

'Can I speak?' Lifted his arms in anticipation.

She sat back raising her arms huge scowl on her coupon not happy with his intervention seething but allowing him to carry on. Smiled, rather more of a sneer, nodded.

Patrick objected. 'No you are hear to listen,' he squeaked like an injured rat.

'The oil company rep agreed with me,' ignoring Patrick, 'mill ran out of dope. No use without the coal tar. Course you knew that full well. Watched and caught them red handed recycling rubbish from the floor that was not on. You are forgetting it was my responsibility to make sure everything was done by the book. Not my fault it took them two days to get their supply. Plain to me you are looking for a scapegoat which is fine by me. You don't have to sack me I resign as from this minute. Shove it more on my plate to worry about. And what you know about or are… I give up. I'm out of it,' turned to leave saw Night and Day standing listening behind the half closed door wondering am I in trouble, have I blown it?

'Not only that.' Patrick said.

Frank looked at him, 'fuck me,' he muttered. Was if Patrick hadn't listened to a word that had been said. His face was as red as a beetroot Frank could see it was about to burst. Like the needle on his boiler was on the red ready to explode. Stand by for his brain to explode any minute now he wished. Turned saw the door closed gave a sigh 'thanks for that,' he murmured who knows what Night and Day had been thinking?

'Your brother lost us a lucrative contract with the English council,' said Patrick, 'a paint job on the bridge undone because he never showed. Never appeared hadn't the guts to phone to keep us right. Workers waiting every day not doing any work whatsoever because there was no inspector on site. It took the council two weeks to find out what happened.'

'Cancelled contracts caused by you and your brother,' Mary said. 'You've heard of the domino effect? Well it's happened. Another three councils in England have cancelled. How many more and now the word is out we could be facing bankruptcy. Thank you very much for that.'

He thought she was going to start the waterworks was famous like the weather going from one extreme to the other whenever the mood took her.

'I'm not responsible for what my brother did or didn't do you were responsible for his actions not me. I know I was perfectly in my right to halt what was going on in the mill. The right thing and the company rep was one hundred percent behind me.' His reply he knew would infuriate Patrick he waited to see if the steam was going to erupt from the top of his head.

227

'This is not a good way to treat us after what we have done for the two of you. I'm afraid you're days are over,' she said, 'there will be no more work coming from this office. Once the word is out you will find it hard to get any employment. We will make sure of it mark my words you'll rue the day.'

'Mary give it a rest,' Night and Day returned and entered the fray, 'give the lad a break about to put his brother into the ground heard enough of your crap staying ben the hoose till the pair of you calm doon,' placed a reassuring hand on Franks back as he walked past.

Patrick screwed his face and looked at her waiting to see how she was going to respond to the interruption by their gadgie.

She nodded and waved her hand giving him the opportunity to speak.

Frank stayed silent.

Patrick waited till Night and Day was out the room then said, 'You can depend on it no more handouts from us. Get going you know where the door is we are glad to see the back of you.'

'Wait,' Mary said, 'what makes you think we had a hand in what happened to your brother what have you heard who have you been talking with? Let's have it who?'

'Why are you bringing my brother into this conversation forgot his name already have you got a lapse of memory have you?'

'We heard you were asking questions about us regarding your brother,' she snarled and turned to look at Patrick who sat with a sneer so big Frank held back from putting him on the floor and not caring the consequences witness or no witness!

'No. A police matter. I'm sure if you were under suspicion they would have been on to you don't you think or you hiding information? Not like to think so.'

'The police, no. Not spoken to us.'

'Have you inclination of who or suspicion of what happened you would say after all in spite of everything.'

'No not a clue. Now you can leave. Get out go and if we hear you are spreading rumours, well, you do not need me to spell it out do you.'

'Take it this is some kind of threat you are issuing?'

'Read it as you like.'

228

'You are wasting your time if you think will take any notice of your threats.'

'You are not telling me you… Are you threatening me?'

'Did I threaten can't remember doing that?'

'Get out of my sight. Don't come here with your threats get out now!'.

He stood outside for a moment on the top stair hearing them screaming at each other. 'Good. Can get stuffed,' muttering to himself. Heard Mary say she was going to kill him. Patrick egging her to do it. She said she would be better with a cat for company better than having him on her coat tails.

Entered the Tip the public house at Granton Square.

'You knew about Jamie when we met at the docks why did you not put me wise?' Frank put her drink, Moscow mule, in front of her and saw the expression of guilt on her face.

'Thought you already got the information. Mary Mckenzie I assumed would have been in touch with Captain McPherson. That is why I met at the docks.'

'You were there to meet me you knew was on my way?'

'Yes. How otherwise would be there waiting. Mary said.'

'Would have been better you had told me. Found out at Mary's place was a terrible shock.'

'If had said we wouldn't have enjoyed the evening got to give me that.'

'True. That's very true. Enjoyable no was better than that.'

'How sad. Your poor brother and of course the girl.'

'We won't dwell on it drink up let's go.'

'Thanks for the drink but no.'

'Why you tell me, no?'

'Got to stay. Work to do money to make.'

'Not the rumours?'

'Rumours what rumours?'

'Talk not fit to be seen with these rumours, bye,' up and storms out she's lucky not nice to be near when the devil is in him.

THIRTY SEVEN

Frank made his way to Berts. The hands on the clock on the wall showed 7pm.

The gang were there. The public house a home from home for the pipe men of Leith. Any day, any time, pipe men would be in there drinking. Depending on their shift pattern, of course, er, ah, some it was said slinked out to slake their thirst but not wise to be heard saying so.

In a public bar frequented by golfers you lower your head when you enter. Golf balls are flying all over the place. In this public bar duck, it's talk of rusty steel tubes. Oil pipes for a North Sea contract and here it's the pipes being over your head. If the conversation is not about pipes it's, about conundrums.

'How you get from Main Street Newhaven to the fit, O' the Walk without going over or under a bridge?' Tam the bam, crane driver, wanted to know.

Alex, Phsyco, Bates, and Spider, Hughie, Webb, wracked their brains.

'You could maybe do it by boat,' said Phsyco.

'Don't be daft,' said Spider, 'has to be shankies pony on your feet silly loon but maybe on a bike or a bus not by boat.' Getting up from the table gathered the empty glasses and approached the bar smiling and shaking his head. 'Same again Boaby the ejits slate.'

'Which one?' Boaby asked with a shake of his head and a wry smile.

Glesga Mary wanted to know how many picture houses were in Edinburgh and did Sauchihall street in Glasgow have more shops than Edinburgh's Princess street in the nineteen forties. Her pal 'Marlyn, Hettie Munro, wanted to know how many dance halls Mary danced in and how many yanks had she been with? And did she keep a diary if so where was it or was it a state secret? Knowing her definitely a state secret.'

'If she's got one about time the slag presented it and give us a good laugh,' said Spider causing a mixed response.

A ladies voice shouted, 'shame on you Spider. Let's see your diary or too thick to have one, aye too thick.'

Boaby wants to know, 'what is a bowtow?' Get your bowtow here two a penny their cheap as fish. What is a bowtow? form a line at the end of the bar get yours for only the small sum of two for a penny.'

He is greeted with lots of laughter.

'Save me two,' Glesga Mary cried out and smiling at Marlyn, 'four for her.'

This rubbish or good banter if you prefer goes on all night answers wanted the dafter the better.

Was the man who done Jesus a Scotsman? Where was Harry Lauder born?

Did Scarlet, gone with the wind, drink tea in a Newhaven fishers house?

Some wag searched newspapers to seek out stories about all this nonsense.

Some of the answers giving more unbelievable than the questions. Ah well. It's more entertaining than playing bingo some would say.

'You know we're sitting in Berts?'

Tam the bam and Spider carried on the conversation.

'We are in Junction Street do you know it should be Junction Road, said Tam in all seriousness.

'How come?' Asked Spider wearily.

'Granny said they got it wrong.'

'So, who got it wrong?' Spider said giving Frank a sly wink.

'Let's hear him,' Frank said, this has to be good.'

'Continue, the man has spoke.'

'Them, the head guys. There's Newhaven Road then Ferry Road. North Junction street. You with me and please no more.'

'Aye, get on with it.'

'Then the The Water O' Leith.'

'Is, this a geography lesson?'

'Spider will you just let me tell it. This side the water is South Leith, ay. The side over the bridge is North Leith, okay? You know along this side,' he points left, 'that's the Fit O',The Walk. From North Junction Street to the Fit O',The Walk is a road. So should it not be Junction Road?'

'Aye, okay but it's still Junction Street. Can you remember when your mother sent you for a fourpit tatties and a half loaf and five woodbine? I can,' said Spider.

'Ladies and gentlemen and other's…For your entertainment we have spared no time and let me say Bert your host has gone to a lot of expense to get you the best in entertainment from across the pond… What?' A long pause and looking to his left, supposedly been interrupted in his spiel… 'He's no coming?' I thought, heard the helicopter landing out the back… What?... was a bus passing the door,' another long look at the audience with a sorry expression. Of course it's part of the patter not unusual but similar to other establishments in the vicinity.

'Awe well, it will have to be your old…give it up for… Jordan with his squeeze box and the wee smasher…The one and only, wait for it, your own, wee, Lizzie.'

He left with a beaming smile on his face leaving the pair to get on with it.

'Old, Walter Auld, announced the turn a regular occurrence in this establishment.

Lizzie adjusted the mike down to her height. Smiling and greeting them with her usual happy enthusiasm. 'I want to hear you so all join in. Don't be shy now we're all gadgies here ye ken. It's back tae sunny Leith,' she raised her arms, 'lets go. Don't be shy. You can all join in let's hear it for return to sunny Leith. Loud as you please.'

Lots of whistling and clapping, shook his head, f… Me!'

Ive seen the southern cross at night lit by the milky way
Ive seen the sun rise up above the table mountain bay
Ive seen the shark seen the whale
Ive watched the seals at play
From good queen bess and Durban
East London to Dundee
Across the forth to sunny Leith is where I long to be.

THIRTY EIGHT

'See yer up?' Mary was surprised to see him sitting at the kitchen table.

Swung round in the chair, 'think it's me. Who the hell were you hoping to see your fancy man. Sorry to disappoint only me.'

'Don't start that again it's not funny.'

'You come to spy again?'

She pulled a chair sat down thinking when is he going to bloody well grow up?

'Take a seat and make yourself comfy. You come to give me grief?'

'Have you seen him? The police are looking It's no like him to be missing this long,' hoping he'll act responsible hoping for a grown up conversation.

'You on about Jakie Ross? Wont be missing don't worry he'll turn up wondering what all the fuss is about bet he's lying somewhere smashed out of his skull again.'

'Aye well. Maybe so. It would be just like the rascal to make a meal of it if he finds out people were concerned.'

She was worried knowing he was the last as far as she knew the last to see him. The pair of them seen staggering up the Whale Brae drunk as coots.

'What you want Mary not like you to be here this late in the afternoon have you no other business to be getting on with keeping your punters happy, ay.'

'Just going,' rising and pushed the chair under the table with her knee ' kept the place tidy I see. No dishes cluttering the sink. Got a grip at last. If only you could…Ach, wasting my time. I'm out see you when see you.'

'There was me thinking praise coming from you, my my, what next?'

'Heard you were at it again last night is that why you got drunk after seeing you know who they Greenes?'

.'Don't go there, Mary. Nothing, to be said about it.'

'Is that why you ended up at Berts making a fool of yourself again never learn.'

'Hell! Nothing sacred have you been listening to the jungle drums or have you got your spies on to me, no, whoever said was drunk got it wrong.'

'Came to ask if you had seen him and before I forget got to give you a message from Walter Auld. Knows something about Jamie and the quine. Wants you to go and see him urgent by sounds of it appeared to me to be a worried man that's told to me by Amy last night in the pub. A bit concerned about Walter Auld.'

'Old? He never said anything to me last night in the pub had the opportunity more puzzling secrets that'll come to nothing I dare say.'

'Well now you know. It's up to you see or no go see.'

'I've solved the problem you've got about uncle Jonny.'

'Oh, what was that then what was the problem had with the bold boy?'

'The southern cross thingy. Lit by the Milky Way problem.'

'You've solved a problem go on then don't keep me in anxious suspense.'

'Song wee lizzie sings. Heard it rather some of it last night nut jobs giving it laldy in Berts place. How they love the wee quine and her singalong they sure can raise the roof got to hear it for yourself seems she can't do any wrong.'

'Good for Bert might get the two of them her and Jordan to play in my place. Might attract more arses on the seats could do with something to liven the place up.'

'Last time I saw him he was in a huff wouldn't give him the price of a swally.'

'If he's not found soon McDougall said he would organise a search. Will you join and help look for him?' Have to watch her words having to be careful if he agreed she would need to let kaiser know in case he came across Frank on the hunt. His disguise would have to be very good to be able to fool every body. Only snag she could see was McDougall likely wanting to know who was on the hunt. Kaiser being a stranger easily attract his attention would have to convince him not to go on the hunt. The way he was following him about would be a hard task to convince Kaiser not to join better if he and McDougall did not meet.

'Yes will help look for him but if he turns up before it you will let me know. May be otherwise engaged so knock before entering.'

'I'll kill the old bowtow myself when he's found. Honest swing for him. Going into hiding is not like him wonder what's got into him going off on walk about.'

'Don't you think, the cops have something to do with him going awol?'

'I don't. He's lots of things but afraid of the police no never.'

'Well, you would know. You seem to know all that goes on in this place.'

'Are you saying me a nosey Parker how dare you of all the cheek expect more than that.'

'Your pub is a hive all things can I say...All bright wonderful and beautiful.'

'Don't be daft.'

'There are a few tales told in your shop. You can't tell me you turn a blind eye to all the gossip you hear do you think they two rat bags radio local where they get it from? Hell's Kitchen, that's where. What goes on in the bar the men give it them when they get home after a good session. Bet isn't all they get when the men get home most likely another good session.'

'That's not a nice thing to say Frankie. Surprised at you but there again to be expected I'm leaving goodbye.'

Why he wondered why does she always leave scornful why are the two of them always at loggerheads maybe he should be the first to let her know how much, naw. Not a good idea. Rubbing her up the wrong way is part of the game. If she wants to be a surrogate mother why shouldn't he go along with her. The important thought now is Jakie Ross. Where he wondered was the old fool and if he was being watched he thought the old man could be in danger. If someone knew he had spent the night here in his house just maybe was a warning. Maybe whoever were now showing their hand hoped he was wrong. After all he has gone walk about before. Some time if and when sober could make some money out for a few days on the boats and nobody giving a thought but now why the urgency what was McDougall really after?'

Made up his mind to ask at the pier someone there may have got a glimpse and if not no didn't want to think the unthinkable. Hopefully he would show up soon and wonder what the fuss was about. The way he knew him the way he knows the old fool knew how he could scrounge enough drink to last a week or longer. Telling about his latest adventure at the police station could entertain some who would fall for his rouse, aye, the rascal would make many a muckle oot oh a mickle, old soak could tell a tale or two wasn't so long since he was invited to the primary school in the village to let the children know his wartime exploits. How he had to water down the stories telling them how he was one of the many who helped to liberate the horror camps at the end of the Second World War. How it was stupid and hoped they would never experience the like. Prey never again was his message to the school bairns.

Jaunt round the pier came to nothing people he spoke with no joy he hadn't been seen recently not for a few days. Stopped to speak with, Walter Lyle a retired fisherman.

'Hear you're looking for Jakie lot of people have suddenly taken to caring about him what's the interest know what's he up to now silly old bowtow.'

'Aye, gone missing nobody has seen hide nor hair of him.'

'Nothing new in that par for the course what he's like.'

'It's suspicious, you know how he saw my brother in the car going into the harbour.'

'The police had him they must have been satisfied.'

'Mary thinks going over the top.'

'Why are you looking for him not get enough when you had him.? Waste of time I know. You can't rely on a word he utters just wasting your time would be looking somewhere else forget him if were you.'

'Think the cops gave him a fright but she is in the opinion he's got nothing to fear from them, typical Mary, says can take care of himself the cops are not a worry.'

'Knowing him she is correct but that young whelp of a copper who hangs about here hiding from the other one, McDougall. The rookie one always asking questions about Jakie but wouldn't say why he was looking?'

'It's sure a mystery all what's going on,' Frank said, 'got me worried.'

'The talk you're right to be worried.'

'You mean?'

'The last to see him. You so it was said why I say look other places forget him.'

'F… these jungle drums.'

'What you expect but put the pep back into this place no doubt about it this intrigue sure has them all guessing some even afraid to go out at night.'

'Change you say, where? Where do you think should look?'

Walter rubbed his chin with his right hand examined his stick for a moment before laying it on the bench adjusted his hat back to rubbing his chin… 'Betty.'

'Betty you mean at the café?'

'Keep this to yourself,' touched his nose and winked, 'the daughter. That crazy one. Thick as thieves. Won't surprise me if they are hiding out.'

'You mean Dilly? No, you've got the wrong end of that nonsense. No, impossible have to be half daft to be into that game. Jakie? No can't believe it impossible!'

'Have to be going,' collected his stick said cheerio.

Frank watched him making for the market his mind going over what had been said was unbelievable not possible.

Continued walking round the pier but got no joy. No one had seen the old fool and now he was concerned. If he didn't show soon well couldn't bare the thought.

'You seen anything of your pal?' Rookie cop stopped him at the slip end.

'Pal?' Looked at him then glancing looked over his shoulder, 'your Sergeant is looking for you seen him over at the lighthouse five minutes ago. McDougall. I said hadn't seen you. Better have a good excuse he thinks your absent without leave thinks your skiving. Thinks your in Bettys place drinking tea all day,' how good a lie was that. Will give the rookie something to chew over.

Rookie took off. Frank saw him disappear behind the fish market building into the darkness. Smiled muttered 'doesn't take much to get him worried. Why he doesn't stand up to the Sergeant, oh, why am I bothered he muttered.'

Leaving the pier at the road end sees McDougall at the police box. 'Sergeant McDougall, you looking for me by any chance,' thinks to have the first word before he collars him. Give him something to rattle his brain.

'Someone say otherwise,' says gruffly and standing to his full height as he closes the police box door

Walked away wondering why McDougall never mentioned old Jakie?

Cup of coffee please Betty.'

'Something for eating?'

'No.'

'Not going to get my fortune from you. One coffee my my,' shakes her head turns muttering 'another taking space all day on one cup of coffee,' bothered, not me.'

'Having a rotten day sorry to hear it.'

'Here's you're cup. Take a seat and behave yourself.'

'Someone rattled your case, oh dear.'

'What you been up to now?'

'As in?'

'So many you can't say.'

'Not a clue what you are on about.' Takes a seat looks out the window sees three old ladies, strangers, approaching the café. One draws the other two aside. Standing in a huddle each turn to look at him then decide the café is not for them and walk off in the opposite direction.

'Saw that,' Betty says, 'that's it. Lost customers drink up and leave will have no customers at this rate'.

THIRTY NINE

'I've good news and bad, what do you prefer,' Rutherford took a bite out of a fat beef burger picked up the plastic cup of steaming coffee from the bench struggled to remove the lid from the cup.

'My, it's bit early for junk food. Have you not had a decent breakfast? thought you coppers had a regime. Not like the like of me with my irregular life,' Tony, rubbing his stomach burping, 'plagued with indigestion do me one of these days.'

They met in the park military band was in full swing. Music playing to only a few die hards who occupied the wooden seats separated from each other here and there among the many empty rows. He looked at the clouds reckoned soon would rain. Could see the band having no audience to play to.

'Your tip-off proved spot on,' said Rutherford jumping up suddenly. dropped the burger. The coffee cup fell on the ground spilling the contents.

'Burnt my lip! The bloody coffee is red hot and my hand burnt my bloody hand!' Waving and blowing on it same time stamping his feet and muttering more expletives.

Tony watched, shook his head laughing, 'should be aware of these plastic cups never learn do you,' said, turning away hiding a smile. 'Useless you really are know by now what these plastic cups are like.'

Four ducks came out of the water waddling furiously heading for a share of the spilt food joined by a couple of gulls who appeared from nowhere landing with wings flapping and sliding in to each other in their eagerness to get to the free food. Wings outstretched they came screeching like banshees.

Kicking furiously at them, 'get out of it, you… vultures get, get,' waving his arms chasing but without much luck.

A swan appeared flapping it's wings neck low to attack his legs it's feet slithering on the gravel knocking over a waste bin in the process spilling the contents around the bench.

Rutherford retreated fast. Tony couldn't help laughing at his misfortune.

'The birds really love you would be better if you go and see Landa and get yourself a cool ice cream to sort you out blood pressure is getting the better of you. Oh, the poor ducks. Not a good way to treat them a good job the park ranger didn't witness your outburst.'

He laughed out loud was not long to get over the problem he was having with his stomach. 'Certainly showed who's boss. The swan had you on the hop.'

'I'll survive no need for ice cream thanks for your sympathy not much help were you my so called friend.' Wiped his lips with his handkerchief resumed his seat on the bench. Watching and glowering at the swan waddling away with it's head held high at a job well done. 'He's Leaving, look, the victor retreats,' Tony said, 'wont forget this in a hurry.'

Calm restored 'As you were saying give me the good news first. Need a lift not had much of a night.' Tony said.

'You've had it rough don't know the half.'

'That's to be debated. Are you gonna say what your on about or what?'

'Your information. Good result. Picked up the Irishman Docherty from the Harwich nick early this morning. Traveled overnight and now he's in custody but he's not singing. Others have that task if they succeed,' shook his shoulders, 'wait and see.'

'Good, hope you remember in future.'

'A lucky hit is no guarantee that's it for the future. I'm not saying it was not helpful.'

'You're sure, oh, wasting time with you Rutherford. My help got you the desired and with more contacts there is more to get from my grass but you are just an ungrateful B......!'

'You want to hear me out or else could be somewhere more important than swanning about in this park you understand.'

'Very funny realise you just made a funny. Swanning about in a park. Have a sense of humour after all who would have thought it? Swanning in the park you're a comedian not a copper.'

'Customs caught him with a shedload of money, he said, ignoring the remark. 'Have to give credit to the officer's for their due diligence.'

'Burke's money?'

'Not positive. As I said not talking. Customs vigilance getting to know about this gang taking laundered cash to the continent. Different ports have been alerted round the country and ports in Ireland. Money out and diamonds back is the first collar they've managed to get. Thanks to my help, er yes you, as said, he's not singing yet. Sure is scared clammed up from the beginning.'

'Burke is a very shrewd customer. How come you and your band of brothers can't get anything on him. Surely it doesn't take a genius to flush him out. How he continues to outsmart you is beyond me?'

'One day it will happen. Empire one day will come crashing about him. All we need is some positive proof about his activities. Officers are gathering information as we speak but as said hopefully soon we may get a result.'

'Goodness sake he's running girls and bookie betting shops as well as the high class casino up west something has to snap. Kids in the streets know he's a drug dealer. If children know the score why not you?'

'Everything he is doing is as safe as he makes it. Everything is above board. Everything he runs is licensed has it tight as a drum. No one got the guts to squeal. It's too dangerous to go against him.'

'Who gives him these licenses?'

'You are at it again. Conspiracy.'

'Don't you think there is more? Some higher source?'

'Bent coppers you think? Not privy to that can't say.'

'Let's have the bad part of your story then maybe grab some coffee or in your case more coffee,' stood up, 'come on let's walk and talk. Exercise will do you good. I'll buy you a replacement from Landa.'

'You're off the hook concerning the Irish girl, Walters, with my help.'

'What do you mean of the hook was never on the hook. What are you saying?'

'You should be thanking me. The ends had to go with my boss would curl your hair. I succeeded in getting him off your back was convinced you somehow involved with her demise took lots on my part for him to think otherwise. Keeping information to yourself will not go down well if he finds you out Walker is on his back you can imagine.'

'Okay, thanks. Grateful but so should you be grateful to me for getting you the lowdown on Alex Docherty.'

'You never explained were the info came from you traveling with some dodgy customers? You better mind your back. This guy Burke has the where for all to glean information you will have to be very careful my friend.'

'My lad came out after his a stretch up in Manchester people in that camp have scores to settle with Burke. My boy kept his ear to the ground and with his contacts inside he has given me the goods, me, then you, the goods. Can only give what I get. Let me remind you about the danger. The risk taken. I'm giving up to you to use the information to get results.'

'Pity he did not get on the ball sooner?'

'What do you mean sooner?'

'Might have got something about the girl. Maybe could have saved her.'

'Don't think so it was random. Something to do with Burke's old lady. Could be the girl was trying to free herself from their clutches and now seems the Irish girl who worked in the bar shopped her. Somehow they could have been searching and the Irish dame spotted her and got in touch. Angelica Burke is not the sort to be just a casual customer in the sort of bar not like Tracy lords over.'

'Sad to say she was murdered. Nothing to do with sleeping pills a needle inserted between her toes.'

'Poison? Telling me she was poisoned?'

'No not poison bubbles pure air. Injection. Don't ask how it works but it's the official explanation. I'm in the dark as well as you are.'

'Again! I told you of my friend in Scotland. His friends brother and girlfriend done the same way. Got to be the hand of Burke at work here no doubt.'

'At least not losing their heads,' Rutherford said, taking the cup and dabbing his lips with his handkerchief and blowing into the hot coffee.

'It's a pity your lot did not liaison with the custom officers and followed the trail.They could have put someone on to him to

242

his final destination. Or is that to much to ask when are you going to end this racket how much information do you need?'

'Not got the man power.'

'The Dutch and the German police could have done it and got Interpol involved.'

'I don't have any influence to set up such an operation.'

'If they're out to get this guy Oldersum. If he is the cog in the wheel along with his Irish Frau. Would think they would pull out all the stops to crush their set up,' said with a bit of irony in his voice watching him blowing into the coffee cup.

'How do you know the guys name is Oldersum?'

'Boy Van Oldersum? You said or something like it. Positive you said.'

'No never gave you a name.'

'Irish niece of mother Burke you…'

'No never. Pity your nark didn't spill about the other dame. Dead, same as.'

'What you say dead how the hell did that come about you telling me she is dead?' His jaw dropped the information took him completely by surprise.

'Another tip off. Found in the same gaffe as you're first Irish hooker. Needle between the toes. Clean and quick. A professional hit no better evidence a sure fire guarantee.'

'The place could be one belonging to Burke. It's obvious making a fool of you. If I had the authority would have had his, you no what, by now. How long are you going to wait to pull him in it's getting weirder and weirder by the minute. How long to find the answer. Pull him in get some fear into him.'

'I've said already. You don't listen. This is not the States. We do things different here need facts. Get me Burke or the grand dame bang to rights. They have lawyers. If it's not water tight we haven't a hope in hell. Proof we need proof.'

'Again. Proof on about proof. Get proof!'

They left the bench walked to another scanned the area the usual people in the park sat down still blowing on his coffee in the plastic cup.

'You gonna drink it or make love to it never seen such an old woman and how much proof do you need beginning to think this is a stalling game.wasting my time with you. Positive someone is not hindering the investigation?'

'You again there is no conspiracy. Simple proof that's what we need anxious as you to get it over and done without there being anymore fatalities. Get it out your head that we are being, as you would say stymied.'

'Looking from my side think something stinks.'

'Well, if that is your take on the situation prove it.'

'I think you are in a better position than me to find out.'

'I'll ignore that.'

'What next?'

'Meaning?'

'Meaning what?'

'You gonna say what happens next? Gotta pump you for information!'

'No crystal ball. How the hell do you expect me to get the future?'

'You waiting till something happens then what?'

'You keep your ear to the ground and when you have something you know how to get in touch.'

'Can't you do anything without my input?'

'My head... My head is all over the place. Don't you realise the pressure I'm under? If only you had my worries don't know the half!'

'The half. You don't know your arse from your elbow!'

'If you say so but you've got to understand my position.'

'Position?'

'Pressure keep saying.'

'The longer this takes the worse it's going to get.'

'Someone or something will break.'

'There you go again hoping!'

FORTY

The pots were coming up with good results. Large partan crabs nice size lobsters a plenty. Binky is pleased he took the chance to drop his gear nearer Inchkeith island. The sun was on the up. He was on the up thinking of the reception he would get when he got to the market. It was a good haul the opposition would slap him on the back and congratulate him also expected full well there would be a little bit of jealousy in their banter. Good for them but it will be easy to knock the smile of their faces he was thinking had the broadest smile on his face nothing would detract him from jubilation.

A flight of seabirds tagged along waiting the opportunity of free scraps.

Only a couple of pots to come was sure like the last these pots have to be same, bulging. One pot left to get on board suddenly realised something was amiss the motor on the winch began to labour. Seen smoke... The winch stopped… got hold of the rope started to pull. Hard going. The weight of the pot made him wonder what the hell! Thinking the pot is exceptional he was anxious to get it on board though in his mind disasters that had taken place in the past when boats dragged up mines left over from the Second World War. Mines that had escaped the clean up and exploded resulting in many lives being lost.

'Please, no, not that,' he said loudly. The pot had to be full of bounty to banish his fears. Struggling with the task beginning to think the worst. Got the pot near the side of the boat saw the rope go slack. He straightened. 'What the?' The rope was free floating on the surface followed by the pot popping up turning over and over. The water bubbling as if air pressure was rushing up from the sea bed. The water boiled the pot swirled in the motion. He saw the clouds darken the waves getting angrier. The swell rocked the boat. Fearing the worst decided to cut the rope and forgo the pot. With no help in sight decided to make for the safety of theharbour.

Removing his hat scratching his head he removed the rag he had round his neck. Wiped his face then sat on a pot recovering his breath wondering what had happened.

As the water bubbled in the flotsam he saw a body floating in the tangle of ropes covered by bits and pieces of ripped fishing net. Watched It move to the stern then all at once he and the body being attacked by the gulls. They landed on the dead body screeching and screaming and attracting a flock of Gannets scaring the life out of him. Had never witnessed such a scene and prayed it would never happen again. Never saw anything like it seagulls on the boat scrambling about causing mayhem. He grabbed the boat hook swung up, sideways, down, screaming, shouting lashing out to clear them off the deck. Some flew others landing It was the mother of all his disasters. Just when was it all going to end?

In the confusion two seals appeared on the surface near the body. Their black heads twisted turning as they appeared to be eyeing up the situation. Waiting silently he thought to take the opportunity of a free meal.

Waving his arms attempting to shoo them away suddenly saw the body of a man trapped in the flotsam, 'Help. My goodness,' muttering dumbfounded. No head the body was headless!'

He reached with the boat hook found pulling was as hard as pulling the pots.

Puffing and blowing he strained to get the corpse alongside then bending he managed to tie a rope round the gory bundle securing it to the side of the boat. The gulls circled, watching and screaming. They followed swooping over the body while another three seals appeared, in single file like mourners going to a funeral.

McDougall and the rookie cop on the slipway waiting for the doctor to give them the okay when he finished his examination of the headless corpse.

'Head could be anywhere,' he said, standing and removing his spectacles. 'I've seen the likes before could be the result of a boats propeller it's not been in the water very long.' He returned and bent over the body. Lifting the dead mans right arm he examined it then stood up. 'Lot of bruising here. To me, looks like it could have happened before the body went into the water. Take it away done here.'

Collected his bag, said, 'till tomorrow afternoon let you know what I find. Someone must know who it is? The state of it makes it a puzzle but think it's local. Aye could be the one you're searching for.'

Rooney arrived on the scene in a foul mood.

'Why the hell you got me here? How can I help with this business deal with it!'

The sudden outburst took McDougall by surprise he watched and wondered why Rooney turned away from the body without looking at it,

'You not do this without me? Get something right for once. Take charge move these spectators out of it don't let them see what's lying here.'

He walked got into his car and drove away.

'Wait I.' McDougall was too late to get his attention.

'It's the alky, Jakie Ross,' the rookie said.

'How do you know thing has no head,' McDougall stared and shook his head, muttered, 'strength give me strength.'

'It's the clothes recognise the mans clothes.'

The crowd gathered above the slipway talking excitedly amongst themselves giving opinions who the deceased could be was it Jakie or not or was it a woman? Speculation was rife. Busybodies craning their necks eager to see the spectre.

Sudden noise of a car backfiring made the spectators scatter for safety thinking they heard a shot from a gun.

The noise from the car and of the sea birds circling above their heads twisting watching swooping waiting for the opportunity to land on the grisly scene below on the cold wet cobbles put a shiver up the rookies back, 'what do now sarge never witnessed anything like it in my life,' he said glancing at the birds expecting a sudden attack and seeing the pier was empty and silent wondered where everyone had gone.

'Get the thing covered see if anyone up there in the crowd if they've surfaced out of hiding places if any can help or if anyone can confirm who it is. Maybe someone else will recognise the clothes, you may get lucky,' was going to make the rookie suffer.

The dressing down he got from Rooney was not called for not in front of a subordinate. He didn't take kindly to his nose being put out of joint Rooney was overstepping the mark. 'Do what the inspector wants you to do. Going to speak to Binky why he brought it back here goodness sake he should have left it were he found it.' Took off muttering to himself. As he got down the slipway towards the boat he was thinking Binky would not be in any fit state to be interviewed but he had to find out exactly the sorry circumstances.

'Need to ask you some questions need answers if your up to it. Sooner best,' he said climbing onto the boat deck.

'Was ready to leave but if you must.'

'Not take long. Best while still…'

'In my brain? Think don't know why?'

'Not come to lay blame just get the facts that's all. Binky, you know how it is. Got Rooney on my back and having to put up with this idiot,' nodded towards the rookie.

'Get to it but dinnae ken what else to say except what's been said already.'

'Who? Who you been talking to?'

'Told it to the other's.'

'Cmon who? Others what other's?'

'Policemen. Said they were. Two of them.'

'Someone pulling it they were not newspaper men wouldn't put it past them kinda stunt they would pull.'

'Not got time to stand here talking to you. Policemen or newspaper reporters don't know two men asking said what a said you find out what the situation is.'

'Okay leave it for now speak to you later. I'm sorry. You know really sorry. The situation you are in but got to find who would do what has been done. Jakie was a pest but didn't deserve this ending.'

FORTY ONE

Mary Mckenzie was banging on Franks front door.

'What now Mary not use the key come in why the commotion got a key why are you hammering on the door not deaf your key, f… me. Fright! Thought was being invaded by the Stasi.'

'They found him have him on the slipway at the pier. She was out of breath like had been running. Her voice is dry was having difficulty getting the words out. Wiping the tears from her eyes sobbed and shivered. He got hold of her arms sat her down at the kitchen table. 'Sit make you a nice cup of tea. Stop blubbering and start at the beginning. Who have they found you going to say take your time,' went to the stove and put the kettle on to boil. Turned and looked at her he knew it must be bad the state she was in.

'Jakie. Binky. Out the water. When he was fetching his pots.' She wiped the tears used the handkerchief to blow her nose continued sobbing uncontrollably.

He had never seen her like this before she was the one who always appeared to be the pillar of strength but now he saw her in a different light. 'So that's what happened to him not hiding and not on the lash,' said rubbing her shoulder stroking the back of her head. 'Why so upset Mary, as far as it goes you hadn't a good word to say about him was just a pest in your eyes. I don't see why you've taken the news so badly, don't cry. Things will work out,' head in turmoil, 'another one when will the nightmare end,' he's shaking his head and muttering, 'nightmare bloody nightmare!'

'You don't know nobody knows?'

'What Mary? What you saying tell me get it out,' maybe, he thought shouldn't have been so blunt should be letting her know he was there to give her support and was taken aback by the sad news she was telling him.

'No as bad like everyone said he was but he was my mother's uncle. He was family and now the only one left,' face in her hands rocking back and forward on the chair.

'Kept that quite. Funny thing all the time known you you never once. You never let it be known he was a relation thought you were only on your own had you down as the grumpy spinster,' trying hard to ease the situation he said it but she wasn't listening, 'not many people knew and would like to keep it that way promise me!'

'You will have to make the arrangements. Funeral and things. There's got to be a wake despite him. He did have a lot of friends didn't he aye?.'

'They're saying no head has no head. Who would do that to a human being why? No head!'

He helped her stand gently brushed the hair away from her forehead.

'Go home Mary will have to let McDougall know you are kin he will keep you right and anyway if you don't tell him well you know what it's like round here. Someone will be there before you telling tales and McDougall will be asking you, why? Why took you so long to come forward.'

'Are you sure, McDougall said, 'you have told me all the facts? You can't say if you so him on a boat when you were out. He wasn't on this boat was he? Would say wouldn't you? After all has been known to doss on the boats in the harbour nothing new in that,' trying to set the scene in his head but Binky wasn't ready to speak of the horror he had witnessed he needed a drink. A drink would help him get over it. One drink but he was thinking one is no good was ready to get hammered.

'No definitely not. Never on this boat and no there was no other boats out there except me. Just me and these screaming gulls and those honking seals. I thought they the seals were going to join me in the boat. People are right when they say the gulls are the offspring of the dinosaurs. If you had seen what I seen you would not be going anywhere near the sea again. Talk about man eaters. You have not not met the like believe me. Gulls and seals. Monsters of the deep and monsters in the air. Unbelievable don't want to go through that ever again,' covered his face with his cap 'Now if you have no more questions got to get away from here.'

'Okay. Leave you now but might have to ask more later when you're ready. And yes know how you feel what's left of the poor…'

'Aye but what about me? I've got to live with what happened. The good haul is now one big waste of time. Who wants to have sea food associated with it? Would you like it if I served you and you knew where it came from? No don't think so.'

'Oh, Binky. You poor bowtow ,' said dryly, 'how sad for you dear dear,' walked away looked up at the sky saw the black clouds and wanted out before the rain. He hurried up the slipway approached the rookie, 'any joy from the mob on the pier see not many left there, gone, now the fun is over.'

'No, you know what it's like. No one has anything to say.'

'I see they have taken the body away.' Looking up at the pier seeing the last of the people leaving how easily was thinking how they are distracted now there is nothing to gape at.

'Van left a minute ago when you were on the boat. Did you get any sense from him the fish guy?' asked but McDougall wasn't listening something more on his mind.

'Rooney he's gone? You see what the time was when he left. Did you see what direction he took didn't take him long to scoot out of it. Must have been important,' had no time for any of the rookies questions writing in his notebook was mulling over what Binky had said. Was he legit more interested in loosing his catch than the plight of the dead man he brought up from the deep wrapped in fish nets. Rooney doing a runner perplexed him. Something more important must have cropped up but what could be more important A doubt if he will ever find out.

The rookie interrupted his thought, 'no, a hunch he took off sickened. I bet we'll find him at Maggie Shaws. What do we do now? Is there anything more you want me to be getting on with?'

In Maggie Shaws the talk all about Jakie Ross. The public house is full of people there to gawp at Mary and to see how she was baring up after the news.

Rogan Josh and her pal from radio la la are listening to hear as much gossip as possible. They keep moving punters out of their vision to keep their attention on Mary hoping to see something to their advantage.

'You can have one drink. To settle your nerves after the ordeal. Then you go it's a good job Rooney isn't here you wouldn't get any that's for sure.'

'No sarge. Not bother have to be somewhere else.'

McDougall watched him leave and wondered why refuse the drink. Rooney and the Rookie? What's going on?

Next morning small fishing smack chugged into the harbour and tied at the slipway. Two fisherman on board got busy unloading boxes of fish.

McDougall walked towards them waved for their attention.

'Hi Brodie. Anymore boats still out there any coming into Newhaven with their catches? Know of any coming to catch tomorrow's sales. Late ones or otherwise?'

They stopped unloading. Brodie stretched and yawned gave the impression he had had a hard night and now thinking why was he being sought by this incompetent fool McDougall. What does he want can't he see how busy we are got no time for this. Oh well better to humour him to get him out of the way.

'No the last,' said, hoping it would be enough to get on with what he was doing and not wanting to be seen talking to a copper, 'need to go south with my catch can't waste time blathering to you.'

'Did you see other boats,' asked again, 'any kind out there,' pointing towards the sea, suspicious, why is he landing here not further south he was thinking.

'No, no other boat. Ah, in the distance sure one at the back end of Inchkeith island. Not a fishing boat, no, not fishing.'

'That should get him off my back,' muttered, 'got to make him believe. Got to make the market before the price drops,' muttering, 'don't need him asking questions'

'Thanks Brodie. If you remember anything else you know how to get in touch. Not me then the rookie is here ready to assist if needed.'

He fingered the notebook flicking through the pages. Curious about something else Brodie hadn't said. Funny not enquiring about the incident. the word had spread like wildfire he would know what went down curious not asked the latest news.

The pier above the slipway was practically empty only few people wandering about not one interested in what had taken place the day before novelty factor was short lived.

Standing looking in his notebook heard loud angry voices saw Brodie speaking with a civilian dressed in a black suit wearing a black trilby. He wondered who the stranger was started towards them. They saw him approaching the stranger walked hurriedly and was soon out of sight. McDougall thought it strange the guy took off so quick.

'Am I in any trouble?' Brodie asked, 'what you want got nothing to say can't help.'

He was thinking he was not gonna get peace. like a dog with a bone he knew how the copper persisted and the sooner he was away from here the better.

Standing on the slipway his hands embraced a length of tarry rope lovingly caressing it like a favourite pet.

'Have you done anything wrong something I should know.'

'Why you asking not done anything to bother you with.'

McDougall knew this was a hostile witness. For a long time he was on this guys case but drew a blank, ' asking cause asking. So have you done anything I will find out later. You telling me you have done nothing wrong if that's it well okay.'

'No, got a clear conscience,' pulled himself up to his full height was willing to spit in the coppers eye. Changed his mind, spat at his feet.

'Well then nothing to worry about,' McDougall said side stepping the spit.

'Who was it you were talking to a minute ago sure was in a hurry.' Walked a few yards stopped, 'when was the last time you saw Jakie Ross?' Asking as he looked over his shoulder hoping to trip him with the direct question.

'The last time saw him,' thinks for a moment. Who?'

FORTY TWO

'Done yourself good by coming in Rooney said,'

For two hours they kept asking the same questions over and over again. But he was sticking to his word, 'no comment.'

McDougall was doing all the talking and loosing it showing his anger at the repeat, no comment.

Frank could see only time was on his side. Asking the same rubbish was going nowhere. Soon he knew he would be out of there free and exonerated what mattered most he was thinking do with a drink and considering what boozer and remembering his date with Jeannie the barmaid.

'You were the last to see him had him in your place must have got the lowdown. Who did he say he saw or who did he hear who else was there beside the two he told us about quicker you talk quicker we're done and you're out of it.'

'No comment.'

'Give us a break Frankie have to see you do yourself no good taking this attitude.' McDougall mellowed his voice knowing the interview was going nowhere.

'Rooney said done good by coming in what has changed? How long have I got to sit here? You got something on me then charge me or getting out of here.'

'You want to know who was responsible for your brother and the girl? Help us get something because up till know we are totally in the dark.'

'No comment.'

'He told you there was another person on the slipway in the car didn't he, Jakie Ross.'

'Who said?'

'The constable heard what he said to you. There was someone in the back of the car. Who was it? You know what he said?'

'No comment.'

'When did you see him when the last time? Your in trouble you know it.'

'No comment.'

'You want a lawyer? Rooney asked.

254

'Any idea who the alky was meeting?' McDougall asked.

'The Alky? You mean, Jakie Ross. Give the old guy some respect,' he said shaking his head surprised at his attitude.

'Okay Frankie we know your upset. Have you any idea?

'Don't need a lawyer. No comment.'

'No comment,' McDougall tapped his pen angrily on the table and shook his head, 'Is that it? Is all you will say, is, no comment. We'll be here forever if you do not lighten up.'

'No comment.'

'If you are shielding someone it will do you no good because we will get to it eventually. You'll see so come on?'

There was a knock cop stuck his head round the door, sir,' he said.

'Carry on don't wait,' said Rooney going out of the room.

'How long you going to keep me here? Are you going to charge me?'

'You're here to help with you know what's needed.'

McDougall was up to the teeth with the whole business and Rooney well what could be said he had no right to leave him acting the bad cop.

'This is rubbish you know it and if am here just to help with your stupid enquiries and you're not going to charge me? Well out of it getting out of here.'

He stood up and pushed the chair back getting ready to leave.

'Sit down. We're not finished. There maybe more when the inspector comes back relax.'

'Okay, how much longer are you going to keep me here?'

'Anything?' Rooney asked when he returned.

'The inspector wants to know if you've had second thoughts?' He glanced at Rooney and saw he was not paying attention to the proceedings but doodling with his pen on the papers in the folder.

'Do you want to ask a question inspector?' asked McDougall wearily. Looked at Rooney and thinking he is not here. Obvious wants to be somewhere else.

'Get on with it,' Rooney said, taking notice of the situation.

'When are you gonna let me out of here? Had it. You let me go or are you going to charge me with something?'

'You'll go when we say you can go,' said Rooney, 'why did you have him in your place overnight and don't repeat the crap it was the kindness of your heart. The guy was a mess. Not only was he a mess he stank to high heaven.

'You must have had a good reason to put up with him in your house?' You must have had good reason to find out who the third man was?' McDougall said.

'No comment.'

Rooney stood, 'let him go wasting our time.' Grabbing the folder from the table he hurried out the room.

McDougall got up, 'keep your nose clean. We will see you again. Were not finished here. He will have you back.' He gathered his documents, 'remember keep it clean. Pay you to cooperate. Got to wise up.'

'I always keep It clean.'

'Don't be flippant be careful.'

'Nothing to hide when you going to get off my back.'

'Only trying to help if you know something don't keep it to yourself.'

'You can help telling me why you think am responsible for Jakie Ross?'

'The whole thing is getting out of hand should not be talking to you this way and the quicker come to your senses the better.'

'You would tell me if you knew someone on my tail?'

'On your tail, my my. Report it to the police if you think your being followed.'

'Following me. A black Mercedes on my case it seems.'

'You think someone is following you,' looked at him a queer look on his face.

'That's what saying. The police? If them couldn't be a better alibi could it?'

'Report it but you need to get a story straight think you're paranoid black car you say?'

'No not paranoid. See what a see and why you say report it to the police that's what bloody well doing!'

'Keep it down keep quiet. Don't give him,' nods and looks up the corridor, 'if anything is said will keep my ear to the ground. If as I say. About a black car will let you know. A Mercedes a black one not many them about. A Mercedes aye right,' he was thinking how the hell going to see such a thing not many about.

'Will tell if you get the lowdown on Jakie won't you?'

256

'On your way. What you think this is?'

'Not to much to ask need to know what's what.'

'Get more information the usual place. Radio, la la, will be your best bet!'

'Why no help?'

'I'm not going to tell you again.'

Frank stopped him from leaving.

'How long this going on for? I haven't, not, don't know why. Your keeping me back got better things to be getting on with so get going.' He said.

'You don't really believe,' Frank said, 'it's all down to me do you?' He watched him hurry away along the corridor wondering who or what was next on the agenda?

Drinking coffee with Binky in his fisherman's cottage after leaving the police station.

'Glad to see you a bit more calm after it skipper.'

'No Frank son. Never get over it. This will live with me forever never get it out of my head.'

'Could imagine how shocking seeing what you saw. They had me in asking questions. How they expect me to fill in the details beats me.'

'McDougall is at me all the time told him from start to finish what was what. Sick hearing myself repeating over it again and again and that young copper now he is at it.'

'You mean behind McDougalls back?'

'Aye, like scoring points.'

'The inquest will settle it.'

'Not for me bloody nightmare. Inquest won't find who was responsible won't get the truth of the matter.'

FORTY THREE

'Did they give you a hard time son?'

Put down a plate of Cullen Skink on the table, 'it'll do you the world of good. If that doesn't sober you but sure it will. Well try it anyway.' Sat opposite with her elbows on the table hands under chin watching and waiting for his response.

'Nothing couldn't handle.'

Held the fork in his right hand the fish is so soft he had trouble keeping it under control 'blast' he said

'Dip the crusty bread you are such a loon seen bairns with better manners,' she scolded pushing the bread over, 'or use a spoon you stupid loon.'

'Stop it Mary. Back clucking you've over cooked it crumbled out of all recognition look. he said swirling the fork side to side squishing the fish on the plate

'Get on with it. It'll do you fine just sup it. Did the two, you know, beat you up or anything like the Gestapo? Did they shine a light into your eyes and threaten you with doing something bad?' She waited anticipating details of the gory event.

'You've watched to many old movies. No not on me. Who's been filling your head with nonsense, Gestapo? where you get it, beats me. You have to stop reading those crime novels. You'll be having nightmares. Gestapo get a grip!'

'They two numpties are capable of anything would keep out of their way from now on try to get something on you. Ken what they're like. A film a seen years ago. A fat man outwitting the Germans. He was if remember a British spy.'

'Yes, know,' a shake of his head, 'this is really good,' pointed the fork at the plate, 'more, could eat more of this Mary.Realy good. Surpassed yourself.'

'No more that's your lot.' Lifting the plate walked to the sink, 'have to buy they two so called pals of yours a drink when you see them.'

'Pals? What two pals?'

'That man Spider and the hussy, Glesga Mary.'

' Are you kidding me get them a drink why goodness sake?'

'Because it was they let the police at the police station know they saw him getting chucked out the pub at the fit of the Walk after you saw him and a good job too you've got a cast iron alibi, ay. Nothing as solid as that me thinks.'

'Did they now was good of them. Nice to have friends who care, ay,' gave her the usual look waited to see what her response would be but as usual no response.

'I will do it when I see them sure was good of them.'

'When they heard you were in they wasted no time telling and the packed pub was easy to confirm it was true. Why do they call the quine Glesga Mary if you don't mind me asking.'

The look on her face said it all he was at a loss to understand why couldn't suss it out for herself, 'it's better than hairy Mary,' said shaking his head.

'That's a drink,' she said giving him a knowing smile, 'a well known swally.'

'A drink?'

'Aye, hairy Mary... Aunty Mary... Antiquary... A twelve year old whisky. Got you!'

She laughed he shook his head, 'I could go with some more fish this goes down well,' giving her a reassuring nod.

'You promise to do what I said.'

'What? What was it?'

'The alibi you forgot already? Useless bloody useless.'

Next day early morning walking along Commercial street after leaving Betty's café on his way to meet with Old, Auld.

A black Mercedes slowing came alongside. The driver wound down the window had a long look.

Frank watched as it gradually picked up speed. It stopped further along the street and a tall thin man in a black suit wearing a black trilby got out and crossed to the opposite pavement quickly walking in the direction of the bridge making for Bernard street. He carried on walking now and then looking over his shoulder when he turned the man was out of sight.

Reached Bernard Street bridge turned right then left into Water Street stopped at the tower block for a moment was not being followed but where the stranger had got to was a mystery.

Shrugging he carried on. Soon was out through the Kirkgate reached the foot of the Walk entered the tenement sprinting up the stair to the second floor apartment and chapped on the door.

'Hello Frankie come in it's nice to see you got my message okay?' thought no maybe not said.'

'Something to tell me Mary said.'

'Get you something, drink, vodka or a wee whisky perhaps?'

Sitting down in the easy chair beside the electric fire glowing in the blocked up fireplace, 'no thanks not now bit early.'

Record player on the table the vinyl spinning the male crooner singing about a rip tide, 'that brings back memories. My mother played him all the time was her favourite crooner,' he said to lighten the mood.

'Can't get enough of him. Unfortunately the young ones don't see it as I do. Not today's scene,' he said pouring a drink and sitting down at the table.

He stopped the record spinning put it back into it's sleeve, then said, 'Want to speak to you about Jamie god bless his wee soul.' Lifting the glass he knocked back the drink so quick Frank was surprised at how fast he downed it never seen the old man so nervous and wondered what was worrying him.

'Mary said was, what you…'

Old interrupted him, 'saw him the day before it happened.'

Rose up poured himself another drink and as before drank it over in one gulp.

He sat forward… 'Go on what did he tell you must have said what trouble he was in what it was about?'

Old reached for his pipe on the mantelpiece stood in silence filling the pipe tapping the tobacco down with his finger struck a match puffed hard filling the living room with sweet smelling tobacco.

Frank crossed to the window raised it from the bottom a few inches. Looking out he saw a black Mercedes parked on the opposite side of the street outside the grocer store.

'Heh Old, come here. Take a look black car over there.'

Coming alongside lifted the window a bit higher leaned out.

'Saw it before any chance you know who it belongs?'

'No, not before,' ducked back under the window closing it 'can't see if there is anyone in it the windows are black.'

Frank resumed his seat. 'The windows are tinted,' he said , then, 'go on you were going to tell me about the particular day he showed up.'

'The day before…'He hesitated, his words came slowly, 'he was here uneasy a bit of a state gave him a whisky just to calm him. He said he was in trouble big trouble. Appeared twitchy. Kept going over to the window if he was looking for something or someone. Said he was on the run with a lassie from Germany. Really felt for him seeing his state agitated like.'

'Was the quine here you see her or was it her he was looking for out the window. Did she arrive when he was waiting, show up or not?'

'No, was waiting up town in a hotel think he said in George street he was taking her away from there and taking her to Spider, in Stockbridge. His wee house in Stokeree you know where it is in Stevens street.'

'I've seen Spider he never. Not a word.'

'No no, don't blame him. He kept his word. He knew you would get the gist at the right time. The laddie was in hiding. The least who knew the better and you not here at the time

'Very true but someone certainly new.'

'They traveled from London in a hire, that car, one out the harbour,' He moved looked out the window shielding the tears. 'Why they came here should have gone somewhere else not here. Wrong thinking got them done in,' said taking short quick puffs on his pipe showing a worried look.

Frank reached for the whisky bottle. 'do you mind?'

'Help yourself, have a double,' he puffed and puffed on the pipe watching the smoke billowing to the ceiling.

'Thanks for that,' moved to the door, 'it's time to go.'

'Wait something want you to see,' crossed the room opened a drawer in the tall standing writing bureau fetching a small white square cardboard box and handed it over.

An astonishing look on his face holding it. Looking at it for what Old thought a long time and wondered if he was going to open it. He smiled nodded indicating. Inside nestling on white cotton wool large blue diamond attached to a long gold chain He wondered at the size of it, 'wow!' he said quietly.

'It's for you, Jamie said he was sorry and to give you the stone. Proud he was said you like a surprise.'

'No. no you keep it don't want it.' He took it from the box turned it over in his hand then gave it back. 'You have it don't want it. See you tonight at Berts,' hiding a tear he said, 'thanks for that see you later take care of yourself.'

When he reached the street the Mercedes had gone. Looked both ways thinking it probably was a coincidence should have taken more notice of the car number plate. Would be sure to take more care in the future because taking his eye off the ball was a mistake. Being street wise had to be earned. Was thinking he was getting out of touch got to be more vigilant can't afford any slip ups in deep and things not getting any easier.'

'What is a bowtow?' Boaby, the barman shouted when Frank came into Berts.

'Oh, okay now. Here is one. Here's, the BOWTOW,' he cried.

'Very funny. A pint of your best please when your ready.'

'There you are a pint of the best. First one on the house, enjoy.'

From the corner of his eye he spied Old. It was 5 after 7 on the clock and he knew what was coming stepped back to let Old come past watched him step up on to the stage to arrange the mike for the act to get underway.

'Ladies and gentlemen and others. For your entertainment tonight privileged, yes privileged to bring to you the one and only… and accompanying oan the squeeze box... Wee Lizzie and Jordan. Let's hear it from you, give you, wee Lizzie. Now some in here, been reported, not behaving when the acts are on. Got to stop. Now here she is. Give you again Jordan and Lizzie.'

She adjusted the standing mike down to her height.

'Tonight gonnie give you a song all about broken love. If you want to join in cause looking round here there's quite a few of youse. No, a better no say it. But if you want to join in feel free. If you want to shed a tear that's swell. That's all right. The more you greet the more you'll, awe, you ken what a mean so let's get oan wi it.'

Loud whistling and much clapping round the room.

'Here we go,' raising her arms. 'You're edged oot,' she shouted pointing a finger at Frank and smiling.

I would never edge you out like you edged me out
Can you forgive and try to give another chance
A passing glance a knowing smile
A pleasing word to mend a broken heart

'I'm edged out, right out,' he said to Boaby.
'I don't understand.'
'Why, what you saying?'
'Why you have a dislike to the quine. She's not all that bad.'
'If you say so but as Old says not my scene.'
'Old? He said that did he, Auld the... hypocrite.'
'Anyway better things to be getting on with.'
'Such as the opposition.'
'What opposition what you on about?'
'A certain quine serving you whisky in a bar that opposition.'
'How the hell!'
'Oh, you know. Don't know the quine personally just what people said that's all. And good things not bad.'
'Mary Mckenzie will kill her the old...'
'No, not saying,' giving a wink and a smile.
Old came to his side, 'see you tomorrow?'
'Frank nodded, 'got to be somewhere else.'
'Jumping ship to another boozer,' said Boaby.
'You didn't say had you in,' Old said, caring look waiting on the details.
'Well, from other people unbelievable, ay.'
'You must be serious with this one,' said Old.
'Serious?'
'Come off it you know what he means,' said Boaby.
'Nice girl. You'll do...'
'Hold it Mr Old. Who you been talking too?'
'The way your acting makes it positive,' said Boaby.
'You didn't let me finish. She is a nice girl you could do worse.'

'Like Dilly,' Boaby said, hand over his mouth to suppress a laugh.

'I'm out of here,' he says, 'Between you pair and you know,' nodded at her who he sees scowling at them for interrupting her performance.

'As could do worse,' Old reiterated. 'Dilly? You mean'

'Aye, gossip at the café. Betty is not pleased.'

'Boaby I don't believe that. You think? That desperate?'

'There's always someone for someone. Nothing new in it stranger things. You know stranger things do happen.'

'That Mary will kill her,' said Frank.

'No, don't you say it,' Boaby said clocking who was near. 'If something. God forbid it doesn't.'

'Stupid thing to say Frankie,' Old interrupted as he squinted round seeing who was close and if they were overheard.

'Anything, possible,' Boaby said, looking at him and shaking his head.

'Youse pair paranoid, like superstitious which is nonsense. Grown men, jeese.'

'Tell that to the others,' said Boaby.

'You'll be off to meet the new one then, Old said smiling, ' not superstitious you know that never been.'

'He's off. See her in Stockbridge hope he keeps out of trouble you never guess trouble follows him.'

'I'm here Boaby you speak if not here take care of myself you know that.'

'Aye, others, do they know it,' Old said touching his right shoulder, 'be careful son never know who.'

'Frank interrupted him, 'don't need for you to worry.'

FORTY FOUR

'Mary, you know the fisherman Brodie?'

Kaiser finishing his breakfast pushed the empty plate across the table.

She stood up gathered the dishes and walked to the sink.

'I'll leave these till come back going to see what state he is in this morning. If he was doing what you saw him doing last night. What state he is going be in is for me to find out. Wish you could see to it, get him told about the amount of drink he's swallowing. He's going to rue the day mark my words.' She said and he could see the worry appearing on her line wrinkled face.

He was glad someone else was looking out for him. The only doubt he had was would she slip up and open her mouth and give him away. He knew the danger.

It was a risk he was having to take. If only he had the people round him he could rely on like ones in Holland and London. But here he was on his own. Perhaps when this situation is done and finished he may have some reliable connections. He got up from the table and put on his coat. Today he was looking respectable wearing a blue pinstriped suit a crisp clean white shirt and sporting a blue tie.

'You're looking dapper the day.'

Lifted his hat posed in front of the mirror tilting it this way that way till he thought it was just right a little smile seeing her reflection standing at the sink doing the dishes noticing had changed her mind about the dishes she didn't see him posing, preening, looking at himself smiling at his reflection. He turned towards her. 'Mary the way you treat me thinking going to move in here with you on a permanent basis. Good to me even mastered the secret of perfect coffee. I'm afraid he doesn't know what he's missing no mam.' A little flirting goes a long way he was thinking. Keeping her happy he would keep hopefully her worry at bay, 'would have a word if on speaking terms you know isn't possible but the more you goad him the more not going to take any notice so best leaving it.'

'My. You are certainly getting your head round our Scottish sayings the couthie language. But not listen to your silver tongue ya loon. Know when your business is finished you will be long gone. When it's over you will take the other loon with you. Be sorry to see the both of you going out of my life forever.' She held the handkerchief to her eyes.

He felt embarrassed. Not in the position to be the one to console her. He sat down at the table and glanced over the newspaper she had brought from the newsagents. Pushing the paper aside he sat back looking at her. 'He doesn't know how much he's missing. You're mothering him too much. It's grief he's having to get over and it will happen time will heal you'll see.'

'Do think you are looking dapper the day,' not taking a word what he said returned her handkerchief into her apron pocket then on with her coat and hat pulled a chair and sat down.

'Do you know this guy, Brodie a fisherman?' He reminded her. 'It's I have to find him. Could be an advantage.'

'Thinking earlier when you asked one I know who sometimes lands his haul here at the harbour but not live here no down the coast. South, not here. Brodie Flucker no not from here,' she said shaking her head. 'How come you have got on to Flucker what does he have to do with anything a man would not give the time of day to. Just what heard. Not to be trusted. Saying that never had any dealings with him. Just gossip pub gossip that's all. What I hear down there we'll honest lot of rubbish. Stories my. Wishful thinking no worth bothering about honestly.'

'I was down stairs in the bar and heard part of a conversation between three guys from the fish market. One said the guy Brodie made a bundle renting his boat to foreigners would very much like to have a word with this guy Flucker maybe know something about the old man who died. Sure you don't know where I can find him it might be important the only lead.'

Now her attention was at a high leaned forward eager for more information. 'Tell me have you got a clue you think he killed him?'

He raised his hand. 'No shouldn't go there. The less you know the better. Remember we have to be careful. Up to now we're getting away with it. But think whoever is behind what's going on here and are leaving Bowtow alone must be after something important to them. Something they think he has got and how long before they make a move is anyone's guess?'

'Okay, won't ask anymore.' She made ready to leave walked to the mirror and adjusted her coat squared her hat picked her message bag 'Going to the butcher's,' she said.

'Have you any idea we're this guy does come from if not from here you could ask, discreetly not to raise any alarms. Wouldn't do to upset the investigation at this particular time. Less people, you know the better. Get some information fast things getting out of hand. Not good.'

'One of they wee villages on the coast somewhere between Musselburgh and North Berwick. Got to warn though. Lots of they places are such clannish will have to have your wits about you to find him.'

'Got to give it a try. No luck hanging about getting nowhere fast.'

'Still canny see it. Think you will be on a fool's errand.'

10 am, Main Street. Unfortunately his hire car is between a bakers van and a luxury coach. The coach passengers going to a wedding fabulously dressed in their best. The ladies with their ridiculous hats... Why do men see woman's hats as ridiculous was thinking they looked great. Men in suits with flowers in their lapels. Some in shirt sleeve order standing about the street in little groups talking and laughing waiting in anticipation for the journey to begin.

A small mixed crowd on the pavement watching and waiting to wish them bon voyage, children doing the usual running about chasing each other. Girls dressed as fairies boys dressed as elf's. Four teenage girls looked rather smart dressed as fishwives in white and pink costumes. All in all it was a happy scene.

He stood in the stair entrance of a tenement watching two drunk men hand in hand frolicking dancing a jig to the delight of the many spectators.

Everyone in a jolly mood having a wonderful time except one small boy who was crying being comforted by his mother after he fell when being chased result a skint knee. She's kneeling spitting on her handkerchief rubbing his knee. Two small boys looking with wide eyes at the boy with sorry expressions on their faces but not so innocent.

Looked at the sky. Not promising won't be very nice if it rains shame would spoil the brides day.

The driver came out from the coach gathered the youngsters together announcing the bride would soon be leaving it was time for the guests to be on their way. They had to be gone to arrive before the bride and her maids reached the final destination.

'So if you please will you get on board and we can get going on our way.' Call it fate or a lucky coincidence. The bakers van reversed the driver opened his window shouted to two men the last boarding the coach giving them his good wishes to one Brodie who turned smiled and waved in response.

Kaiser followed the coach joining others going to the wedding in cars knowing some guests on the list would be unknown to each other one's from the grooms side and some from the brides side always the case that strangers would introduce themselves to each other but some stayed within their own groups.

The convoy traveled along at a nice comfortable speed giving him time to wonder at the names he saw as he passed the sign posts, Portobello, Musselburgh, Preston Pans. He knew Preston Pans a famous battle was fought. Some guy called, Bonnie Prince Charlie was the winner. What ever happened to him he thought? A sign for Wallyford. Who the heck was Wally? Still more, Cockenzie Longniddry Port Seton. The names fascinated him and another strange one, Gullane. He knew it was famous for the game of golf? Thinking the whole east coast of Scotland had numerous famous golf venues and he knew Gullane was one of those places..

He followed the coach on the A1 road before it turned onto the A68 route to the village of Ormiston. They came to a halt in the Main Street were the passengers left the coach.

The cars stopped behind the coach he drove past finding a parking place further on up the street where he could see what was about to happen.

The rain began to fall as he stood on the pavement watching the groups mingle with each other the children playing ignoring the soft drizzle.

The Main Street flanked on each side by pretty stone fronted houses. At the end of the street a small bridge over a fast flowing river. Half a dozen shops on the Main Street satisfied the curious as they walked up and down to the delight of the locals who admired the costumes of the children in their fancy dress.

The teenage girls dressed as fishwives gathered the children together escorting them to the driver who was on the steps of the coach giving out instructions. Some children being unruly others happy but the usual ones who got in a strop over nothing. The instructions, walk a little way down the street turn right follow the lane into the field bit of a squeeze he told them but they would manage okay. Just keep hold of the children. Follow through the field and wonders of wonder you will see one of the oldest yew trees in Scotland. The official who is conducting the wedding is waiting for the wedding couple there. Under the branches of this huge tree, the wedding will be performed. Not to worry if anyone feels the strain. Chairs have been placed in convenient positions for the weary to watch the proceedings. Also, you will see a lady harpist playing on her ancient harp tunes of old Scottish aires, he was telling them with a large smile and when he finished instructing them said he would be back in a couple of hours to take them to Dunbar for the wedding feast and to be sure they were all back here ready to go because time was important schedule on a time limit, he reminded them. Not good to upset the planned proceedings and when he left the guests gathered together into a long line reminding him school children being led by the teacher going to class this time they set off singing… return to sunny Leith.

The man Brodie and another stayed behind. He reckoned they were waiting for the wedding cars to arrive.

The two entered into the shop in the middle row of shops. He followed. Walked slowly. Casually picking up brochures from a pile displayed on a side table. He glanced at them whilst keeping sight of his prey. Clearly the information on the leaflets was about the village history. The yew tree was hundreds of years old. Famous men of the village included, Wishart the evangelist who preached under it at one time. Mr William Beg a teacher the nephew of the world famous poet Robert Burns. Mr Moffat the father in law of David Livingstone born in 1745. Among the great and good the celebrated Col, Burd of the French Indian war of the Pennsylvania American revolution.

To think this village only fifteen or so miles from Edinburgh, Kaiser was surprised to think very little people had heard of the village.

The first wedding car arrived shortly after he followed the two men out of the shop. The groom a fisherman he had seen in Newhaven came from the car and was greeted by the two men who rushed forward to congratulate him with hands outstretched they embraced him slapping his back enthusiastically.

'You got here okay then, Mr Mason?' the groom said.

A wasted journey he realised was on the wrong trail walked up and got into the car looked at his watch still early.

As he drove away he saw the bride and her father get out of the limousine followed by another with the bridesmaids and a chaperone. The bride was resplendent in white. He wondered how she might struggle to get through the field with the long grass to reach the ancient Yew unfortunate for her on such a wet rainy day.

'So you drew a blank did you told you it would be hard going,' she said putting a plate of thick hot broth and slices of well fired crusty bread on the table.

'That looks good,' he said, 'but it's late didn't expect you to wait up. You must be tired Mary? I've had a tiring day but at least scored one guy of the list. One less to bother with. How many men with that name can't be many, ay.'

'I'm not long from downstairs thought about food for myself but you're welcome there is enough for two.'

Thought she would be asleep when he returned not expect her to be there with the offering of soup all he desired was his own bed he was bushed after driving all over the place and coming up with zero.driving to Dunbar asking the same question of people thought could be of assistance. Like the two old codgers, retired fishermen sitting on a bench overlooking the harbour. No, not

270

heard of the guy with the name. Anyway if this man Brodie was a small one man operator he would not land his catch at Dunbar large boats in the harbour no wouldn't compete here one old man said better to head back up the coast to the smaller ports.

At the few public houses where he stopped he asked the same question. Wanting to hire a boat to go on a days fishing. Heard it was the man Flucker the one to oblige. Blank stares and tight mouths was the result. At port Seaton he parked outside a pretty ivy covered public house noticed eight cars, thought the pub was probably a well known watering hole. Possible the restaurant could be a haven for good sea food and he was hungry. The smell was overwhelming. Fresh fish nothing beats the smell of fresh seafood but better is eating it.

A few yards from the entrance a small elderly lady tour guide giving her group a history lesson. Standing a little way back listened to what was being said. Two ladies a teenage daughter beside what looked like a grandmother with grandpa. A dad and a teenage son hanging on to the guides every word Americans possibly on the trail of their ancestry. The guides name was Becky her name on a blue badge pinned on her bosom directed their attention to the name above the ivy covered door.

'The Caryatid takes it's name from two mermaid stone figures that we will see later at the church,' she said.

The boy wanted to know about witches. 'Was it true Scotland had hundreds and hundreds of witches put to death?' She stopped talking about mermaids and agreed with him, 'later we will learn about witches and the case put forward by a Scottish king in England. A king made a lot of fuss about witches in Scotland,' she said with a lift of her left eyebrow and a hint of a scowl clearly not happy in the least with the boys interruption.

He spoke with a man standing near and asked if he was local found the man was the mini coach driver with the group. Said he enjoyed the different guides his boss got to accompany the tours… A bit of a coincidence the company is Butler chauffeur tours based outside Edinburgh airport. The driver said was okay with the history tour but preferred the golf tours. Being a player and enjoyed watching also getting paid for doing so, a dream job, he said, who could ask for more.

271

Walking past four small windows beneath the scrambling ivy he peered into the dark interior. Too dark couldn't see much so strolled casually to the main door where he lingered taking in the surroundings.

When he entered the tavern found out to get food in this establishment would have to make reservations. The reputation was so good to get a table would take at least a couple of weeks for a reservation. The staff in front house were run of their feet and he had the idea, which proved correct, the man behind the bar would give him no joy. Was paying attention to the paying punters having no time for giving out information to a stranger he thought was acting suspicious.

'Looking to hire a boat for a days fishing,' he said standing at the bar holding a half pint glass of beer but being ignored as if invisible.

The smell from the kitchen was so good it made him long for food he decided to ask the question the last time then head back to Newhaven.

The barman behind the bar abruptly explained he was too busy for idle chit chat and no he did not know anyone who hired out a boat small or otherwise and wasn't familiar with the name Flucker. The harbour was the place to hire boats he said not here.

'So you learnt nothing,' she cleared away his empty plate, 'bed time,' she said.

'I saw the house of John Muir in Dunbar. The father of the parks in the U.S.A. I believe he was born in Dunbar. A really famous guy. I learnt that much.'

'I don't think you will ever find Brodie Flucker,'

'He noted doubt in her voice. 'I've had a long night need sleep,' she said yawning.

'Why do you think won't succeed?'

'Och, just a hunch coast is full of wee coves. Plenty hidden beaches you are not going to find it easy to find a yawl landing a catch,' she said, followed by an act of stretching and more yawning hoping he would take the hint.

'Looks as if you really need your bed Mary can have this conversation tomorrow. Don't want to keep you any longer.'

'What are you going to do now? It looks like you won't get anywhere with your investigation and it looks like the mystery is not going to be solved.'

'I'll keep on it got all the time in the world to carry on.' Why does she think I would give up he thought, 'so we will get a result one way or the other,' he said, 'go to bed see you later.'

Not tired anymore thinking of what his next move will be. He could phone Tony. No, too late. Guessed he would maybe otherwise be engaged and wouldn't like to be distracted from whatever. Anyway he hadn't anything new to tell. He could get in touch with Karli but realised would be a no no considering the late hour. His thoughts turned to Beeny wondering if he was behaving himself now he was out the picture. Hoped he was not giving Karli any grief trying his ideas on her. Like trying to assume the role of being in charge. No, he thought, she wouldn't take any of his nonsense, knew she was wise to his mad schemes. Anyway maybe she held her word and seen to uncle Winter and taken him in hand. All this thinking was not good. His brain was in over active drive all over the place anxious to get results his heart racing. Let down at each turn was infuriating hoped he would get a result any result how small wouldn't matter be worth something big or small something may have came about to get a clue he needed a handle on the situation. Going to bed was not the answer he knew sleep was out the question. He turned on the radio fiddling with the knob till he heard the female voice rambling away in Dutch. 'Get a grip,' muttered to himself, 'too young to be feeling nostalgic too young to be wanting the comfort of my own language.'

'Hey, you, quit the bloody noise turn it off and get to your bed,' she shouted

He smiled reached and opened the cabinet a bottle of malt would be just what the doctor ordered he was happy just to get a small sample.

'No you don't. Don't think about it. Bed I said not booze.'

'How the hell?' He Shouted out, 'right mother hear you bed it is good night see you in the morning. I know it's morning now but you know what I mean sleep tight.'

FORTY FIVE

'I'm sorry missed you in Berts the other night Spider had to be somewhere else.' Frank said. 'When the wee lassie Lizzie came on to do her act had to get out of there fast had a previous appointment to fulfil couldn't risk being late.'

'Yeah I know Frankie, Old explained after you left.'

'He said you wanted to tell me about…'

'Find it hard It's hard for me to keep a secret and then find out what happened is choking me up.'

'I'm okay with it sometimes other times feel out of my depth. Getting pissed heals for a wee while but the hangover keep saying never again then back.'

It was if he was appealing for sympathy and wondered why he would seek solace from a man such as Spider. Couldn't get into his head why his brother thought he was a man to trust?

'Loosing our baby so hard for a while took a long time to get over it. Honestly I thought Annie would never recover. It was touch and go if we would stay together yet we did somehow though the memory always there I know exactly how you feel.'

'It's not knowing the facts what's bugging me.'

Spider Webb's front parlour at the house in Stockbridge Frank is waiting to find if Spider was going to give him some useful information but realised it was a bad move. How much help do I need? Old let him into what Jamie said. At the moment he is drowning. Don't know if coming or going. There doesn't seem to be much information coming from anywhere. The cops don't seem to have a clue. Bloody useless it's as if they don't care.' He was wondering what he was doing there. Spider was not going to be any help nothing he said was no more what he already knew himself. Keeping in touch, he thought might come in useful some other time so he was going to sit there and listen and show respect before getting out.

'And looks like the girl was responsible getting him involved in the crazy scheme in the first place. Seeing them together is hard to believe how they thought how on earth would get away with it?' Of the opinion having Frank there was embarrassing what could he say give him one drink might go before Annie returns from her shopping spree.

'Oh, not lay all the blame on her knew what he was getting into. What is it love is blind so they say.'

Spider smiled, 'when you see some who are together well the saying so apt. Me saying it like the font of all knowledge. Marriage, me, wow!'

'Not like you and Annie of course.'

Spider quickly changed the subject. 'Are the police in touch? Keeping you up to speed about old Jakie?'

'Your guess is as good as mine. McDougall doesn't seem to know much. If he does keeping it to himself. There is nothing so far about Jakie. They had me in but couldn't help with their enquiry.'

'Yeah I know. Good job we saw him in the fit the Walk. Whole pub saw him.'

'Thanks for that and as you say plenty seen him.'

'You don't need to thank me. Anyone would have done the same,' walked into the kitchen returning with a pint bottle of whisky and two nip glasses. 'A wee one will not do any harm. Was surprised when Jamie turned up here. Pleasantly surprised let me say not contain himself really enamoured with the lassie...' gestured ready to pour looked for approval.

'Why did he bring her to your door not think it strange he came here must have gave you a shock him arriving out of the blue.'

'From the hotel in George Street. Afraid they had been followed from London. A nice quine Annie was all over her. You know not having any kids of our own. She wanted to mother her but not stay long enough would have soon tired of the experience. Know how she is being on her own queen of her abode.'

Not waited for him to say when he put as much as half a pinkie amount of whisky into the glass and handed it over.

Miserable he thought, then asked 'Find out where they were going when they left?'

He looked long at the offering of whisky before putting the glass down on the table. He can have it he was thinking bet it goes back into the bottle when I leave such a miser he can stick his whisky!

'No turned up with the car. Took her away the last I saw can guess a shock when we heard what happened.'

'Was along the road in the boozer with McDougall the other day afraid to say it turned out to be a waste of time.'

'If had known would have joined you.'

Yes, maybe he would have enjoyed his company but possibly not. Wary of the approach thinking having difficulty in reading the mans thoughts. 'Quizzed about Jakie by McDougall at the morgue. There seeing about Jamie and the girl. Could see why Jamie fell for her. Why, Mary Mckenzie under the impression they were going to get wed but maybe wishful thinking on her part we'll never know.'

'Don't know no clue. Should have called in here after you met up with McDougall. Bit lonely just Annie and me.' Suddenly changed the subject, 'any idea if the mill will soon be back in production any signs of a new contract?'

'Wrong person to ask.'

'The Greenes you in bad. Heard about your latest spat.'

'Yeah in bad.' Now is sick of the conversation time he was getting out.

'No one likes that pillock Patrick. The weasel needs a long walk of a short pier,'

Refilled his empty glass, 'there's lots of guys in the job who would happily oblige,' he stretched his arms with his palms demonstrating the push position. 'Many waiting for the call. For a fact Patrick got lot of people wishing he would disappear out of it. A long walk you know the rest.'

'Got a shadow. No, think got a shadow coincidence maybe. Black Mercedes in my space wherever I turn round. Two guys in the car. Don't suppose you've seen a smart car like the one hanging about this street sure would like to know once and for all if in any danger.'

'No, not a motor like that.'

Walked over to the door to leave, 'see you later on my way to Berts. Give Annie my love say sorry to have missed her tell her I'll call again,' of course he was good at it, lying.

Talk of the devil. When reaching the street from the tenement building saw a Mercedes with the two black suited gentlemen inside turn the corner into Hamilton Place. Did they see him if they did why no confrontation. Why they keeping tabs on him he went down the steps into the pub.

She wasn't there disappointed would have one drink then call on her.

'You just missed them lucky you, ay,' the barman, Ian, said.

'Who was that then?'

'They two coppers Rooney and McDougall here asking if you had been in told no lies when said you hadn't.'

'What did they want did they say?'

'No, didn't ask. Not my business.'

'The other day you see the guy who McDougall had bother with you know him?'

'Yes, and?'

'Who is he?'

'Why, you interested thought, you know, Jeannie.'

'No not that. Was it one of his regulars?'

'No, you don't need me to spell it out.'

'You say …?'

'The penny at last has dropped.'

'Many?'

'Yes. Different all the time too many to count.'

'Well well, who would believe it. Thanks Ian.'

'I'll tell her you called.'

'No need.'

'Starting her shift soon. Not a problem. You're not going off are you it's not, you know, you're not giving her a dizzy are you. So soon. Be getting a reputation.'

Up steps muttering, 'in a boozer and not a drink who would believe it not me. A reputation? Thought had one already!'

FORTY SIX

'It's twelve o'clock on the dot at least you are punctual I'll give you that. Glad you are here when you said you would be hate people who don't do what they say. I'm so busy down stairs. You know it cant tolerate time wasters.'

She was watching the clock. Fearing Kaiser would suddenly appear and be seen by prying eyes. It would be a disaster if it happened.

The afternoon session was in full swing at Maggie Shaws. The fish market was closed workers from the market were in the pub celebrating the days bumper harvest. The market prices were above average giving Mary more strangers than regulars in her place. But of course happy her sales were on the up.

Lizzie was being interviewed in the upstairs apartment about a singing date on the strength what Mary had heard about the girls good performance and decided to give her a try with the accordionist Jordan

'Frankie Butler he said he saw you in Berts. You had a good crowd there,' said it to build up her ego a little encouragement would not go amiss.

'It's always good there they pipe men you know easily entertained. House always full. Some mind you a bit on the crude side but good natured with it. You could say a captured audience like to think the punters come just for me.'

'I hear there is some daft going's on in there, is that so?' This wee quine knows the time of day she's thinking money in the bank If play my cards right might get a deal to make it worth my while. Could be okay if not nothing lost.

'When they start the conundrums,' said Lizzie, 'so crazy hard workers who play hard You have to be there to experience it. You could have conundrum nights? Good for laughs'

'I've tried a quiz night but no good no one was interested fishing is all the talk that's about the strength of it.' She laughed, 'who would think it fishing in a fishing village conundrums no.'

'Think a sing song night would work?'

'Well Lizzie, up to you to make it a success up to you dear.'
She was taking a liking to the quine and if it works out good if it
brings the punters well yes.

'We won't manage an afternoon session Jordan works at the
market during the day.' She said hoping it wouldn't make a
difference better be honest from the start she thought not good to
get off on the wrong foot. The problem was convincing Jordan.
Lately he hinted the act was engaging in two many gigs.

'No dear not in the afternoon guarantee it dear. No, it has to
be at night would clear out my fish salesmen if they thought a
sing song was on the agenda afternoon no has to be the evening.'

'I wonder what has happened to him, Walter Auld. He was
supposed to meet me to talk about the contract. I've got him
acting as my agent at the moment. Not that got one you know
just volunteered to help only done it to humour him. Something
to keep him busy. The poor old soul bit lonely since retirement.
He takes control in Berts gives him a kind of satisfaction taking
charge.' She was now thinking the contract to entertain was
forthcoming and excited to think the old grouch was willing to
give her and Jordan a chance.

'Walter? Oh you mean, Old. Old Auld. Is he still on the go?
My goodness haven't seen him. Oh dear so many years ago.'

Her smile had Lizzie thinking the way she smiled maybe she
had a pleasant memory of Walter Auld.

'Yeah, not like him not to show. Supposed to meet at Betty's
café. Looked in only for a moment but he wasn't there. Couldn't
wait had to be here on time not like him not to get in touch.'

'Oh well suppose he will have an excuse. Won't surprise me
if been waylaid by the loon Frankie Butler. Worried about him,
been hitting the bottle lately. Won't surprise me if they met then
decided to go on a bender. Not in mine worst luck,' she said,
laughing letting Lizzie see her lighter side.

'Didn't think it would take much for him to go on the booze
seeing what he has been going through and Old doesn't need an
excuse should have got in touch though say if he was coming or
not coming. It's a worry so it is!'

'Well dear would have offered you a cup of tea but you see
how I'm fixed run off my feet down there,' she said, 'see how it
goes dear be in touch soon.'

In the street Lizzie got a glimpse of Mary's pot man hurrying away from the pub after locking the door. 'Strange?' She said Knowing Mary she wont like it that her premises are shut. Missing punters not spending will stick in her craw wouldn't like to be in his shoes when Mary finds done a runner not like him to leave so early.

Reached the café hoping to see or hear anything about Old
'Can I have a cup of coffee please Betty'
'Anything to go a cake or scone?'
'No ta Betty. I'm too excited to eat anything.'
'Why is that good news that'll make a change.'
'Got my fingers crossed. Shouldn't be saying but wait and see. Could be what I need. Had a very interesting talk with Mary at her apartment above the Shaws. If it has gone like I think soon be playing there a couple of nights a week. I've not told Jordan want to keep it secret to surprise him.'
'Good for you dear. Whatever floats your boat.'
'Walter Auld said he would represent me. He never showed up and to tell the truth I'm a bit worried. Not like him at all.'
'Typical is all I could say dear.'
'You never thought of having some…'
'No dear. Not have a music licence. Beggar the thought.'
'Don't suppose he has been in has he? Old.'
'No. Haven't seen him in ages.'
'Hope nothing has happened.'
'Why do you say that dear?'
'Mary thought he may have met up with Frankie Butler.'
'That would explain it dear.'
'You think?'
'You were up stairs at Mary's nothing unusual a lodger say?'
'No but she said a strange thing just before leaving.'
'Strange? What was it what was strange?'
'How busy she was. Heard the noise from below in the pub when I met her but suddenly a wee bit later nothing just silence no voices coming from downstairs. Saw Jonny lock the place up when coming out the stair.'
'Strange that was strange dear, my, closed you say?'
'Aye, strange. Hope it's not serious.'

'You think serious? My what next? Getting worse goodness knows what she'll think losing money won't be happy.'

'Wonder what's going on?'

'Not ours to worry about.'

'It's just scary what's been happening lately.'

'Village no the same. Queer things happening.'

'Aye. You think that Frankie Butler has something to do with it. Since he's been back?'

'Canny say but watch what your saying!'

'Jordan keeps at me to be careful thinks talking to a bairn.'

'Nice to have someone looking out for you. How lucky you.'

'Worried now come to think. Old, you know?'

'Canny tell them. Know what they're like.'

'Aye. They never listen.'

'More tea dear nothing beats a nice cuppa.'

'No thanks Betty better be on my way.'

'He's not going to show now dear.'

'Yeah if he was coming he'd be here by now.'

'Maybe right enough.'

'On the booze?'

'With Butler anything is possible dear.' She touched her hand, 'Lizzie don't think? No to horrible to think about it. Not think going to say it he's come to some harm you don't think that do you?'

'Frankie Butler?'

'No, silly quine…Walter Auld.'

FORTY SEVEN

Ten after seven in the evening at Berts. Tam, the bam was at the bar ordering pints of beer when he saw Frank enter.

'Hi Frankie sit down there beside the ejit. 'A pint is it?'

'Thanks Tam,' sat on the seat next Phsyco Bates.

Berts was as usual very busy he was lucky to get a place at the table.

'He's got something to say,' said Tam looking over his shoulder smiling at him.

'To your advantage,' said Phsyco a large grin on his face.

'Me, my advantage?' Smiled at the thought of it, 'could do with some good news at the present canny wait.'

'Tell him go on tell him,' said the impatient Phsyco when Tam returned, 'go on, tell him he's waiting,' said excitedly like a child on Christmas morning, ripping the presents from their wrappings.

'Let me get seated,' said Tam, 'you couldn't keep a secret if you tried truly useless ya bam.'

'Yeah, tell I'm all ears,' said slowly sipping the beer waiting what the hell was coming next.

'The conundrum,' said Tam, 'about A young lassie drinking tea in Newhaven. There's something in it. English quine came for a holiday many occasions it so happens. Came to visit relations and the villagers who sometimes took her on fishing trips. Your people could have known her the long time they been in Newhaven. Over time this quine became a famous actress emigrated to America and married a guy of Irish descent who just happened to have a huge plantation with hundreds of slaves. A quine visiting Newhaven and going on fishing trips? No, sailing trip but not fishing. They wouldn't dare too dangerous,'

Phsyco butted in, 'would have liked that quine. Strong willed. No me on a fishing boat can you guess what his name was?... Butler thingy you get it?'

He bounced up and down with glee saving himself from falling off the seat by holding on to the table.. 'Sorry,' he said, 'making a fool of myself, sorry.'

'My advantage? Off your head or what?' Frank said.

Phsyco prompted Tam to explain he thought Pontius Pilate was Scottish? 'Tam found the guys dad had been the governor at a fort in Killin in Perthshire. Was Pilate born there, maybe? Could be fact,' looked at Frank a kind of told you so.'

'It's your shout Phsyco get drams we've heard enough. Nae mair of your nonsense,' Tam said shaking his head..

Boaby the barman made the case of why he was about to tell the punters he was going to introduce wee Lizzie and Jordan, with his squeeze box because Old has been reported missing. Possibility lying in a drunken stupor somewhere, ha ha, laughter came loud followed by lots of clapping.

Lizzie took the mike. Put it down to her size and smiled at them. She scanned round the room seeing the friendly faces.

'If you know it join in and let me say if any know where the old fool is tell him am gonna kill him when I clap eyes oan him. But for now the song is called edged out and when I find him he will be edged right oot as well the rascal.'

The proceedings interrupted by sergeant McDougall and the rookie cop. The silence was deafening when the punters saw them entering. People stared others hid their faces. Ladies disappeared to the ladies and men sneaked off to the men's.

McDougall spoke with Boaby and after a few minutes left followed by the rookie who making himself seem important lingered a few moments eyeing up the clientele.

Murmurs went round the bar. The Rookie took the hint and left. Things got back to normal the talking got louder. People wondered what the police wanted with Boaby who seemed to some to be a little perturbed at the police presence.

Lizzie adjusted the mike.

I would never never edge you out like you edged me out
Can you not forgive and try to give another chance
A passing glance a knowing smile
A pleasing word to mend an aching heart
You edged me out knowing I was not the one to blame
Cut my love like embers of a dying flame...

Glesga Mary interrupted her and took the mike. No one seen her come into Berts and when the music stopped they looked and they could see she had been crying.

'You all know do some cleaning for the Old yin. Well went to his place,' she announced tearfully, 'used my key to get in.' Here she stopped and wiped her eyes and pushed back the hair from her face, 'have to say house was ransacked. Phoned the polis.' Fighting back her tears, she whispered into the mike… 'Dead…Found on that wee bit oh sand at the Tally Toor at the back of the docks. A man walking his dog found him. He thought it was a seal lying on the beach. The dog went mental. The man ran down after it. It was Old. Lying there dead,' after pausing, 'no head he has no head!'

Mark the barman helped her from the stage.

Silence lasted all of five minute before the yapping started again seemed no one one interested what was said.

Boaby took a deep breath, 'shut up!' He shouted over the Mike, 'there's been another one.' This got their attention. The barman Jimmy sat Mary down at a table then mounted the stage stood beside Boaby, 'have you people not got any sympathy for the old yin think you should show a little respect and vacate the premises?' He was met with silence, 'also to tell you, McDougall was looking for Willie Combe.' Here Jimmy took over, 'you know Willie, the cousin of Mary's pot man, Jonny? Well, Jonny has been found dead also. Same as what Glesga said. Not far from the Tally Toor. He like Old head…Cut off.'

 Punters began to leave slowly one by one couple by couple.

Boaby returned behind the bar. You better have a drink then leave. I'll have to inform Bert and get closed up,' he said to Frank.

'Wouldn't want to be in your shoes, Frankie,' said Tam.

'Why is that?'

'Cause the rate you are losing friends you are a dangerous person to be with.'

'You think it is down to me?'

'We going to Mary's place?' asked Phsyco.

'Why would we do that?' Frank asked him.

' About Jonny to let her know.'

284

'I think McDougall will have done that course you think what the hell!'

'We could get a drink at Mary's place.'

'Shut up,' they said in unison.

'I've got more,' ignoring what they said.

'Conundrums from a pro' said Tam, 'Maxi Mum think she's foreign that sums her up. No more oh your nonsense at this time. Things serious getting out of hand.'

'A canny win. See what like he treats me Frank.'

'What a shame,' Boaby said, 'go the pair of you. Need a word in private with Frank.' They watched them go pleading for one last drink but Boaby stood his ground telling them to go home.

'Your telling me Lizzie saw Jonny lock up Mary's place she mentioned to Betty at the café?' Frank said somewhat surprised.

'Aye, Betty phoned Mary to find out what was going on and Mary told her she had wondered why the silence came from down below in the bar and why there was no sound. It was so strange it happened suddenly. She didn't understand and went to investigate. Found they two lumps the two Marie's,sitting behind the bar not realising that Jonny had cleared out the punters and locked them in. You imagine the pair oh them. Doing their nails and gossiping.'

'No punters. And them sitting there not finding it queer what was going on they must have guessed something was not right?'

'No kidding bloody useless the pair of them. Bar staff gie me strength. And Robbie must have been on a different shift.'

'Mary? Could imagine wouldn't be happy not at all at losing punters. Her punters leaving she'd be mortified.'

'Ballistic. Threatened to sack them on the spot when they said Jonny ushered the punters from the bar then took off it was nothing to do with them. They said he had been having words with Patrick Greene and the last thing he said to the two Marie's was ye canny have bananas oan a fishing boat. Would you believe it bananas on a fishing boat. I'm thinking it's bad luck to say it yeah real bad luck and whistling!'

FORTY EIGHT

'You've got to let me get this slug.'

Tony's meeting with Rutherford was not working. Kaiser phoned to let him know about Old and Jonny. Was trying to drum into the coppers head that now enough was enough. And if the Met was not going to act? Well he was ready to step in to clear up the mess. In his opinion the way it had been handled now looked like they were all just a bunch of, no good, two bit rookies. As useless as the proverbial chocolate fire guard. 'How many more before something is done to end this slaughter of innocents?' He argued but guessed too well was backing a loser.

'Get of your high horse Tony said before we need proof.'

'Another one,' said Tony, 'same as the others. Two old men found with heads missing the other found in the sea… without bloody heads! You have to let me get after Burke.' How long is he going to stall was thinking. Why is it taking so long to get the low down. If he got Burke in a locked room it wouldn't take long before he got him screaming. He would make sure the fink would squeal like the rat he is.

'What you described happened in Scotland. We have no authority there. They have their own police force. What makes you think Burke has anything to do with it up there? Get down your high horse can't listen to your threats. You know it makes no sense. You can't go beyond the law you do something stupid can't help.' Was sick of it as well as Tony knew or thought he knew someone dragging their feet was running out of excuses. Fed up to the back teeth his friend going on at him.

'What about the copper who lost her boyfriend? If she is giving you the amount of grief, you say why don't you give her to me?'

'Gladly. Would give to you in a moment, but,' he shrugged and turned to leave 'it's out of my hands. She wants to get back to work know it's better if she stays in lockdown in a safe house. No one will be responsible for her safety. Not if she leaves. You know how it goes, system is there to save that's that.'

'She's a witness. Why can't I use her can't you give her time off and If she is agreeable can use her. A partner who knows what Burke looks like. I will make him confess you can bet your coppers boots on it.'

'You haven't convinced me Burke has his fingers wrapped round anyone in Scotland or anywhere else. Proof get me proof.'

'Much proof do you need you make me boak you don't half take the biscuit.'

'I'll do a deal with you if she agrees,' he hesitated, 'I will turn a blind eye up to you. No need to know what transpires between both of you don't want to know. You will be responsible and if you make a mess of it, well, it will be the end of a long friendship be warned. I wash my hands and know nothing. You will be on your own. Know it don't you?' They shook hands, 'Will call,' he said, 'stay within the law.'

Walked off and was wondering just what had he let himself in for. He stopped, turned, 'remember what was said got to be legal or it's curtains. Will be down to you.'

Tony smiled, 'you will be loving me when this is all over. Have the glory give you the head on a plate. Not literally but you know banged to rights proof,' walked after him turning him and hugging him hard.

'Go steady! Your like a grizzly took my breath away can hardly breathe,' he stepped away rubbing his chest. 'If the girl agrees,' he continued, 'don't count on it but speak with her and just remember I know nothing it's a terrible risk your embarking on be careful. My back will be out for a week. Maybe need some sick leave. I'm not promising a good outcome and what Walker will say if he finds out dare to think.'

The meeting with Rutherford proved fruitful. Sissy Maitland was sick of being cooked up in the safe house and jumped at the chance to help nail Burke.

Nearing nine o'clock the following evening. The heavens throwing it down. People hurriedly getting off the street seeking shelter. Shop doorways full of people who got caught out. Some brave enough to stand on the pavement trying to get taxis. Unfortunately the cabs were passing with hire signs switched off and other traffic on the road trailed nose to tail.

'Want to introduce you to my friend Billy Main,' he said, when Billy got into the car. 'Sissy Maitland meet Billy Main. All you need to know Billy she won't be with us long the weather is not helping he may not even show?'

'Hi Billy don't know what you're friend is trying to say but need Burke as much as he does. What I don't understand is why I'm dressed like a tart got me showing too much. What do you think? Think he's perverted?'

'Because Sissy when he gets out the car need him to take notice of you. I want you to bump into him. Give him some excuse to apologise. Drop your purse or something get round his feet make a fuss.' He was trying to get into her head how important it was not to go wrong and would be okay if she did what he said.

'If he recognises me what do I do and if he's got that brute of a driver Malky then I'll be in real trouble there will be no where for me to hide. I wouldn't like that man to get his hands round my neck,' says as she puts her hand on her neck and squirmed.

'Billy will be there don't worry he will see you okay you take care of what you have to do, that's all. Do you see the cab waiting over there parked near the entrance to the casino. The driver looks like he's getting rid of that man and woman who are trying to get into the taxi.'

'Yes, okay see it,' she said, screwing her eyes and peering through the rain splatter on the windscreen.

'Well as soon as I arrive you focus on the cab and what you are supposed to do. Then you get going. Will meet at Tony's flat,' said Billy, 'no matter how long. You wait. You savvy? We can't have you getting in the way let us take care of it. Just you walk get into the motor and the driver will see you right.'

She nodded, 'Just fall at his feet is that it? With this short skirt? It's so short it's up to my…'

'Nice knees,' said Billy giving out a low whistle.

Tony said, 'get on with it Sissy. Burke he will be here any moment,' looking at his watch, 'now listen. You approach and distract him. Sure you can identify him? We don't need a case of mistaken you know... Billy will be there by your side. You go to the taxi have you got it its got to be him Burke make sure can't have a case of mistaken identity.'

She nodded in agreement, 'I get it don't go on. I've got it!'

'I'll be there. Billy will grab him and bundle him into the car. It's simple.'

They watched her leave hurrying across the road hunched against the rain and making for a shop doorway next to the casino. Watched her squeeze in beside the other people who sheltered there. 'So far so good,' said Tony, 'it's a waiting game now. Burke is going to get a shock when we get him. Got an old score to settle. Wished for this day for a long time and at last if everything goes right will have closure. So let's see just how you look Mr Burke. You have eluded me for too long it's going to be my Christmas and birthday rolled into one!'

'Sissy was having second thoughts. She knew how important it was to get her revenge. Made up her mind if she got the opportunity she would make Burke pay. But now feeling unsure. Would her nerve hold? Sure, it was time. She wasn't happy too many people in the way and not happy and second thoughts about the skirt and it's length.

'What makes you think he will be here at nine o'clock?' Billy asked. 'How come you are positive it will happen?'

'She phoned for an appointment to work in the casino. He told her he would be there at nine that is why. And if you heard her talking on the phone, you would be a fool not to be where you said you would be.'

'What is she going to do in the casino? Has she got the credentials?'

'Serving food and drinks. That's it. You don't need a brain to do that. If she wears a skirt like the one she's got on wow! They won't be eyeing her tray would you? No don't think so. Anyway is not going to be working in the casino.'

Billy got out the car. Crossed the street and stood beside a shop door a couple of yards away on the other side of the casino entrance pushing in past a couple of lovebirds who take umbrage.

Tony started the engine when he saw the Rolls Royce stop opposite the casino got ready to move into position he watched the wipers scratch over the windscreen, 'bloody rain,' he said, waiting for the moment to nail him once and for all.

289

The driver Malky got out the rolls walked round and opened the passenger door. Held his hand as if to assist. Burke shooed him away as he got out waving his arms It was obvious to Tony they were having some kind of an argument. He wound the window down and heard Burke shouting at his driver over the noise of the traffic.

The Irishman stood in the pouring rain watching the Rolls drive off and he angrier as his umbrella is refusing to open.

Sissy approached as he turned to go into the casino. She walked towards him, her right hand inside her purse.

He looked at her in surprise and recognised her. Suddenly he screamed. He raised his hands to his eyes and walked out into the road dropping to his knees.

She heard the taxi screech to a halt Burke was lying on the road in a mangled heap with cars passing washing the rain over his lifeless body.

Billy rushed to her side pushing her in the direction of the waiting cab.

She walked away slowly with her head bowed through the advancing crowd.

The people ignored the rain and rushed forward to see what had happened.

A young man with a young woman bending over examining the body.

'I'm a nurse,' she said putting two fingers on Burke's neck feeling for a pulse. In a moment looked at her partner, 'he's dead,' she said.

The taxi driver said he didn't have a chance, 'the guy was just there in front of me.' He repeated it over and over again, 'it was an accident, honest, just an accident,' he turned away ignoring the body and appealing to the crowd.

Someone said, 'the man, wow! Six feet into the air. Dead before he hit the ground poor guy not a chance in hell to avoid it. What was he doing out on the road in the rain, like he wanted to end it sure case of suicide we'll performed.'

Billy rushed to meet Tony. 'Certainly was not on the agenda? Burke, he's dead, now what.?' Stood looking at the crowd gathered round the body. Cars coming to a halt and a police sirens wailing in the near distance..

What the hell was she thinking? Certainly cocked it up. What now?' Billy asked as Tony drove from the scene driving fast following Sissy in the fleeing cab.

'Pepper,' Tony said, 'didn't see it coming hit him between the eyes rather we got him alive but dead? Oh well.'

Two large bouncers came running out of the casino when they were alerted to the accident and when they saw Burke lying on the road one asked the question of the other. 'Are you going to phone her highness with the news?'

'Why not you?' The other said meekly. 'Why does it have to be me? You know she doesn't take to me.'

'Because it is me telling you,' he said, 'doesn't take to you my my. Who the hell does she take to?'

Someone in the crowd asked if anyone had phoned the police, or for an ambulance. 'Cant leave it there should do something?'

'Not nice to see the body lying there, like that,' a woman said, 'Police car has arrived that was quick someone on the ball.'

The rain washed over Burke's body as he lay a tortured mess. The wind blew his half open umbrella and it nestled beside him like a puppy snuggling for warmth.

'Who is he you know?' Said another to her girl friend as they moved slowly away making a path through the onlookers.

At ten the next morning they met in the park.

'You won't need the assistance of Maitland,' said Rutherford, 'do know Burke is dead? You're theory up in the air I warned you I said it.'

'You did you said it right enough.'

'Burke was not the one. Was the mother we have to get the mother. Still waiting for proof but Burke was of no consequence. Maitland will resume her duties. Now I say she is one happy bunny. Woman? Beats me knew she would not have been of any use to you a good job too stopped her from getting into any kind of trouble. Proof Tony get me proof.' He said it with a hint of, told you so. 'When you going to take what I say getting tired of the same old same old nonsense.'

'At least had an idea to do something and not playing with her fingers.' He would keep Rutherford in the dark, Maitland a different story. Not at the flat when he showed. Should have been there waiting like been told to wait. Played it cool getting revenge for her lovers death was high on her agenda and she sure pulled the wool over Tony's eyes. Pepper, scored a maximum ten. In out, he couldn't have done it better himself. To think subordinate to Rutherford. True saying woman scorned. According to the cab driver he saw her go into the flat lost sight after had done what was required. How was he supposed to know she did what she did or didn't do?

'Now the Irish man is no longer with us we will have all sorts of scum kneeling in front of the old girl looking to fill the vacancy,' said Rutherford. 'Maybe better luck now he is out the picture. We'll see who pops up.'

'You must have an idea who will apply or is it going to be another excuse for you to wait and see. The only concern now is Maitland she is going back to work too soon out there someone knows who she is.'

'If she is determined to return to her duties who am I to stand in her way up to her and will get her off my bloody back. Sore bloody back may remind you.'

'I thought it was someone higher who would say if it was okay for her to return not you? I understood she was from a different part of the force a country bumpkin,' he never could get his head round the difference between the many departments, city or village coppers.

'My chief has more clout than her village bumpkin.'

'Why don't you let me have her for a couple of days? Seems to me you have the clout could be quite an asset for me.'

'What you up to Tony? Why you so keen?'

'Get help you get the help you need from me then you get the glory.'

'You will put her in danger can't let it happen. My boss wants to give her a desk job to keep her safe.'

'You have her cooked up in an office on duty but what happens off duty?'

'What do you mean?'

'Off duty she could be a mark.'

'Burke is dead say no more. Final. End of story. No more about it got it

FORTY NINE

'Get up get dressed coming with us to answer some questions.'
McDougall was standing at the end of Franks bed.

Sitting up and yawning bewildered. Slowly taking in the situation, 'what now and how did you get in here? Never heard you knock,' Frank said. 'What do you want why won't you leave me alone sick of this. You know it's harassment need to see my lawyer. You do know have one don't you?'

'McDougall turned and stared at him. Oh yeah, good. Get up your wasting time.'

Rubbing his eyes looking round the room seeing the rookie cop rifling through the drawers and cupboards, wondering, what the hell?'

A female copper stood sentry at the bedroom door.

He stretched and picked up the clock from the bedside table it was exactly six o'clock he rolled over got out the bed.

'Get dressed,' McDougall said again, 'shift yourself gotta get out of here be quick can't keep him waiting.'

'What is he looking for at this time in the morning hope he leaves things as he finds them. Maybe if you tell me what is going on I could help. Still waiting for an answer. How did you get in here? If you've bust my door you'll be hearing from my lawyer. Be warned giving fair…What you call it.'

'Yeah yeah hear you,' said the Rookie.

'Get yourself organised. The quicker we get out of here the quicker you will be, you know, released,' said McDougall, 'For your information door was not locked. We knocked it was open we entered to make sure everything was in order. You must have had a good night forgot or incapable of locking it so come on. I'm repeating myself here. Shift it.'

Twenty minutes later in the interview room McDougall sitting opposite glancing through papers and twiddling with a biro pen. The young female constable on sentry duty at the door.

Leaning back on the chair eyes searching round the room. One minute up at the ceiling then diverted to the female cop. 'Is she there for your safety or to stop me escaping how long am I

293

going to be here this time? This is a farce and you know it. Why am I here? Many times do I have to ask the same question, come on how long don't you have better to do like catching criminals or something useful?'

'When we are through,' said McDougall, 'not before so be patient and shut it. You'll have your chance sit quietly. Wait and be quiet won't say again.'

Looking at the sentry who hadn't moved. Rigid her eyes fixed straight ahead in a trance.

He looked round the walls small blue and white tiles perspiring. His eyes fixed on a couple of rivulets sliding slowly down he watched to see which one would hit the floor first.

Rooney entered put a green folder on the table opened it took out papers then sat for a moment in silence studying the contents.

'Why am I here if this is a prelude to a silent movie I'm out of here for your information seen it all before don't wish to sit through it again so, if you are not ready to begin, leaving,' he pushed the chair back and stood up. 'Got to be at another venue. Party will wonder if I gave her a dizzy. Your playing havoc with my love life you know that don't you. Your upsetting my love life.'

McDougall said, 'behave. Suppose your lady friend is as real as your lawyer?'

'Sit down,' said Rooney closing the folder.

'How long we going to be here?' Asked slowly resuming his seat. Treating everything as a joke. Finding the episode hilarious he knows they are scratching at thin air.

'Mr Auld. We know you knew him so don't try to deny it. And you knew the man, believe you knew him as, uncle Jonny,' McDougall said, 'what can you tell us about uncle Jonny?'

'If you knew I did know them why are you saying I would deny knowing them never heard anything so daft in my life. Come on get to it why have you got me here you know your wasting my time.'

Rooney, looked at McDougall. McDougall, looked at Rooney and Frank looked once more at the constable and was thinking she could be good for a date. He reckoned she knew how to keep her mouth shut would be ideal remaining silent when he hung one on not like Mary Mckenzie who complains forever and a day would be a change and would be most pleasant.'

'Don't you think it's strange that you knew…'He stopped opened and closed the folder opened it and with his finger moving down the page…'The drunk Ross who's body was fished out the sea,' looked at McDougall to confirm.

'Yes, knew Jakie Ross knew Old and Jonny so did a lot of people,' Frank said.

'Old, you said,Old you mean Mr Auld,' said McDougall.

'Is that why I'm here because I knew them? Give me a break do you really think I had something to do with their deaths give me a break!'

You were the last to see him, Jakie Ross,' said McDougall.

'No, think you are forgetting dozen or more people saw him in the boozer at, oh, you know perfectly well where.' The last time you had me here if you remember you had to release me.'

'You were the last to see Mr Auld,' said Rooney, 'we have a witness who seen you leaving his flat. You were seen lingering at the stair entrance. Also seen over the road looking up at the windows of the tenement casing the scene.'

'Wrong, understood he was found at the Tally Toor in the docks not in his flat What are you trying to do to me was it the flat or the docks? Are you going to fit me up for Jonny as well and for you're information I haven't got any information on him whatsoever.'

'You could have done it in the flat then when it got dark got rid of the body in the docks. You were seen coming out of a public house on the Shore shortly after ten The night a night when the fog was thick'

'I must have been drunk. Can't remember any fog.'

'Definitely it was a really bad fog,' said McDougall.

'It was so bad,' Rooney continued, 'disability was down to, would say only a couple of yards. We know it's only a hop skip and a jump from the place where the deceased was found.' He glanced once more at the papers in the folder waiting for a reply looking again at McDougall who sat dumb was somewhere else just like the sentry staring into space.

Rooney coughed to get his attention.

'You have a witness saw me coming out a pub in the fog who are you trying to kid who is this witness is he in the building get him here, now. Like to meet your reliable witness. Go on let's see him or her. That's if you've got a witness? If not saying no more. Let's have it out with your grass and got some legs if you think a hop a skip and a jump will take you to the Tally Toor. You are in the wrong job pal would be sure of gold in the games If you think you're so good. It's probably a half a mile away from the pub you say I was in. I was in cuckoo land right enough…A hop a skip and… me,' he said with a laugh.

'We can keep you for forty eight hours.' Rooney said.

'You want to be here all night?' Said McDougall.

'You can produce a reliable witness to say you were not there can you? Cast iron alibi and tell me how you know the distance from the pub to where he was found? One you say you were not in,' Roonie chipped in.

'Not me. You said was there. Did not say was there. It was you who said I was in that particular boozer you sarge or was it him Rooney not me?'

'Now your at it,' said Rooney now riled and like the last time sick of him repeatedly saying, no comment, asking the question and getting no answer just no comment.

'Not this again, Butler. Enough of you before so will you please answer the questions put to you by the Sergeant and stop saying bloody no comment!'

'Is this conversation on tape? I don't see a tape machine is it being written down? I don't see that happening either. Is it a joke, or what? I'm out of here.'

'Where were you on the night in question, if you say you were not where we said. Where were you?' McDougall asked.

'No comment.'

'Answer the sergeant.'

'No comment.'

'Have you a contact we can get to verify your alibi?'

'Not said anything about an alibi. No comment.'

'This is getting ridiculous wasting our time.'

'And my time, also, No comment.'

'Just tell the Sergeant if you had anything to do with the three men. If you can throw a light on who you think was responsible if you say it wasn't you done the deed.' Who do you think is responsible? Come along.'

'Don't know anything about any murders or deeds as you call them. Cmon get it over with.'

Rooney gathered the papers and made for the door. 'Go but let the desk know if you are thinking of leaving the country,'

McDougall said, 'don't want to be wasting our time chasing after you. Don't disappear.'

At Berts two punters moving tables and chairs to make space for a piano and wee Lizzie was getting ready for a rehearsal.

The piano player ran his fingers along the keys.Smiled, nodded, 'Lets go,' he said.

'Ready as ever been though how do I convince Jordan about the piano? Think be pleased do you? Can see an argument on the horizon.'

'He can join in. Not see there being a problem don't worry.'

'Your right worry about it at the time.'

'That's the spirit you'll swing it.' His fingers ran along the keys. He looked she smiled and touched his shoulder, 'ready, let's as you say, swing it.'

The punters took no notice of her having a rehearsal with the piano and she was thinking if they don't show an interest now maybe it was not a good idea after all.

I am down in dreams
down in dreams
The night is day the day is night
Nothing is as it seems
The night is day
The day is night
And how I dread the dawn…

'Heh Boaby, what's this, a piano.? Not staying here listening to this why is it I bump into her all the time do you think she's on my case following me you'd say wouldn't you? I'm not staying. What a man has to suffer I tell you.'

'Good news Frankie,' he said, giving him the broadest of smiles, 'will be entertaining you at Mary's place next week.'

He turned to the door, waved. 'Is there no peace give me strength! More of it. Escape how can I escape it tell me?'

Ten minutes later was in the crowded pub at the Foot of the Walk. Made for a seat put his pint of beer on the table stood and watched a commotion with Sandy the barman. Two gadjies, arguing about not getting the correct change from a ten pound note. Punters silent listening to what was what. Waiting the outcome. Who was in the right Sandy or the gadgies his bet was on Sandy would be sure of that.

The place came to life again as Sandy escorted the two from the premises.

'Hi Frankie take a pew pal,' greeted by an old friend, Guy O'Brien.

'Hello Guy,' he said, 'my, how long is it imagine bumping into you here. Coincidence or what was going to give this place a swerve but decided to come in at the last minute. Gee it's good to see you pal.'

'A long time Frankie only been one day back from the states. Came back yesterday. Another contract finished. Now, I'm at a loose end again.'

'Join the club back a couple of days myself. Just back from Holland. As you see nothing changes.'

'How right you are. All the same faces. Before sitting down was asked to make up a four on the bones. It was as if nobody had missed me. No one was bothered had been away for so long…Strange ay nothing queer as folk.'

'Same situation. Know how it is. Came for a quiet pint only get bloody situations. People staring wanting the dirt. Distraction not wanted or need any time soon.'

'I was going to go over to Berts when leave here. You want to come we could make a time of it can hang one on and celebrate if you feel the need up for it if you are? Talk about the old days could get to oh find out you know.'

'No reminiscing Forget the past anyway can't oblige got a date waiting but we could have a session another day. You'll get a nice reception over there. They've got a piano and wee Lizzie singing. Well, she was when I was there half an hour ago. Sure the crack will be good but what you heard I know what you are leading up to…But don't advise it.'

'I've heard you've been having a hard time of it and sorry about your brother. The news about Old and Jakie Ross. It's getting more like Chicago every day. Have you no idea who is responsible for what's going on? Jonny…Who?'

'What makes you think it has anything to do with me Guy?'

'I heard it has something to do with your brother and a tart was the start of it I believe.' Looked for a sign on his face sat back in the seat gone too far he was thinking, reputation…Not wanting a pint glass on his coupon knowing what he knows about his friend Frank Butler.

'Your only back one day. You think down to me and mine, great, ay. Tongues are surely out in force. I wish they would mind their own.'

'Think you could do with some help,' relieved Frank let what he said go over his head. Was safe from any retaliation.

'It's the cops who need the help not me.'

'Remember when we had the gang in the village when we were kids. It wouldn't take much to get the word out for old time sake.'

'No not a good move.'

'Why, not take much to get the word out.'

'Better left as it is. Can't have too many running about like headless chickens.'

'See what you mean. Far too many loose dunder heeds.'

'I would appreciate it if you forget this conversation. Have to be safe.'

'Serious as that loose talk all that business.'

'Yes Guy. It is as bad as that. Really serious.'

'What about the problem you're having with, you know who gruesome twosome.'

'Don't go there.'

'Why they need sorting.'

'Is nothing sacred it's like smoke signals and jungle drums on the go all the time!'

'Sacred what do you mean sacred people looking out that's how I see it.'

'People. How fast the news goes round. Jeese unbelievable!'

299

'The Greenes spreading the dirt wouldn't bother about it. They sure have you in their thoughts like it or not.'

'It's not taken long only back yet you've certainly got all the gossip.'

'The usual suspects are spreading.'

'Putting blame on me but you know sticks and stains breaks the brains but name will never hurt as the saying goes.'

'Yeah, dangerous all the same some people can't be trusted.'

'You know it's why I'm telling you not to get involved stay far away further the better.'

'Okay, as you say. I'm only back but you take care.'

'I think will love and leave keep in touch.'

'Already? Oh well if you must. Remember know where I am. Make it priority and you keep in touch. Don't think be heeding advice though,' smiling, relaxed, now he was leaving it could have been unpleasant but decided to go and gave Frank a five minute start.

Tam the bam was sitting with Guy in Berts. The place was mobbed. No sign of wee lizzie he was disappointed not to have seen her was expecting to see Jordan but Tam said Jordan hadn't shown. Something said about the piano. Seems he wasn't pleased with the idea. The act, way it was was fine. Not needed bleedin piano. Looks like the end of a perfect relationship.'

'Some going on. Any ideas?'

'About him, the one who needs no help? Keeping it shut mums you know.'

'Yeah about Frankie. What's going on desperate times.'

'He won't ease up. Keep things close to his chest.'

'Has anybody tried to get on to it he needs help.'

'No he's not asking. Nobody dare get involved at this time.'

'Why?'

'The ones, you know want to help but he's playing the lone wolf. Won't discus or get anyone involved, stubborn, not the word for it.'

'I see. Playing the fool. Oh well get the drinks. Get a pint and a nip seeing your on the bell.'

'Word listen. Someone said, he was in a boozer not far from here it went something like…Approached the German bartender who asks his pleasure…'

'A German!'

'Aye. He says a pint of your best. Barman says, stranger, not seen you in here before. Staying long are you?'

'Would like that I imagine.'

'Holds on to the pint as it sits on the counter. Looks him in the eyes. Lingers a bit too long. Barman, uneasy, walks down the bar. Frank is watching him..

'Can see it just picture it in my minds eye.'

'Long bench along the wall. Three gadgies staring at half empty pint glasses.'

'Oh no don't say it.'

'One at end rises and offers a seat. He sits and takes a sip of the beer.'

'I'm still waiting you getting them in?'

'A minute…One says without looking, should go to where he came from not a regular. No welcome comes from other side of Junction bridge across the water.'

'Getting better.'

'Two in hospital, one, nobody got any any idea. Shutting time barman ends up with a cracked head also in hospital. Polis no idea how or who an invisible man, it happened. Non saying who cause don't know who. Understand? Words all I'm saying. Best keeping quiet, ay.

'After all that, think I'm due a swally. Getting them or no getting them?'

'Aye, in a minute. What you think possibly or no?'

'Asking me?'

'You seen him did he say?'

'What was it that war time saying careless talk cost lives.'

'Thought it was dig for victory?'

FIFTY

'I've got to do a delivery over the border a pub in Jever.'

Beeny was excited. Was acting overly enthusiastic as he sat her down at a seat in the restaurant could hardly contain himself with the news.

'You are going to Germany why tell me good for you going to Germany.'

'Want you to come with me.' He was smiling and giving her the impression he was doing her a big favour.

'Me? Why on your wildest dreams would you need me to go with you for heavens sake,' didn't appreciate the proposition had no intentions of going. The thought of it sent shivers down her spine. It was bad enough she had to work in the place but go with him. No thanks. No never in a million years.

He stopped her from leaving, 'sit down please Karli let me explain. It's like this....'

Nine thirty a.m, in the restaurant. Was being prepared for opening. The cleaning woman was driving her noisy sweeper in and out the tables and getting in the way of a young waitress who was busy arranging the seating.

'What's got into you?' She got up and walked pushing past him. 'I've work to do your keeping me. She returned behind the bar continued washing and drying the beer glasses at the sink below the gantry.

He followed her, 'listen,' he pleaded, 'stop what your doing and listen. Come back. Why are you so against what I have to say. You'll enjoy the change of scenery could be worthwhile this trip. It's a nice day to take your mind of things.'

'No haven't got time for you're mad cap schemes.'

'Come come and sit and let me explain,' he was hoping she would be up for his idea only she would let him explain would she see the sense in it.

'I'll give you five minutes this better be good your keeping me back from my work.'

'Are you two still here?' His father, Harry, came into the restaurant from the kitchen and approached them. 'I expected you to be on your way' he said, 'why are you still here come now business to run no time for hilarity.'

Before Beeny could answer he rounded on her 'Karli you have work to be getting on with you've no time for gossiping. We'll be opening soon so please. Stop what you're doing and get on with what is more important. Customers will be knocking the door down stop loitering.'

'Before you go,' said Beeny, 'it's important,' he held her arm to stop her from leaving, 'possibility to get into you know good books,' he said.

Two thirty or thereabouts in the afternoon they arrived at the yacht EUPHAMEIA berthed at Wilhelmshaven Docks. He eyed the situation as they got out the van. For some reason there was no one about. The dock area had an eerie silence except for the splish splash of the waves below the wooden pier against the hull of the vessel.

Karli carried a large bouquet of red roses on board and walked onto the owner's private deck putting the flowers on the table.

'For Mr Oldersum Trudi,' she said to the pretty blonde girl who was in the process of giving the large spacious cabin the once over with a feather duster.

She walked over giving her a hug and whispering, 'quick Trudi we haven't much time got to do it fast.'

'Yes, hurry. I'm expecting him to be here soon. He won't like it if he sees us here. You know the instructions are to be strictly observed. Cleaners have to be out before the crew arrive. So, come get it done.'

Beeny carried the last case of Jever pilsner into the galley when he heard the car arrive at the gangway. Car door slamming and raised voices shouts one louder than the other the wheels screeching as the car drives away.

'The boss is here early,' the chef said, 'in a bad mood by the sounds. Going to be one of these days.'

'Sailing soon? lucky you sailing off to the sun.'

'Yeah, you better get out of here. He doesn't like non people on his boat.'

He was hoping to get some information from the chef now he was not sure what to do because Oldersum was making his way up the gangway giving him no time to warn Karli or the blonde Trudi, who he knew was another in Kaisers game of spies.

'What you doing in here?' Oldersum demanded when he saw the two girls.

Trudi was busy going over a bundle of papers and gasped tried hurriedly to put the papers into the open drawer.

Karli across the other side of the cabin froze when she saw him enter.

Trudi trying to gather the papers together looked at him saw him coming and before she could turn away he pushed her hard. She fell hitting her head on the corner of a small table loaded with liquor bottles scattering them over the floor.

He knelt and turned her over touched the back of her head, 'she's dead,' he said looking at Karli with hate in is eyes.

She saw his blood stained right hand tried to scream nothing came, stood rooted frozen to the spot not knowing what to do and thinking he won't leave me here as a witness and Been she is hoping he would come to her rescue or was he dead too? Petrified she watched him move to the door now she has no escape route.

'Who are you who sent you,' demanding, his voice menacing frightening broken English mixed with a harsh German dialect.

Boss is early,' the chef said, 'no one is expected until later tonight. We sail on the midnight tide. Nothing new about him coming early he lives on this blooming yacht. Not a surprise comes and goes and always in a bad mood. Trusts no one would make a move if I were you get going before he sees you.'

Karli coming to her senses didn't answer. Looking round to escape spied a bronze statue of the naked Venus on a sideboard made a dash grabbed it rushing at him before she got near saw a small revolver in his blood soaked hand stopped raised the statue above her head ready to strike.

Without hesitating once twice he fired.

They ran when they heard the shots Beeny first on the scene.

'Phone the police,' he shouted to the chef who turned and ran back to the galley.

Entered the cabin saw Oldersum kneeling over Karli. Caught a glimpse of Trudi lying on the floor behind the desk took two steps forward saw the man turn looking up at him sees the gun in his hand rushed him kicked it heard the sickening thud as his foot hit his hand sending the gun sliding along the floor at once saw him rising holding his injured hand Beeny stepped forward delivered a blow to his face.

Oldersum looked, smiled and retaliated with a straight punch Beeny went flying over a chair lay on his back as Oldersum dived.

Beeny rolled out of reach got to his feet grabbed the Venus statue from the floor beside the dead Karli rushed and hit him with a vicious cracking sound to the back of his head, 'got you you b...... that's for the girls,' he said, standing for a moment in shock looked round the cabin at the scene he was witnessing sat down hands over his face tears running down his cheeks.

The chef being interviewed by the police inspector saying he knew nothing of what had taken place was in the galley along with the beer delivery man when they both heard shots. Now was worried he was going to be unemployed and no, he did not know the girl who came with the flowers. The blonde Trudi was a cleaner from a local agency who held the contract for cleaning boats in the harbour and this was nothing out the ordinary was daily routine and normal procedure.

Oldersum was slumped in a chair moaning.

The doctor finished bandaging his wound. 'The ambulance will be here soon,' he said to the police inspector, 'need an X-ray to estimate the full damage. He's in no state to answer your questions at this time.'

'And you, what is your take on the situation?' The inspector asked Beeny.

'Just a delivery. Flowers, wines and beers. First time may add.'

'You the girl the one Karli?'

'Yes. From Holland. I deliver in Germany from our place in Leeuwarden. Our last delivery was in Jever. I don't know who this guy is,' he nodded towards Oldersum while rubbing his chin with his right hand. 'All I know is he has killed two innocent girls who were doing what they were supposed to be doing. The guy is nothing but a monster…A two bit monster.'

The ambulance men arrived. The doctor gave them the go ahead. 'Take care of this patient. Arranged for the bodies to be moved. I'll follow you to the hospital.'

'Read him his rights Sergeant,' the inspector said, 'charge him with murder. Cuff him to the stretcher get him out of my sight make sure you stay with him.'

To two other uniformed policemen he said, 'cuff the chef. Read him his rights take him to the station.' As he spoke the doctor returned. 'Inspector, sorry to say, your man is dead. I'm sorry worse than thought head wound done for him I'm afraid.'

Beeny still in a state of shock how was he going to explain the situation, Kaiser and the others would have to know what had taken place was dreading the outcome what would the backlash be?. If only he had left her at the restaurant this shambles would not have happened. The police had their hands on the gangster Oldersum and about to bring the ring down but was it worth the death of Karli or Trudi? His head was in turmoil what would happen how could he explain the situation he was thinking what of his future what blame would be heaped on him shuddered to think. Retribution came easy to them and who were, them, ones who come out from the shadows. Now he was afraid for his own life.

'You say you have no idea who you were dealing with?' the inspector asked.

'No. Don't know who he is. All I know is he has killed my friend and the girl.'

'I've waited a long time to get my hands on that man.' The inspector said, 'too bad it's come to this. I'm sorry for the loss of your friend. We are on the verge of taking out a gang of vicious thugs. Drug dealers here in Germany. The many connections in

England. The British police are ready to hoover up the other's and close the operation down for good. Tonight we will have the rest of the crew when they arrive on board. Will be squealing like pigs now we have the head boar, dead roast, a good joke don't you think and the sow will be taken care of when she reaches England. Good results all round.'

'Am I free to go? What will happen now he's dead?'

'Yes. My man has your statement and home details you will be informed in due course. What will happen next I say case of self defence will be recorded.'

When he informed his father Harry, his father said, 'it's now time to remember.' When Harry informed Kaiser, Kaiser said, 'it's time to mourn and when Kaiser informed Tony, he said, 'it's time for revenge.' When Tony informed Rutherford, Rutherford said, 'if they were not looking for information on the yacht?'

Tony was furious with Rutherford as his snide remarks did not go down well and shortly after the meeting he contacted his young friend Billy Main.

'We have a little bit of work to carry out on the Kent coast.'

'Have we? Not recall the conversation?'

Don't you well telling you now.'

'No, if we had the conversation it's slipped my mind.'

'That is typical of you Billy you never listen.'

'If you mean Burke's place whats the point dead ain't he nothing to be had.'

'That's the point you don't listen.'

'Okay, why are we going to the Kent coast If I may ask cause got other things to do. A friend of a friend got something big on the boil.'

'Just be prepared explain it will come clear.'

'Not Scotland?'

'Scotland, who mentioned going there, no, not jockland.'

'Sorry. It's only you are on about it all the time. And put two and two together and came up with the idea that's all.'

'Came up with five, dozy. What happened to you on your holiday at her Majesty's, bad, or you're not saying. Pleasure park change to scary park got me thinking.'

'Why you asking?'

'Words, some said, suspicions.'

'What you on about?'

Looked at him for his reaction. Was what he heard true or idle gossip. Dig a little more and get the truth once and for all. 'Getting friendly with the wrong types.'

'Me? Why you saying? Thought you wanted me to help in a deal not the third degree.'

'Nitty gritty are you hold up with Burkes organisation?' Best he thought head on. Ask get his story see if it's believable. Knows the man too well. Can tell if he's genuine or otherwise.

'Burke no. Got that handle wrong. No not true whatever it was you heard.'

'Some in the same cell convert you?'

'You know I'm freelance. Always will be,' trying his hardest to convince him.

'Okay, now about this idea I have.'

'Burke's place. Kent coast you...'

'You have been listening. Yes that's it. Little jaunt to the coast. A nice night to go bat hunting in the country.'

Tracy approached them flicking his yellow duster here there and anywhere he saw imaginary dust. Now and then give some of his men regulars a little flick here there and anywhere in a playful mood.

He took a seat beside them and smiled at Tony.

'Get another two beers on the house,' he said to Billy.

'What you know about the demise of one called Burke?' He asked Tony.

'Why you asking? What makes you think heard anything about a guy called Burke said before no nothing about the guy.'

'These dames I thought well seeing what you done...'

'Burke and dames. In the past. Now go and fuss with someone else. Think your duster could do with a clean seeing where it's been in and out of you know where you put it.'

FIFTY ONE

Angelica Burke decreed the funeral for her son would be for family only and of course the unseen behind the scene.'

In attendance was the niece her two girls and an old wizened dottery Irish priest.

When the four bearers Burke's so called gardeners lowered the coffin at the side of the grave they left making for the big house. A single line walking heads down in silence.

Malky was behind Angela Burke slobbering like a little boy wiping away the tears in a large white handkerchief. The priest lingered a moment as the assembled walked back to the house. Soft rain fell as they proceeded in their moment of grief. Mist rolled in fast from the woods the sky darkened they hurried except one girl continuing behind and then in a shrill voice sang an eerie dirge haunting words singing in a German accent.

Tea and cake in the library was interrupted by the arrival of inspector Walker with Sergeant Rutherford and Maitland

In the drive three police cars and three police vans. A dozen or so police in riot gear ready all waiting to raid the premises and arrest the many, secret, mourners who were hold up in the house.

Maitland was new to this situation. Wondered how she would feel about the experience. The thought of her being responsible prayed on her mind. No one any the wiser. Could rely on Gissertini was sure. He was implicated so was positive would keep quiet about the episode.

Mother Burke was perfectly calm and when the maid ushered the police into her presence. 'Was expecting you, inspector,' she said, 'and news is not good from Willemshaven. Not good for my niece or her girls.You will appreciate she is in shock and awaits the outcome. Not forgetting due to attend her girl in Scotland arrangements for the girl to be sent home to Germany. But now suppose come to do your duty.' She was standing at the bay window seeing the police rounding up her staff and her hench men the mourners who tried a dash for the woods.

Unfortunately they were no match for the police who caught them before any could escape. She saw them rounded up along with her maid and her cook.

Walking to the middle of the room she raised her hands smiling, 'ready to go with you inspector.'

Walker smiled raised his arms to usher her out.'

'Take them. Read them their rights,' he said pointing at the others waiting their fate. The girls burst into tears, 'now now girls be brave nothing to be afraid of,' Mother Burke assured them, 'come along no one will harm you.'

Frau Oldersum, stopped the proceedings by asking a question.

'Inspector will you grant me a wish?'

'What makes you think you are entitled to a wish you horrible excuse for a human being? If it was up to me you would be leaving here in a pine box.'

Rutherford was angry at the bare face cheek of the woman, who dared to ask the question. It was obvious the lady could play the innocent game with ease.

The woman said something in German to the two girls. They looked at Rutherford if he was a piece of dirt.

Walker glared. First shooting a look at Maitland then turning his attention to Rutherford who couldn't wait to get out fast. He gave Maitland a sign she took to mean he got Walkers back up good and proper.

'Go and wait in the car Rutherford' Walker said, 'Take this man Malky with you.'

Maitland was showing surprise at what Rutherford had said, knowing how Walker hated him. Thought it was a stupid thing to do to get on his wrong side at this time and she wondered what would happen next wished the day was over. Pleased when this whole episode will be done and dusted.'

'Has he the right to speak to my niece in that manner? Has he no compassion? She is an innocent in this matter. Cant he see she is in mourning?' said Angelica Burke.

'What do you want me to do? If it's in my power will try to oblige,' Walker said walking towards the exit door.

'I know my aunt won't ask but my cousin is waiting in his box at the graveside. Waiting for the grave to be filled in. Would like you to allow some of aunties men to return to complete the task,' Frau Oldersum said in her soft Irish lilt. The caring way she come over caused Maitland to gasp at the woman presenting herself as the sweet Irish rose traipsing barefoot through the green lush grass.

'Sorry, ' Walker said, 'afraid will not happen. Will get the local undertaker to finish the job in due course. When the van returns you people will be taken to the station and will make a call to let the Scottish police know what to do about the deceased girl,' took Maitland aside, 'watch them closely, follow on to the station relying on you to do it right. The sooner Rutherford is out of my face not come quick enough. I'll see you at the nick later tonight for your report.'

Did she feel guilty about being there? No, was glad. Burke's demise down to the part she played. What Gissertini thought? Well their secret was safe with her. Not that she would be seeing him anytime soon or possibly ever again.

'Thought he would have granted her request,' she said to Rutherford who now was a worried man.

The old lady and the niece with her two girls were in the police van.

They followed in the unmarked police car.

'You showing your mummy side, again?' He said, somewhat scornfully and dreading the coming showdown.

'It wasn't too much to ask. How would you have reacted if the man in the box was your responsibility?'

'No Maitland. These people do not deserve any of your kind words. They are evil. Worse than evil.'

'Are you going to see them into the station when we get there? A show of strength?'

'Not a good idea drop you when we're there.'

'He, Walker will be waiting.'

'Yeah and I will be gone.'

'You will be when he gets in touch with your boss.'

'My boss is off to Germany.'

'Why?'

'I should have been with him.'

'Yes would have given me peace if you had gone.'

'Sent me to spy on Walker. What a fiasco.'

'Spy, on my chief, well I never. Why?'

'Spying to see how he treats Angelica Burke'

'The devious…And you never said.'

'No Sissy you know how it's played out.'

'Spying? This is no way to run an operation. What is going on aren't we supposed to be all in the same force but might have guessed the half of it.'

'Not privileged to let you know. Least said you know the rest. The instructions from my chief. Fortunately for my ears only.'

She turned her face to the window. Sighed, shook her head. What the deuce is going on here she thought. Her mind into overdraft thinking past events that did not add up. Was the rivalry between Walker and Rutherford going to end badly and what was the influence Rutherford over his own chief and how come he seemed to be one alone and master of all she couldn't wait to find out.

'You going to level? Bring me into the picture no didn't think so. The moon will turn pink when I fathom you out.'

'No.'

'All you're saying, is, no. Guessed that would be your answer nothing new in it.'

'Yes that's it. Now keep quiet.'

'What do I tell Walker, oh dear, will be expecting me!'

Routine procedure the woman were separated from the men. Walker took charge of Angelica Burke. Sissy was surprised not to be asked to sit in at the interview.

She watched over the two girls who wouldn't stop crying. Had an idea they were making a fool of her. Ask her questions they spoke to each other in German. She knew they spoke English very well. Tried asking about Oldersum and what kind of father he was. Waste of time. Waterworks got worse. A visit from the children's department relieved her of the duty. On her way to the canteen. She saw Angelica Burke and her maid. Frau Oldersum and her girls accompanied by two suits getting into two vehicles. 'Well that was quick', she muttered, 'Rutherford will be pleased at that I don't think!'

FIFTY TWO

Hi Mary is he there?

'Hello Tony, yes, he is here... It's for you. Your American friend,' she said, handing Kaiser the phone.

'I'm here.' Was pleased to get the call because he was sure everything would now come to a head and the worms would be coming to the surface. The buck he was sure would be passed amongst the ones who needed to save themselves. A falling out of the brethren trying to save their skins as per usual.

He waited and listened. Knew something was not right, 'come on out with it why the silence you there speak or forever hold your... you know get on with it!' His expectations were about to be shattered. The outcome not what he expected.

'No afraid not. Lot has happened in the last thirty six hours.'

'You sound despondent expected to hear…'

'I know what you expected,' long pause, 'the whole thing has been one big fiasco after another.'

'Oh don't tell me! There was me thinking the end was in sight but your going to tell me it isn't. Are you that's right is it can feel it in my you know where.'

He sighed, Tony could tell Kaiser was as much, maybe more, disappointed. 'The whole kit and kaboodle have walked except the driver who is still helping with Walkers inquiries'

'The driver Malky you mean the ex wrestler?'

'Yes, that's the one. He's spilling his guts and as far as can see he is spewing a lot of crap and you know who is lapping it up. Walker that's who.'

'How can things be so complicated as you say? Did they not get anything when they searched the Burke's mansion?'

'That is how things have panned out.'

'I knew, thought, what happened to Oldersum it would be a open and shut case.'

'No worry there. He was going down for murder. But you know he is no more along with his mob on the continent.'

'Well If the Gerry cops had closed down the organisation how come the English are dragging their feet?'

313

'Proof Rutherford keeps telling me over and over he needs proof. Sick hearing it. On his brain, proof, proof wants proof!'

'They have the females of the clan. Why nothing sticking to them they must be in it as much as the rest. Guilty they have to be. How, tell me no one taking any notice of the situation?'

'The driver has said that the whole thing was down to Burke and now he is no more. The driver is the only witness so far Walker has.'

'Are you saying Burke is the one responsible for all the murders in England,? Do not believe that's possible, no way.'

'You have to get what's being said. Burke learned his trade with the knives and needles on the continent with the help of his cousin. His cousin the Frau and Oldersum. I take it with a pinch of salt myself.'

'And the needles? Some boy this guy Burke. Has to be more. Walker is he only person to interview them. Something doesn't add up. Is anything else going to come out of this?'

'Yes trick with the needles,' he waited for Kaiser to say something… after another pause, he said, 'you there? Hello are you still there speak to me.'

'Aye, here. Trying to get my head round this. Are you saying, was no pairs of German hit men operating in England we on the wrong track? No something not add up,'

'That's what i'm saying. The driver has confirmed it was all down to Burke.'

'Wait a minute. What about the two who managed to get from Amsterdam. I thought it was these who were responsible fishy that's for sure.'

'Apprehend by the police when they got out of the plane at London airport. The Dutch alerted the English Met immediately they learned what flight they were on. Sent back to Holland under escort and straight into the pokey.'

'And Scotland? Who are the two hit men on the loose here?'

'Don't know about that. Looks like have a case of copycats. What other explanation is there?'

"No Germans responsible.The murders are being done the same way and can't see it being the work of copycats? No, no way. Too much coincidence.'

'It looks like you have got your work cut out for you there.'

'Phew what now where do I go from here situation has now became impossible. It looks like, now, will have to change my way of thinking got to start at the beginning.'

'Yeah looks likely but a feeling things here will surface again feel it my water.'

'Have you been talking to Rutherford and do you think he will carry on with the investigation?'

'Rutherford he's bloody useless thinks the information given to Walker by the driver will be the end of it. Or so he tells me. He is confident it will be what a mug!'

'The old lady Burke she'll continue? Think it possible she'll resurface hope not!'

'The old Lady Burke and her niece according to her lawyer have nothing whatsoever to do with anything. They didn't know of any of Burke's misdemeanours. Said they were shocked when they found out.'

'And do you believe that? Hard to believe.'

'Can only go what's said,' said Tony. Gives him a moment to ponder and he's thinking something not right with Rutherford . All this carry on about proof needing proof before they notch up a gear doesn't to him ring true. How long and how many more is going to be before something is taken seriously?

FIFTY THREE

'You, were in the Tip at Granton, last night?' Guy O'Brien asked.

The look on his face let Frank know he was not going to like what he was about to hear. The tone of his voice certainly one of doom. He waited, anxiously to hear the reason for the question. Was getting used to these types of questions but not liking it one little bit.

'How do you know was there nosey Parker's again on my case I presume?'

He asked the question. Was thinking if his friend had looked in the mirror, wow! What a mess his face. Looks as if went ten rounds with a prize fighter and didn't he come of worse. A corker of a black eye his nose covered in yellow blue cuts resembling a road map. It was obvious he was suffering pain in his joints as he squirmed in the chair trying to make himself comfortable.

'Better give him a black coffee, Betty.'

She stopped serving the fish salesman who was standing at the counter in his white coat and yellow rubber boots who's order all day breakfast was suspended not happy to be kept waiting turned round spied the man responsible for it's delay and was not pleased in the least for having to take second best what looked to him a vandal who shouldn't be there in the first place.

When she saw over the fish salesman's shoulder she came from behind the counter, 'my goodness,' she said amazed at the sight of his injury, 'how on earth did they let you out of the hospital looking like that I take it you did go to the hospital, ay should have staid in your bed stead of coming here, oh with Butler with him I'm not surprised.'

'Just coffee, Betty, if you please,' he said trying a smile.

'What happened?' Frank asked when he saw Betty retreat behind the counter and before she returned with a cup of coffee. 'Enjoy if that's possible?' She said, placing the cup on the table stirring it with a little white plastic spoon. She stood watching and waiting as the coffee whirled round and round. 'With him I suppose,' of course Frank in her eyes most likely to be involved with Guy's bad luck.

316

They watched in silence as she played the spoon the opposite way round the cup. She stopped and removed the spoon when she saw them looking at her.

'Haven't you heard what happened yesterday?' O'Brien said, squinting and wincing. Twisted on the seat pulling a face the words said in a hurtful whisper.

Frank listened. Guy was doing his talking through the pain. It was a sure thing a kicking was the reason he was in such a sorry plight.

'No. Did I miss something? The state your in. I'm glad I missed whatever it was. Must have been some party. Remind me to leave off your invitations. Some party you attended. Have you been for an X-ray? If not you should because it looks to me your ribs have been caved in.'

O'Brien tried sipping the coffee but found it to painful. He pushed the cup out of reach. 'Fine,' he lied. 'The Greenes, you know, recruiting yesterday. I'm surprised you never showed,' he said.

'They were responsible for doing that to you goodness,' Betty asked pointing at his face, 'take it you went to the police? Have to be checked and get it reported.'

'Why? They're not going to give him a job,' Frank reminded, with a wry smile. 'Betty go see to your customers. Like a woman to think of the police if that would help it's a no brainer.'

'Your telling me you were in the Tip and didn't hear what happened and no Betty they didn't do this to me. Yes, but in a roundabout way.'

'No all was quiet except the usual cat fights with the ladies. Who pinched who's mark. You know what goes on with these girls since their Queen has given up the game to become a Madame in a high class brothel. Rule has broken down. That's the entertainment I witnessed yesterday in the Tip. If you can call it entertainment. Plenty of fun and games, of the usual pleasures. What you mean roundabout way I bet it all to do with them. What did I say stay clear you not listen thought not pig headed never learn but appreciate the move.'

'There was a commotion. No, more than that, a riot, outside the Greenes office.'

'I would like to see what the other guy looked like,'said Frank.

'Guy's I'm sorry to say. It was as you rightly said one hell of a party.'

'Must have been. The state of your coupon hospital is right go it's going to take some time for your face to heal. Can't see you having much luck with you know what. Looking like how you are looking right now.'

'Thanks for the vote of confidence was doing okay till Night and Day waded in. The first I realised who was up against was on the deck, bang, out of it.'

'Oh didn't did you not him? Why you pick him when will you learn?'

'I didn't. He was just there in front of me in the mix if you must know. Not remember much after that. Tam the bam got me out of it before the cops arrived. It was a real punch up. Quite a few got lifted by the coppers.'

'A new contract for the mill?' Frank asked with a hint of a smile remembering his conversation with Spider. 'I guess the usuals were in the line up. Up front fighting to get their jobs back. All the jealous greedy ones to the forefront no doubt about it.'

'Yeah a two year contract. But thanks to you,' pointed his finger at him.

'Me what have I got to be thankful for don't thank me nowt to do with me,' giving him a quizzical look, 'you don't have to thank me for anything.'

'It was all down to you. You were responsible.'

'In the Tip yesterday. How is it my fault someone started a riot f...... nonsense.'

'Not long after the recruitment started the line was slowly moving up the stairs. Some in the line-up thought the Greenes were taking too long giving out contracts. Then your old pal Spider stood at the top of the stairs and announced to one and all in a loud angry voice that any friend of Butler need not apply. Well, you can imagine all hell broke out. The majority of your friends so no work for them. Suddenly the rumour went round like wild fire. The Greenes had a couple of coach loads of foreigners waiting at the middle pier. Cheap labour waiting to be signed up. Just after the announcement was made the coaches drove up and all hell was unleashed.'

'Can't blame me. It's down to the devious Greenes for pulling that stroke. It serves them right for what they've done. Hope the cops got involved. It's down to the Greenes. Now you know why they won't allow any union reps in the works.'

'The rumour is Mary Greene has lost the contract. The mill won't be opening for a while. Doubt if it will happen at all. The word the oil company is going to take the work to the continent. Leith will be down for a long time after this sorry state of affairs and the Greene family have a lot to answer for.'

'Wow it looks like my old friend Willie back in Holland had a crystal ball. He told me the mill over there was in for a large contract. Who would have thought old Dutchman forecasting the f...... future.'

'Where were you, later, after the Tip, still don't know how you got no wind of it,' He turned in his seat and caught her attention to bring him another coffee and when she brought it to the table.

'Betty were you in Franks company last night and did you get it on say yes.'

She smiled. Her eyes glinted in anticipation of what he was thinking.

She felt a soft flutter in her bosom wondering what he was playing at with his cheeky question.

Frank thought she would explode at the cheek of the question.

'Are you jealous, I bet wish it was you but not in that state,' sighed eyes lit up smiled you saucy boy,' she said

'Betty!' He rasped, 'behave please it's serious.'

'No harm in dreaming is there. If you think you are man enough well will look in my diary,' She said going behind the counter.

Frank taking a long look at his battered face and thinking, what the hell what's he cooking up? He was surprised at her response and thought, not bad, could be productive. Now and again had had an inkling of having a wee liaison with her but hadn't the courage to approach her.

'What are you scheming let's hear what's on that tiny brain of yours.' He said. 'Better be good cause you do realise what you're proposing?'

'Have it on good faith you know who is on your tail. Surprised they don't have you inside already,' said Guy.

'Do tell,' Betty said excitedly. Returning pulling a chair. She sat down beside them. Waited eagerly for him to come up with what she expected a fabulous story of intrigue. First she looked at Frank then her gaze lingered on Guy willing him to come up with the goods to satisfy her inquisitive mind. 'Cmon, you know waiting for the punch line get on with it.'

'Would you be willing to give him an alibi and stick to it whatever happens say yes.'

'Wait on here. Why do I need an alibi can take care of it don't need any alibi plenty saw me in the boozer.'

'Will you Betty go on, yes, you know you want.' Guy said again. Having trouble sitting.

'Yes but why does he need one what is the reason you want me to play your game. Tell me what's what then maybe give it some thought,' she said giving Frank a smile with her red luscious moist lips and he felt a little flutter. The thought of a little romance. After all even if she was a little just a little bit older not much and anyway it was only wishful thinking on his part but well, maybe.

'Not only is Night and Day in a comma in the Kranken house not expected to recover. But they found Patrick Greene last night dead. He was found with a silver handled flick knife stuck in what had been his neck. He was on the Wirdie staircase, just along from Granton Square opposite the entrance to the beach were his minder was found with a similar knife slash to his throat. But as I said not dead yet. Mary Greene is shouting from the rooftops. It's you Butler who is responsible.'

His head was spinning. Knives like the ones Kaiser got from the hit men made him think they were now getting closer. Why was Mary Greene out for his blood. Was she so certain it had something to do with him. Now he was thinking an alibi was needed. If Betty was up for it he would have a lot to be thankful for. It would would give him an excuse to get more cosy with her. The alibi would need to be solid because the night in

320

question was a night of drunken stupor. He had put away so much, he woke up in the ally at the back of the Kirkgate shopping mall sleeping between a couple of over filled waste food bins wrapped in a filthy green blanket he realised he had no proof to go to the police with. Now he was truly up the creek without a paddle. A foolproof alibi was needed urgently. The Tip is just a short walk from the Wirdie steps now he was in deep trouble Things certainly not looking good.

Kaiser brought Mary up to speed the information he had received from Tony.

Over breakfast she was trying with his assistance to get her head round the situation. The news was getting worse by the minute so it seemed to her.

'Surely you'll have to let him know what has happened he's got to be told.'

'No got to get another angle rethink and start from scratch.'

'Where how can you start again when you hadn't a clue in the first place, crazy!' Gathered the breakfast things from the table shaking her head. Scowling as she chucked the dishes into the sink. 'How you going to do it?' stood with her back to him turning from the sink when she heard the door close. What is going to happen know she was thinking. How will it end, pulled a chair and sat at the table wiping tears from her eyes.

Kaiser put the plate with the bread roll containing fried egg on the table. He sat down and lifted the large white mug of tea to his lips and gave the man across from him a smile and a quick nod at the same time clocking his surrounds.

'Have you got back to work in the mill?' He asked casual.

Was obvious to him the man was a product of the pipe mill.

In the greasy spoon café outside the dock gates. The elderly man, sitting across the table wearing a silver safety helmet. Had a red bandana tied round his neck burnt face was craggy a sure result of being too much in the sun. The accent was definitely Aussie. Had on a Khaki shirt with broad pockets on his breast. Khaki trousers tucked into his safety rigger boots. A gaffer was sure of it seen the likes at the mill at Delzijle when he visited Frank on occasions.

'No, not at the moment. Still on standby.' He said giving him a smile and looking round pulling his seat getting ready to leave. 'Is that so thought a contract was in the offing might have got it wrong.'

'It was, it is,' he stuttered the words, 'there was a bit of a to-do about recruiting workers and things are on hold at the moment. Soon, maybe get the outcome just waiting.'

'Bloody unions! Always holding things up.'

'No not at all nothing to do with them.' He lifted and finished his coffee put the empty mug on the table.

Kaiser watched him through the window as he made towards the dock gates. He imagined the guy was whistling Waltzing Matilda as he swaggered on his way.

'You're set up. You're job is safe,' he mumbled when deciding to leave. A quite stroll was on the agenda to clear and get his brain into gear.

Four men sitting at the adjacent table eating egg rolls and drinking mugs of tea, heard what he said.

'You know him do you were looking to get back? The mill back to the graft.'

'No. What makes you think I know him just having a friendly conversation that's all. Exchanging pleasantries. Nice to be you know. Doesn't cost to be friendly.'

'You're foreign, aren't you? From the mill we're all from the mill,' One interrupted.

'Dutch. Yeah foreign you are correct but from the mill no not there. Don't fancy it. Working there understand.'

'Why the interest it's a great place to work I tell you.' another said but in a gruff manner.

'We are on the beach out of work pipe men,' said another, sneering as if pointing blame.

'Sorry about that was just making conversation that's it.'

'What did you learn from the Australian we were going to chat with him but you beat us to it,' first guy said.

'Not a friendly way to be you being foreign as well,' another one said giving him a hint of malice.

Kaiser had his suspicions, realised, they were not pipe men from the factory,

'Contract still under review. So that man said,' he said.

'You looking to get work at the mill if not already. The third man asked. Said not up to the work but maybe putting us off.'

When the first man, who asked the question, rose up from his place at the table he adjusted his coat and Kaiser saw the head of a baseball bat secreted inside. Checking the rest of the gang he could see the tell tale bulge of bats under their coats. He smiled to himself fun and games here recon he mused.

'You guys are giving out bad vibes.' He said, 'hope you are not thinking about anything that is not going to be good for my health? If you are would like to introduce you to my friend.' He gave them a glance of the revolver in his underarm holster as he slowly sauntered past on his way out the exit.

He decided to walk through the docks and soon found himself nearing the local, council sewage works. The smell that greeted him made it obvious what was in front of him. The smell was overwhelming. On the deserted road he was aware the men from the greasy spoon were on his tail. Slowing he let them get closer. Seeing each carrying their choice of weapons the baseball bats he wasn't lingering. Sure what to do and not waiting for or expecting an explanation.

They came after him shouting at the top of their voices whooping as they came.

A leisurely stroll to Portobello, he thought, would give him time to ponder to get his head into some sort of closure about the situations he found himself. He was not expecting to find himself in any kind like the present situation with this gang of thugs. This he did not need but was ready to meet the situation head on. The four gadgies he was not sure if were separate from the present caper he was engaged in. But then, who knows, so to be safe he was not taking any chances. They were out to get him and if they were involved well they would be less to worry about.

He saw the wire fence spied a large hole leading into an empty field a short distance from the sea wall. He ducked under and scrambled through the nettles and weeds and waited for them to follow.

Like mice leaving their hole. One after the other they came in single file one then the second followed by the third and finally the fourth falling over each other eager to do what they wanted to do. As they hurried to get through the hole in the fence the first fell and the others fell over him cursing. Surprised not knowing how fast the man they were after acted, swift and without hesitation, fast, perfect aimed shots. Easy as shooting fish in a barrel. Three lay dead one lay moaning and asking why? He smiled down at him and answered by putting a bullet through his brain then he walked out under the fence. The street was deserted was glad no one to witness what had taken place. But why? For what reason did they come after him would he ever find out. So only got what they desired to do to him but why? Was it something to do with the man named Brodie? Possibly he thought but certainly was a mystery.

Later sitting on a bench on the promenade at the beach watching the family's enjoying the summer day. Drinking coffee in a plastic cup and eating a large beef burger. He was there seeing and admiring the crowds on the sands enjoying the warm weather. The children having fun. Donkey rides and bucket and spade gangs running here and there. To him the pleasure, of them not having any cares whatsoever. He was brought to mind his care the last victim dying asking why and not giving the answer.

'You had a nice day for it, said Mary. Lucky you, sitting in the sun at Portobello beach. Takes some to get the cream ay.'

'Yes Mary but was thinking about you.'

'Me, Goodness.

'Thinking about you being stuck down there in a stuffy public house and me sitting at the beach eating burgers sun shining. Yes, was thinking about you. Just thought how nice to have your company and not have to worry about anything.'

'Go on with yourself spect you were watching all the quines lazing about in their nearly swim suits. They ones that don't see the water. Go on thinking about me, never,' she came over all coy and giggled like a teenager.

324

'I was Mary. How many hours days nights your in that place you should delegate and have some time off now and again get some fun.'

'With they numpties got working in there no way. I'd be bankrupt within the week. They are clock watchers. Yes that's it. Just clock watchers. No interest. Not got my interest just waiting for the hands of the clock to reach the end of a shift. Out and away. No interest whatsoever.'

'A wee bit much of the sun. Think call it a day and have a kip. See you in the morning.'

'Okay, glad you've had a nice day. Sleep tight.'

'How you get on with him today Frank I haven't seen him since last night. Missed the gang fight that took place some dead I heard.'

'Terrible news wasn't it. That poor Patrick his sister Mary is in a terrible state poor quine.'

'He was not there. Know for a fact he was not there.'

'Surprised at that he's in bad with the Greenes.'

'Saw his pal Guy both in the café.'

'The loon his face bashed. In the pub downstairs Archie McDougall was quizzing him wanted to know how he was in that condition must have been satisfied with the answer. Not quizzed him for long. Was surprised? Came off a motorbike lucky not to be killed. That's the story I heard but maybe there is something different in that story.'

'You got a better explanation? If McDougall took it as said then why you think differently?'

'Motor bikes, ask you.' Wonder he wasn't with him, Frankie, my the two always thick as thieves since they were bairns. Crazy loons the pair of them.'

FIFTY FOUR

'You sit there as bold as brass pleased with yourself expecting me to congratulate you on a job well done must be bloody mad don't get you not at all.'

They met in the park at their usual bench discussing the Burke case and how Rutherford handled the affair.

Tony was scathing, pointing out if he had been in charge the outcome would have been a very very different outcome.

'They had no case to answer. The lawyer said it was down to the son. Unless Walker had any information to the contrary he had to let them go.'

'Let them go? That's it free as the birds out goodbye cheerio move nothing to see here. Strength give me strength!' Tucked the newspaper under his arm and walked off.

'It was not my decision. I'm not in control,' said Rutherford. Too late. Tony was out of earshot making his way out the park.

Later in the day drinking coffee in the Blue Star.

'Do you want a beer,' asked Tracy going through the ritual of lifting and wiping the bar with a flair of urgency like he does when listening for gossip. Not seeing Tony for a while needed to learn what was new on the Burke case.

'Not at the moment we're having a conversation. Go and bother someone else,' he had no time or patience for his put on act at this time.

'You had a let down sounds like it my my don't count on any sympathy from *moi*. Serves you bloody well right bad tempered person,' was not a happy bunny.

'What are you on about let down go annoy someone else get out my face.'

'Oh dear. We are in a mood. Sorry for asking. I'll get out your face you bad tempered person,' said again but this time with a smile and a flick of his yellow duster leaving them as he minced his way down to the other end of the bar.

They lifted their coffee cups and moved to a vacant table.

326

Tony said in a low voice. 'The bruiser Malky has been let loose after he done a deal with Walker so this is what we do.'

'Go after him then what bash his brains in shoot him or what I'm up for whatever.'

'Get information that is what have to find out what is going on in Scotland.'

'We talking about Kaiser? You never said he was in Scotland. Wondered why he was in the flat for such a short time. Thought he was in Dutchland.'

'Yes now you got it got to get to the bottom of what's going on once and for all.'

'Will we be going there, Scotland, keep on about it Scotland.'

'No listen. Rutherford said the Burke's have their place on the market. The casino is no more has been closed down and the licenses revoked. The bruiser has taken his employers by road in their Rolls to Holyhead they caught the ferry to Dublin. He has to return to be a sort of caretaker until the place that Mount something and other properties belonging to the Burke's, is in the hands of the estate agents until they are sold. But mark my words we will have a surprise waiting for him when he gets back and bet he'll be surprised to meet up with you.'

'Why do we need him let's go to Scotland.'

'Go and get two beers, then I will give you the low-down,' shook his head as he watched him go to the bar and returning with two bottles of beer.

'I know he knows more than he's told Walker. Must find who is responsible for what's going on up North. Kaiser needs to solve the mystery once and for all. The bruiser he will, sure, be in for a surprise when he returns.'

The local church bell struck ten booming across the quite warm evening just as they stopped at the gates of Mount Kenny.

'What now?' asked Billy when he found the gates locked.

'Get in. We'll drive further up the road and look for a place to park out the way. There must be a gap somewhere in the fence or the wall,' an impatient Tony said. A closed gate was not going to scupper the project he had in mind.

They traveled only a short distance before getting out the car and walked along the estate wall searching for somewhere to get access into the grounds. Not long before they came across a small wooden door covered in wild blackberry bushes they pulled making a passageway through didn't take Tony long to kick open the door unfortunately for Billy who complained bitterly about his hands suffering from many sore scratches by the thorns on the bushes. The moon in shadow they sneaked hurriedly through a small part of the wood then crossed a field to the well manicured lawn in front of the dark deserted house.

Billy used his expertise opening the french window next to the bay windows leading into the library still complaining about the scratches on his hands and seeing Tony wearing gloves he said, 'gloves you should have said needed gloves should have warned me my hands look at my hands these are my tools,' going on and on about his hands.

'Quite, stop moaning maybe someone will hear keep it down.'

Once inside Tony closed the curtain shone his torch found the light switch and put on the lights. 'Careful. No one here. Leave no clues be careful.'

'Wow! Posh or what,' said Billy hands forgotten. Wasn't listening to Tony.

He picked up a large blue vase...Crash let it slip when he turned it over to see it's maker's marks it shattered into a hundred pieces, 'whoops there goes a few thousand. Oh well easy come easy go. Plenty more where that came from. A little treasure house here ready to be plucked Wow!' he said pulling the cover from the nearest display cabinet. 'Gold and silver Roman by the looks.'

'We're not here for that purpose. Hands his tools who's he kidding,' Tony muttered, 'will you stop playing the fool keep your mind on the job. Go upstairs make sure we don't have company but first put back the covers on the glass case before you go,' now whispering, 'leave the mess on the floor,' not happy with Billy eyeing the treasures, 'might have guessed you would get distracted plenty time later.'

Moved from room to room. White dust sheets covered the furniture the windows shuttered the house locked down tight. Tony was surprised to find there was no security system in place, it seems the Burke's failed on that score, or were they so secure in their thinking too important for such things but thankfully he and Billy were now free to wander over the premises knowing the mansion was deserted.

They came down the stairs making their way to the kitchen.

After a short time they heard a car approaching scrunching on the gravel drive.

'Hello Malky.' Billy surprised him coming into the house carrying two suitcases.

'Put down,' he showed him the revolver, 'there's a friend waiting for you in the kitchen. You know the way get going move don't look back go.'

'Billy Main what are you doing here?' he said surprised, smiled, 'why the shooter Billy? No need pal going.'

'Just hurry. Don't make me use it walk.'

'Thought we had an understanding you going back on it?'

Tony tied him to an upright wooden kitchen chair with a silk cord taken from one of the bedroom curtains.

'A few questions,' said Billy. 'If you tell me what we need to know you won't be harmed. But no need to tell you. You know what will happen so spill.'

'I know who you are. You're that dick Gissertini. What do you want can't help you. Whatever it is your after I don't know know nothing. And Billy you're an arse!'

Going over to the stove spooned some coffee into a pot and filled it with water from the tap. When the coffee was ready, he poured two cups. Handed one to Tony then approached Malky.

'If you say what's what will give you this cup but if you don't tell us what we need to know, well, Tony here will not be happy with you. Understand it's simple.'

'No thanks. You can't stay here expecting people.'

Billy put the cup on the table turned faced him then with the butt of his gun smashed it down on the bruisers right kneecap.

He screamed as the blow cracked the bone sending out a loud sickening noise.

'Just a few questions that is all we want,' he said smiling holding the gun over the other kneecap, watching, waiting for a response. Thinking the first blow would get the desired result no but the second was sure it would.

'Okay ask your questions no need for violence. I don't know what can add only the driver for the old girl. Only doing as I was told that's all. You know me Billy thought we were friends why are you doing this said already know nothing,'

'Who killed the people who got in Burke's way,' asked Tony, rising from the table walking menacingly towards him.

'Burke that's who was just the driver you know. Honest and Billy knows it. Tell him Billy it's the truth tell him.'

'Germans?' Tony surprised him with the question.

'What Germans? I know nothing about Germans.'

'Who killed the girls I know you know,' quickly changing tack trying to trip him.

'Burke said Burke. He did it and the dealers. Please, Billy, tell him go on you know don't you.'

'Scotland, what about Scotland?' Tony quickly changed tack again.

'Haven't a clue what your talking about... My leg... I won't be able to walk,' moaned and whimpered like a pup being removed from the bitch.

'You should never had done that Billy. I won't forget what you've done. You forget what I've done for you. Remember?'

'Get to it. Tell him what he wants to hear, or, you know it'll be worse for you.'

Tony retreated. Billy sidestepped then approaching struck the other kneecap with so much force another cracking sound was heard. The chair and the man went flying backwards. He lay in agony moaning and working his hands loose. Billy moved to raise him from the floor Malky got his hands round Billy's neck and squeezed hard choking him.

Tony rushed to free him saw Billy's lifeless body sprawled on the floor blood oozing from his mouth eyes wide open staring 'you've done and killed him.'

The bruiser swung forward grabbed him round the waist lifted him up. Both fell with a thud on the floor had him in a bear hug squeezing the life out of him. Moaning and grunting he squeezed and squeezed.

Stretching his arm Tony feeling the life leave his body searched with his open hand back and forth reaching retrieved the pistol from where Billy dropped it. He fired point blank into the bruiser killing him instantly pushed the dead heavyweight to one side got up sat for what seemed forever gathering himself together shocked trying to fathom just what had happened. Walked to check on Billy moved and turned the bruiser over. Still in shock wandered outside saw the Rolls approached and opened the trunk then back into the house returned carrying Billy put him into the trunk fetched Malky pulling by his feet dragged him, struggling, shoving pushing, got him into the the drivers seat and positioned as if was caught unawares.

Crossing the yard entered the double garage found a five gallon can filled with petrol. Back to the Rolls poured the petrol over it setting it alight.

The flames engulfed the smoke billowed hovering over the car then suddenly explosion scattered the remnants high into the night sky.

He casually walked back to the house. Inside the door he spied the two suitcases the Malky brought into the house..

In the kitchen he opened the first case it was full of clothes to suggest he was going on a long journey, passport, a handful of pound notes and a single ticket for the Dublin ferry most likely on his way to join Angelica Burke.

The second smaller case was a real eye opener two tightly packed bundles containing fifty thousand in used bank notes.

Returning upstairs to the bedroom collected another silk cord from the curtain.

Back in the kitchen upended another chair wrapping the cord round as if it had been used like the other on the floor.

Emptying the clothes the passport and small amount of pound notes onto the floor leaving signs of mayhem taking place.

Left the house and for a few minutes watched the car burn, removed his gloves threw them into the flames. 'Bye Billy,' he said quietly.

The rain came on stronger. Hurrying crossed into the wood turning now and then picking his way through the tangle of bushes and fallen branches stopping to look at the scene behind him no sign of life only the red glow showing in the distance from the fire he started in the double garage was thinking the rain may save the fire reaching the main house. Would need to hurry. Got to be on his way no time for lingering done what had to be.

331

Reached his flat without incident. Was surprised he drove from the Kent coast not seeing or hearing any signs of fire engines or any police activity on the way.

Stayed up late drank a full pint of whisky. In the process of wracking his brains on what had gone wrong why had Billy died? Blamed himself for what happened. Muttering on about getting to old to stupid playing this foolish game. Woke in the afternoon and vowed never to touch the stuff, whisky, again. Head felt if it was in another room.

The rest of his body was numb. He thought if he wanted could stab himself with the bread knife and not do himself any harm. Not that he was going to try it. But he reckoned that would be what would happen nothing.

He stuck his head under the cold tap and of course that was no use was no good still had the daddy of all hangovers knew the solution would be a return to bed and sleep let the headache take care of itself.

12 Noon next day Rutherford was looking at the suitcases. One large one small standing on the floor inside of the outside door. Brain into overdrive wondering the reason.

'Going somewhere?' He asked still wondering the occasion for the fat man to be getting his head into gear. A holiday well well. Why? Not like you to be doing something as brave as a holiday?'

Tony feeling much better after getting over his hangover but not in a good place. Not happy to have visitors not as such as Rutherford when he had much to think about.

'You did not say you were going anywhere,' surprised he found him to be in a seemingly quite mood not his usual gruff smart aleck way he had to put up with on occasions. 'By the look you look as if you had a hard night. Serves you right thinking not in that doss house were you…No don't need to know!'

'Scotland having a short break,' poured two small measures of whisky gave him one then sat opposite in the easy chair. Faced him looked but kept silent. Waited.

'See you took my advice and got the place tidied.'

'I'm off to Edinburgh recharge my libido. If you must know,' he said forcing a grin. 'You can have another then go got to get going. Must be out soon.'

'Two cases?' Rutherford nodded in their direction, 'sure it's a short break?'

'You spying on me are you when did it come about had to let you privy to my coming and going's gee what have to put up with should be glad getting out your hair.'

'You wont be going to stick your nose into the Scottish constabulary dealings, no don't. Another answer do not need to know. Nosing into what's ongoing with their problems will get you into trouble you will have to keep your wits about you,' said suspiciously and hoping to get to the bottom of why the sudden urgency. Feeling more to be had if he persisted.

'A bit of fishing with my friends been planned for sometime now. I'm curious to see the place where the game of golf was first played hundreds of years ago. It's in or near Leith. I'm led to believe. That's if you are interested in such things.'

He wondered just what Rutherford was going to lead up to next why the visit good news or bad news, knew his journey back from Kent was faultless so okay on that score.

'All very well but have to ask. Your young pal Billy Main.'

'What about Billy not in trouble again the silly fool won't learn. Is he in trouble the idiot. Not long out. Won't learn the fool.'

'I've just come from Burke's place in Kent. The agency for the sale, Dooley Dooley and Dooley of Dublin, been in touch with Walker when they found nothing but half the house left after a fire engulfed it. A fire deliberately started may say. My boss sent me to have a look when he heard, arson no doubt about it.'

'What's it got to do with Billy you think he has got a hand in it, not arson, no?'

'Malky the driver and your pal, rather, the remains were found torched in Burke's Rolls Royce. Someone had a bonfire party. I don't suppose you have any idea what the young mug was doing there in the company of Malky. But not really surprised, knowing who he was associating with in Manchester.'

'Nope, haven't seen him much since he got back. Are you sure it was Billy. No, think you're barking at the wrong tree. Billy not Billy not an arsonist.'

'You don't come over as if you are shocked at my news are not hiding anything are you and yes was him dental records confirmed it.'

'I've nothing to hide. I've said haven't seen him for a while. Time you were leaving. I've got things to get done,' he now knew Rutherford hadn't fitted the pieces together and being careful to keep it that way.

'The Oldersum woman is ready to carry on from a new base in Ireland. Someone is ready to take over here. The fire was a warning no doubt about it'

'You mean Billy and the driver at the house at the wrong time? What an idiot.'

'Certainly. They walked into a nest of vipers who have sent a strong message. Understand Billy but the driver. I'm flummoxed scratching my head for a reason.'

'Poor Billy what was he doing there have you any idea go over to the Burke's if so that's one hell of a surprise to me,' waited, Rutherford ignored the question then he said, 'I really need this break don't you think. Really looking forward to it.'

'Where will I get you if I need you? Will keep in touch send a card. Can't get it in my head are not doing a runner are you would say if coming back?'

Wittering on as he ushered him to the door reluctant to be moved out. He's suspicious of the suddenness of it. Tony is hiding something he's sure of it.

'The JAMES in George Street that's where a good cop like you won't find it hard to find me. So get going. I've a train to catch for Edinburgh so move it you are keeping me late.'

'I'm going better things to be getting on with but remember will expect the postcard. One to bring back the happy memories when there as a student.'

'Join me the case is closed and you will have time on your hands. You come and enjoy yourself. A double room booked in a swell hotel. It wouldn't cost you anything to stay as my guest come and relax a while.' He asked knowing Rutherford would decline the offer.

'No time for a holiday the Burke's are ready to start again. The boss is on the warpath had a trip to Germany but turned out a waste of time. Going there to learn the wherewithal about the gangster Oldersum. The police not happy they guessed he was interfering. Came back with a flea you know where. No, it was a bad move. Walker is reading the riot act. Screaming for an enquiry and my head. Sissy Maitland is on my back giving me grief. You don't know the half of it.'

'I'll think about you when on the golf course or when lazing on a grassy bank doing some quite fishing.'

'You make me sick!'

'Good. Get going things to get on with.'

'So you said all ready don't go on going.'

'Give my love to Sissy and long may you suffer... Her grief,' he smiled.

'Sissy no please leave it. Wits end and having Walker after my guts is no picnic. My boss is hinting should be putting in for a post. Preferably somewhere far away the better. He's had it with Walker putting where he is not wanted.'

'Asked and you you knocked it back. I could have taken her in hand but no you couldn't see it.'

'Not that again.'

'I was willing to take her but no you knew best.'

'Is the offer of a holiday still on the agenda?'

'What, what holiday?'

'You said certainly heard you offered.'

'It's not as bad as you are making out. You are making a nonsense of this.'

'You think do you? I'm testing your reaction something your not saying got the hunch.'

The job is getting to you relax a little,'

'When you get back may take you up on your offer.... Regarding Sissy.

'Is Walker keeping her safe don't understand it she would be better out of his grasp.'

'Got my doubts about him. This carry on with the Burke's, something smells.'

'You gonna ask me to postpone it's why you're here, knew it got a hunch you a hunch. After something not a casual call is it, devious….Not the word for it!'

'Wanted to know about Billy seeing how you two were hipped together like peened on as they say.'

'Walker what's your beef now you've got me roped.'

'Nothing can't take care off.'

'Your not involving her Sissy I mean?'

'What time is your train? Let you get on with it, I'm out of here. Nothing here to write home about.'

'Not so fast. What about the Burke's place? You can't open the can and not sample the goods what have you found out?'

'Nothing more to be said.'

'Come off it.'

'Not on it nothing.'

'You came knocking on my door wanting to know about Billy Main. Got to be more in it than that and teasing with Maitland, something doesn't add up.'

'I was thinking a visit to your haunt might throw a light on the situation.'

'Honestly? You think it a good idea? No wouldn't chance it.'

'Your going on holiday.'

'Yes, but you were not aware of it before you turned up here.'

'You've just told me what you were doing.'

'You're checking on me.'

'No, thought you had knowledge of what went down.'

'Because my association with him you thought…'

'Okay guilty. What you think about my visit going to the Blue Star?'

'Go, yes. Five minutes in the place you would clear it out quicker than you could say Jack the Ripper.'

'Robinson Jack Robinson is the saying.'

'What else are you not saying? Ripper, Robinson, wtf.'

'Think won't get good reception, do you, agree but have to see what this guy Tracy is it give him the once over.'

'If he knows you know me that'll be me with arse oot the windy as my Scots pal would say. Not a good idea going there.'

'What do you suggest I do? If you have an alternative all ears.

FIFTY FIVE

Came out the shower woke him from a deep sleep he lay back yawning watching her dry her naked body with the shortest of white towel. Her breasts wobbled as they sagged and could see the fat across her stomach ripple as she stood in front of him stretching shaking the water from her long black hair. The top of her legs seemed larger as they tapered down to her knees. He was musing over how she had reacted to the night of passion just what was he thinking? It was good for a one night session, but… he wouldn't be in a hurry to go through with it again. Even though she displayed the joy of one who had been long time starved of the fruits of love and male companionship. Thankful she had agreed to the ploy of an alibi but was not going to let himself be railroaded to her station again. He realised how much woman's clothes hid a multitude of magic trickery.

'Up, so early, why?' He asked as she came to him.

'Hurry, you, get up nearly six o'clock.'

'Good. I've got time. It's early. What you think? You want more of the same do you if you get the meaning,' he's good at lying.

'You know have to get the café ready for the salesmen from the market. It wouldn't look good if I didn't open on time. You ken what they're like Frankie. So hurry and get a shift on there is no time for lazing about shift it.'

'Im waiting here in anticipation of much more of the same and you're hustling me out,' got out the bed took her in his arms and kissed the tip of her nose.

'Enough. Stop. Take a telling get going.'

He made a grab pulled her towards the bed.

She gave him a playful shove moving out his reach. 'It was good of my brother Paton to have the girl overnight will be bringing her back soon don't want her to see you here you must go. No time for this.' Her attitude changed.

'Have time for breakfast or are you so embarrassed what people will say surely that's not it. Know you don't give a fig for what anyone says.'

She pushed him back onto the bed, 'get going no time for this. have to get dressed want you out of here.'

He noticed the hint of urgency in her voice. Could see she was serious in her request for him to leave.

'Will get Paton to contact Sergeant McDougall and tell him to come and see me. Let him know about the whereabouts of the two of us on the night in question. Suppose he will end up at yours to get your part in the affair. You can tell him what you like will back you.'

Fully dressed she tied her apron round her waist adjusted her small head piece then strolled through the door into the café.

Dressed and joined her. She was busy frying bacon and eggs… sausages and tomatoes on the large flat electric hob type cooker. Her back to him, ignoring, was as if he was invisible.

'Can at least get coffee?' He asked showing a hint of frustration surprised at her attitude.

'Go home no time for this have to open soon. Not good to be seen here at this time. Know how they old hags would have a field day if they got a whiff of you being in here at this time in the morning.'

'Okay going. Thanks a glorious night of fun,' he lied again, 'Only hope you can convince you know who.'

'Not a problem assure you,' she said with an air of authority.

'Are you telling me he has been after you has not tried to get into your…'

'No! Don't be stupid. Have you not wondered why he has never married, well, where have you been all these years it's common knowledge.'

'Heard McDougall was round poking about. What is it this time looks like he's looking to move in.'

It was four in the afternoon. Mary there eyeing the situation and fussing as usual. Yes, there but not in a good mood.

'Jungle drums haven't a patch on the grape vine that operates in this place. Jeese, Mary, is there nothing that gets past you sure you're not an agent for MFI?'

'Don't be silly. But glad to see your sober and behaved yourself last night. Not that prying understand,' she said, walking to the sink, filled the kettle making ready to organise a tea time treat of coffee and the home made scones she retrieved from her medium size canvas message bag, 'what was his purpose this time? Don't you realise he, they, are not gonna leave you alone anytime soon. You better watch it. My, the scrapes you get into, my my.'

He sat at the kitchen table rolling a tea spoon round his fingers then dropped it into the saucer.

'Tying up loose ends thats all loose ends.'

'Oh, yes, heard. Terrible wasn't it. I hope he didn't think you were involved in it? Not many will be sad that these two have passed. What's it coming to. People afraid to go about their business. Gangsters everywhere.

'Passed? What are you talking about, who?' She stopped what she was doing laid the kettle on the hob. 'You haven't heard have you about the murders Greene and Watson. You know Night and Day that Gadgie. Not sorry to see the back of him.'

Picked up and rattled the tea spoon into the empty cup making a clattering noise giving her the signal that what she had said had taken him by surprise.

'Well McDougall never mentioned that he was asking were was but was vague on the purpose certainly never let it out about what you say.'

'And was he happy with you?'

'I'm here ain't I what do you think be locked up otherwise. Are we having coffee or tea or what and put plenty jam on the scones please you know partial to your scones.'

Nine in the evening the bar packed and in the Hell's Kitchen was standing room only all waiting to hear if the word that had gone round about the little girl singer was as good as was said by the usual gossip mongers.

She was halfway through her second rendition. The first had received a standing ovation, she was certainly in a swinging mood. Giving it laldy as they say.

When Frank came into the bar. The smile disappeared from his face as he looked about the packed room. What is it about

339

wee Lizzie and her pal Jordan with his accordion that appeals to so many he was thinking.

Sunny Leith brought them to their feet followed by…

I'll stay I'll stay I'll stay now you say you need me
Ill stay I'll stay I'll stay because I loved you
Ill stay I'll stay I'll stay now you say you love me…

He couldn't understand why the two were so popular. Was like Old had said was not his kind of music and catchin Mary's eye, let her know by a wave of his hand he was out of there and would see her in the morning sober or otherwise. Made his way to Berts. Got an unexpected surprise in Main Street under the street lamp saw the familiar tall guy in the black suit wearing his black hat standing beside the black Mercedes. He decided to brass it out 'nothing gained oh shut it,' he muttered.

'Please get in the car Mr Butler,' the tall man speaking in a German accent opening the car door and inviting him to get in.

How stupid or what was thinking now at last they've caught up. What the outcome? Is it time for a showdown was certainly ready for it. He was going to get the answers one way or another someone's final solution would make sure but not his, muttering to himself as he ducked his head getting into the rear passenger seat content in the knowledge the gun in his underarm holster was fully loaded.

An hour and some minutes past they dropped him outside Berts.

It was her night off Jeannie the barmaid with the blouse not pleased was ready to leave. Waiting there in this bar where she was being eyed up somewhat unholy suspiciously she knew a complete stranger has to take the consequences entering strange territory. Relieved when she saw him come in approaching to where she was sitting. He was not smiling though glad to see him she was ready to lay it hard for being late liked him but wasn't prepared to stand being taken for granted.

'Hi,' he said, 'been waiting long a bit late sorry,' forced a smile as he approached.

'She thought if he is not glad to see me she would leave.

Boaby the barman shouted, 'time let's have you no homes to go to?'

When he saw Frank and his companion ready to leave he was pleasantly surprised... 'Well seen it all now,' he called out to the punters, 'Do you see the boy is leaving the bowtow not a word no argument no saying to get stuffed...Love conquerors all or so they say. Is it or is it? Get your raffle tickets here cheap.'

'Ignore him. He has to have his fun you know how it is,'Frank is assuring her as they go out the door.

'Your place or mine or whatever?' She asks as she takes his arm snuggling against him as they walk.

'Not mine. No privacy,' kisses her cheek and gives her a squeeze as he wraps his arm round her shoulder.

'A taxi look for a taxi.' Pulled away from him looking up and down the street.

'Walk. Not far to get to a lock in. Five minutes that's all.'

'Have you not had enough?'

'Enough? What enough you got something on your mind?'

'Mine. Have a lock in there.'

'You sure? What you want it's okay with you it's okay with me. No argument there.'

FIFTY SIX

Tony was waiting on the platform at the Waverley station. He spent a much needed few hours sleep was fit and wide awake. Can't you smell it,' he said to Kaiser. Sweet fresh air.' Laid his luggage on the ground started to take short sharp breathing in out. We in heaven?' he said.

'Let's go. You'll get more of it when we walk into Princes Street,' Kaiser said lifting one of the suitcases taking Tony by his arm making their way out the station.

'Walking? No taxi to the hotel?'

'You want fresh air don't you walk will do you good be there shortly stroll will give you a sense of the scenery.'

'Okay let's go.'

They crossed the road and he stood for a moment with his eyes closed in the warm sunshine relaxed and up for anything that might come his way.

The crowds on the walkway reminded Tony of the busy streets like Oxford street and the many other's in London. But nothing like what he was looking at here. To be in the middle of the city catching a glimpse high above them majestic castle above the park. Towering peaks of the extinct volcano, Arthur Seat, sprawling above the building's. Turning his head to the left seeing the monument standing proud on Calton hill, old Reekie,s disgrace unfinished columns designated as Athens of the North. Unfinished cause the city ran out of money, so said?

'Wow! Am I dreaming? Truly. I'm in paradise the scenery is magical nothing like it beautiful.'

Kaiser took him by the arm guiding him through the throng of people ambling along in and out of the many shops on the broad Princes Street. In a short time they entered the plush foyer of the, JAMES on George Street.

'Killed the Burke's driver,' he said as casual as you like.

They settled down to sample the plates of fancy cakes. Kaiser pouring the tea looked in astonishment at what he said, 'was him or me got lucky after he done away with Billy. I torched the place

342

and it was Rutherford who took charge of the inquiry didn't go over it with the proverbial fine tooth comb not a clue it was me only problem was convincing him why Billy was there thought he had been got at by the Burke's when doing his time up North. Manchester has a lot to answer for, Silly Billy. Sad he's gone, silly Billy,' he said again.

'Certainly kept that episode quiet was you who done it good but sorry about Billy. Lucky you got out. Rutherford never found out? you were careful!'

'Paid me a visit. Knows nothing.'

'Who does he think is responsible?'

'Now the old woman is in Dublin thinks her niece the bitch Oldersum has taken charge. Someone, a climber out the ranks in London is trying to muscle into the empty seat Burke has left.'

'What I don't get if Burke was doing the business down there in London what is going on here can't fathom out any connection whatsoever. The mystery of the two hitmen caught at London airport sure is a mystery. Who followed the boy with the frauline here? Why is the deaths done in the same manner? Headache right enough,' rose from the table retrieved whisky miniature bottles from the drinks cabinet poured two bottles into each glass handing one to Tony.

'There has to be a connection to Burke here in Scotland,' said Tony, 'can't be copycats. I've found out the press up here have not published the full facts of what has occurred down south really is a puzzle. Found nothing whatsoever to connect anything to anyone. Stumped. But hey? When are you going to introduce me to your friend, Frank. What you've said got to think it's time for a meet to get our heads together, don't you agree? Three better than two and two… you know.'

'You to sit down and listen to what got to tell you.'

'Oh goodness sake Mary not more scolding please.'

'No. Far from it listen.'

'Okay listening but no havering not in the mood.'

It was early evening Mary in the kitchen getting ready to prepare a meal. 'What got to say I know it's going to upset you but you'll see it's for your own good. Rant and rave all you want still be your friend,' she watched the expression on his face change from frivolous clown to one of bewilderment.

'You better explain yourself never seen you so genuinely serious. If you don't mind be quick. I've a heavy date and need to be elsewhere very soon.'

Moved the kitchen chair next to him taking his left hand in her hand looked into his eyes stroking his arm. 'Your friend one in Holland,' she said slowly, 'have to say you will not like…'

'You mean Kaiser don't you not going to tell me something has happened to him are you it's not bad news? Could not stand much more of this if that is what's on your mind not him,' he said. 'He took too many risks no not him, no!'

She had never seen him fall apart like he was doing now. Not even when he got the news of his brother. Well maybe it was but was afraid he would go on the booze knowing how easy it was at the slightest excuse. Things in the past not easy to change. The culture of drink… we'll she couldn't complain. She after all was in the business of supply and demand.

FIFTY SEVEN

Ten minutes after nine the same evening he was on Edinburgh castle esplanade.

When he saw Kaiser he rushed at him and hugged and hugged. Twirled him round and round all the time saying was great he was here in Scotland.

Tony stepped in and separated them.

'How long has it been since you two were together talk about lost souls.'

I take it your glad to see each other, Yeah, thought so.'

Overwhelmed an under statement he stood wiping away the tears, 'pier 11 in Rotterdam docks the last time with Beeny in the van honestly thought would never see him again. When Mary told me what the score was so mad vowed to kill him but that was frustration, Her, Mary, couldn't believe how she managed to hide what was going on from me surpassed herself can't believe he has been shadowing me all this time though knew creepy going's on somewhere in the background and had a sense something not as it should be.'

'This is Tony, said Kaiser, ' with the three of us hopefully we will get to the bottom of what's been happening. Three brains have to be better than one don't you think? Say so wouldn't youse, ay?'

They mingled with the tourists taking in the sights of the castle. They stopped before reaching the drawbridge agreed they retreat from the castle to a favoured watering hole and slake their thirst whilst discussing their next move.

Kaiser stopped huddled them closer together whispering said, 'the tall guy with the blonde girl over Tony's shoulder someone I've been looking for. He was with a fisherman in Mary's place. I'm sure he had something to do with the old man, drunk old man who died. It is him in Mary's with a couple of guys from the fish market, I'm positive it's the same one,' he said eyeing the man and the woman seeing them arm in arm walking and laughing together like they hadn't a care in the world. Carrying on like a couple of young lovers all over each other unaware they had been

345

spotted not knowing at this moment fate would deal the wrong hand of cards. Was it fate or coincidence?

Tony having a long look and anxious to stop them he was ready to move, 'same man but not wanting to make fools of ourselves if this is the same guy, could be a help.'

Frank couldn't contain himself. He rushed forward, pushing past knocking people out of his way desperate to get hold of the guy who saw him coming and in the stramash the man turned and ran from his pursuer. He took to his heels pushing his girl friend so hard she stumbled onto the ground. He looked back and saw her sprawled on the ground but did not stop he took off running through the entrance into the castle.

The girl screamed shaking and wondering what was going on scrambled to her feet and stood rooted to the ground in a bewildered state shocked by the suddenness of it and saw them running after her boyfriend.

Two elderly ladies went to her assistance fussing about her asking if she was okay and like mother hens consoling her.

Kaiser followed Frank who was behind Tony going through the crowds. Slithering and sliding over the cobblestones in their determination to catch the fugitive, 'Dam and dam,' Tony shouted. In his eagerness he fell onto his knees losing sight of the prey. Frank helped pick him up.

Kaiser stopped running. Slowly walked to a raised part of the steep road scanning over the heads of the many. He waved to Frank to go to his left while he would go into the middle of the crowd searching amongst them casually looking here and there hoping to catch a glimpse. Was surprised how the guy vanished so quickly.

Tony caught their attention waving his arm and pointing vigorously letting them know the man was among the crowd who swarmed round the barrel of the giant Mons Meg. He was kneeling pretending to have a problem with a shoe when he saw them coming. He jumped up onto the parapet. Like an acrobat with arms outstretched he scurried along keeping his balance glancing at the spectators who watched in amazement. They thought the guy was putting on a show thinking was one of the many street performers who were performing up and down the Royal Mile.

The three separated and spaced out slowly walking along the wall cutting off his escape route watching him move one way then the other trying to evade them.

Kaiser shouted the game was up just wanted information from him no harm would come to him he promised information was all they wanted.

Tony pleaded for him to get down. 'Stupid could be killed if you fall.'

'Only making it hard for yourself what have you to hide?' asked Frank.

The spectators moved like a swarm of starlings opening a void moving as one in silence as two soldiers came running out of nowhere shouting for him to give himself up to get of the wall it's against regulations being there could face prosecution causing a disturbance advise come down immediately.

Kaiser was the nearest made a grab for his legs. The man turned and looked over his shoulder at the oncoming soldiers. Silent and without hesitation he leapt. A perfect spectacular swallow dive. The people rushed forward looking down they saw him plummeting and bouncing off the rocks landing on the ground far below. The silence was deafening at first then all at once women in the crowd began to scream. The soldiers looked over the wall and saw the body lying lifeless in a mangled mess they looked at each other amazed what had taken place.

Policeman taking the statement from the girlfriend of the man who jumped. They were alongside one of the two police vans on the esplanade.

'No, don't know why he ran away from me,' she said more composed and assuring the policeman she was as much in the dark as he was why her boyfriend suddenly ran away from her

'Not having words wasn't an argument that made him leave you funny what he done jumping the way he did.' Tony standing near heard what she said. The guy's name was, Mark Flucker. 'A fisherman and his address, Rose Cottage, outside Coldingham on the east coast. Not married lived with his brothers family all fishermen doesn't know how to contact them, so sorry,' she said, 'today was to be the start of a short holiday feeling guilty because her boyfriend was not keen to visit the castle. Was not sure many people came to the castle was always crowded with tourists. They argued and he relented. Now, because of her he was dead.'

'You were not responsible for him jumping. Are you sure you have no knowledge of why he decided to jump anything anything to show some light why he did it?'

'The three men chasing him,' she said, slowly remembering.

'I thought you said you did not know why he fled now you're saying three men?'

'Was so confused. So quick thought I was going to murdered. Have you caught them. What will I do if you can't find them? Why did they do what they did.?'

'Would you recognise them again or do you know who or why the chased him. It doesn't add up nobody has come forward to say they saw three men chasing him.'

'No, it happened too quickly. Said it to you already so quick.'

The policeman a little bewildered, 'you don't know of any reason why he was running from these three men? Okay miss, have a seat in the van boss will want to speak with you later.'

'Are you sure it was the right guy we were chasing wouldn't like to think we were responsible for an innocent man jumping to his death,' Frank asking first Tony then Kaiser and passing the three pints of beer across the table.

Sitting in the well known robbers pub not far from the castle esplanade filled with tourists the talk was all about the leaper.

'No worry on that score,' said Kaiser, ' jumped he must have been guilty.'

'Good thinking meeting at the castle like we did. Invisible in the crowd,' Tony, chipped in, 'result,' he said taking a large swill of the beer.

'What next?' Kaiser asked.

'We're still in the dark who knows,' said Frank.

A crowd packed together at the front door of the pub. Lady escort with them in a shrill sounding voice telling the story of the notorious robber, the man who's name was, Deacon Brodie.

The name incidentally above the entrance of this particular establishment and yes same name as the Brodie the person they were desperate to get hold of. The pub was full of punters the tourist mob outside ready to come in made up their minds they agreed to go elsewhere as the public houses on the Royal Mile from the castle to the Palace of Holyrood at the bottom beside Arthur's seat would all be the same jam packed.

'Make for Newhaven,' Frank said.

'Who is brave enough to try this wheeze?'

'A wheeze?' Kaiser all ears to Tony's suggestion.

'You'll have to explain,' said Frank.

'I don't think it possible but there again, it could be.'

'What?' They both said.

'Do it,' said Tony.

They looked and waited.

'You gonna tell?' Kaiser asked.

'For goodness sake,' Frank said swivelling on the bench, 'let's go.'

'Rutherford said when he was here in Edinburgh he and a pal done a pub crawl. Leith street to the very bottom of the walk. A half pint in every pub,' said Tony.

'Can't be done. You'd be unconscious only a short way down too many on both sides no impossible,' said Frank.

'I bet we could get away with it give it a try,' said Kaiser.

'If Rutherford done it can't be so hard,' Tony said.

'Could be he was pulling your you know,' said Kaiser.

'That's decided then,' said a smiling Tony, 'up for it. A tenner for last man standing and I know who it will be. Write a name and keep it. We'll see.'

Tony was back in the room at the, JAMES Kaiser stayed overnight at Franks.

Shortly after seven that morning Mary was in the kitchen preparing plates of fried eggs bacon black coffee and buttered toast. As usual berating them both for staying up all night hanging one on. 'A pub crawl on Leith walk? I ask you. Loons off your heads. I'm glad it's good to see you suffering from it. n Serves you bloody well right no sympathy none whatsoever. And don't suppose you heard the news buzzing out and about out there. Four copped it along the Seafield road. Along there,' she

349

pointed, 'at the waste ground. McDougall says it's the usual gangsters having a hit. My goodness, when will it all end I ask you and you lot supposed to be grown up men when you going to change? This drinking will be the ruin of you mark my words' she plonked the plates down on the table in her angry way knowing they were not listening to a word she said. 'Drunks and gangsters hit men my my. Murder incorporated right enough.'

Kaiser peaked through his fingers, 'she's been seeing too many gangster movies again. Wants to know what the fat man has to do with Finkle Jones the detective. What he has to do with it my oh my,' he quipped.

'Goodness Mary give it a rest will you,' Frank said,' can't you leave us in peace still the middle of the night for… sake. Why are you here so early getting us out of our beds and hey didn't know Tony's name was Finkle when did that happen? Fat man Tony Finkle wait till I tell him he'll be delighted, him being a gum shoe and all ha ha. Oh my head gonna bust gonna die.'

'You're not funny Frankie,' she scolded, 'shame on you. Good job he's not here would be unhappy hearing you saying a thing like that.'

He moaned and groaned, 'Oh, my head,' he wailed again, avoiding her scowling face. 'You leaving? Not time you were seeing to your pub?'

'The state of the both of you. I suppose the other one in the same drunken stupor. How you managed to get him into a taxi to go back up town must have taken all your strength. The size of him my goodness. Pity the taxi driver if he had to manhandle him in and out his cab. What the people in the hotel will say if they saw the state of him I don't like to think. And you pair when you going to get it into your heads you are in trouble you haven't a clue what is waiting out there,' said angrily.

Pushed his plate to the side of the table, 'making fun of him Mary,' he said, 'and I can't eat this Mary, it's too early. What I need is the hair of the dog, please, give me a wee one will you please a wee one it'll do the trick.'

'No Frankie afraid both your erses, are oot the windie.'

She drained the bottle into the sink. 'No more booze. Not now no not for a while. You better get sober. Drink the coffee. There is plenty more where it came from.' She put the mugs on the table, 'better get your act together tout sweet. I still think, no, doubt, if you are thinking straight. Going after they Flucker brothers without proof of their involvement seems daft to me. Anyway he's not in good shape to be driving. And you Kaiser son are as bad as him. Your other pal? Well, expect he won't be able to do anything for a further twenty four hours I bet,' being her usual self she knew perfectly well they would not take the slightest notice of what was said but thought she had the right to say it. Feeling superior now she has both of them to chide.

'He jumped,' Frank said, 'from the battlements not what an innocent would have done. He knew the game was up when he saw the three of us after him. I guess the two army guys helped him to make his mind up. Fly like a bird. The swallow. Is my theory anyway what it's worth. He must have known something. A bairn wi a biscuit erse could fathom that.'

'Took the gamble and jumped,' said Kaiser finishing the coffee and asking for a refill smiling at her, sad, he knew she told the truth about the whisky going down the drain.

'We will have to go Mary have to get a handle on it. It's the only way we will get any further. Have to go down the coast. What we got, nothing? The Fluckers are the only lead so far. You may doubt are doing the right thing but what is our alternative? Tell me, you want us to succeed don't you find the truth, ay.'

'We have to know,' said Kaiser.

'The police why not the police?' She said as she gathered the dishes from the table.

'Archie McDougall? You kidding Mary? Better with Finkle Jones,' said Kaiser.

'You will please yourselves won't listen to me. Recommend you wait a while before going in like a bull in the china shop. If you must go please stay out of any pubs on the way. You have no idea what you maybe getting into going against those people will be careful won't you,' draped her coat over her shoulders adjusted her hat, 'be very careful,' walked to the door and out into the street.

Frank caught a glimpse of a tear as she walked past him, 'she'll be okay,' he said to Kaiser who nodded. He sprawled across the table arms stretched, 'finished,' he moaned, lifted his head looking at him, 'wanna die,' he said.

They met up with Tony a little after four in the afternoon. The journey was done mainly in silence except for the occasional burp and complaining about sore heads and going over the coming event.

'Who won the Tenner? Reckon the off side rule. Nobody won it. Trying it was impossible. Agree or not agree,' Tony said, waiting, 'no answer. Take it all agree then?'

'We are clear know what we have to do you guys ay,' Kaiser reminding them.

'Tony nodded, ready as ever will be,' looked over his shoulder Frank was sleeping,' he's out of it,' he said, 'and can't feel my legs. Too much beer. That's what it is. I'm sure it's that.'

'Stay on the whisky. Vodka doesn't agree with you,' Frank said as he woke doing a good stretch and wide yawn.

Before long they reached the village. Drove the A1 road through Musselburgh and Haddington to Coldingham an easy free from trouble ride lasting just over an hour with Kaiser and Tony taking turns at driving most of the journey.

They stopped opposite an old man who was sitting on a bench beside the village church. Put the newspaper he was reading on the bench then he rubbed the ears of the dog at his feet asleep. An aged black and white collie dog with a lot of grey hairs round it's muzzle. Frank reckoned was as old as the old man.

'Excuse me sir. Can you point me in the direction of Rose cottage?'

Lifted the paper slight pause looked suspiciously up at him. Shuffled the paper gave the impression hadn't heard what was said. Rubbed the dogs ears who continued to sleep.

Frank waited.

'It's a boat your after, looking to get a boat?'

'Aye, that's about the much of it.'

'I doubt if it can happen. Doubt it very much.'

Looked at the dog who woke giving a mighty yawn then a little yelp before settling down,

'Just the way to the cottage if you do not mind not too much to ask is it?'

'Take that road there,' pointed to the road on his right, 'follow along to the sands. A white painted building on your left. You can't miss it. It's the only building on the way to the sands but I doubt it very much. Use yer een. Canny miss.'

'Another doubting Mary,' he said to Kaiser as he got into the car. 'Use yer een.'He repeated, 'that's what the man said.'

They parked in a lay-by a couple of hundred yards from the cottage.

Walked slowly towards the building it was obvious the place was deserted.

Tony approached the locked front door. A rusty sliding bolt with an old brass padlock. Yale lock with the remnants of a spiderweb convinced him that this was not the entrance to the house. He looked in the windows on each side of the door but couldn't see anything he was looking into empty darkness. In the garden, a row-boat turned upside down with a gaping hole on it's bottom. A pile of lobster pots stacked along the perimeter wall and a bundle of heavy fish nets,with four old wooden broken oars nestling on top of the nets.

They emerged from behind the cottage, 'deserted,' Kaiser said when the three met up making their way to the car.

'A pub in the village when we passed,' Tony said, 'what do you think? Will we give it a try. Someone there may know of their whereabouts never know let's try.'

The old man from the bench at the church was there with his dog at his feet sitting beside the log fire watching the sparks from the logs scurrying up the black hole in the chimney.

Frank gave him a nod as he sat down.

The barmaid put three pints of beer on the table.

'You didn't believe me, did you?' The man with the dog said. 'I said I guessed not you getting a boat at this time.' His tone was…I told you but you wouldn't listen.

'Thanks for that,' Frank said 'you don't happen to know where we can contact the Flucker brothers do you the house is closed up deserted. Derelict by the looks.'

'Fishing trip is it?' Leaned over put some potato crisps on the floor the dog gobbled them greedily looked up at him with sad eyes, eens, hoping for more of the same and gave another mighty tired yawn.

The half dozen men present in the bar minding their own silent their een,s staring looking elsewhere and not at them.

The barmaid who had listened to the conversation with the old man came from behind the bar, 'you are too late gentlemen,' she said removing their empty glasses.

'Lifted this morning early. Two detectives from Edinburgh. Something to do with their dead brother it was said. You will have to go elsewhere to hire a boat for your fishing trip,' she said, giving them a smile before making her way back behind the bar.

'Maybe if you left your number may have a contact who sometimes organises fishing trips.' A large giant of a man sitting at the bar said.

'Warned you that it was futile to go hell for leather all down the coast on a wild goose chase. If you had listened to me you would have saved all that energy. But no. Off and never mind the consequences. Away without a plan making fools of yourself,' was on the warpath and gingerly placing three plates of her favourite dish, Cullen Skink on the table.

'You were right Mary,' Frank replied sheepishly looking to Kaiser and Tony who all agreed their heads going down over the plates in silence supping the feast.

'Before I go,' she said 'McDougall in the pub looking for you Frankie. And to save face think it would be a good idea if you called on him, instead of him searching for you.'

'Not again...I've already had words with him. What now what does the man want with me this time I think it is time him to retire and get of my back ay.'

'And what is this gossip going around about you and Betty?' She said with a sly look. Waiting but knowing he's going to deny it all day long.

'What me and Betty? What you heard you got something good to say? Whatever it is innocent. Time you stopped listening to gossip.'

'Should be ashamed of yourself! Wasn't it her daughter you were after, you did, you hinted as much,' she said.

'Betty? The one with the café well well. Who would have thought you rascal Frank,' said Tony giving him a hearty slap on the back… 'you rascal!'

'And? the daughter?' Kaiser laughed, 'rascal right on it Tony. Both quines well blow me.'

'All round the village,' she said. 'They busy buddies are tormenting poor Betty. Quizzing her. The good thing though she seems to have a full shop most of the day.'

'Can I have some more of this delicious soup please Mary,' asked Tony who didn't really care much about Franks love life. Found her good meals doing a lot of kindness to his troublesome oversized stomach.

She left them sitting at the table knowing she wouldn't get much change out of them and made her way down the stair to the bar.

When she was gone Kaiser asked Frank if he was happy to present himself to the police? Would it be a wise move? he suggested it would be. Letting them know he had nothing to hide would be best. Get it over with brazen it out he advised.

'Get it done,' said Tony, 'have to make progress waiting to get to the bottom of all this is getting tedious,' waved his arm concentrated on his soup the while hoping Mary left more on the stove.

'I agree,' said Frank, 'tedious frustrating give it a go.'

'Has your pal Rutherford been in touch?' Kaiser asked Tony.

'Don't get me started on that useless excuse for a human being. Hell he will be keeping a low profile cause I'm not there to hold his hand consoling him. The fact is his boss is trying to get rid. The other one Walker he's out to crucify him at the first opportunity he gets. But saying that I think Rutherford is on to something the easy ride Walker dished out to the Burke's there may be hidden reasons into it.'

'Skullduggery you think, ay,' said Kaiser pulling a face.

'Asked Rutherford about it. Asked if he thought someone higher was involved got short shrift accused me of looking for a conspiracy me of all people.'

'I appreciate it you're here on your own terms need a few more answers to your statement. And thanks not getting us involved Frankie not having to look for you. Now you sure you have not left anything out your statement positive don't wont to change anything we're giving you the chance.'

The woman copper was as usual on duty at the door staring into space. Rooney with McDougall sitting across from him in the interview room at the Leith nick. Rooney doing the talking

'I can't add anything to what I've already said.' He pushed on the table sliding his chair backwards making a screeching noise on the floor. Standing he looked at the sentry but as expected never wavered from her stanc. 'Is she for real? He asked sitting looking first the McDougall then Rooney but got no response to his question. He shrugged waited to see what was coming next stood for a second pulled at the sleeves on his reefer sat down. The chair screeched on the floor as he pulled it under the table.

'How long you keeping me this time don't need to change anything so finished aye or no. Have lots to be getting on with can't hang about you know times money so it's said, ay.'

'Witness says you were in the boozer at Granton Square the night Greene and Watson were assaulted you still saying you spent the night in the company of the café owner?'

'Yes. Couldn't put it plainer. You want to know the in and outs if it was satisfactory? Don't think she would like me to give all the details you think?'

Rooney up and left the room walked to the end of the corridor counted out quietly pone to twenty returned to the interview room. 'It's repeated you were in the Tip at Granton on that night,' opening the folder looked over the statement taking time slowly turning the pages. 'you still stand by what you said?' Disbelief in his voice thinking have to get something on this man Butler quickly. Also thinking McDougall is useless has to put up with him warts and all worst luck.

'Yes. How many times?' Desperate to get the grilling over with. Looks at the clock on the wall, 'getting late he says.'

'As long as it takes,' said McDougall, 'if and when you go don't think of doing a disappearing act. Don't think you can get away with anything underhand you understand we are watching you on to you. Is serious business and we will get to the bottom of it sooner we can wait.'

'Not going anywhere you're wasting your time if you think don't know what's going on here.'

'What you think is going on?' Rooney closed the folder stood up and left the room barging past the sentry without waiting for an answer.

McDougall said, 'you don't want to get his back up Frankie. Don't make an enemy of him. You're backing a deuce take my word on it son,'

'You've stooped to threats now why don't you get your witness in here let me challenge his or her statement.'

'Impossible. You know it doesn't work like that.'

'Can go? You finished? I said already better things to be getting on with forever saying to you lot wasting your time.'

'No, not yet. You want more time to think it over?'

'Not need time,' looked at his watch, 'they're open. I'm missing valuable drinking hours. The only important time. So ask again when are you going to let me out of here when is the chief coming back is he away consulting his imaginary witness? Don't forget I came on my own terms. I think should go the same. If you have something on me well charge or otherwise. Out of here decide yes or…Get on with it.'

McDougall opened the folder thumbed through the pages in silence.

'What are you doing tonight missy?' He asked the sentry on the door all he got was more of the same a silent stare.

McDougall lifted his head giving him a hard look, 'will you never learn?' He said, returning to thumbing the documents.

'If you don't ask you never get,' he said cheekily, 'you never know sarge might have agreed to a night on the tiles. Could've surprised even you,' smiled and a stare letting him know yes sir know about you.

After a lapse of about five minutes Rooney came in placing his folder on the table, 'leave us,' he said nodding to McDougall to go, 'give me some time to speak to him.'

'It's good cop bad cop time is it? Missy. You are a witness to this. I hope you are taking note of what is going on here,' he said but guessed it nothing stirred.

357

'I'll ask you again do you need to change anything on your statement,' said it coming over as the concerned uncle tone mellow with concern.

'No comment.'

'Your digging yourself into a hole.'

'You say but it's me digging the hole,' had the idea the next question would be fired at him with a hint of malice.

'Things starting to stack up against you. You don't honestly think your alibi is going to stand do you? You need to be very careful before you answer.'

'No comment,' said again as Rooney left the room leaving a trail of papers falling from the bundle in the folder. He could see the anger as he rushed from the room.

Almost immediately McDougall entered, 'You can go for now,' he said standing beside the open door indicating to the lady cop to leave.

At the end of the corridor saw Rooney speaking with Betty. When they saw him she hurried to the exit. Before he could catch up to her McDougall pulled him aside. Was angry blustering and stammering. 'A word. He's after you,' pointed to the retreating Rooney, 'you have to be careful not having this conversation remember be very careful!'

'Aye, okay noted. Take it he has upset you but can ask…'

'Quick,' looked along the corridor giving the impression he shouldn't be seen speaking with him, 'what you need to know?'

'Flucker brothers. You know the same. One who jumped from the castle walls. These brothers.'

'Flucker, no. Cant help you there.' He started up the corridor.

'You don't know or your not saying?' Caught his arm, turning him looking, 'brothers from Coldingham the Fluckers?'

'Don't know what you are going on about. Let go off my arm. Get out of here.'

Scared and what is he hiding or does he genuinely not have a clue to what Frank asked.

'They brothers you arrested. Coldingham the other morning. Those two who were helping with your enquiries. You know the one that Brodie one. You had words at the pier.'

'Don't know what you're talking about. Who said had words with this man you say Brodie or whatever?'

'Your not saying or your kidding me you would say, ay.'

'No. Said already haven't a clue don't know what it is you're asking me. I'm out of it get going.'

'Detectives arresting the brothers maybe not arrested but to help with enquiries about the guy who took a swallow dive off the battlements. Not you or Rooney and if not…Who? You do know, aye, say it.'

'I think you better go. You don't know what your getting yourself into, don't get involved take my word for it keep out of his way he's out to lay it on you. You are getting deeper in the mire so heed my warning.'

Halfway up the corridor McDougall stopped and turned…
'All I'm saying is,be very careful warning you as a favour.'

Five minutes later was in the Copper Cup sitting nursing a pint of lager and thinking about Betty. Had she changed her statement and let him down seemed highly unlikely she had done the dirty they let him go. Who, he wondered was this anonymous witness who supposedly came out the blue or was Rooney bluffing His brain was into overdrive and seeing her there could be just a coincidence The night Patrick Greene and Night and Day bought it he was really out of it. Recalling his movements was proving to be just a blurry dream of inconsistency. In the Tip girls were squabbling over punters. Couple of guys were ready for a fight and he didn't like the look of them and add to that the noise from the juke box. High pitched talk from the crowd at the bar he remembered he had to get out and go somewhere with a quieter clientele before the noise scrambled his head. Hard thinking is called for. Danger is catching him up. Got to find the solution. Hits his brow with the palm of his hand, 'think dam you think,' he's muttering. If he stayed at Berts would have saved all this bother or if only he had met with Jeannie. Stayed till her shift ended at the pub outcome would be entirely different. But he knew plenty punters saw him in the tip and would give him an alibi. Twisting the facts. He couldn't take the chance. He knew the antics police used. The fault was his own. The wee quine, Lizzie was the reason he left. Now if he had stayed would save himself all this grief.

The Wirdie the local boozer only minutes away from the Tip was the place he made tracks for. Drunk tracks no doubt about it. The tunnel on the opposite side of the street was lit by an old cast iron lamppost and the wide tunnel under the rail line leads the way to Granton beach. The foreshore were with pals he had loads of adventures. The memory of smell the aroma of hot new baked bread rolls reminded how good they tasted. A feast only a halfpenny each bought from the bakery next door to the public house the Tip round the corner from the square.

Remembering in his minds eye a train passed overhead sounding it's whistle twice, so loud it would have woken up the dead from their graves.

From the lit up entrance at the Wirdie looking over at the tunnel he heard another train pass. Things coming back. He was getting a clearer picture of what took place that night. Five or more pushing and shoving could hear the raised voices shouting angrily. Men just shadows creeping about in a swirling mist. A mist he experienced as if, maybe, something added to his drink?

Now things falling into focus the large man he saw he now realised was Night and Day some other's he didn't recognise. Another he guessed must have been Patrick Greene and where his body was found on the Wirdie steps only a short distance from the tunnel. Now was thinking someone he was sure saw him on the street at the entrance to the boozer. Wracking his brain yes there was a woman, not young, with what he thought a cat draped round her shoulder. Now he knew it to be a fox fur wrap-around her shoulder. A small hat on the side of her head. Now remembered he nearly knocked it off when she offered to help him. She proposed a night of passion which he thought was hilarious at the time. Did she come forward to report seeing him at what he now knew was the crime scene. Not be the answer Rooney would have used her to embellish the story and use her to nail him good and proper would be locked in the cooler.

Remembered a blanket the tramp at Stockbridge had a green blanket no too daft to think it.'

Was he there at the shopping mall did he cover him with the same smelly rag? Could not get his head round it. And if it was the Flucker brothers responsible for the killing he thought They were the masterminds, not, he sussed the Greenes. Why, why

360

was Mary Greene letting out he had something to do with the killing of Night and Day and the weasel Patrick? Time is getting short quicker the three of them get their act together he thought.

A slight detour to allay the gloom.

'Did you hear about the poor man with his donkey?'

'Oh no. Not more rubbish please, spare us!' Tam the bam said appealing to Frank.

Phsyco with a quizzical look on his face put three pints of beer on the table sitting down scrutinised each one waiting in anticipation willing them to listen. What he was going to say he thought was to take the edge of the gloom. Something needed to be done to get his friends minds of the situation of the mill being closed.

'A man and his donkey? When did you see a man and a donkey in Leith?' Tam the Bam looked at Frank, 'he's getting dafter and dafter I ask you a donkey in Leith. A poor man, aye. But a donkey?' He lifted his glass drank half in one go. 'Send for three men in white coats. Make sure it's white coats not green had enough of them they Greenes has to be white.'

Frank, smiling, waited on Phsyco for a further explanation

The punters near stopped talking fascinated to learn what was coming next.

'It's a fable read it and if youse hadn't heard it would, what's the word….enlighten you.'

'Oh, listen to him enlighten us. Go on then get on with it enlighten us, ay, he's going to enlighten us how grand lets hear it, ay, long time since been enlightened.'

'He asked a rich man for a job with the donkey cause he was skint and needed money to buy food for his family.'

'What rich man was this? Me and Frank we're skint let us know who he is and where we can find him?'

'Give a chance,' said Frank, 'haven't the time. Waiting for my friends to show so keep quite let him get on with it.'

'You heard the man do as he says. He's in a hurry so hurry and git oan wi it.'

'Are you going to listen or what, why you have to muck things up all the time are you trying to belittle me. If, och, won't bother now,' he said was in a huff lifting his pint of beer turned in the seat showing them his back.

'Bert has just told me Mary Greene has lost the contract for the mill. The company is looking to recruit workers to make them full time employees.' Boaby the barman informed them, 'you better get down there if you want to get your old jobs back. Get there quick before the news is all over Leith. And you know how fast that can be so if you hurry drink up and get there fast.'

'Me,and Phsyco will go, when we're finished here,' said Tam. 'Frank, what you think coming with us. We can't miss the opportunity.'

'Things to attend to don't think working at the mill is on my immediate agenda. Anyway good luck to you two. You should be safe might get a better deal working for the company. I see you as good company men,' took Phsyco by the shoulder and turned him round, 'are you going to finish what you started got us waiting on tenterhooks here get on with it.'

'Tell him to keep it shut always trying to make a fool of me disnae appreciate that I'm smarter than he is,' he scowled stuck his finger on the others right shoulder and pushed it twice, 'smarter, ay, smarter than you,' laughed making out it was all one big deal to keep the punters enthralled.

'All right. I'll keep quiet tell us your tale then we will have another pint before we make our way into the docks,' he said, giving Frank a wink.

'As I said the poor guy wanted the rich man to give him a job with his donkey.'

'What kind of jo, would that be what could he do with a donkey?'

'I thought you was keeping it shut,' he said, giving the long stare.

'The way you two keep ribbing each other, pals, how long have you been pals a class act the pair of you.'

'Ignore him. The rich man told the guy…'

'The guy with the donkey, ay.'

'Frank tell him his mother is ootside looking for him. He's wanted for his tea.'

'Got a job on been dead for a few years now. Making my tea, I ask you would take some doing,' brushing away a pretend tear.

Lets hear it or have you stopped havering and talking of miracles.'

'The guy wanted a job. And, if you say… the guy with the donkey… I'll kill you. Now keep quiet. Anyway, the rich man said if you can walk with the donkey through my front door...'

'Sure it was a door not a needle?'

'Ignore him Frank see what have to put up with all the time he would try the patience of a saint.'

'Better than listening to you talking the hind leg of….'

'A donkey! You were going to say it weren't you goodness sake!'

'It's getting boring now hurry and get it over with,' Tam yawning.

'How long?' Frank asked checking his watch with the clock on the wall.

'If he walked with the beast through the door. He would give him hundred pounds. And before you chip in again,' he paused, 'British pounds, okay?'

'I was not going to interrupt you so there,' made a face stuck out his tongue, 'I'm thirsty get on with it we've somewhere else to be. Hurry up.'

'The guy walked through the door with the donkey and asked for the hundred pounds but the rich man said he didn't see him do it. What he saw was the man walk with a pig.'

'A pig how the hell did that get in here.?'

Frank shook his head highly amused at their antics. Was waiting for Tony and Kaiser to arrive to get back on track of their next move. The two pals had the punters waiting with baited breath on the punch line listening to them was giving him a respite from what was praying on his mind. 'Pleas, my friends will be here soon. How long is it going to take till the end?'

'The rich man asked his servant,' Phsyco continued, 'who was standing near what did he see and the servant said he saw a pig.'

'He would say that wouldn't he. His boss would fire him for not being loyal.'

'Tam I'm nearly finished will you keep quiet. I won't ask again all right.'

'All right. I'm bored again,' gave a longer yawn and a shrug.

'I am a poor man but an honest man he said to the servant. Your master has so much wealth if he saw a pig I will bow to his judgement. But, if you saw a pig it is sitting on his high chair before me or observe a donkey!'

'Is that it. Is that what we've all been waiting for,'Tam looked to the punters who were now disinterested everything was as usual.

They rose to leave when Kaiser and Tony entered, 'see you later Frank,' they said, Tam pushing his pal before him. 'We could maybe put a word if you want?'

Frank shook his head and gave them the usual, 'get out of it, ya bams.'

Boaby the barman brought three drams of whisky. 'On me boys. Drink up better them on their way than sitting here talking rubbish and maybe losing out.'

'Out?'Kaiser making a face at Frank.

'The mill is opening up.'

'Oh that,' says 'don't think so.'

'Heard different? Tony asked.

'Frank studied his face. 'You up to your tricks?'

'What tricks would that be?' Tony taking an interest.

'What you heard?' Asked Frank.

'Met with a guy from Australia got to talking about things.'

'Things what things?'

'Where this going,' said Tony, 'came for the drink not to here things and you repeating things.'

'Well the Australian what wisdom did he part?' Frank asked again. 'The mill opening or not?'

'Not sure. A skeleton staff to keep the place in good shape but a contract… was very doubtful.'

FIFTY EIGHT

'I've convinced Binky Mason to give us a few hours tomorrow a spot of fishing will give us a relaxing period to get our brains working,' Frank announced

'Good, I'll look forward to it with immense joy,' said Tony smiling, 'it will be something to tell that useless… of a sergeant, Rutherford. Only hope to get something big to brag about put his peep at low I'm up for this fishing trip yeah baby.'

Twelve noon. The sun was high in the cloudless blue sky.

They chugged out of the harbour. The sea was calm. Colours in the water changing from greens, blues to white and silvery shades as the sprats raced alongside chased by the mackerel.

The spectacular diving of the sea birds. Sight of inquisitive seals following honking and snorting loudly. A group of dolphins in the near distance showing their acrobatic skills added to their pleasure.

'This is perfect,' said Frank, 'certainly a good way to calm the nerves.'

'We'll try our luck behind the island,' said Binky, pointing to the far distance, 'we're on the Roads. Have to keep an eye out for other traffic.'

'He means, Leith Roads. This stretch of the river,' said Frank.

'River, thought we were on the sea not a road?' Said Kaiser, bemused and giving Tony a friendly elbow, 'you understand I don't.' Made ready baiting a rod gave Tony a high five, 'noise in this country is hard to understand,' he laughed, looked at Frank shook his head. 'Why the road not the strath make your mind up road or strath?'

'What do we do when we catch some? Tony asked, 'Throw them back or take them too Mary for a fry up? The sea air will give us an appetite. I'm sure looking forward to her fish soup. My stomach can't get enough of the stuff.'

'Better catch lots to feed him,' Kaiser said, clapping and honking, 'honk, honk,' he cried, mimicking seals.

They fished for a couple of hours without any luck. Binky shifted position a few times found themselves leaving the mouth of the river and heading out to the North Sea. The sea, though like a pond in the distance they could see a bank of fog coming fast nice to see in the distance but not under.

'We safe?' Tony asked Binky who was on his way to the wheelhouse.

'Time to go,' Binky said, firing the engine while they stowed the fishing gear. 'Hurry lads soon be in a race with that stuff coming at the back of us.'

'They watched the fog rolling towards them. 'Coming fast,' Frank said, 'hope we make it. The speed of it. Thick like smoke. Binky knows what he's doing. Be okay.'

Twenty minutes later and miles from safety of the harbour the fog quickly engulfed them. In the distance they could hear the intermittent sound of ship's horns the eerie sounds bouncing back as if the wall of fog warned of imminent disaster. How near or far they couldn't tell the nearness of other vessels sounded as if they were trapped in the middle of a circle of a fleet of ships. the presence of other ships the sounds near enough to make them aware just how dangerous being out on the Roads could be.

'No need for any worry. We'll make it back, trust me.' Binky set out to put them at ease and was surprised how easy they adapted to the situation.

Kaiser was at the bow keeping watch peering through the fog shouted to Binky to cut the engine, 'listen, someone calling for help dead ahead,' made his way back to the wheelhouse.

'Did you have to say dead this nightmare will remind Frankie of an old Hollywood movie we will get some kind of monster bearing down on us even a giant octopus with tentacles wrapped round the stern pulling us under you know how he likes to drag up these old pictures he keeps reminding us.' He was on lookout port side Frank at starboard Kaiser returned to the bow.

High above they heard the cry of a gannet, 'scary or what?' Tony shouted, 'what was it don't know roads bloody place is haunted sure is scary.'

'Quiet, listen, hear something,' Kaiser shouted.

The dim light came clearer as it came into view Kaiser saw the fishing boat loom ghost like in the shadowy blanket of fog.

The scene being highlighted by the haunting echoes of the ships horns.

Binky steered in front Frank passed a line to the man on the stricken boat.

'Captain John Lyle fishing boat Maddie out of Eyemouth engine trouble, thanks for your assistance skipper. Very glad you came along. Yes sir very glad.'

He shouted his voice mixed in competition with the sounds of the ships horns.

'We'll give you a tow into Newhaven,' Binky shouted restarting the engine slowly steering a passage through the fog.

The sky was clear the pale moon was rising as the sun was going down. Hard to believe the crazy weather all was calm after the fog lifted and thankfully they got back to Newhaven without any problems.

'I can sure go with something to eat,' Tony said to Kaiser as they watched Frank tie up watched him do the same for the Maddie out of Eyemouth.

The skipper of the Maddie and his two crewmen unloaded their catch of lobsters onto the slipway. 'Not bad for the amount of time we were out. Could've been much better if my engine hadn't developed a break down,' he was speaking with Binky, 'my son and my fitter are on their way. When I'm sorted will go back to retrieve the rest of my pots. My lad will transport this bit of catch home for the market tomorrow thank you again skipper for coming to our rescue.'

Early the next morning they met up at the harbour. Kaiser, spotted the Maddie out of Eyemouth sailing outward bound through the calm water...It was high tide. The water was as mirrored glass. Suddenly he spotted a man on board the departing vessel. He dropped his fishing rod down on the deck and ran along the slipway scrambling up the ladder onto the pier above shouting at the top of his voice.

Binky caught the attraction of the other two. Were amazed at what Kaiser was doing, running, sprinting, waving his arms and

367

shouting. They looked in amazement as he ran towards the lighthouse at the end of the pier.

'What the hell what is going on?' Binky asked, when Kaiser returned.

'The guy standing on the deck of that boat the third man is the one saw in Mary's place,' he said catching his breath. 'He's the one who fixed the engine on their boat. Guaranteed to be another one of those brothers the Fluckers. You think we could catch up to them skipper?'

'Certainly give it a try,' into the wheelhouse fired the engine, 'let go fo,ard let go aft,' shouted at Frank,' who quickly cast off the ropes and jumped on board.

Furiously spinning the wheel full speed ahead made for the harbour exit.

'No fishing now, drat,' said Tony.

Binky steered west and soon had the fugitives in sight.

Kaiser handed binoculars to Binky who slowed back the engine watched the Maddie, out of Eyemouth sail west.

'There are no pots or any fishing gear on deck,' said Kaiser.

'They are making for Queensferry. Well well,' Binky said, 'what on earth are they up to? We'll make nearer to the Fife side of the Forth. Burntisland is near, A good place to keep them under observation..

Tony once more got busy baiting the hooks on the fishing rods, 'we can try our luck skipper. If they are watching us we won't be on their radar. Just another fishing expedition,' he said, with renewed enthusiasm.

'This side of Hound point is a good place to fish,' said Binky, 'a good advantage to keep watch. We may have a long wait will have to take turn on look out don't need a tanker rolling us over.'

'A tanker?' Kaiser piped up sounding surprised.

'That's what I said. Hound point is the tanker filling station. This is where they fill up with the crude. The black gold comes down the pipe line from the Forties field.'

'There is no danger. The skipper knows this place like the back of his hands,' Frank said putting them at ease.

Tony stopped baiting the rods when he heard what Binky, said. 'Is that possible? All this way to be ending up run over by a massive tanker, wow! How often does it happen? All I want to do is fish not be food for the fishes.'

'It will not happen the skipper will not let it happen,' Frank, assured again.

'We'll anchor away from the shipping lane but will still have to be very watchful. There is bacon and eggs for tea. And if you can provide some, haddies we will survive. We may have a bit of wait to see what they are up to?'

'Haddies skipper,' Tony said, 'haddies?' He repeated.

'Haddock,' said Frank.

'If you say so skipper. I'll take your word for it. I'll try for the haddies,' rehearsing with the rod unaware wasn't going to be fly fishing. 'I'll get the hang of this fishing lark even if it does kill me and what a surprise Mary will get when she sees my catch, soup, fish soup lovely.'

Six o'clock the next morning Binky woke them, 'they're anchored off Silverknows beach on the other side of Cramond island,' he said, 'two men in a row boat have gone ashore. I'll let you Frank and Kaiser ashore at Barnbougle bay. You can get onto the island. The tide is low you can walk over the causeway and follow them.'

'Wait skipper,' Tony handed him the binoculars, 'a man with a hand cart and a couple of wooden crates they are having a conversation wooden crates are being loaded on the row boat they are going to take them aboard the Maddie. It looks like getting ready to leave what's your take on it skipper? You think definitely they are crooks on the make. Like to know what is in those crates? If we could get a hold of them would soon find out.' Binky was holding the binoculars watching the man with the empty cart make his way towards the walkway beside the river Almond, 'Fort. That's it. They are shifting artifacts from the dig at the Roman Fort,' he said.

'Got what they came for they are leaving,' Frank said making ready with the dingy beckoning Kaiser to join him.

'You will be careful boys. Play it cool we don't want to loose you,' said Tony pushing the dingy away from the side of the boat.

'Okay skipper,' Kaiser smiling up at Tony, 'nothing to worry about got the handle on it.'

'Forget the causeway,' Said Binky follow the guy with the cart,' pointing to the mouth of the Almond, 'the Fort is along the walkway not far be quick. There's a large car park there won't surprise me if there will be a van waiting to go south. Edinburgh, is only a five mile drive from here but bet they'll be going further south. I'll let the coast guard take care of the Maddie also will alert the Edinburgh polis about the van. A help will be if you get the registration.'

They pulled the dingy up the beach and hurried through the deserted village on their way along the walkway by the riverside.

Binky was right his thinking was spot on. A small blue van was there waiting in the empty car park.

Frank ran at the man who was about to enter the van.

Seeing Frank he shouted to the driver to go. The wheels on the van screeched, speeding and churning up the gravel as it drove away.

When he saw Frank rush after him the man ran into the Roman ruins.

They ran after him shouting for him to stop.

The roar of the adjacent waterfall pouring into the river drowned out their cries for the fugitive to give himself up.

Kaiser said it was another of the same men he saw in Mary's place.

They separated each taking a different route into the ruins.

The guy ran from the Roman bath house like a rat scurrying from a burning building with shoulders drooped thinking looked invisible. He looked at them following saw them catching up to him took off along the rim of the waterfall his arms outstretched slowly walking pitting his wits against the rushing flow.

Kaiser let him get half way across before he extended his arm above his head and fired into the air. The shot could be heard echoing from the steep banks along the riverside. The swans and the ducks took flight. Frank watched them lifting out the water going a short distance then landing again.

The man stopped and turned, looked at them defying them suddenly tried to run slipped and fell headlong down into the foaming river his scream echoing like the pistol shot. They ran and looked over the falls but was nowhere to be seen. He disappeared from their view.

'You get him?' Asked Frank. 'Shoot him, you think he's dead good shot you think?'

'No. If aimed would have killed him. No, shot in the air.'

They got down below the waterfall searching the bank found no sign of the body.

'What now?' Frank,shook his head. 'If not dead he's gone Escaped.'

'Forget it. Who cares. He'll surface eventually.'

When they reached the walkway Kaiser said, 'got the number of the van.'

'Where has he got too? Not ran we would have spotted him,' said Frank looking this way and the other way wondering.

'Beats me. Trapped in weeds at the bottom. Or caught in rocks' said Kaiser, 'get out of here before we're spotted. Someone must have heard the shot and the piercing scream let's get back. The quicker Binky reports it the better.'

'Good you got the registration,' Binky said it won't take the polis long to get the van and the driver. The sheer cheek of it in broad daylight too. Nerve they've got it.'

'Roman pieces in broad day light? How did they think they would get away with it? Frank said to Binky whilst admiring the pail of mackerel Tony had caught when he and Kaiser were on the trail of the elusive crooks.

'No idea what happened to the guy who fell?'

'Mystery skipper,' said Kaiser.

'Back square one no further forward. Pity, not getting hands on that guy at least you can tell your grandchildren about our adventures,' joked Tony.

Kaiser gave Frank a quizzical look 'adventure don't ever see that coming to fruition do you Tony? Not the adventure ii mean the children,' he laughed

'No chance.' Frank said, 'You nailed it but the fish what we going to do with the fish are we going to give them to Mary well No,' held up the pail full of squirming mackerel. 'Feed the seabirds,' he said, taking the pail from Tony and emptying it over the side of the boat. Stood back and looked skyward, 'in a minute' he said, 'here they come. Watch your heads,' jumped back from the side of the boat laughing.

Seagulls came swooping from nowhere screaming fighting over the free food. Tony stood with his mouth open, 'what we say to Mary?'

The three rushed falling over each other scrambling into the wheelhouse.

Birds on the deck upturned the bucket wings flapping beaks biting, 'see,' Binky said, 'see what was up against. Now you know how it feels. You'll laugh on the other side of your faces now you see what I was up against and that is not the half of it.' They watched the scrummage. Lasted only matter of minutes till the birds flew away. 'Wonder of nature,' said Tony, 'how cruel it could be.'

'Must have been a nightmare for you Binky,' said Frank 'real nightmare.'

'In Scott and Stevenson's neck of the woods many a tale has been woven in this area,' Binky informed them after consoling Tony on the loss of his catch and thanking him on what he had said about his sad experience.

'You mean Sir Walter Scott and Robert Louis Stevenson roamed round this place?' Tony was all ears.

'Aye,' said Binky, 'the Hound point has a ghost.'

'A ghost? Now I've heard everything,' said Tony.

'When the laird of Barnbougle Castle dies. The howling of a great hound is heard from the point going out across the Forth,' he said.

'My goodness what next? Witches and ghosts? Something just walked over me bet will not sleep tonight,' Tony shrugged, 'something just walked up my spine... How long before we get back?'

'Will make for Granton expect the polis will be waiting to get my report. I'll see you later on just hope they've got a result?'

'Some fishermen you bunch are. Might have guessed the trip would be a waste of time,' said Mary pouring coffee into the mugs and putting a plate of biscuits on the table. 'There was me waiting in anticipation of a good kettle of fish.'

'Mary if you only knew,' said Tony 'I kid you not. Had loads of fish. Loads to bring you but Frankie boy he tipped them back said mackerel was no good.'

'Excuses excuses but if you say so I believe you,' she said, making her way out, 'a pub to run. I'll love youse and leave youse bye bye nae mair bother mind!'

'Anyone know what she is saying it's double Dutch to me,' Tony said. 'take it kin leave youse no tae git intae any mair bother. What on earth?'

'Would enjoyed some of her fish thingy,' Kaiser, saying how hungry he is.

'Getting as bad as him. Why you two always on about your stomachs?' Frank said reaching for the whisky bottle.

'Fish supper,' Tony said, 'go with a fish supper from what you say when you want one? The shop what you say?'

'Chippy,' Frank said.

'Yes or a Scotch pie. Like the pies,'

They looked at Tony, 'you're drooling,' Kaiser said.

'Large white handkerchief wiped his mouth. 'Dreaming of food,' he said.

'Sorry to disappoint but it's whisky or nothing,' Frank said pouring into the glasses. You'll no say no to that I bet,'

'No, doesn't mean couldn't have both. I'm hungry,' Tony said rubbing his stomach. 'Think to give the chipper a visit.'

'Chippy,' said Kaiser.

'Whatever,' he said reaching for his overcoat.

FIFTY NINE

Next morning early they were out on an early stroll made their way above the Starbank Park to a secluded wood the grounds of Jinty Lodge old Victoria building once part of the Trinity estates. Now with it's modern frontage and clear view across the Firth well placed for Captain McPherson to use his fixed spy glass to look out the bay window watching the comings and going's of the many vessels sailing up and down the river.

They accepted the skippers kind invitation to a meeting, he said would be to their advantage and of course sample his good selection of different Malt whiskies.

Unfortunately today the sky is overcast and a steady sheet of soft rain makes watching ships through the glass a pastime for another day.

The three sit enjoying the skippers malt whisky in comfort leaving their troubles for now behind them. Round the cosy fire sitting and speculating what news to their advantage was going to be forthcoming?

Kaiser left his seat and took a peek through the telescope.

'Can see very clear the entrance of the public house down there at the park.'

'Aye,' said Frank, Mary would have a great time spying on us with one of these spy glasses don't you think?'

Mrs Morton a comely soul with her blue eyes and cheery smile showing her appreciation to the company who sit around busy putting the world to rights. She is pleased, as housekeeper to the Captain, finds life lonely in the house due to the Captain spending so much time at sea. After dispensing more good measures of the Captain's Malt Whisky to the assembled she retired to the kitchen to prepare a feast of afternoon tea. A good selection of sandwiches and tea cakes with cream and strawberry jam filled scones.

From the kitchen window she saw a car stop in the drive and was pleasantly surprised to see more visitors arriving. She took of her apron tidied her hair hurried to greet the two strangers approaching the steps to the entrance hall.

McDougall knocked loudly on the door she opened up and smiled but wondered why did he knock so loudly? Muttering to herself her smile changed to a scowl when she recognised the pair of them. Was about to enquire what did he think he was doing banging on her door in that manner when he forcibly barged in.

'Sergeant McDougall and Inspector Rooney to see Captain McPherson may we come in to have a word if he is at home?' Not stopping showing her a glimpse of his warrant card pushing past. Rooney walking a few steps behind entered the lounge taking them by surprise.

'Well! How rude,' she said closing the door.

Immediately after the arrival of Rooney and his sergeant she saw more police arriving. A black Mercedes car with two plain clothes policemen and a police van with two uniformed policemen stopping a good distance from Rooneys car.

Wondering what? Realising wasn't tea and scones they were after but something serious. If the Captain was aware what was happening she wondered why she hadn't been informed. It was not like Eckie McPherson to keep things from her.

She was aware of what had happened in the village. The murders and the strange going's on. The mystery of the men killed at Seafield. Knew the police were baffled by it all. Was wondering if the one responsible was sitting in the Captains lounge? My goodness she's thinking not in the lounge drinking the Captains treasured Malt whisky. No that wouldn't do at all. Wondered who it could be, Frank? Known him since a boy but his companions? Well strangers maybe one of them. Would go and complain to the Captain about how rude McDougall was, barging in like he did.

'What's the meaning of this intrusion!' McPherson demanded when Rooney and McDougall entered the room in a not a quiet as expected way but in a hurried and aggravated state.

'Want Butler to come with us,' McDougall said approaching motioning him to get on his feet. An anonymous phone call received at the station gave us his whereabouts. Information saying he was visiting you Captain. We have it on good authority his statement is false. Have information from a reliable witness.'

Kaiser and Tony stood up. Tony asked the reason why the urgency and how dare they barge into a private meeting.

Rooney ignored him, 'Frank Butler,' he said, 'want you to accompany us to the police station to help with our enquiries into the deaths of Patrick Greene and the man Watson known as you know Night and Day. You don't have to say anything at this time but warn you could be charged later depending on the extent of the answers you give.'

'Okay but you are wasting your time. I've an alibi and you know it,' said a bewildered but smiling Frank.

'We'll see,' McDougall said, taking his arm and walking with him to the door.

'He has an alibi what's changed?' Kaiser blurted out.

'Helping with inquiries. Who are you?' McDougall asked.

Kaiser sat down pouring himself another whisky.

Tony moved to the door stood between the two of them his large physique getting in the way of McDougall.

'Who? Who has come forward with information?' He took hold of Frank and released him from the McDougalls grip.

'Ask questions here instead of disturbing our afternoon?' Captain McPherson said. Nodding to Mrs Morton who came to the door of the lounge in a state wondering and wringing her hands and asking what all the fuss was about. 'it's fine Jeannie, you can leave us. I'll give you a call if we need you further,' he said watching her come in ducking under Tony's arm then saw her squeeze past them on her way back to the kitchen she was in a rage disgusted by the way the policemen had brushed her aside when they swept past her at the door. Never had she witnessed such behaviour this way before and was mortified at the behaviour the policemen especially the loon McDougall. Who she just happened to know since he was still in his mothers arms he should have known better.

'Now now inspector,' said the Captain, 'lets sit and get to the bottom of this. Come in nearer the fire and have some tea. Mrs Morton will be happy to oblige I'm sure come and sit. Lets get to the bottom of the situation. You Sergeant can sit over there,' he said pointing to a chair beside the bay window.

They both declined his suggestion.

Kaiser watched the proceedings and decided to pour himself another whisky.

'You won't get away with trying to stop us taking Butler out of here,' Rooney said, 'I can have a police presence down here fast if you try to hinder us. You know that don't you won't get away with trying to stop doing our duty understand don't you Captain McPherson. Giving fair warning have a warrant for his arrest.'

'Precisely Chief Inspector we have no intention of trying to stop you doing your duty. All we ask is do your must here. We are all grown men. We will give willingly any questions you wish to ask. May I remind you you haven't shown me your warrant to enter these premises but don't worry could ask you to leave but will agree to holding the enquiry here, otherwise, well get out will have to ask you to return with a warrant.'

'To make it legal we have to take him to the station. Come on Sergeant take him to the car,' he stood in front of Tony shrugging and indicating he wanted to pass.

McDougall held Franks arm just as Mrs Morton came back into the room squeezing past the group of bodies.

'Captain McPherson there is another two policemen in the library. Foreign ones. Germans and a young lady. They want to see you,' she said, 'my my what's going on? I've never seen the likes in my life. Captain are you okay?'

'You better wait till I find out what's going on,' McPherson, said to Rooney as he made to leave.

McDougall glanced over at Rooney and gave the look that said, what do we do now what is your next move if you've got one?

After a short spell McPherson returned. 'This is Sergeant Den Berg of the Dutch National police and sergeant Hoffman of the German special crime unit. I think you will want to hear what these gentlemen have to say Inspector Rooney.'

Hoffman stepped forward to the middle of the room as his companion took up station at the door. 'Sergeant you can stay out of Mr Butlers reach he can resume his seat. We come to explain the reason for our visit. We are assured the guilty person responsible many fatalities is here present 'We have a witness a young lady from the public house in the village of Coldingham, who we believe can help with our enquiries pertaining to vicious acts of violence against certain individuals.'

Tony and Kaiser glanced at each other with a worrying look.

Frank recognised the policemen, his shadows, who he lately had a conversation with in the back of their black Mercedes.

'Please ask the lady to come in Mrs Morton please,' said Captain McPherson.

When the woman entered it was the one who served them when they were in Coldingham looking for the Flucker brothers.

'Miss Alex Robertson if you please,' Den Berg said, as she came to his side.

Looking at each one she slowly raised her arm and pointed her finger at McPherson. Who immediately moved to his left. She held fast and continued pointing.

The Captain took a further two steps nodded and winked at Kaiser who was wondering what the hell! He turned to look at the woman to see who she was pointing at...her finger was pointing at Rooney.

Smiling looked to Den Berg and nodded. She didn't speak but left the room with the German policeman.

All eyes were focused on Rooney who was complaining profusely about the nonsense of the situation.

The Captain smiled. They sat dumbfounded at what had taken place. When the penny dropped sheer delight on their faces looking at each other bewildered still not what the hell happened, completely taken by surprise by the outcome.

Den Berg looked to McDougall, 'read him his rights Sergeant and put the handcuffs on him take him out of here will see you at the police station in the High Street. The van is in the drive. No need to keep the officer's out there waiting any longer not needed. Quickly as you can we do not want to disturb the good Captain McPherson. I'm positive Mrs Morton will be delighted to furnish her guests with as much more of her delicious tea and scones.'

'Excuse,' McDougall said who hadn't a clue what was what.

'Read him his rights what am I supposed to charge him with? He's my boss for goodness sake.'

'What you doing? Never seen this woman before are you mad this is a stitch up. What's going on here? It's Butler you want not me Butler!' Rooney said, He was falling apart and making much fuss complaining and struggling with McDougall who pushed and shoved him out the house to the waiting van.

Rooney couldn't see the delight on the Sergeants face. Fame at last he was thinking. After all these years was about to make a name for himself he could see the headlines, Local Sergeant McDougall with the help of foreign policemen spectacular arrest. The policeman very thankful for the help with enquiries that led to the result of taking a dangerous gang member off the streets. Which was all nonsense of course.

In the evening, at Mary's place. 'I'll leave you in peace. Those old hags in Bettys café will be having a field day. Three men in the house my goodness that's my reputation up in the air. I'll never live it down.' She was saying but secretly lapping up the attention. 'Never hear the end of it, oh dear.'

'Yes you will,' said Frank as she made for the door, 'jealousy is to be expected. Envy will be more to the fore. They'll be wishing they could get three men into their houses don't worry about it Mary.'

Tony was on his second helping of Cullen Skink and his two hands tearing a crusty loaf praising her for giving his stomach relief from his problem a problem he kept on about at every waking moment but Mary said his problem would go away if he ate less. Frank and Kaiser were quick to agree.

Kaiser was on his third whisky 'okay Bowtow are you gonna get it off your chest, now it's over. Don't you think you have some explaining to do?'

'Certainly pulled the wool over my eyes but it was a good ending couldn't have done better myself,' Tony said, 'if I could only have seen Rutherfords face when I phoned him with the result. My my what a treat that would be.'

'Come on guys surprised just as you are. The last couple of days have been the clincher. I honestly thought we were never going to get any kind of closure. Honest what a relief it's now

379

over lets get out of here. Lets do a pub crawl to celebrate think we've earned it.'

'I know,' said Kaiser, 'I know where the wee quine Lizzie, is playing.'

'Oh, for f…sake not that please!' Frank let them know in no uncertain terms what he thought of that idea.

Next day, hangovers to the fore. They gathered in Tony's room at the, JAMES on George street.

'Do you think the coast guard brought the whole thing to an end when they caught the fishing boat berthed at Coldingham sands or was it the cops who trailed the van with the Roman things in it?' asked Tony.

'Binky has to get some credit for his quick action in alerting the authorities. It's giving him back a little bit of strength after his ordeal with the headless corpse of old Jakie, bless his soul,' said Frank.

'Poor guy. Why was he killed can't see the sense. What had Rooney against him.

And how many deaths was the scumbag Rooney charged with?' Kaiser asked. He poured each a double whisky drowning them with a rush of cold water from the tap. 'Rooney who would think it, ay?' He said.

'Watch it. Leave some whisky in the glass too much water you'll spoil it,' said Tony. 'If want water get it myself. It's whisky I want.'

'Six, we know of but who knows how many more there are? According to the two cops from the continent who were tailing me it could've been dozens the gang carried out here and in England.'

'You were well catered for Bowtow two cops and me keeping you safe have to feel privileged, ay,' a smiling Kaiser reminded him.

'Rutherford he's not out the wood yet,' said Tony. 'He's sure the Burke's will resurface in Ireland. The Oldersum woman is free to recruit in England. He thinks the cell will be back in Oldenburg pretty soon. He's asking me when I'm coming to join him down the smoke guess he can't do without my help. And Walker well, he's still suspicious about him. Rutherford wants my help. Needs me back. Letting me know how he could get a hand on a pretty cop woman thrown in for inducement. Wants me to take her in hand, as well as get the goods on Walker. Says he has information about some crap the superintendent was involved in with the Burke's. Especially Mother Burke.'

'Might amount to something who would have guessed Rooney being involved. A feather in your cap if you get to the bottom of it,' said Frank.

'Yankee doodle dandy mit der feather in his hat I see it,' said Kaiser.

'Your not funny cousin. I don't see me with a feather in my hat. Anyway like it here. Rutherford he can go and jump in a loch all I care.'

'Now then, Frankie the lowdown on how it panned out. Get it out your system. We're waiting to hear the full facts,' said Kaiser.

'The two cops in the Mercedes who were always somewhere in the background, that mystery, was solved thank goodness. They stayed on my tail giving me the occasional glimpse letting me think they were gangsters on the watch. They were hoping someone would be out to get me. They didn't have much to go on. I was being used as a decoy. Good job you were on my case. I don't think they had much time for me cause they wanted to catch anyone. They had no concern for my safety but explained when they picked me up, I thought when they got me into the car this is it my time is up. They said how they were getting near the bottom of it and had enough evidence to get the case over and done with. Got to thank skipper McPherson. Something he let them know. They told me to wait and keep a low profile but to take care as things were going to come to a head soon.'

'How on earth did they latch on to Rooney,' Tony asked, shaking his head in disbelief at the outrageous conclusion.

'The guy who fell from the waterfall was another Flucker brother' said Frank. He survived the fall only to be huckled by the village cop when he went to investigate the gun shot. Found the guy lying unconscious on the bank of the river further down where we lost him. When the cops told another member of the gang about the apparent suicide at the castle the guy was quick to spill the beans on Brodie. Who, of course in turn done a deal and grassed Rooney. The mystery is McDougall. All these years not knowing what was going on unbelievable ay. There you are that's the rub. And the gang member who fell in the river was afraid. Couldn't trust his brother Brodie. Thought he was going to be the next victim for getting things so wrong. He knew what Brodie and Rooney were capable of. He was quick to spill the beans.'

'And surprise of surprises Rooney just happens to be a cousin of the Burke's. Cousin in the clan who learned his apprenticeship in Germany with the Nazi Boy, Oldersum,' said Kaiser. 'Who would have thought the Dutch cop to be the hero getting all that information.'

'Others have done deals and now the Burke's and the rest of the clan have been apprehended in Ireland,' said Frank, 'so now hopefully it's over for good.'

'Rutherford has other ideas. Doesn't trust Angelica Burke,' said Tony.

'Anything is possible 'Frank said, 'Forget it have a proposal to make to the two of you. And you better not let me down cause having no kin not forgetting Mary of course who has already turned me down.'

'You didn't propose to Mary, did you?' They both said with a surprise look on their faces. He looked at them shaking his head and said, 'Captain McPherson received a package from my brother when the ship was in Rotterdam docks explaining. Inside was another letter for me. He let the skipper know if anything happened to him and the girl he would know what to do. It was Rooney had his claws into Jamie the lure of easy money was the catch. He knew the arrangements we had with the skipper from the trips did as kids. The skipper gave me the letter after Rooney was taken from his house. He took everything in hand warned me to keep quite until he got it cleared with his contacts. I don't know how he worked it the barmaid from the pub in Coldingham, who saw us just the once but saw Rooney many times in the company of the Flucker brothers helped in her way to put it to bed.'

'Don't get how she got into the picture?' Tony said.

'Remember she said two detectives had Flucker taken to Edinburgh to help with enquiries it was our friends who got the nod from a member of the gang. They hightailed south and got lucky. Caught him in the boozer. After grilling him they went back later and got the griff about Rooney from the barmaid.'

'Well that clears that up why did Rooney do away with the man Greene and his minder that been explained?' Asked Tony.

'The Roman idols,' Frank said. 'Patrick Greene welched on a shipment. Tried cut Rooney and the Fluckers out the loop. Mary Greene now blaming it all on her brother who wanted to keep dealing with the Burke's on his own.' And of course the other things happened. Rooney and his gang watching me. Watching see if the money my brother had stolen was somehow coming to me. They needed that money. Done what they done thinking people near to me knew where the money was. Killing them came easy they couldn't trust any of the poor souls keeping quiet about being in contact.'

'Now it's all panned out what is your proposition?' Tony asked shrugged turned to Kaiser 'your all ears aren't you?'

'Yes of course want to hear what he has to say for himself.'

'Talk of opening a boozer in Spain how many times have you laid it on me? Obsessed it's your dream. I don't know about Tony we'll get on to that. How about us in the sunshine?'

The two looked at each other and smiled, 'yes, it's on but… what about the money? You need money for such foolishness,' said Kaiser.

'A bar in Spain wouldn't come cheap,' chipped in Tony.

'All down to hard cash afraid,' said Kaiser.

'Let's hear him out,' said Tony. 'The floor is yours, pally,' he motioned by bowing and giving a sweep of his arm.

'Drug money. The deposit. Three hundred and fifty thousand pounds deposited in the Appingadam bank in my name left by my brother. Also in the letter I got from the skipper just happens to be a ticket. A wee red ticket gets me, er, us, a share of the proceeds. Waiting in a brown coloured large suitcase waiting to be collected at the left luggage Waverley rail station on Princes Street. At least half a million used pound notes to be rescued from the hands of they dastardly Burke's, proceeds of their ill gotten gains. Filthy luchre you might say.'

Kaiser reached for more whisky, 'the wee bowtow I would have liked your wee brother. What a great surprise. Sorry, the way it has happened though.'

'Snap. Drug money. Fifty thousand donated by the Burke's I salvaged from their Kent Mansion,' said Tony, 'we could use it right enough. Who's to know where it came from?'

'Wait', Kaiser frowned, 'idea just hit me. The money it's not ours. Could we get away with it? Don't you think it could be illegal for us to use?'

'Kaiser have you suddenly got religion, well, didn't see that coming,' said Frank.

'He's got a point there,' said Tony, 'but, there might be a way. A reward we could hand it over got to be some kind of reward don't you think?'

'We'll think about it,' Frank said.

'We could suss it out first. See if any reward is on the cards?' said Tony.

'What.' Kaiser said, 'always wanted to live in Spain. All my efforts the gun running and the other things too long to mention was, thought, going to get me enough to realise my dream.'

'And now you have the chance,' said Frank encouraged by the good response pleased both were agreeable to the idea.

Captain McPherson was right when he said your brother was on his way to see you. Remember what he said when we visited him in Rotterdam.'

'Yeah and wondered why he never showed.'

'He must have realised he was being followed and was lucky if can say that making it to the bank was a courageous thing for him to do,' said Kaiser.

'How did it come across for you, money?' asked Frank.

'I killed the Burke's driver after he strangled poor Billy. I done him in self defence. He had the money in a suitcase at the Burke's mansion in Kent was baby sitting the place. Waiting for agents to come and view the joint before putting it on the market. I thought at the time he was taking the money to the Frau and the old woman in Ireland or he was going to do a runner with it.'

'He didn't get far did he,' said Kaiser, 'you arranged a funeral pyre for him and Billy. Good thinking but pity about the Rolls Royce bet it was a nice car.'

Frank smiled, 'have to phone Nikki in Leuwarden might like to join me what you think good idea or not what you think Kaiser?'

'Oh, I could add a few to the list... There's, Stacy and Jossi and Margie and...'

'Stop had it with you lot,' she said as she entered the room. They didn't see her smile until she stepped into the middle of the room. She raised her arms and could hardly contain herself. Waving a copy of the evening paper. 'Look look,' she cried all exited. 'It's here in the paper look front page.'

They looked at her in astonishment. 'Calm down Mary you'll do yourself an injury watch it,' said Tony. 'Sit and get a nice cup of tea or would you rather a whisky?'

Frank took the paper from her, 'we'll would you believe.'

'What,' Kaiser wanted to know, 'you gonna say or...'

'Well,' Frank said again, 'Mary Greene has been arrested for multiple murders. Rooney has grassed her. A fisher lassie with remarkable skills with filleting knives. Would you believe it done some along with Rooney her fancy man.'

They raised a glass to the victims. Mary now was sad. Now she was losing all three. She expected only the two would go but now Tony was going as well.

She had her memories to console her specially the time when Kaiser tried to make a spy out of her. Finkle Jones he had said, when she was sure it was the Fat Man. She couldn't fathom it at all. Something else, McDougall, oh dear wasn't looking to him to be making a fool of himself bending the ears of her punters. Not now he had been promoted to Detective Inspector. And the rookie being made a Sergeant. The only good the episode brought lots of nosy people from far and wide to see the pub were it all happened. Of course she was prone to exaggerating and wee Lizzie got her afternoon slot to keep the tourists happy but not Jordan who only performed at night. Money was the prime factor and Mary she was well pleased with the outcome. Berts bar is now just a ordinary run of the mill bar now the pipe factory is no more.

'What a surprise never heard you coming in Mary. I knew it, spying again,' said a bemused Frank who had to have a say. Had to say something.

'I invited her,' said Tony. 'Mary. A happy reunion. Know what I have to do. Tried the fish and chips...I've done the Cullen Skink but before we go... has to be Haggis Neeps and Tatties.'

'But the icing on the cake has to be The dastardly Mary Greene,' said Frank.

Tony,' Kaiser said with a puzzled look, 'Burke all this time you never set eyes on the man how come? The main man and you...'

'Don't ask him that,' Frank stopped him, 'stories you'll get fairy stories, I warn you. Let's savour the hour. Get more whisky. Mary fill up the glasses.'

'Let him speak want to hear his version,' Kaiser repeated.

'Well? Mary said, giving Tony all her attention eager to hear.

'No,' Frank again chipped in, 'don't want to be in for the long haul.'

'Ignore him,' said Kaiser.

'The fat man took it on,' Frank said groaning.

'I knew Kaiser would come through,' said Tony. 'pulled the strings and greased some palms and Meerka. We got the hell out of Amsterdam, as quick as, you know the saying. The towns of Groningen and Leuwarden would see the last of us, no sir, not us again. Anyway that was the plan. Soon we were established in a seedy part of Soho. On a London street where the barrow boys hang out and the prostitutes to be seen as far as the baby blues could focus. We thought, wrongly, no one in their right skull would give us the time of day never mind any kind of business. You guessed wasn't long before Rutherford Sergeant that is from the City Met came calling one late evening. I was surprised to see him. We had done some good business and got good results but didn't expect he remembered. The sky was chucking it down. Meerka spied him lurking peering through the misted window she getting my attention from the back office. I crossed to the door... 'Why are you standing there getting soaked come and have a coffee.'

'I was admiring the brass plate on the door, Gissertini Private Investigator. Not take long to arrive back settled take it'.

'You gonna stand or come in?'

Came in took of and hung his coat and hat on the stand. Kissed her said was glad to see her. Hoped it was the start of good things to come. The way he was acting, you know, spinning things out. Knew he was up to something. No one in their right mind would be out hanging about our door if they hadn't something desperate on their mind.

'Got anything on the books,' he asked.

'Something brewing, you?' I asked.

Meerka, obliged with coffee and it didn't take him long to come out with the caper. Me to take possession. 'Right up your street,' he said, 'a few quid for very little effort,' he said. 'Ill let you know if it's worth it,' I said, 'when you spill the story.' Meerka ready with the notepad. Rutherford asked for more coffee, she got up got the pot poured more then sat down again waiting the details.

'Simple routine,' he said, 'you'll be, in out you know simple, as I said.'

'So simple why the Met why you not on it?'

'Party no police involved. Get my reason.' He winked when he said it. Came over all coy. You see it. Rutherford coy. No, didn't think so. You guessed, pulling a fast one. You can guess, he was pulling a fast one, 'Lady, er, no need to know information will come clear due course,' he said. 'Want something doing.'

'Not divulging the road map,' I said, 'something smells of rotten fish,' I said and waited to see his reaction. Watched him squirm in the seat.

Meerka closed the notebook rose up made for the back stair to the upstairs apartment. He clammed till he saw her go up the steps closing the door behind her. I waited wondered. He lit a cigarette and asked for more coffee. Took pity didn't know how long he was waiting outside in the rain. Got his coffee and sat down. 'Irishman indulging in a bit of blackmail. You do the carrying and get the goods,' he said.

'know full well,' I said, 'the deal me the mule you watch when it was made clear not too watch. Must have seen the movie a hundred times never fails. Ends up in disaster. Someone gets hurt and you want me for a patsy?'

'All right. Okay I done the deal. Money was tight. Meerka on my back going on about grocery money and rent money you know the score. Getting cold feet but I reminded her she agreed to get out of Holland. Guessed London would be a slam dunk. Looked forward to lots of corruption to keep us busy but now she was having doubts. Me, contacts would come sure I was sure. Did not leave the favoured precinct in New York, knowing I would fall for the Dutch blonde and get involved with the family of equalisers him sitting there, Kaiser, her cousin and the others of that particular clan. Me Sergeant Gissertini, left the force after the success a huge drug bust in Amsterdam. Expected to return stateside and take up duties where I left off. Work as a private dick appealed, saw the sense in it. After all, working with Interpol made many contacts in London's underworld. Anyway much later made the effort. Braved the fog and made my way through the park to the Blue Star watering hole were I had an understanding with the clientele specifically with the owner of the establishment the very likeable fag, Tracy.'

'Hello, nice you to give us the pleasure your company. My my can't see your hand in front of it' he said but I did not ask what he meant. He was there with usual friendly smile, 'beer is it dear?' He asked in his theatrical manner.

'What you know about a dame used to be a show girl married a Lord or something in that guise. Went by the name Rusty something or other. The dame not the Duke or the Lord take your pick,' I enquired of him.

'Had a bottle of beer in front of me. I lifted to drink and clocked the place. Some tipplers standing at the bar others sitting in deep conversation with whoever get the picture? Seems forever before get an answer. Wait while he goes through his routine remembering or not remembering. Just have to wait till he gets it together.

'Can you concentrate,' I say, 'plenty time to be chummy with the rest. Asked you a question.'

'Grumpy Tony,' he says, 'no patience. Do you mean, oh, I know. The one who's necklace worth kings ransom yes scandal or what. Old chestnut surprised they keep falling for it. Caught in bed in a shady hotel. Naked with her lover door burst in photo taken flash flash flash. Gems swiped of the bed cabinet. Oh dear what will his Lordship say? Blackmailer knows she'll pay to keep the old man in the dark. Spin the usual, gems darling? Took to be cleaned darling. She'll be cleaned all right for plenty. You on the case, my, lucky ducky.'

'Get useful information and leave. Force myself to go into the park the fog is worse my chest is playing up and my stomach, no don't ask. Anyway Rutherford is in the park at the usual bench. Tells me Billy Main back from doing another stretch. Wants me to keep him under wraps, cheek, tell him not in the business of grassing people up. I know what he's after, information, wants me to relay the goods but he's not on. What Billy tells me I try, try mind, keep to myself. Anyway forward?' I tell him thinking about it.'

'Where you go from here' he asks,

'Out of here I say now the fog is lifting. Leave him sitting on the bench promising to keep in touch. Look back see him going in the opposite direction.'

'I find Billy. In a low dive near the railway station. Waste of time wants a handout till something big comes to fruition. Wont spill tell like him we are two of a kind on the beach together. Comes over all pally suggests seek Milly Dick. Madam of a joint up west. Leave Billy dreaming about his big score, he'll make out, I know but not be surprised he gets another stretch soon knowing him. I hail a cab. Tell the driver the address, oh, he says, not there crawling with cops raided early morning a shooting cops still on the premises. We do a turn round tell him who I'm looking for. Drops me at the dog track. Meet who I was seeking shady character no need for you to know, anyway, he suggests Dublin. Two nights Dublin get information. Go to Kilkenny when I get there, too late, the man Burke is found in the river NORE drowned.'

'And he never saw the body,' Frank said smiling, 'not laid eyes on Burke to this day. Got his jolly in Ireland as well of making money. Typical ay but no her ladyships jewels.'

'Saw Burke a fleeting glance another story for another time,' Tony said, 'little do you know. Surprising how little you know.'

'Why? I'm confused,' said Mary, 'why go after this man what's his name?'

'Burke,' said Frank.

'Aye Burke. why were you after him, I don't understand.'

Tony gave her his famous smile,' Burke was the blackmailer. Slimy as they come. Lady, er, not need for you to know. Burke got lot of money. Big one off payment. Lady, got back a replica, glass and paste. She asked Rutherford if he could help. He got me. Poor woman no insurance. Her husband thinks trinket is genuine. She can't claim insurance for something that isn't lost.'

'I get it clear as mud,' said Mary.

'No Tony you're not getting away with it you can't change the story to make it fit your ramblings. Can't alter the details the facts don't stack,' Frank said.

'You mean he's telling lies,' Mary shaking her head puzzled.

'Yes,' Tony said, 'no Mary, don't mean I'm telling untruths, things do stack. Your forgetting, four gadgies. Books. Millions upon millions sold. Same subject same story four versions. Do they stack. If they can get away with it so can yours truly. Now food what was I saying?'

'Yeah yeah,' said Frank, 'has to be haggis neeps and tatties!'

SIXTY

The songs wee Lizzie sang.

EDGED OUT
I would never ever ever
Edge you out like you edged me out
Can you not forgive and try to give another chance
A passing glance a knowing smile
A pleasing word to mend an aching heart
You edged me out knowing that I was not the one to blame
You cut our love you stopped our love like embers of a dying flame
You hurt my heart although you knew you were the one who shamed
Can't you forgive and let us stay to put your love to give our love
A chance to love another day

SIXTY ONE

RETURN TO SUNNY LEITH. A sea shanty

I've seen the southern cross at night lit by the Milky Way
I've seen the sun rise up above the table mountain bay
I've seen the shark I've seen the whale and watched the seals at play
From good queen Bess to Durban east London to Dundee
Across the Forth to sunny Leith is were I long to be

I've seen the sun rise up above the Table mountain bay
I've seen the Southern Cross at night lit by the Milky Way
I've seen the shark I've seen the whale
I've tigged a dolphin on it's tail
From good queen Bess and Durban east London to Dundee
Across the Forth to sunny Leith is were I long to be

The Jackass skip on Boulder,s beach
From harbour walls they're out of reach
I've seen the shark I've seen the whale
But beware a Mantas tail
From good queen Bess and Durban east London to Dundee
Across the Forth to sunny Leith is were I soon will be
Across the Forth to sunny Leith is were I soon will be

Good queen Bess…. Port Elizabeth… Jackass… Penguins

SIXTY TWO

STAY FAR AWAY FROM YOU

I'll stay I'll stay I'll stay
I'll stay because I love you
I'll stay I'll stay I'll stay
I'll stay now you say you need me
You locked me down then played around
Your lies convinced this fool
You played the part from the start
On set you knew you could change the rule
I'll stay I'll stay even though I know you will forever haunt me
I'll stay I'll stay now you say you want me
I know you'll write you'll write and say
Come what may your love could be much better
But I know your worth and your worth
Your worth is not worth the letter
I'll stay I'll stay
Knowing how much you need me
I'll stay I'll stay
Knowing how you will demean me
I know my right and with all my might
I know just what to do
I'll stay I'll stay I'll stay I'll stay far far far away from you

SIXTY THREE

HURRY ON

Hurry on hurry on come on you played the ace
Now it's your place to hurry hurry on
Speed along speed along fly or catch a train
But hurry hurry on
Hitch a ride sail a boat even hop a bus
Hurry on hurry on it's just you know for us
Our ups and downs our highs and lows
Our round the block and back
Hurry on hurry on free now from attack
The chasm small but oh so wide kept us both aside
Won't matter now don't matter now when you are by my side
So hurry on hurry on come fast with the tide
For soon to be soon we'll be
The happy groom and bride

SIXTY FOUR

DOWN IN DREAMS

Down in dreams down in dreams
I am down in dreams the night is black
The day is black
And nothing is as it seems
The night is day
The day is night
And how I dread the dawn
I'm down in dreams down in dreams
Worn down and torn
Now you've gone although I'm strong
My life is now it means
Forever down forever down
Let down forever in my dreams

SIXTY FIVE

This is a work of fiction. Place names are reserved for effect. Any resemblance to actual persons living or dead is entirely coincidental.